Anywhere

Sarah Sprinz was born in 1996. After studying medicine in Aachen, she returned to her hometown by Lake Constance in southern Germany. When she's not writing, Sarah finds inspiration for new stories during long walks along the lake shore and enjoys planning her next trips to Canada and Scotland.

Dunbridge Academy: Book 1

Anywhere

SARAH SPRINZ

Translated by Rachel Ward

QUERCUS

First published in Germany in 2022 by LYX, an imprint of Bastei Lübbe
First published in Great Britain in 2023 by

QUERCUS

Quercus Editions Ltd
Carmelite House
50 Victoria Embankment
London EC4Y 0DZ

An Hachette UK company

A CIP catalogue record for this book is available
from the British Library

PB ISBN 978 1 52943 159 9
EB ISBN 978 1 52943 160 5

10 9 8 7 6 5 4 3 2 1

Typeset by Jouve (UK), Milton Keynes
Printed and bound in Great Britain by Clays Ltd, Elcograf S.p.A.

MIX
Paper | Supporting
responsible forestry
FSC® C104740

Papers used by Quercus are from well-managed forests and other responsible sources.

Dear Readers,

Because this book contains elements that could be triggering, you will find a trigger warning on page 481. We hope that you will enjoy the book!

Happy reading, from
Sarah and the team at Quercus

*For all of you
who just keep on running.
I hope you find someone
who makes it worth
stopping.*

Everything I've never done,
I want to do with you.

William Chapman

Playlist

baby luv – nilüfer yanya
apricots – may-a
older – shallou and daya
hope is a dangerous thing for a woman – lana del rey
stone – jaymes young
all three – noah cyrus
happier than ever – billie eilish
edge of midnight (midnight sky remix) – miley cyrus feat.
stevie nicks
meet me in the hallway – harry styles
a. m. – one direction
wonderland – taylor swift
runaway – aurora
perfectly out of place – dreams we've had
talk – hozier
sweat – zayn
a little death – the neighbourhood
fine line – harry styles
my tears are becoming a sea – m83
mind over matter (reprise) – young the giant
the beach – wolf alice
run boy run – woodkid
right where you left me – taylor swift
ready to run – one direction

Anywhere

'I'm sorry,' I say, although that isn't actually what I mean. It absolutely isn't. It's capitulation of the worst kind, but I have no choice.

My voice has never sounded as flat. As if I didn't care about what this means right now, when the opposite is true. I do care, I care more than anything.

What have you done, what have you done, what have you done?

The right thing. It was the right thing. Wasn't it? A moment ago, I'd been sure of that, but now I'm overcome by doubts.

I turn around. I grab the heavy black iron doorknob. I don't know how my legs carry me. I don't know how I push open the door and walk out of the head teacher's office without losing my composure. I don't know. I don't know anything any more.

I hear the voices in the corridor, the laughter that echoes off the high walls. The sounds of rapid footsteps on the old, uneven tiles in the arcaded walkways. Sunbeams fall through the panes of the lancet windows; dust glitters in the air.

Faces turn towards me: my fellow pupils smile at me, say, 'Hi,' the same as ever, and I don't reply because I can't. I run blindly past them. I have to get away but I don't know where to go. I no longer have a home.

The thought hits me like a punch in the belly, but it's true. For a moment I feel the need to stop and curl up. But I keep on running.

My feet fly over the tiles, taking routes I could walk with my eyes shut. Across the courtyard to my dorm wing, brown brick façades covered with twining ivy. High lattice windows, dark roofs, pointed towers. I see it all but feel nothing. Coming towards me down the worn stairs from the first floor are the fourth-formers; they slow as they recognize me, then run all the faster once they're past. The heavy dark wooden door to our wing is shut. I have to lean my whole weight against it as I reach for the key in my trouser pocket and open it.

Silence.

And then I pull my suitcase over beside the wardrobe and start packing.

1

EMMA

It didn't go off. My stupid alarm clock just didn't go off. It stayed silent because my phone's dead. How can you forget to charge it overnight when tomorrow you're flying to Scotland for a year abroad at boarding school? How? This probably sounds like a bad joke but, sadly, I have to confirm that it's not.

I just plain overslept. On the day I'm travelling. And there's no way Mum can find out about this or she'll freak. She was so doubtful yesterday, after it had been confirmed that, with the stupid ground crew being on strike in France, she couldn't get back in time to fly to Edinburgh with me. Like an eighteen-year-old was totally incapable of getting to the airport alone and flying to Scotland. Mind you, I'd be going into a class with people younger than me because

I needed to start at the beginning of the A-level course, not halfway through.

What can I say? Looks like she was right.

I always plug my phone in before I go to sleep but yesterday I forgot. After all, it's not that common to spend half the night crying your eyes out because you've suddenly realized that going to Scotland for a year might actually be a crappy idea. Maybe my subconscious was trying to give me one last chance to come to my senses. Don't catch the plane, don't be the new girl at Dunbridge Academy tomorrow, just enjoy the rest of the summer holidays, and start my *Abitur* at the Heinrich Heine grammar school in September as if I hadn't been about to make a major mistake. But that's impossible because all my friends know I'm going to be away for a year. If I bailed now, I'd really make an idiot of myself. It'd look like I didn't know what I wanted. But I know exactly what I want. And for that I have to get to Edinburgh.

I chuck the last few things carelessly into my washbag while I brush my teeth.

I have to get there. I've known it since I found that cassette and lay awake into the early hours of the morning listening to that song on my old Walkman. 'For Emma'. The title was like a mocking promise.

That was ten weeks ago now and, deep down, I'm sure I only got a place at this school at such short notice because Mum pulled some strings somewhere. She's super-good at that. As a lawyer, she always seems to know someone somewhere who owes her a favour. And I was totally sure that I was doing the right thing. Even though Mum didn't understand why I suddenly wanted to go to boarding school after years of rejecting any such suggestion. I can't tell her that I have to find my dad. That his voice on the tape sounded totally different from the way I remember it. That it sounded so close, as if his lips had been brushing the mike the whole time he was singing 'For Emma'. That I listened to the song with goosebumps and a fluttering heart for a whole night, and never again.

That 'For Emma' wouldn't leave me, not even once I googled his name, for the first time in years. Jacob Wiley, still waiting for his big break, still just a man with a guitar and no conscience – there's no way you can have a conscience if you leave your family for a dream and don't look back.

Jacob Wiley was born in Glasgow and is a Scottish singer-songwriter.

And he's living back there again, at least according to his Wikipedia entry. He's in Scotland, so I have to go to Scotland. I knew it the first time I voluntarily pulled up the Dunbridge Academy website.

'Airport, please,' I pant, a little later, as I clamber into the taxi. I want to close my eyes, not to have to look at the time, but unfortunately it shines reproachfully at me the moment I reach for my phone. This is going to be seriously tight. I'm such an idiot. I have to get to baggage check-in and hope it's still open, then through security, and make it to my gate.

All inside an hour and twenty minutes, after which the plane is due to take off – ideally with me on board.

No idea what I'll do if it doesn't work out. I'm sure there'll be another flight to Edinburgh later on, but do you just get rescheduled if you miss your flight entirely through your own fault?

Mum would know this stuff. But unless I absolutely have to tell her, she's never going to find out that I'm not even capable of catching my plane. She'd end up interpreting it as a sign that I don't want to go to Dunbridge Academy. And it's not a sign. It's just a stupid, stupid fuck-up.

I send her a WhatsApp claiming to be on the way to my gate – which is kind of true.

It's seven thirty on a Sunday morning but even now the Frankfurt traffic is remorseless. I shut my eyes as the taxi slows down more and more. Oh, God, I'm so screwed. I'm going to miss the flight and be late to the school. Right from the start I'm going to be the new girl who couldn't even make it to the first day of term on time.

My pulse is racing when, an eternity later, I jump out of the taxi, grab my luggage and pay the driver. I've flown millions of times, but Frankfurt airport is and always will be above and beyond, even when you have plenty of time in hand.

I start running. People and their suitcases are standing around all over the departure hall. They can see I'm in a hurry, but hardly anyone gets out of my way. My inner thigh muscles are still complaining after training on Friday. One last coordination and speed workout with the girls in my club. *You'll love it, Emmi. I was on the Dunbridge athletics team, too.* I hear Mum's voice in my head and pray that she's right.

My legs are like lead. It's hard work pushing two suitcases and I can feel a slight stitch in my side. It's harder than normal to pick up my feet, but I don't stop. I never stop before I've reached my goal. It's the only thing I ever really persist at. Keep on running, even when I'm almost puking with exhaustion. Keep on running, keep on running, no matter where I'm headed. My dad on the regional express train, in a red carriage, speeding up, faster and faster as I run faster and faster after him. But never fast enough.

Apparently, I look desperate enough that the airline staff open a new window, and I heave my first suitcase onto the belt. The woman behind the counter raises an eyebrow at the number on the digital display, but slaps on the sticky label without a word. Maybe she'll have pity on me. I *hope* she'll have pity on me.

'You'll have to hurry – the gate is closing, but I'll let my colleagues know you're on your way.'

'Thank you,' I gasp, reaching for my documents, then turn and do the one thing I could manage in my sleep.

I run, as fast as I can.

2

HENRY

I hate running.

Hate it, hate it, hate it.

It's stressful enough even when you're not trying to race from one end of this gigantic airport to the other after a delayed ten-hour flight. Now I remember why I normally avoid having to transfer in Frankfurt: an hour and a half's transit time is never long enough. Least of all if your flight gets delayed. I ought to write it out somewhere in big fat letters as a reminder next time I book my return flight from Nairobi to Edinburgh.

'Excuse me, sorry . . .' For fuck's sake, why's it so hard to stick to the stand-on-the-right-walk-on-the-left rule on these endless conveyor-belts? 'Connecting flight, sorry.'

I barge into elbows and ignore the tightness in my

chest. It's so embarrassing that I can't run even for five minutes without feeling like I'm about to have an asthma attack. The rucksack on my back suddenly weighs a ton, my hoodie is way too thick, but obviously I didn't realize that until earlier when I was jammed in with all the other passengers in the cramped aisle of the Boeing, waiting to disembark. I wish I could stop and pull it off but, one, I haven't got time and, two, I'm past caring.

I stumble as I set foot on solid ground at the end of the travelator. My body wants to carry on – my muscles are barely capable of absorbing the sudden deceleration – and, God, I have to start running more often: I'm so unfit! Maybe I ought to follow Theo's example. My older brother used to do his revision on the treadmills in the school gym. *The brain takes in new information much quicker when you're moving, Henry, it's scientifically proven.* And it's scientifically proven that my heart is going to jump out of my chest any moment if I don't slow down and . . .

Hang on. Gate B 20. *B.*

I stop so abruptly that a wave of German-sounding swearwords washes over me. My pulse is pounding in my ears again as I stare at the signs above me. Maybe my brain isn't getting enough blood and I'm hallucinating. Or maybe that actually says Gates C–D.

Fuck. Where did I go wrong? Why is my connecting gate always at the far end of the airport, wherever I'm transferring, and why–

The second I turn around – without looking – there's a dull thud. That doesn't sound good. And it doesn't feel good either. I'd forgotten the way all the air gets crushed out of your lungs when someone runs into you with their full weight. I land on the slippery tiles between a girl's knees. One of my rucksack straps flies open and the contents scatter over the floor in front of us. Water bottle, headphones, chewing gum, the bag of mini pretzels from the other plane, phone charger, my passport. But I don't see any of that. All I see is pale blonde chin-length hair and very grey-blue eyes.

'Sorry, sorry . . .' she begins, and she keeps talking. I can't understand her, and I hope that's not because I got a bang on the head when we fell. The words sound like German, but from her mouth they're not as harsh.

'Are you OK?' I ask in reply. I'm expecting her to pause as she realizes she'll need to answer in English for me to understand her. But she switches languages without a moment's hesitation, and, oh, God, why's that so attractive?

'Yeah, I think so,' she says. 'How about you? Sorry, I shouldn't have been running like that, but–'

'No, it's fine. I wasn't paying attention.' My brain fires up again. I bend instinctively to rescue my bottle, which is rolling perilously towards the people hurrying past. As I reach for it, her eyes flit over my things. Almost as if she were silently weighing up whether or not she should help me collect them.

'Sorry, I . . .' She pauses as I look at her again. 'I'm so late, my flight's leaving and—'

The leaden voice of the airport announcement system interrupts her. She jumps up wildly as the German words echo from the loudspeaker. Then I hold my breath as they're repeated in English.

'Last call for passengers Bennington and Wiley. Please go immediately to Gate B 20. Last call.'

'I'm sorry.' The girl's look is as apologetic as it is desperate.

'Is that you?' I ask, and she nods. 'Edinburgh?'

'You too?'

'Yes,' I reply.

She hesitates, then reaches for my stuff. 'OK, we have to hurry.'

We grab my things – three handfuls each. I stuff my headphones into my rucksack upside down, then jump up too. I keep my passport in hand.

'Wiley?' I ask, looking at her.

'Emma,' she says, pointing to the direction I've just come from. 'And you?'

'Henry. Pleased to meet you.' I can only stutter out a few words because my lungs are on fire again. Or still. Either way. 'Is it far?' I gasp, gradually dropping back behind her. Emma. The grey-eyed girl. Wow, she's fast.

'Don't know.' She glances back, gripping her rucksack straps firmly. 'We have to speed up.'

'I can't.'

'Yes, you can.'

Like hell I can. Unlike her.

She makes it look effortless.

'No, this way.' Just before the next travelator, she grabs my wrist and pulls me to the right.

Oh. yeah. *Gates B35–1*, the sign reads. I must have run right past it before.

Emma mumbles very German and apologetic-sounding words as we run past people with hand-luggage trolleys and dodge small children.

I'm embarrassingly out of breath, while Emma has no more than a clearly rising and falling chest and somewhat flushed cheeks. Can't be more than a few hundred metres, but this airport corridor seems to be going on for ever.

B31

B29

B27

They've already started boarding at gate B24 and there are people everywhere. Right in our way. I thank them from the bottom of my heart because I'm forced to walk a few paces. Emma vanishes into the crowd ahead of me and I make myself run on.

Our gate is empty. It sticks out like a sore thumb amid the other waiting areas, which are full to bursting. I can see the plane through the window, but there's nobody at the desk.

Fuck . . . I've got a stitch and I press my hand to my side.

'Seriously?' murmurs Emma. Her voice sounds way too normal after the sprint we've just done. 'They only just called us and . . .'

'LH 962 to Edinburgh?' calls a man.

A flight attendant appears, and at that moment, I'd like to fling my arms around his neck.

'Yes!'

'Great. This way, please.'

I'm trying to suppress my wheezing as I pull my phone out of the kangaroo pocket on my hoodie. I bet my face is bright red. Emma looks almost fresh. How the hell is she even human?

I pull up my boarding pass on my phone and hand the flight attendant my passport. Once he's given it back, I move away slightly to wait for her. Emma's got her boarding pass printed out on paper and something about that makes me smile. It's kind of sweet.

She thanks him and she's blushing a little after all as she looks at me. I think she's surprised that I waited. And at that moment it happens. Her eyes drop from my face to my chest. I see her stare at the white logo embroidered on the dark blue sweat fabric of my hoodie. The entwined initials of Dunbridge Academy within a simple, ivy-framed shield. Emma recognizes it. I can see it in her eyes. Before she can speak, I've scanned through every year group in my mind. No, it's impossible. She has to be new, or I'd have seen her somewhere before. I might not know all 423 pupils at

Dunbridge by name, but I know them by sight. And I never forget a face.

'You're at Dunbridge Academy?' asks Emma, and her voice sounds so awestruck that I'm now absolutely certain.

She's definitely new. You wouldn't ask like that unless you only knew the school from the glowing reports on the web.

'Yes,' I say, and the flight attendant appears behind Emma.

'Quickly, please!' He's all smiles and gleaming white teeth, but his insistent yet friendly manner gets us both moving again. Emma's eyes are still fixed on me. I don't like the way she suddenly seems so abashed.

'Is this your first year?'

'Yes.' Emma gives a thin smile, and suddenly I want to hug her. Or I would if I wasn't dripping with sweat. And, actually, not even then. We've only just met. But why is she alone here? Newbies are usually brought by their parents. Even when they're from Saudi Arabia or Mexico. Germany is hardly far-flung by the standards of our school.

'I'm just on a year abroad,' she says, as we hurry down the long corridor. The walls are close and the carpet swallows our footsteps. I don't like the way she stares at the floor as she speaks. She seems kind of . . . unhappy.

'Cool. Your English is great.'

I immediately sense I've said something wrong.

'Thanks,' she mumbles, as she raises her eyes.

I want to ask her so many questions – where exactly she's from, if she's excited, all that stuff – but I can't because we've now reached the plane door. Another flight attendant is waiting for us.

'Welcome on board,' she greets us with, but her smile is impatient.

'Where are you sitting?' I ask Emma. All the other passengers have their seatbelts fastened. They're staring at phones already in 'airplane' mode or looking towards us in annoyance.

'Twenty-seven D,' says Emma, glancing over her shoulder at me. 'How about you?'

Blast . . . For a moment I seriously wonder how cheeky it would be to ask someone to change places.

'Here,' I reply, as we reach twenty-two C. The aisle seat, and obviously there's nothing free anywhere nearby. The woman in the middle has already got chunky noise-cancelling headphones on and doesn't look like she wants to be spoken to.

'Oh, OK.' Emma doesn't stop. 'Enjoy the flight. See you later, Henry.'

'Yeah.' I gulp. 'You too.'

EMMA

The middle seat in my row is free. Of course it is. It's booked in Mum's name, but Mum's stuck somewhere in Nice, not here beside me.

I realize that only after Henry's sat down and a flight

attendant is telling me not to undo my seatbelt until we've reached cruising altitude.

So I sit there, ignoring the cabin crew's safety announcements and trying to send Henry a message with my eyes, begging him to turn around.

It doesn't work. He's on his phone, I can see him typing, then looking up guiltily, presumably because the flight attendant has told him to put it into 'airplane' mode.

Turn around, turn around, turn around.

I could gesture to him to come and sit next to me later. Well, if he wants. Would he want to? No idea. Doesn't matter anyway. I don't even know if I want him to. No, that's not true. I do know. I don't want him to. No way. He seems nice but why should I care? He's a man. And we all know what that means. Broken hearts and tears shed that we can never get back. Being with someone for six months, only to get a text message out of the blue saying he isn't feeling it any more. I've had enough of guys like Noah from my old school, or my dad who left and never got back in touch. Yet here I am, flying to Scotland to look for him, unable to stop gazing at Henry. Why am I doing this?

Henry doesn't turn around, and the longer I hope he will, the sillier I feel. We might not even be in the same year. It's a big enough school that we might never bump into each other again. Which would be a shame ... God, Emma! Enough now.

I stare at his shoulder in that dark blue hoodie and wonder

how old he is. Must be in his final year. There's something about him. Something self-assured and relaxed. The way the *Abitur* students stroll down the corridors at home, because they're so grown-up, so casual, like the whole fucking school belongs to them. But maybe everyone at this boarding school is like that. I guess I'll soon find out.

Either way, he doesn't turn. Not that it would mean anything if he did. I pull my headphones out of my bag and play an old One Direction song cos it's almost time for take-off and I could do with a bit of chill.

Why isn't he turning round? If he sat beside me, I could start asking him about the school. Or other questions. Why he's flying from Frankfurt to Edinburgh when he sounds so clearly British that I didn't even need to ask him where he's from. Was he on holiday? What's boarding school like, then, and, oh, do you happen to know a guy named Jacob Wiley? No? Oh, well, never mind, doesn't matter . . .

I'm so obsessed.

The plane stops taxiing and the engines roar more loudly. I'm pressed back into my seat and, because I'm always a bit nervous about take-offs and landings, I shut my eyes. Just for a moment, just until we've levelled out and I can feel half-way confident that we're all going to survive. Mind you, I've heard that landings are more dangerous than take-offs. Whatever . . . Stop thinking about it. I'll listen to my music and that's all that matters. Taylor Swift takes over from One Direction, then Lana del Rey from Taylor.

I squint over occasionally. In case Henry turns round. But all I can see are his elbow on the armrest and part of his face resting on his hand. And I can see that he must be seriously tired because his head nods forwards every twenty seconds.

Has he just got off a night flight? The dark rings under his eyes and the fact that he's wearing jogging bottoms suggest that.

When he pulls up his hood and leans back in the seat with his arms linked behind his head, I turn my eyes away. It's rude to watch a stranger sleeping, but his brown hair curls under his hood and his eyes really were very green. Dark moss green. Like the green in the school tartan, in the uniform I'm going to wear from tomorrow. Dark blue blazer with a blue-and-green-checked lining and the school crest embroidered on the breast pocket. White shirt and a matching tartan tie.

I can't stop imagining Henry in that uniform, which I guess suits him very well, as his head sinks further and further towards his chest every minute. If he were sitting beside me, he could rest it on my–

God, Wiley. I shut my eyes again and Lana sings 'Hope Is A Dangerous Thing For A Woman Like Me To Have'. She doesn't know how right she is. Or maybe she does. If you write songs like that, you know how it goes. Noah, at school the next day. Saying there was no point to it any more. Me nodding, very calm, no emotions, no tears. Anything not to be the hysterical ex, begging him to stay. Because I should have known. Because everything always repeats itself, always, always, always, and you never figure that out, no matter how much you want to believe in the good in people. When it gets tough, they just leave and no one can stop them.

We don't need any more men in our lives, Emmi-Mouse. Mum's voice, and part of me wants to believe her. Because she truly doesn't need men, just her job and to keep busy, so that she forgets how much it hurts. I can't forget. Because I'd been unable to breathe as I changed into running clothes – even though it had been a rest day. But a Noah's-dumped-you day can never be a rest day. It was a day when I had to run to stop myself losing my mind. Because the only way my thoughts stand still is if I do the running for them. But I can't run now. I can only force myself not to look at Henry. Just as well he's not sitting next to me. That would be fatal. No way can he sit next to me, fall asleep and lay his head on my shoulder. I've got no time for that stuff. Noah ended it and I'm on a mission. It's perfectly simple. One year, one goal. For me, everything in Scotland has an expiry date. I have to keep reminding myself of that, can't let myself forget.

I blink.

And, no, he hasn't turned around.

3

EMMA

It's a two-hour flight from Frankfurt to Edinburgh, and half an hour before we land, I stand up to go to the toilet. Maybe I'm obsessed, but just wiggling my toes up and down in my trainers and jiggling my feet nervously isn't enough. I don't normally have a problem with sitting still for hours at a time, but I don't normally fly to Scotland to be the new girl at a posh boarding school. I wonder if it'll really be like the school's incredibly fancy website. Smiling girls and boys, sitting on the lawn with their books, or strolling across the grounds in uniform. Super-high-tech equipment in the classrooms, within ancient walls. Community not competition, no pressure to achieve. Not that my old school was like that either. Not many people cared enough about their lessons for that, but if Mum's memories are anything to go by, Dunbridge is different. *Dunbridge Obliges*. A weird motto, but somehow it fits my image of the school. And Henry. He definitely seems very conscientious, but not in a teacher's-pet kind of way. Either way, as I walk down the plane's central aisle, I'm planning to try to make the most of my time in Scotland.

The plane's only aisle, in fact. On bigger planes and longer flights, you can sneak through the little galley kitchen to the other side of the seats and do a few laps. Here, there's only the route to the loo and back, but that's better than nothing.

I close the door on the tiny cabin and stare at myself in the mirror while my head buzzes. In the harsh light, my blonde bobbed hair looks almost white. I tuck a strand behind my ear and press the flush even though I didn't go. Then I wash my hands, dry them on the stiff paper towels that reject the water rather than absorbing it, and rattle at the door. It opens inwards with a complicated folding mechanism. It fascinates me so much that I don't spot Henry standing out there until it's too late.

'Oh, hi,' he says, and his voice sounds kind of different over the noise of the plane. He's smiling but he looks tired, like he's only just woken up, with slightly puffy eyes and messed-up hair peeking out under his hood.

'Sleep well?' I ask, instantly regretting it because now he knows I was watching him.

Henry hesitates, then his smile changes. He shrugs and steps to the side as another woman pushes past him. I don't understand what she says: her English is unclear and she's speaking fast. When Henry answers, his English is even faster and less clear. Suddenly, I remember again that I'm going to be living in a foreign country for the next ten months. A foreign country that's also kind of my home but, let's be honest, I've never even been there.

You're bilingual – your English is perfect. Isi's voice in my head makes my stomach lurch. I have a British surname and a German accent, because I haven't spoken English regularly since I was a child. When he left. I might always be top of the class in English in a German school, but anytime anyone asks me why I'm so good, it's like a punch in the guts.

'Didn't you want to . . .?' I ask, to take my mind off my thoughts. I point to the toilet door, which the other passenger has just pulled shut.

Henry's eyes come back to me. 'No, I . . . I just want to stretch my legs a bit.'

'Oh, right.' I gulp.

'Are you nervous?'

He wants to chat, in this little kitchen at the back of a plane, and that's fine by me. I've read that you have the best chance of surviving a plane crash if you're sitting right at the back. Sitting, hmm. We're standing. We're not even strapped in. I have to stop thinking.

'No,' I say, meaning yes.

Henry nods like he knew that. 'It'll be fine,' he says. It's unfair of him to smile like that. 'Everyone's really nice.'

He turns aside slightly, hand over his mouth to cover a yawn. 'Sorry . . .'

'Jetlag?' I ask, and Henry nods. Then he shakes his head.

'No, not really. There's no major time difference.'

'Where have you been then?'

'Nairobi,' he replies. 'It's only three hours ahead. But it was a night flight.'

'Couldn't you sleep?'

'The woman next to me had a baby in her arms and, well, it was a bit stressful.'

'What were you doing in Nairobi?' I ask, running my fin-gertips over the metal drawers beside me. They're seriously cold. Henry's eyes follow my hand and I'm not sure if he heard my question or not. Then he tears his eyes away and looks at me again.

'Visiting my parents. They work for Médecins Sans Fron-tières.' He says it the way you say stuff you've said a hundred times before. Like the way I say I barely know my dad because he left when I was eleven.

'Oh, nice.'

Henry smiles. 'What do your parents do?'

'My mum's a lawyer,' I reply. Henry doesn't ask about my dad. In the silence, I'm thanking him for that. He eyes me briefly, like he's understood something that nobody ever gets.

'Didn't you want her to come with you?' he asks instead.

'To the school? . . . Yeah,' I admit. 'But she couldn't. She's in Nice for work and the French ground crew are on strike.'

23

'Bummer,' he says.

'Not a problem.' I grin, but Henry's watching me like he doesn't believe me. 'OK, maybe it's a bit of a problem, but it can't be helped.'

'It might be better that way – then you don't have to say goodbye to anyone.' He leans his shoulders on the wall beside us.

'True.' I've never had to say that kind of goodbye to anyone. Not even from Isi, who didn't offer to come to the airport with me, which feels kind of weird because if she, my best friend, was going away for a year, I'd have done that for her. But I didn't want to get into an argument, and it *was* a very early flight.

'That was always the worst part for me,' Henry says. 'When Mum and Dad used to drop us off at school and drive away again. The half-hour after that ... not great. Till you move into your room and catch up with your friends and forget that you're sad.'

I nod, even if I don't have any friends there to meet up with. There'll be nobody at Dunbridge Academy to meet me, and suddenly, the idea chokes me up. Maybe Henry reads my thoughts because he goes on speaking.

'I'll show you around when we get there. There are times when I wish I could be starting at the school all over again. Everything's so exciting. It's like coming home, even if you don't know it yet.'

I have my doubts about that, and even if he's right, I'm

only staying a year. Maybe I ought to tell him so, but something inside me holds me back. Maybe I'm scared that he'd stop talking like we're on the same team.

'I'll show you everything,' Henry repeats.

I don't have time to reply because one of the cabin crew comes towards us.

'Please take your seats. We'll be coming in to land shortly.'

Henry nods. His gaze flits over me and I follow him down the aisle back to our seats.

As the aeroplane descends, I start – slowly but surely – to feel the nerves. Once we touch down at the airport, I'll be in a strange city. Then it'll really be true. My new reality.

All of the passengers are on their feet as soon as the plane parks. People standing in the aisle cut off my view of Henry and when I eventually get up and pull my rucksack out of the overhead locker, he's gone. Of course he has. What was I expecting? That he'd play babysitter and wait for me? But then again we're going to the same school, and he did say he'd show me around, so it's not unreasonable to expect him to hang about, or is it?

I walk through the plane to the front, making a mental to-do list. It's dead easy. Walk to the luggage carousel, then through Passport Control and out. Find the shuttle bus that meets Dunbridge pupils at the airport to take us to school.

Will Henry be on the bus? He's sure to know where—

'Hey.' I jump as I spot him out in the passageway leading to the terminal building. He waited. 'There you are.'

I feel my cheeks flush. 'You waited! Thanks.'

'Of course.' He smiles, and my racing heart calms slightly.

As we walk through the airport, I learn that Henry's been at the academy since he was twelve but started a year behind because of his messed-up education before that, and this year he's school captain. I don't know much about him, but it seems to fit.

Chatting with him, I don't feel as if we've only known each other two hours. Most of which we spent apart. He's very easy to like, and something about that makes me uneasy. This could get dangerous if I don't watch out. Henry's nice, sure, but that's probably exactly why he's school captain. Don't go reading too much into it. He's probably just as friendly to everyone.

As we wait for our bags, I quickly message Mum to tell her I've landed. I hesitate when I see my chat thread with Isi under hers. But then I open it and send her the exact same words. My best friend and I don't message much, so it can sometimes feel like we've grown apart over the holidays. Things are different when we see each other every day at school. So I'd better not think about what that'll mean for the year ahead.

Henry's and my suitcases are some of the first off, probably because they were the last to be loaded into the hold. Henry seems almost surprised that his has made it too, after such a short transit time.

Once we're through Passport Control, I realize I haven't

asked how he's getting to the school. I'm about to do that when we reach the arrivals hall. Henry's eyes scan the people waiting there and a figure steps out of the crowd. Then it all just happens.

The girl is our age. There's something fairylike and seriously elegant about her as she runs towards Henry. He drops his suitcase. A few seconds later, she's in his arms.

'Hey, you,' I hear him say, and turn away as they kiss. I don't know why I suddenly feel so much like a spare part.

He's got a girlfriend. She's gorgeous – she has these dark, glossy curls and shining brown eyes that beam at him as she strokes a strand of hair off his forehead and kisses him again.

'Excuse me, please!'

Startled, I move aside as people push past. I hastily make room, and Henry reaches for his case. His eyes are fixed on the girl and I can't hear what he's saying. Maybe because of the airport noise, or maybe it's the roaring in my head.

Suddenly I grasp that I'm in Edinburgh. Totally alone, nobody came with me. And nobody's here to meet me, like Henry's girlfriend. Not even my dad has the faintest clue that I'm in his home country to look for him. My fingers tighten on the handle of my suitcase. What am I even doing here?

I don't want to bother Henry and his girlfriend, but it feels kind of wrong to just walk on and look for the bus the way I'd been planning. As I glance uncertainly at them,

Henry turns to me. He smiles this warm, open smile that I should read nothing into. 'Grace, this is Emma.' He tows her by the hand as he walks towards me. 'She's here on a year abroad with us.'

'Hi, Emma, how nice to meet you.' Grace is beaming, and I don't know what's happening as she gives me a hug. 'Welcome!'

I'm caught a bit off guard. 'Thanks.'

'How do you two know each other?' she asks, with no suspicion in her voice.

'We met in Frankfurt – we were both seriously late for the flight.' Henry shrugs. 'I really thought I was going to miss my connection.'

'I'm glad it all worked out.' Grace turns to me. 'Are you coming on the bus, Emma?'

I hesitate. 'Yes, I . . . I was planning to.'

She grabs one of my suitcases. 'Great. I'll take this one, OK? I pestered Mr Burgess into letting me come and surprise Henry. The bus is really only meant for boarders.' I frown, but Grace carries on. 'I'm a day girl – I stay with my parents in Ebrington.'

'That's the nearest town,' Henry explains. 'Most of the local kids go to school in Edinburgh but a lucky few get a scholarship to Dunbridge.'

I follow them. I'm not normally the kind to get easily into conversation with new people, but Henry and Grace don't make me feel like a stranger. Maybe all the stuff that Mum always said was true – that going to Dunbridge means growing up with loads of brothers and sisters, being part of a community. It wasn't like that at the Heinrich Heine where, no matter how often the head talked about it, I never really felt that way and I don't think any of my friends did either. It was nothing more than a school. A place where you battled through the week, tried to keep your head down and not attract attention. Being the new kid there must be rough. I can't imagine that you'd ever meet such nice, straightforward people as Henry and Grace right away.

Without their help, I'd definitely have got lost. I follow them down the endless bus platform outside the airport, and my heart skips a beat when I see my first double-deckers. OK, so they're pink and blue not red, the way I imagined them, but all the same, they're an unmistakable sign that this isn't Frankfurt. The Dunbridge Academy bus is a small dark coach, with the school logo on the side in white. I could easily have missed it.

'Coming?' Henry asks, and I pause. Grace chats to the driver as he stashes our cases in the luggage locker, then climbs aboard.

'Do we have to pay?' I ask quietly.

Henry seems puzzled, then laughs. 'No, Emma,' he says, taking my wrist. 'You're at the school so just hop on.'

'Oh, right,' I mumble, setting one foot on the step. The front rows are almost all full. Henry's saying hi to people, waving. Pupils seem to come to this school from all over the world. Most of them look exhausted, like they've had just as long a journey as Henry. I smile at them as we make our way to the back.

'Anyone who comes into the airport can let the school know in advance that they need picking up,' Henry says.

'Oh . . . I don't think—'

'It's fine,' he interrupts. 'There's plenty of room.'

Grace gestures invitingly towards the back row, where we can all sit together. Weirdly, she doesn't seem fazed, but I bet she'd rather be alone with Henry in a double seat. He's been away with his parents and they haven't seen each other for weeks. They must have loads to catch up on. But instead, the minute we set off, they start pointing here and there, showing me the road to Edinburgh and the way to the sea. It's about a half-hour drive to the school, which is outside the city, and at first everywhere looks very grey. Then we leave the outskirts and drive through green hills. Up here, it's easy to forget how close we are to Edinburgh. There's not much to see apart from fields, woods and a few lakes.

After we've driven a long way down a narrow country lane in the middle of nowhere, Henry turns to me. 'Round the next bend, up there on the hill, you can get the first glimpse of the school.' It must be so familiar to him, but he still sounds a bit excited. 'It's like coming home, every time,' he murmurs, turning back to the window. Grace nods with a smile.

We reach the hilltop and turn the corner. The road ahead

of us winds through the valley along a river that snakes away to the sea. And then I see it. The former monastery, with the big church in the middle, surrounded by a dark wall. The jumble of rooftops and pointed spires, reaching up into the blue sky. The sun is glittering on the smooth surface of a small lake, and in the background, I can make out the roofs of the next village.

'Wow,' I breathe.

'I know, right?' Henry glances over his shoulder at me. How dare he have such green eyes? 'Welcome home, Emma from Germany.'

4

HENRY

It's the last but one time, Henry. The last but one time that you'll arrive at Dunbridge Academy after the summer holidays, get out of the bus with those excited butterflies in your stomach, and step onto the cobbled courtyard. I really wish I wasn't so aware of this fact.

I spot at least five people I have to say hello to straight away while I wait for my suitcase to be unloaded. Voices and laughter fill the air: parents are chatting, teachers are hurrying to and fro between little groups of people and mountains of luggage. You can easily tell who's new because they seem kind of shy.

I look around for Emma and see that she's already been pounced on by Tori from the welcoming committee. Meanwhile Grace takes my arm.

'You are coming to lunch, aren't you? Mum's really look-ing forward to seeing you,' she says. She asked just now, on the bus, and this time I can't avoid answering.

'Right now?' I glance inconspicuously in Emma's direc-tion. I'd actually been looking forward to showing her around, making sure she didn't have time to feel homesick.

'We can just take your stuff up to your room and then go,' Grace suggests. I hesitate, yet it's what we've always done. 'Or don't you want to come?'

'No, I do,' I say hastily. Her face is browner than before I went away, her hair longer. The fringe is new, though. 'I have to be back by four at the latest. Mrs Sinclair's wel-come speech,' I explain, as Grace frowns.

'Oh, yeah, I'd almost forgotten, Mr School Captain.'

I have to smile. Then I raise my hand and mess up her fringe. 'This is cute.'

'Yeah, d'you like it?' She smooths her hair down again. 'It was a spur-of-the-moment decision I might live to regret. New school year, new me, you know?'

'Hey, lovebirds?' Sinclair calls, before I have time to reply. Soon after that, I'm hugging my best friend, who, like Tori, is wearing a dark blue school polo shirt. 'Want me to show you the way to your room?'

'Shut it, man.'

Grace rolls her eyes before greeting him.

'Excuse me? Is that the kind of tone my mother expects from her new school captain?'

33

'It's just the jetlag,' I say.

'Jetlag? I thought you didn't get jetlagged when—'

'You don't,' remarks Grace, reaching for my case. 'Coming?'

I glance apologetically at Sinclair, who responds with a shrug.

'See ya later, Henry Harold Bennington,' he calls, as I follow Grace.

My room this year is on the third floor of the east wing, but we have to stop a few times on the way as I spot people in our year. I say hi to Omar and Gideon, who are on the rugby team, and Inés, Salome and Amara, who are in my tutor group. Grace glances impatiently at the clock as I finally heave my suitcase through the doorway and step inside the ancient walls.

'Go ahead and I'll come in a bit, if you like,' I suggest.

'No, no.' She shakes her head. 'Unless you want to unpack first?'

I had wanted to, actually. Shower, unpack, maybe have a little nap, although probably better not the last one.

'You can have a shower at mine,' Grace offers, as if she'd read my mind. 'You won't have to use the communal bathroom just yet then.'

'Sixth form now,' I remind her, as I carry my case up the stairs. Everyone at Dunbridge has known what that means since the junior school. No more dorms or shared rooms, and instead a private room with an en-suite. Space to ourselves, so that we can focus on our A levels. This may be

34

Scotland but, like a few private schools here, we do our exams on the English system.

'Lucky you.' Grace sighs, even though she's had the luxury of a room of her own for ages. I wouldn't want to swap with her, though. It might have been rough, sharing a room with so many boys, but I wouldn't miss the memories for anything in the world. Even Sinclair doesn't stay with his parents in Ebrington – since he first started at this school, he's preferred to sleep in the dorms with the rest of us, and I think that says it all. Of course, as the head's son, he has a choice. Sinclair, Omar, Gideon and I shared a room for the last two years, and that really bonded us. It's almost sad that we'll all have our own rooms from now on. But at least we're on the same corridor.

I register with Mr Acevedo, our houseparent for this year, who hands me the key to my new room. The window looks out to the east, and I can see the sports grounds. Apart from that, it's much the same as the other rooms I've lived in here, just a lot smaller, of course.

I do indeed have a shower, and emerge feeling almost reborn.

'Are you ready?' Grace asks, when I appear. She jumps up from my bed and is reaching for the door handle. 'Mum wants to know where we've got to. I think she and Dad missed you more than I did,' she jokes, and I smile, but feel a twinge of pain. Perhaps because I didn't think as much about Grace as I should have during my five weeks in

Kenya. In the past, we'd spent hours on Skype while I was away, but this time whole days had gone by without us even messaging. And I can't exactly say that I minded. I didn't care all that much, and I don't like that.

Then again, I'd wanted to focus fully on my time with my family. When we were younger, Mum and Dad used to spend all the holidays in Scotland, but for the last few summers, Theo, Maeve and I have visited them wherever they're based. Since last autumn, that's been an international hospital a little way outside Nairobi. Not that we spent the whole five weeks there. Mum and Dad took some time off and we travelled to South Africa together. I can just about remember our time in Johannesburg before I started at Dunbridge, back when I always went to school wherever my parents were stationed at the time. I guess it's less usual nowadays to go to boarding school when you're twelve, and only see your parents a few weeks a year. If it hadn't been for my older brother and sister, who started here at the same time as me and are now both studying at St Andrews, I'm sure it would've been way harder. Without Maeve, especially . . . She made friends just as fast as Theo did, but she never made me feel like I was bugging her.

Starting here wasn't easy for me, yet Dunbridge Academy has been the only constant in my life. A place that's always there, never changing when I come back after the holidays. Familiar faces, friends who speak my language.

At that moment, I remember Emma and feel kind of

guilty. Because I know what it's like to be new and feel lost and overwhelmed. I'd wanted to keep an eye out for her, but what am I doing instead?

Exactly what I *should* be doing. I haven't seen my girlfriend for weeks and I'm going round to her house.

EMMA

The Dunbridge Academy courtyard is buzzing. There are huge Land Rovers, dark 4x4s and estate cars everywhere, parents heaving holdalls and suitcases out of the boots, while pupils greet each other excitedly. Some are already in uniform but most are still wearing their everyday clothes.

I lost sight of Henry ages ago. As soon as we got out of the bus, loads of people came to say hello to him and Grace. They seem to know everyone here. Unlike me. But I don't want to cling to them like a limpet.

'Hello, you must be new.'

I turn my head and look into the freckled face of a girl about my age. Her long copper-red hair is done up in a neat plait that falls over her shoulder. 'Hi, I'm Tori. I'm in the lower sixth and I'm on the lookout for new people.'

My heart leaps. Lower sixth, same as me.

'I'm Emma,' I introduce myself. Tori must be able to hear my relief because she smiles reassuringly at me before we shake hands. She's wearing a polo shirt with the school crest embroidered on the left-hand side. Beneath it, there's a name badge.

'Nice to meet you, Emma. Welcome to Dunbridge.'

I think this is the moment when the last part of me that hadn't been completely sure finally grasps that this is real. Before I've worked out whether this is a good or bad thing, Tori's talking again.

'Can I help you with your luggage? What year are you in? I'll introduce you to your houseparent.'

'Lower sixth.' I gulp. 'I'm on a year abroad.'

'Oh, cool! We're the same year, then. I'll take you over.' Tori looks at my suitcases. 'Did you come on your own?'

I nod with a tense smile. 'My mum was going to bring me but it didn't work out.'

'Oh, right.'

'It's OK,' I say, kind of without wanting to. But I *really* don't want to start out with everyone feeling sorry for me.

'Well, you're here now,' says Tori, cheerfully, reaching for one of my cases. 'Come on.'

I follow her through the arcades that link the former church at the heart of the school with the long buildings that entirely enclose the campus. Tori keeps to the left and eventually we reach a curved staircase in smooth stone. Pupils are darting to and fro, some in little groups, others with their parents. Tori's always waving to someone. She seems to know so many people.

'Later on, I'll show you around properly, in peace, if you

like. I started here in the junior school and I know the place like the back of my hand.' She points in the direction we'd come. 'The old church is now the dining room, and over there are the classrooms in the south wing. The girls' dorms are here in the west wing and the boys are over in the east. Once you get to the third form, there's a floor per year, while all the juniors, first- and second-formers, sleep in the north wing.' Tori stops at the foot of the stairs. 'I've got good news and bad news for you. Good news first: we get a great view from our rooms – they're up at the top. Only the upper sixth do better from right under the roof. The bad part is, there's no lift.'

'Oh,' I say, as she reaches for my luggage. 'You don't have to. I mean, I can easily come back down again . . .'

Tori raises her eyebrows disapprovingly. 'Hey! Of course I'm going to help you. You're family now.'

She grins, and I feel like I'm going to burst into tears. It doesn't sound like she's just saying it, especially when I remember how warmly she greeted everyone just now.

'We'll just ask Ms Barnett which room you're in.' Tori's slightly out of breath as she climbs the worn stone steps with the smaller of my cases. 'She's in charge of the third floor and the person to go to for pastoral stuff.'

'My houseparent, then?' I guess. The rapid footsteps of a group of younger girls we meet on the stairs echo off the unplastered walls.

'You learn fast.' Tori points down the second-floor corridor.

'Third form on the first floor, fourth form on the second and so on.'

I glance through one of the lattice windows on the staircase. From here, you can see right into another courtyard, behind the church this time. There's a lawn, criss-crossed by cobbled paths along which pupils are hurrying from here to there and back again.

All the Dunbridge buildings are grouped around the two courtyards. If this is the west wing, the boys' dorms must be on the other side of the archway and the broad bridge that brings you into the school grounds from the road. Henry's wing. Not that that matters to me in anyway.

My knees are wobbly by the time we reach the third floor, an age later. The higher we climb, the quieter it gets. On the lower floors, shouts and laughter are coming from the younger pupils' rooms, but things are clearly much more civilized up here among the sixth-formers. I can't help noticing the awestruck way that Tori glances at the two girls just coming down the stairs from the very top. They must be in the upper sixth and, unlike the younger kids, they seem totally unfazed by the chaos. All the same, they give Tori and me friendly nods as they pass.

'Hi, Ms Barnett!' Tori calls, a moment later, as a slim woman walks away down the corridor. She turns to us. 'I've found a new girl.'

I follow Tori and force myself to smile. Ms Barnett must be

in her sixties, and has her light brown hair tied up in a severe bun, yet there's warmth in her eyes. I like her, even before we've spoken a word.

'You must be Emma Wiley,' she says, holding out her hand. 'Laura and Jacob's daughter, right?'

I feel suddenly cold. 'Yes, I … . You know my parents?'

'I was your mother's houseparent too, and taught them both French and art. Did they come with you? I'd love to say hello.'

I force myself to keep smiling, as I shake my head. 'No, sadly they couldn't make it,' I manage.

I don't know why I don't tell her the truth. Maybe because I don't want the first thing Ms Barnett hears to be that my parents are divorced and that my dad walked out on us.

'What a shame. But I'm so pleased you're here, Emma.' Her smile is so warm that I relax a little. 'Welcome to Dunbridge Academy.'

'Thanks,' I say.

'Did you have a good journey? Let me just get the key to your room. Then you can settle in a bit.'

I stand there next to Tori while Ms Barnett disappears into a room to our left. Maybe she sleeps on this floor, too. When she comes back, she's holding a key and beckons us to follow. At the very end of the long corridor, she stops outside a door in dark wood and unlocks it. 'I hope you like it,' she says, letting me go ahead.

I don't know what I'd been expecting. The words 'boarding school' made me think of gloomy rooms and narrow bunk beds, but this room isn't like that at all. There's a bay window, with lattice panes. The glass is a little misty and the paint is peeling on the frames but that doesn't tarnish the room's charm. Quite the opposite.

As I move further in, old floorboards creak under my feet, and it's wonderful. My eyes take in steep roofs and small gable windows, then move on to the pointed spires of the old church. Below us is the cobbled courtyard; a little further away, I can see the hills and, on the horizon, the sea.

'I love the view from up here.' Ms Barnett steps alongside me. 'I hope you'll soon feel at home, Emma.'

I don't know what's the matter with me. I only know that it's very hard to fight the sting in my eyes. I'm here at this boarding school and everyone I've met so far has been super-nice, but that doesn't stop me feeling seriously overwhelmed.

'Did you bring your own bed linen?' Ms Barnett asks.

'No, I . . .' I falter. Damn. Did I forget? I did, didn't I? At least, I can't remember having packed any. 'I don't think so.'

'Not a problem. I'll bring you a set. We have towels too. I'll give you a moment to get started with your unpacking, then come back to go over the house rules with you, OK?'

'Yes, thank you.'

'Mrs Sinclair is giving a short welcome assembly for all the new pupils at four o'clock. Come and find me beforehand and I'll show you the way.'

'I can show her,' offers Tori, who is still standing in my doorway.

'Really? That would be kind, Victoria, thank you.'

Tori looks as if she's making a serious effort not to roll her eyes. I find myself smiling, then remember that it would be wiser not to warm to her so much. I'm not here to make friends. Everything at this school comes with an end date. I shouldn't start liking everyone or it'll just cause more unnecessary pain when my time's up.

'I'll knock for you later,' Tori promises. 'I have to go back down now and look out for more new kids.'

'Don't let me keep you,' I say.

'After Mrs Sinclair's speech, I'll give you the tour! I promise. Bye, Ms Barnett!'

Ms Barnett watches Tori with a shake of the head, but I can see the corners of her lips twitching. She turns back to me. 'Come to me at any time if you have questions, Emma. Anything at all. Don't be shy. I'll see you again soon.'

She lays the key on the desk, walks out of the door, and I'm on my own, really all-on-my-own alone, and the silence feels oppressive.

I'm truly here. I slowly turn three-sixty degrees. All the furniture is in the same dark wood and looks like it could tell a few tales. I wonder how many generations of boarders have passed through here. There are so many marks on the desktop beside the wall. I kind of like that. Above it is a cork pinboard and above that are two simple shelves. The bed's in

43

the corner opposite the windows, with a small bedside table, a chest of drawers and a plain wardrobe. Just the bare necessities, but it already feels cosy, even with no bedding on the bare mattress and no pictures on the walls. Am I allowed to put stuff up? Suddenly I regret not having packed any photos or strings of fairy lights. Apart from a few Polaroids that I carry around in my diary, all my mementos, photos of Mum and me, Isi, our crowd, and the girls from the athletics club, are at home, stuck up over my desk there. It didn't even occur to me to bring them. Why would I? I'm only here for a year. It's not worth settling in.

I run my fingers over the wooden desk. Then I reach for one of my cases to start unpacking. At least, that's my plan. I've just put it on the floor and undone the zip when my phone buzzes.

It's Mum – I hadn't even told her that I've made it in one piece. I jump up and hastily snatch it off my bed.

'Emmi-Mouse, you didn't forget me, did you?' Mum asks, as her image comes into focus.

'Just for a moment,' I admit. 'It's all so exciting.' I sit on the floor and lean back against the bed. Against *my* bed, in *my* room. 'I've just arrived at the school and I've met hundreds of new people.'

'You made it, then? Everything worked out? Come on, tell me all about it! Or isn't this a good time?'

'No, it's fine, don't worry.' I smile. 'Ms Barnett just showed me to my room.'

'She's still there? That's nice. Give her my love. Maybe she'll remember me.'

'She already asked after you.' And Dad. But I'll keep that part to myself.

'Really?' Mum sighs. 'I do wish I could be there with you, Emmi. What's it like? Have you got a nice room?'

'Yes, it's much bigger than I expected.' I switch the camera around so that I can show her.

'It looks so much like mine back in the day,' Mum says. 'I miss that view.'

'Yes, it's gorgeous,' I say, flipping back to the front camera.

'How was the flight?'

I pause. 'It all went fine.'

'Really?' Mum asks, in the tone that means she's busted me. 'Emma?'

'Really. I only *nearly* missed the plane.'

'You what?'

'My alarm didn't go off.'

'Emma Charlotte Wiley, I hope you're not serious.'

'Yeah, sorry. But I'm here now, so it's all good.' And if I hadn't been running so late, I probably wouldn't have met Henry like that.

'I knew I couldn't leave you to your own devices.' Mum sighs, but I hear the amusement in her voice.

'Ha, too late,' I say, making an effort to sound unconcerned. It's not a hundred per cent successful, and she seems to notice.

'I'm so sorry I couldn't come with you.'

She has to stop sounding regretful if she doesn't want me to burst into tears.

'I really didn't mind,' I repeat, the way I did on the phone yesterday evening.

'I do, though. I'm such a bad mother.'

'You're not,' I retort. 'Anyway, flying on my own was way cooler. I felt mysterious and independent at the airport, not like some little kid being taken to school by her mum.'

Mum laughs, and somehow that just makes everything worse. 'Of course, I ought to have kept my distance and never even dared to call you, Emmi-Mouse.'

'We both know that's a lie,' I reply, blinking so my eyes don't even think of welling up.

'You're probably right.' When Mum speaks again, she's sounding more serious. 'I'll come for a visit in a couple of weekends at the latest.'

'You're invited to dinner with the Herrmanns in a couple of weekends.'

'Exactly. Now I've got the perfect excuse – I have to take an urgent flight to Edinburgh.'

'What kind of example are you setting me, Mum, dreaming up excuses and weaselling out of invitations like that?'

'A very good one, of course. It's your life and you can say no to whatever you like. Besides, extreme reluctance is a perfectly valid excuse.'

'Is that so?'

'Yes. Except in the case of homework, but you know that.

Speaking of which, you'll have a study hour at Dunbridge. Every afternoon at four, an hour with no distractions, just you and your books. Ms Barnett knows no mercy, but she also knows every trick in the book for getting ink out of your uniform.'

Uniform . . . I really need to ask Ms Barnett about that.

'And you're sure that you really want to go through with this?' Mum asks, when I go too long without speaking.

'What?' I ask hastily. 'The year abroad? Yes, of course I'm sure.'

And even if I weren't it's a bit late to change my mind now.

'OK?' Mum says, and I shut my eyes. 'It's just . . . Emmi, you know you don't have to do this. Not for my sake.'

'I know, Mum.'

'Did I pressure you, talking about it all the time? I think going abroad while you're at school is an amazing opportunity, but you don't have to if—'

'Mum,' I say, and she falls silent. 'You didn't pressure me.'

'Are you absolutely sure of that?'

'Absolutely sure,' I say, and deep down, I know she's still trying to find an explanation for my sudden change of mind. Of course she is, because for as long as I can remember, she's been suggesting that I spend some of my school career at Dunbridge Academy. Not because she doesn't have time for me and wants to ship me off to Scotland, but because she's a top lawyer who studied at St Andrews, and it's her goal to make all of that possible for me too. The best education, the best foundation for the best future.

But I didn't want to. I didn't want to be the kind of businesswoman who spends more time on planes and high-speed trains than in her own home. Because that's all she has left. Because it stops people asking questions.

She's divorced, and she threw herself into her career to compensate for that. I don't actually think that, though . . . or maybe I do a bit. All I know is that I don't want to be at a posh British school just so I can put it on my CV. That's not what this is about. This is about getting answers to questions I can't ask anybody else, for which I have to go to this school, the one where my parents met all those years ago. It sounds like a fairy tale: the German girl and the Glasgow boy, meeting at an elite school in Scotland. But there are no fairy tales in real life. There's just Mum, who puts her work above everything else, and Dad, whose laugh I can't even remember.

But I can't tell Mum that. She'd freak out if she knew that every time I listen to Jacob Wiley's 'For Emma' tape I wonder if his fingertips are still rough from playing the guitar. I think that happens if a person lets you down often enough. You want to protect your child from being let down too. But I'm not a child any more. I'm almost an adult and, yeah, maybe my dad won't want anything to do with me. Maybe it'll hurt as much as it did back then, when he'd send me a present and a card at my birthday and Christmas and promise to visit soon. I cancelled riding holidays with friends so that I could go to the seaside with him, and then he forgot. He just forgot.

So what's the worst that can happen? Nothing can shock me now. I want him to look at me and explain why he did it. I want answers to my questions. And until then, I'm praying he can give me some.

5

EMMA

'. . . Smoking, alcohol and drugs are strictly forbidden anywhere within the school grounds. And no boys in girls' rooms after ten o'clock, at which time you must be back in your own wing,' says Ms Barnett. 'And vice versa, of course. Break these rules once and you'll get a warning. A second time in a term and you're facing expulsion. Do you have any questions, Emma?'

I shake my head. I should've brought something to write with to note everything down.

'I'm sure it'll all be a bit confusing at first, but you'll soon find your feet, don't worry. And I'm always here if you need me for anything.'

'Thank you,' I say. 'My mum said to give you her love. I just spoke to her.'

'Oh, that's nice. I hope she and Jacob are well,' replies Ms Barnett.

Ask her. Ask her anything. This is your chance. I'm just opening my mouth, when we hear suitcases being wheeled down the corridor. Ms Barnett immediately turns to the door.

'Well, it sounds like the next batch is arriving.' She smiles. 'You'll soon get to know everyone, Emma.'

As I leave Ms Barnett's office, I spot three more girls my age. She's handing out keys and looks busy, so I head back to my room.

My suitcases are half unpacked and the mess is making me edgy. Although maybe some of that is the realization that I don't even know how I'm going to get the information I need about my father. I ought to come up with some questions so that I can get right in there the next time I have a chance.

I've only had a minute or two crouching on the floor amid all the chaos, sorting my underwear, when there's a single short, hard knock and the door flies open.

'Hey, have you seen Bennington? He's meant to . . . Oh.' The blond guy who's just marched into my room stops abruptly when he sees me sitting there. Me and my knickers. He blushes bright red and stares up at the ceiling. At least for a second. Then his eyes flit to the door and back to me. 'Er, sorry, I thought—'

'Sinclair!' We whirl around at the sound of the outraged voice. A moment later, Tori's standing in the doorway too.

'What's the point of knocking if you're going to walk in without waiting for an answer?'

'I'm sorry but . . .' He looks from me to Tori. 'Weren't you going to have this room?'

'Yeah, but I asked Ms Barnett if I could swap. Weird vibes, I dunno. It's better next door. Emma, you might be able to swap too.'

They're both speaking quickly and I have trouble following them. 'No, I . . . I think I like it,' I falter.

'Are you sure? I could lend you a crystal. That might make it better.'

'You and your crystals! They're so pointless,' says the blond guy.

Tori glares murderously at him. 'Without my pointless crystals you'd be resitting GCSE maths this year.'

I have to fight back a laugh because Tori sounds dead serious.

'No, I'd be resitting maths if Henry hadn't coached me.'

'It was a bit of both,' Tori declares, looking at me. 'Emma, are you ready for a tour?'

I nod, bewildered.

'This is Sinclair, by the way,' she says, pointing at the boy.

'Charles,' he adds, smiling at me. I'm totally lost now.

'He's the head's son, so everyone just calls him Sinclair but nobody knows why.' Tori shrugs. 'Emma, Sinclair – Sinclair, Emma. The new girl from Germany.'

Charles – or Sinclair, I'm not quite sure what I ought to

call him – opens his mouth, but Tori doesn't let him get a word in. 'Spare us your lousy German. Nobody wants to hear you count to ten.'

'Hey,' he protests, but he doesn't say anything more. He looks away again as he catches another glimpse of my under-wear. I hastily shove it under a running top that I've just folded. If Tori spotted it, she's not letting on.

All she says is, 'I don't know where Henry is. He's not in the girls' wing, anyway.'

'I think he's with Grace,' I say, and suddenly they're both looking at me. Sinclair's expression is confused while Tori is clearly surprised. She pushes past him, shoving him aside by the shoulder.

'Wait, you know Grace?'

'And Henry?' asks Sinclair.

'Yeah, well . . . no, not really. Henry was on my flight. He had to change in Frankfurt and we got chatting. Grace came to the airport to meet him and took the bus back here with us. I think Henry was just going to take his things up to his room and go back to her house. They were talking about it earlier.'

'That makes sense,' says Sinclair. 'Grace is a day girl.'

'She knows that, if they've met,' Tori snaps at him. 'Don't you, Emma?'

'Yeah,' I say. 'Are you a day pupil, too?' I ask Sinclair.

He shakes his head. 'No, my dad has a bakery in Ebring-ton and we live there. But I like boarding here. I get kind of bored on my own at home.'

'He moved into the dorm to cheer Henry up when he was homesick in the first form,' Tori explains.

'Hey, you cried your eyes out too when you first started, way more than he did,' Sinclair replies drily.

'Yes, but I didn't have a brother and sister here,' she retorts. I find myself smiling.

Sinclair looks at me. 'Well, either way, he has to be back in twenty minutes because he's got to be at Mum's welcome assembly. Think Henry's forgotten?'

'Isn't he answering his phone?' Tori asks.

'No, he . . .' Sinclair pulls his phone from his trouser pocket. 'Oh, wait. He says he's already there.'

'Oh, yeah, and you thought he'd be here, did you?' murmurs Tori, and I shiver.

'Aren't I meant to go too?' I blurt. 'To the welcome assembly?'

'Oh, bum, yeah.' Tori stares wide-eyed. 'Have you got your uniform ready? You have to wear it.'

'Yeah.' Sinclair nods. 'And to morning assembly too. That's every Monday before breakfast, over there in the hall, for Mum to give out important information and notices. The rest of the time you just have to wear the trousers, polo shirt and jumper. Full uniform's for special occasions.'

'Such as the welcome assembly. So, you need your skirt, blouse and blazer. Shoo!' Tori shoves Sinclair backwards out of my room. 'And your hair has to be tied back, unless it's too short.'

'OK,' I manage.

'I'll come back and check that it's all right in a bit, if you like,' Tori promises. She smiles at me and shuts the door behind her and Sinclair.

I slip out of my jeans and T-shirt and reach for the hanger holding the uniform I've just picked up from Ms Barnett. We had to send the school my measurements in advance so that it could be ordered.

They're just new clothes, yet I feel like an entirely new Emma when, a little later, I study myself in the mirror on the back of the wardrobe door. The hem of the blue-and-green checked, pleated skirt ends just above my knees, and I'm wearing dark tights. I tuck my white blouse neatly into the waistband and knot the tie, which is worn by girls and boys alike. I like the look but I'm glad we can swap the uniform for beige or dark blue trousers, polo shirts and jumpers most of the time.

I put my hair back in a quick, simple plait. I have to get Tori to show me how to do the fiddly style of plait she's wearing, but there isn't time now.

I slip on my blazer and shoes, then open the door. Just as she promised, Tori's waiting in the corridor. Sinclair's leaning on the wall beside her, whispering something to her, and they start to giggle. I can't help smiling, even though I don't know the joke. Somehow, I like the two of them.

'Oh, perfect.' Tori looks me over. 'You can roll the top of your skirt to make it shorter.'

'That's against the rules, Tori,' says Sinclair.

'Yeah, but you love to see it.'

He blushes and rolls his eyes.

'Let me just check the knot,' murmurs Tori, reaching for my blouse collar and straightening my tie a little. 'Very good. This way!'

'Do I need anything else?' I ask, glancing back at my room.

'Only your key,' Tori says, as I pick it up. 'Great. Oh, you'll need a lanyard and your student card.' She holds up her own key, which is hanging from a dark blue fabric strap, printed with the school crest. 'But we'll sort that out later.'

I follow her down the corridor, smiling at all the new faces we pass on our way to the stairs. Tori tells me the names of a dozen girls in our year, and I instantly forget them. My head is already spinning with information.

'Has Valentine arrived yet?' Tori asks us, as we walk down the stairs. Of course I haven't the least idea who that is, but her super-casual tone tells me she likes him.

'Dunno. Why?' Sinclair replies. His voice is chillier now and he digs his hands into his trouser pockets. 'Why should I care when the upper sixth gets here?'

'Just wondering,' mumbles Tori. 'If you see him and he mentions me, tell him I said hi.'

'Why would he mention you?'

'It was so funny.' We reach the foot of the stairs and Tori points to her left. 'He's been following me on Insta for a while. A couple of days ago, he liked one of my posts.'

'Wow, that makes you practically an item.'

She simply ignores Sinclair and looks at me. 'So then I liked his latest post. And he's liked my last two. You don't do that if you're not interested in a person, do you, Emma?'

'I don't think so. Sounds like he's been stalking you,' I reply, because she seems to expect it.

'You see.' Tori turns proudly to Sinclair.

'Yeah, great. So now you reckon he's into you.'

'You think he isn't? He DMed me after that.'

'What did he want?' Sinclair asks, without looking at Tori.

'He asked how my holidays were.' She seems to be holding back a sigh.

'The guy's a weapon,' Sinclair tells me.

'Hey!' Tori glares at him.

'No, really. Just keep away from the upper sixth. They're so arrogant.'

'Apart from Eleanor Attenborough, huh?' I might not have known Tori long but there's no mistaking the hint of mockery in her voice. Sinclair glances sharply at her. 'In the fourth form, he was in undying love with her,' she explains.

'Oh, man, everyone had a crush on Ellie,' mumbles Sinclair. 'But that doesn't change the fact that Valentine's an arse. Hardly surprising with an uncle like Mr Ward. I'll pray you don't get him as a teacher, Emma.'

'Mr Ward is dire,' agrees Tori. 'But Valentine can't help his family.'

'No, he just runs squealing to him about every little thing, and there's no way he'd be rugby captain without him.'

'He's rugby captain because he's class!'

'Puh-lease.'

'What do you know about it?' mutters Tori. We turn a corner and Sinclair stops with a bunch of guys who greet him loudly. Tori leads me up another staircase and down two more corridors. I've lost all sense of direction by the time she stops outside an open set of double doors; next to them on the wall is a sign reading 'Head Teacher's Office'.

'Here you are.' She glances through an outer office to another door, also open, beyond which I can hear quiet voices. 'Mrs Sinclair's office is here, to the left, and the assembly will be next door in the hall. Go right in. You're not the only newbie. Can you find your way back, or shall I come and meet you?'

I'd normally decline at once. I don't want to get on Tori's nerves, but right now, I'm not at all sure that I'd ever find my room again. I'm just opening my mouth to speak when I feel a light touch on my shoulder.

'Don't worry, I'll show her the way back.'

'Hey, there he is!' Tori beams as Henry comes towards us, now in uniform too. My silly, treacherous heart skips a beat at the sound of his voice. 'How was your flight? You look knackered, Bennington.'

Henry laughs and gives her a hug. 'Wow, thanks a bunch, Tori. You're too kind.'

'It's all true.' She smiles at him and her teasing expression shows me what close friends they are.

'How about you? Good journey back? How were the holidays?'

'Yeah, great.' Tori shoves Henry and me towards the door. 'I'll tell you later. You've got a hot date.'

I enter the room. Henry laughs and runs a hand through his freshly washed curls. In all other respects, he does look bleary. Even so, his eyes are infinitely green. I was right. He looks way too good in this uniform.

We walk into the hall where the new pupils are sitting in rows of chairs. Most of them are super-young, but I spot a few older faces further back.

'Does it matter where I sit?' I ask.

'No, no.' Henry turns to me. 'Sit anywhere you like.'

I head down the central aisle to the back and sit in a free seat, while Henry stays at the front.

He's talking to a much younger girl, and I take the chance to watch him inconspicuously. The dark blue blazer fits his slim torso like a second skin.

When Henry's eyes meet mine, I hastily look away. I hope he didn't notice I was watching him.

I mustn't be so pleased to see him. I force myself to remember Grace's hands in his hair. Her lips on his and Henry's beaming face when he saw her. God, it's so messed-up that I'm wasting this much head space on him. I've just been through a break-up and I don't plan to let anyone else play with my emotions like that any time soon. So what's my stupid heart up to, fluttering like that at the first guy I've met here? It's just not fair.

Henry greets every new pupil like he's genuinely thrilled to see them here. I don't know how he does it, but he's everywhere, and making it all look so easy. He even manages to get the little kids smiling shyly and not looking quite so scared.

Henry straightens his shoulders a touch as a blonde woman in her forties enters the room. His eyes flicker along the rows of chairs, and I get the message. I stand up with the others. My heart beats faster as Mrs Sinclair shuts the door, gives Henry a nod and a smile, and comes to stand at the front of the room. It was never this quiet at my school when the head gave a talk, and I'm suddenly feeling ashamed of that. It has something to do with respect.

Mrs Sinclair's eyes rest on each of us in turn. When she looks at me, I can barely hold back a gulp. I want to make a good impression. I don't know why that matters so much to me. She studies me, and somehow I feel like she's looking at me longer than the others. At that moment, the question pops into my head. Does she know my father? She's about my parents' age; if she went to school here too, she might well do. I wish I could ask her right now, but of course that's not an option.

Mrs Sinclair smiles and nods to us to sit down again. She

waits until the scraping of chair legs has stopped and there's quiet.

'On behalf of all the staff, I'd like to wish you all a very warm welcome to Dunbridge Academy.'

HENRY

It's the second time I've heard Mrs Sinclair's welcome speech, but I'm no less impressed than I was back in the first form. Quite the reverse. Once she's introduced me to everyone as school captain and their first port of call if they have any problems, I glance casually over the rows of seats.

It feels like it was just yesterday that I was sitting there. Maeve on my left, holding my hand, Theo on my right, rolling his eyes because I'd been crying again. We'd just arrived from Jordan, where my parents were stationed at the time. I hadn't a clue what would be in store for me at this Scottish boarding school because, although my family are British, this country had never been home to me. I was born in Cape Town and I'd been to school in five different countries. Until I arrived here, I didn't know what it was like to have a permanent home. Or that home isn't just people but places too.

Just like then, the new arrivals are listening to Mrs Sinclair with rapt faces. Her aura, her straight posture and precisely tied-back hair don't allow you to whisper or crack jokes in her presence. At moments like these, she isn't my best friend's mum, she's the head teacher of the school that made me the person I am today.

Emma's sitting one row from the back. Seeing how intently she's listening makes me smile.

'I'm sure that when you think about school, you think about grades,' says Mrs Sinclair. 'And, yes, you will sit exams here too, but as I see it, your academic results are not the most important thing. At Dunbridge Academy, our main aim is to instil values and build character. One day, you will leave this school and go out into the world. For some of you, that won't be for a few years yet, while for others, you are within touching distance of your final exams.' She pauses and her eyes flick to me, which gives me goosebumps. 'When that day comes, I hope you will have positive memories of your time here with us to look back on, and that you will feel fortified and strong. Use your time at this school to sharpen your minds and broaden your horizons. You will have to be disciplined and work hard to get to grips with day-to-day life at Dunbridge Academy. Some of you will find that easier than others. You will have to deal with failures and setbacks. But you should always be aware that at my school your fellow pupils are not rivals but allies.'

Mrs Sinclair is silent for a moment. Through the closed windows, I can hear voices and quiet laughter outside. 'The pupils who make us proudest are those who leave Dunbridge Academy as young adults who stand up for themselves and for their fellow humans. To me, outstanding exam results and places at the top universities are less important than walking mindfully through this life and being kind, getting to know yourselves better and growing. If you achieve that during your time with us then, in my view, you will have succeeded.'

You could have heard a pin drop, and I hardly dare breathe. I feel a warmth in my belly as I see Emma nodding. For some reason, I'm certain she will succeed in all the things Mrs Sinclair is talking about. Even if she's only here for a year.

'It is in your own hands,' says Mrs Sinclair, pacing a few steps to and fro in front of the first row of seats, 'as to whether this time will be the best or the worst period of your life. I demand just one thing of you: make the most of it.'

6

EMMA

After Mrs Sinclair's talk, Henry took me and the others along to the school office. Mr Harper, with snow-white hair and alert brown eyes, handed each of us a dark blue bag with the school logo on it. Inside it we found everything we'd need for everyday life at the school: the lanyard and student card, our timetables, and a planner with a map of the school buildings. I didn't have much time to look at it before Henry brought me back to the girls' wing after a quick tour of the grounds.

He'd advised me always to use the church spire to get my bearings because it marked the centre of the school. That tip has helped me no longer to feel totally lost – although it would be an exaggeration to say I know my way around now. There's a new building next to the west wing, which houses the school hall and modern science rooms. There are more classrooms in the north wing, behind which are the sports facilities. I'm thrilled that, as well as a sports hall, there's a proper fitness centre and pool, and a stadium with an all-weather running track circling the rugby pitch.

To the left-hand side of the playing fields, there's a path to the vegetable garden and greenhouses, which are close to the stables and riding hall. It's huge. Gigantic fields and meadows that stretch down to a wood. There must be some great runs around here. I'd love to change out of my uniform and straight into my running gear the moment I get back to my room. But it's dinnertime soon and I don't want to be late.

'I could take this as an insult, you know,' Tori declares, when she knocks for me a little later and we walk down to the dining room together. 'I wanted to show you around, and Henry could have guessed that.'

'To be fair, he did offer first,' I say, locking my door, 'when we were on the plane.'

She gives me a quizzical look. 'Well, *I* don't think that's fair, Emma.' I have no chance to reply, because a few metres down the corridor, she stops to hammer on another door.

She grins as we hear a muffled 'OK, OK!'

'Come on!' Tori yells, 'Or at least tell us what you're doing in there, Ms Henderson.' She takes a step back as the door flies open.

'You're impossible, Victoria.' The girl glares at her in annoyance.

'Your hair's still down,' Tori remarks, unimpressed. 'And wet.'

'Yeah, cos you're stressing me.'

'Have you been swimming?' Tori asks.

'Obviously. The championship heats are in four weeks,' she says, shutting her door behind her. As we walk down the corridor, she pulls her long brown hair back with her hand and glances at me.

'This is Emma,' says Tori, before I can introduce myself. 'She's new.'

'Ah.' Tori's friend eyes me. 'I'm Olive, hi.' She doesn't sound unfriendly, but she's not smiling. Maybe that's just because she's concentrating on putting her hair into a fish-tail plait in record time.

'Pleased to meet you,' I say.

'What's your star sign?' Tori asks, out of nowhere.

'Er, Aries.'

Tori scrutinizes me, then nods decisively, as if that had been the only correct answer to her question.

'And your rising sign?'

'My what?'

'There are websites where you can look it up. You just have to know the exact time when you were born.'

'I'd have to ask my mum,' I say.

'Then we can look it up together,' Tori says. 'I think you have kind of a Libra energy. So maybe that's your ascendant.

66

Just a hunch. I think you two are going to get on. Olive is a pure Scorpio, but she's very nice really.'

Olive tosses the finished plait back over her shoulder and looks sharply at Tori.

'I'm a Leo,' Tori adds. She's gazing expectantly at me, so I nod like I understand, even though I have no clue what that's meant to tell me about her. 'And my rising sign is Gemini. Like Val's.'

'I thought Geminis were arseholes,' Olive observes.

'Hey!'

'That's what you said before the holidays. That they were two-faced.'

'Some of them.' Tori sighs. 'But my rising sign isn't very strong. And Val's definitely Gemini with an Aquarius vibe.'

'Sinclair's Aquarius, isn't he?' Olive says.

'Yeah, he's totally an air sign.'

'I keep telling you, Sinclair's a much better match for you.'

'Yeah, he's sweet,' Tori agrees. 'Right, Emma?'

'Um, yeah, he – he seems really nice.' And he's the head teacher's son, I remember, the head I have so much respect for. I'd better watch what I say now.

'No way could I date him, though,' Tori continues. 'I cleared up after he boaked on that sailing trip in the first form, and he knows all my secrets.'

'He's your soul-mate. That's a good starting point,' says Olive.

67

'No, no, no danger. Sinclair's like a brother. It'd be like being into Will.' Tori pulls a face. We join a stream of girls heading from the west wing down the corridor towards the dining room.

'Is Will your brother?' I ask.

Tori nods. 'Yeah, he's in the year below us. You'll see him at dinner.'

'Will's very sweet, too,' Olive adds.

'He's too young for you, Olive.'

'Actually, we're the same age, remember?'

'Anyway, I'm not having it. And he's got a crush on this lad Kit in his form. Couldn't talk about anyone else all summer.'

'Do I know him?' asks Olive.

'He's not a boarder, he's an Irvine. His parents run the shop, and he's an Aquarius too, obviously. I mean, he wears leather jackets and smokes in secret,' Tori says. 'If you ever need anything, that place sells everything, Emma. I'll show you when we go to Ebrington.'

'Oh, does he help out there sometimes?' Olive straightens slightly. 'I know who you mean, then. Will ought to get together with him – they'd make such a cute couple.'

'You're right.' Tori falls silent as we head for the dining room, and I stop myself wondering about Henry's star sign. I don't believe in astrology, so why should I care? No way he's a Gemini, though, whatever that means.

The murmur of voices and laughter floats through the large

double doors and mingles with the echo of our footsteps on the stone floor. I gasp involuntarily as we enter the hall. The stained-glass windows at the far end make it very clear that this used to be a church. Golden evening light falls onto the old stone tiles and the countless tables in dark wood, where loads of pupils are already sitting. There are chandeliers hanging from the high ceiling and to the right of the door is a serving hatch, with a tempting aroma wafting from it.

I follow Tori and Olive down the central aisle. The tables seem to be allocated by age group. The long ones at the front are occupied by intimidated-looking juniors, but everyone behind them seems more relaxed. Tori and Olive head towards the back, and my heart skips treacherously as I spot Henry. He's sitting next to Sinclair and they're deep in conversation with another guy, making wild hand gestures.

'Stop havering, Omar!' Sinclair yells, giving him a playful punch on the forearm. Henry looks up as we sit down opposite him. His lips form a silent 'Hi' and I feel calmer. At that moment, the dining-room doors are shut. Conversation ebbs away, and complete silence falls as a gong sounds. The others stand up, so I copy them. I can see Mrs Sinclair right at the front, by the staff tables. She waits a moment, then nods, and we sit.

'Nice to see you all again,' she says, once there's a hush. Her voice has a somewhat solemn tone. 'I know some of you have had a long journey, and that you're all hungry, so all

I will say is: welcome back to Dunbridge Academy, and enjoy your meal.'

I join in the applause, and glance at Tori.

'Oldest first,' she explains, over the noise, nodding at the tables next to us where the upper sixth are standing up. 'After today, there'll be a table-duty rota, which changes every week. When it's your turn, you have to be here a bit early to get everything ready for everyone else. And in return, the rest of the time, you get to sit down with the table already laid.'

I nod.

'Hey, everyone, this is Emma!' Tori calls, to the table in general. I look into a sea of smiling faces and raise my hand to greet them.

'Hi, Emma,' people say around me. I'm glad they haven't all told me their names. There's no way I'd remember them all right now.

'Don't worry about everyone's names,' says Henry, as if he'd read my mind. 'You'll pick them up by osmosis in lessons.'

'What subjects are you doing?' Tori asks, beside me.

'English, maths and PE,' I say, 'plus chemistry and history.'

'PE?' Tori groans. 'God, Emma, do you know what that means?'

'No.'

'A morning run, every day, before breakfast.'

'Doesn't everyone have to do that anyway?'

Tori shrugs. 'Yeah, but you guys get marked down if you don't turn up. I skive as often as I can.'

'Like Ms Barnett's going to fall for you having period pain every week,' murmurs Sinclair.

'Yeah, but there's hay fever too, you know,' Tori reminds him cheerfully.

He raises his eyebrows. 'Not at this time of year there isn't.'

'For *my* hay fever there is,' she retorts.

'Grace and I are doing PE too,' says Olive. I don't know if I'm imagining it, but she still sounds kind of cold. I'm not the only person to notice it because Henry gives her a funny look, then turns to me.

'I'm doing English, maths, biology, chemistry and Latin,' he says, unprompted.

'An interesting combination,' I say.

Henry nods. 'I couldn't choose between humanities and science and I've got another year before I have to drop a couple.'

'He still can't admit to himself that he wants to be a doctor,' says Sinclair. 'Like his parents. His brother and sister are studying medicine too.'

'Bollocks. I'm going to be a teacher,' Henry retorts promptly.

'Really?' I blurt.

Henry nods. 'Ideally, I'd like to come back and teach here one day.'

'You could come back as a doctor too,' says Olive, shortly.

'Her dad's the school doctor,' Tori explains. 'He's a GP in Edinburgh and looks after the sick bay here on the side.'

'But you still board here?' I ask Olive.

She glances briefly at me. 'Obviously. Why else would you have knocked for me just now?'

'I know.' I swallow. 'I just meant . . .'

'Quite a few people have family in Edinburgh,' Henry explains hurriedly, 'so they could get the bus here every day, but most of them find it more convenient to board and go home at weekends.'

'Oh, right.' Olive's looking back at her phone, so I don't say anything more.

'Anyway, I don't want to be a doctor,' Henry explains. 'I see from my parents what a stressful job it is.'

'My dad's seriously chill.' Olive shrugs, not looking up.

'Just wait for the rugby season to start – that'll keep him busy.' Omar's laughing, but Henry looks kind of tense now.

Once the upper sixth have come back to their seats with full plates, it's our turn. I can feel the younger kids watching me as we walk up to the hatch. Henry's constantly saying hi to someone or waving to people, and it feels weird to walk back with him, Tori, Sinclair and Olive.

Twenty-four hours ago, I was still in Frankfurt and everything was normal. I was Emma with the British name, Emma with no dad. Emma, Noah's ex.

I'm still Emma, but it's totally up to me who I'll be here. And there's something I really like about that.

7

HENRY

After such a long journey, I could have slept for twelve hours straight, but nobody goes to bed early on the first night of term. After wing time, Omar, Gideon and I sneaked into Sinclair's room so we could talk the night away, like we used to in the old days. After the eight-week summer holidays, we had a lot to catch up on, but I seriously regretted it when my alarm went off at six this morning. I could hardly keep my eyes open during assembly. Not that there was any important news just yet. There are no new teachers at Dunbridge this year, so Mrs Sinclair stuck to a few motivational words for the start of the academic year, plus a reminder of the morning run that replaces the assembly from Tuesday to Friday. Not even a decent cup of tea at breakfast helped me wake up properly. I feel like there's no way I can get through a whole morning's lessons.

I'm just on my way to English when I hear my name.

'Bennington!' Oh, no! 'How was Namibia?'

'Kenya,' I say, trying not to buckle at the knees as Valentine Ward, from the upper sixth, slaps me on the back. For a rugby captain he's surprisingly slim and athletic – typical winger! – yet the blow is borderline brutal.

'Are you sure? I could've sworn it started with N.'

'Yeah, Nairobi,' I say. 'The capital of Kenya.'

'Oh, yeah. Don't tell Ms Kelleher.'

'No worries.' Even if I did, his uncle would look after him. Or that's what people say.

'Anyway, the point was,' Valentine begins, shoving me aside slightly, 'that Mr Cormack says we might be getting a new winger soon.'

I freeze under his arm. 'Does he?'

'Yep.' His eyes bore right through me and I long to run away. 'I'm seriously assuming that that was a misunderstanding on his part.' He sounds kind of threatening. I step back a bit, but he's pinning me down with his stupid arm. 'You're not getting onto my team just because your surname's Bennington,' he adds.

'I thought Mr Cormack picked *your* team,' I reply. 'Anyway, it was his idea.' Apparently, the PE teacher was impressed by my sprinting last summer, just before the holidays, and thinks I might take after my brother. He'd also suggested

that playing for the school would help my university applica-
tions, but there's no need to tell Valentine that part. Anyway,
I'm still not sure if I should turn up to the open training
session at the end of the week. Just because Theo was rugby
captain, and the team won just about everything in his day,
doesn't mean I give a crap about rugby. Sport is not my
strong point, to put it mildly.

'Don't make a tit of yourself.' Valentine narrows his eyes
to slits. 'Fine. Come to training if you like. Maybe then you'll
figure out that you have to get your hands dirty to achieve
anything with us.'

'Is that right?'

'You bet it is.'

'Pity your uncle doesn't pick the team,' I say, as I turn
away.

Valentine pins me to the wall by the shoulder. 'What do
you mean by that?'

'What d'you think I mean by it?' I just can't help myself.
Valentine Ward makes it way too easy to wind him up. And
I've had it up to here with him acting like he owns the school
just because he likes fighting other guys for some stupid ball
in the mud and gets special treatment. 'That I might get a
genuine chance that way?'

'Don't flatter yourself, Bennington,' he hisses. 'And watch
what you say if you don't want my uncle to hear about it.
I hear you've got him for English and maths this year. You
need good predicted grades, don't you?'

'Shut the fuck up, Ward,' I mutter, finally tearing myself away.

My pulse calms as I walk down the hall. Of course my first lesson this year has to be English with Mr Ward. Because, sadly, Valentine was right. I've got his uncle for two subjects and it's no secret that he hates me. Mind you, Mr Ward hates everyone. Probably including himself – at least, that's the only explanation I can come up with for why he's always so mean. All the teachers at Dunbridge are strict but Mr Ward's in a league of his own. He's the only teacher who always calls every single pupil by their surname. Not even Mrs Sinclair does that, but fine, whatever . . . Unfortunately, he's also my form tutor, when I'd have preferred Mr Ringling. Great.

'Hey.'

I raise my head. Emma's facing me, smiling a little uncertainly. I don't know why but, seeing her, all my irritation dissolves into thin air. Why do I feel so proud at the sight of her in our school uniform?

'Morning,' I say. 'Sleep well?'

She nods. 'Yes, thanks. How about you?'

'Not enough but, yeah, OK.'

'Still the jetlag that isn't jetlag?'

I have to smile. 'Probably.' Her pale blonde hair is tied back and only a few strands fall into her face. Everything about her is so light and soft and gentle. How can you not want to look at her the whole time? 'Are you looking for your classroom?' I ask hastily. 'I'll show you the way.'

'Oh, you don't have to . . .' She stops when the bell goes for the first lesson.

'What have you got?'

'English with Mr Ward,' she says. I'm pleased for myself but sad for her. It doesn't strike me as an ideal start to get a teacher like Mr Ward when you're new at a school. But on the other hand that means we'll be in the same class for six hours a week. And maybe a few others, if I'm in luck. Or out of luck, depending on how you look at it.

'Do you know where that is?' Emma asks.

'Yes, I'm going that way myself,' I say. She smiles, which makes me happier than it should do. 'We have to hurry.'

Emma walks rapidly down the now-empty corridor beside me. Fortunately, our classroom door is still open. I can hear Tori's laugh from out here.

'Emma!' She's right by the door with Inés and Gideon and whirls round towards us. 'I lost sight of you after assembly, sorry! Did you find your way OK?' Then she spots me. 'Oh, you had a guide. That's good.'

'Hi, Tor,' I mumble, glancing past her into the room. Most desks are already taken, but there are two seats together at the back of the classroom, and I turn to Emma. But before I can say anything, Tori's grabbed her arm.

'No danger, Henry. Emma's sitting with me. It's bad enough that Olive's got Ms Ventura.'

Amazement flickers across Emma's face as she looks from Tori to me. I smile and shrug regretfully.

77

'Who am I to contradict Victoria Belhaven-Wynford?'

'Very true.' Tori's smile is sickly sweet as she and Emma walk further into the classroom.

'What did Val want just now?' Gideon draws me aside by the sleeve and nods towards a chair he's been saving for me. Like Omar, he's been on the rugby team for a few years now, and he can tell you a thing or two about what a waste of space Valentine is. Before I can fill him in on our conversation, Mr Ward walks in.

EMMA

'You have to put your phone up here during classes,' Tori explains, pointing at the little shelves where Henry and a couple of others have just left their mobiles. 'Make sure it's definitely on silent,' she adds, dumping hers in one of the pigeonholes. 'Mr Ward's been known to punish us all if anyone gets a call or notification in class. He's merciless.'

'Sounds like a nice guy,' I say, putting my phone on the shelf next to Tori's.

She turns away, and I freeze. At that moment a man walks into the room, and he's looking right at me. His face is inscrutable, his beard perfectly trimmed. His jacket and the brown leather briefcase in his hand are seriously expensive. There's no doubt that this is Alaric Ward, my future English teacher – and he probably heard what I just said. Shit.

Tori's still talking, but suddenly I can't move. He can't be any older than Mum, but he walks with a stick and limps on his left leg. But the thing that sends an ice-cold shiver down the back of my neck is the way he looks at me. Dismissively, coldly.

Is there anything wrong with my uniform? I hastily glance down at myself, but everything's just as it should be. When I look up again, he's putting his briefcase on the desk. Two girls flit into the room as discreetly as possible and one shuts the door. I turn as Tori pulls me by the hand. Silently, I follow her to a table towards the back. Mr Ward hasn't spoken a word, but his very presence has made everyone fall quiet.

I put my bag next to the table but everyone else is standing up, so I don't sit down.

'Good morning, all,' says Mr Ward. It's only after an almost imperceptible nod from him that everyone sits down. 'And welcome to the sixth form.' He pauses. 'How nice that you've all ventured to take A-level English.' Is it coincidence that he's looking at me again? 'I'm sure we're all going to have a lot of fun together.'

I gulp. When Mr Ward turns away, I catch Henry's eye. He and Tori were clearly right. Mr Ward is hardly a ray of sunshine.

'Before we discuss the impending academic year, I'll take the register,' he announces. He's holding an iPad as he turns back to the class. 'Gideon Atwell?'

'Yes.' The guy sitting next to Henry bobs up, then sits down again.

'Henry Bennington?' Mr Ward sounds mildly irritated.

'Here.'

'Where else?' He doesn't even glance at Henry as he ticks off his name. The same procedure is repeated twelve times, and in the end, I seem to be the only one left. But Mr Ward doesn't read out my name. He looks up from the iPad and directly at me.

Should I stand up? Should I have introduced myself at the start of the lesson, or is there some other process for new pupils? Have I forgotten something among all the new information that Ms Barnett gave me yesterday? Oh, please, God, no, I should've asked Henry if . . .

'You're the spitting image of your father.'

At first I wonder if I've just imagined Mr Ward's voice. But as the others turn towards me, I'm sure he did say that. Heat builds in my cheeks as I frantically wonder what to say.

'Jacob Wiley . . . He is your father, yes?' Mr Ward sounds almost mocking now.

'Yes, sir,' I manage. 'He is.'

'I presume that you grew up in Germany with your mother, Ms Wiley? Your accent is unmistakable,' he contin-ues. 'Not that you're the only one, of course – this *is* an international school, after all.' He doesn't go into it any fur-ther, but it's clear what he thinks of that.

My blood runs cold. He's so rude. I'd like to reply, but my mind's gone blank.

'You understand that this is A-level English? "A" for advanced. I only teach the best of the best here, and there will be no time to deal with comprehension problems.' Mr Ward turns away and I see Henry open his mouth in outrage. 'All right, Mr Bennington, there's no need for any commentary from you. I'm quite sure that Ms Wiley will need only a little extra tuition to keep up. You appear all too keenly aware of your duties as school captain.' He looks back at me. 'Ms Wiley, what did you last read in Germany?' He narrows his eyes slightly. 'In school, that is.'

Someone laughs.

I want to get out of here. I just want to get out of here.

'Have you studied *The Picture of Dorian Gray*?' he asks, when I say nothing.

'No,' I admit.

'Very well.' Mr Ward clicks his tongue. 'It looks like you'll have some catching up to do. We did some A-level preparation after GCSEs last year, so you'll have to ask your classmates what you need to read. Alternatively, you still have time to switch courses. It's your decision.'

'No, thank you. I'm sure I can cope. We covered a lot of English literature at home. Although I hope that, here, we won't just study books by dead white men.'

For a moment you could hear a pin drop.

I've gone too far, I'm sure of it.

God, what was I thinking?

'We're doing *Wuthering Heights*,' someone says.

Henry's looking from me to Mr Ward, his head slightly aslant. 'And Jane Austen's *Emma*. Funny coincidence, huh?'

He keeps a totally straight face.

I love him for that.

'You can leave the syllabus to me, Mr Bennington,' the teacher snaps, but Henry doesn't bat an eyelid. When Mr Ward turns to the board, Henry looks at me. Smiles, very fleetingly. It's both appreciative and soothing.

'Don't let him faze you,' Tori whispers, patting my arm. 'He's like that to everyone.'

I just nod, because that's not much consolation.

'He knows your parents, then?' she asks.

'Quiet, please.' Mr Ward glares in our direction, but this time, I'm almost grateful to him.

I wait until he's not looking, then shrug my shoulders.

Apparently he does know my parents. Both of them. And he seems to know that they're divorced. Which might mean he's still in touch with my dad. Or has seen his Wikipedia page . . . Either way, he might have answers to my questions, however horrible he is. I don't take in much of the rest of the lesson. I sit on that chair, wondering how to get those answers.

8

EMMA

The honeymoon's over. That's crystal clear as I head downstairs with Tori and Olive on Wednesday morning. Get
up at six thirty, just time to brush your teeth and pull on
your PE kit, and be down for the morning run on the dot
of a quarter to seven. Sounds brutal, which it is, but I'm
glad the run's on this morning after it was rained off
yesterday.

'I hate my life,' grumbles Tori, wrapping her arms around
herself. Her hoodie is pulled right down over her face as she
blinks at me with narrowed eyes. 'Are you sure you won't
freeze like that?'

And, yeah, I'm shivering in a thin, long-sleeved T-shirt.
August in Scotland isn't like August at home, as I might have
guessed. But on the other hand, if you're cold before a run,

you know you're dressed about right – you'll soon warm up. I'm about to say so, when someone calls to us.

'Hey, guys!' Sinclair trots over, dodging a couple of other girls who've stopped on the courtyard outside our wing. He keeps jogging on the spot when he reaches us. 'Sleep well?'

I nod, but Tori huffs irritably. 'How can you have so much energy this early in the morning? It's boggling.'

Sinclair frowns. 'It's motivational?' he suggests. 'The sun's up, the sky's blue. It's going to be a beautiful day.'

'Not if it starts with a run,' grumbles Tori.

I can't help grinning. Sinclair shrugs his shoulders. Then he takes Tori's hand. 'C'mon.'

'Jeez, Sinclair, I'm taking the shortcut anyway,' she moans, glancing back at me over her shoulder.

'No bother, I'll show you. But don't tell anyone else.'

'Oh, I think I'll go the normal route,' I say.

Tori stares at me like I'm out of my mind. 'The normal route is at least ten minutes longer.'

'Yeah, but I like running.' I smile. 'Honestly.'

'Hi.'

I freeze. Great. I just have to hear his voice and my body betrays me. Or can I kid myself that these goosebumps are entirely down to the single-figure temperature?

Henry's hands are buried in his hoodie pocket, and he looks kind of sleepy. He's wearing a long base-layer under his running shorts, and there's a little hairband holding back his curls to keep them out of his eyes. He looks different like that. Kind of older and . . . Was his jawline that sharp yesterday? You could cut yourself just looking at it.

'Emma doesn't want to take the shortcut,' Tori announces, out of nowhere. I jump.

'I think I'd better start going the long way round too from now on,' Henry says.

Tori and Sinclair stare at him, wide-eyed.

'Hey?' asks Sinclair, turning to me. 'Who are you and what did you do to Henry?' Then he rolls his eyes, although he can't hold back a smile. 'No, seriously,' he says to Henry. 'What's brought this on?'

'There's rugby training coming up,' he says.

'You can't be serious?' Tori exclaims.

Henry shrugs. Before he can say any more, there's a whistle.

'Oh, well, you can run with Emma then,' Tori says.

I hesitate as Henry looks at me. 'Aren't you going to run with Grace?' I ask.

He shakes his head. 'Day pupils don't have to get here until registration at eight thirty.'

'Oh, I see.' I turn around as I hear shouting. Standing in the centre of the courtyard, there's a brawny man, wearing shorts and T-shirt, even in this weather.

'That's Mr Cormack, the rugby coach,' Henry says, as we start running.

'He's straight out of hell,' Tori adds, as Sinclair pulls her aside by the arm. 'See you later, you crazy fools!'

They leave the schoolyard with us through a high gateway, but soon afterwards, they vanish through an inconspicuous door into one of the buildings, while Henry and I follow everybody else. Very soon, the huge grounds of Dunbridge Academy spread out ahead of us. Olive's no longer with us – she's joined a small group of others with *Dunbridge Swimming* emblazoned across their sweatshirts. The path runs along the school walls, the dewdrops are glistening in the sunlight, and threads of mist hang over the fields. The air is clear and cold. I breathe deeply. It's so peaceful, and calm, and very beautiful.

'How was your second night here?' Henry asks, and I have to grin, because he's already breathing hard. I slacken my speed a little. I'm not sure exactly how long the route is and I don't want to outpace him. That would be rude.

'Quiet. It really is super-quiet here,' I say.

Henry laughs. 'Is that a good or a bad thing?'

'I'm not sure. It's weird. I kind of miss the noise of the city.'

'Do you live right in the middle of Frankfurt?'

'No, on the outskirts, but there's always a background noise. And the planes . . .'

'You'll soon get used to the quiet here.'

I nod, overtaking a little group ahead of us.

'Sorry, I'm so out of shape,' he says, once he's caught up again.

'Just say if I'm going too fast.'

'No . . . it's OK.'

Uh-huh. Down to three-word sentences. I slow even more.

'How long does the official route take?' I ask.

'Depends. If you're sporty, fifteen minutes. Otherwise more like twenty.'

'And the shortcut?'

Henry hesitates. 'Um, well, it's a lot shorter.'

I laugh. 'You don't have to come on the full lap with me.'

'Yeah, I do,' he pants. 'I need to get fitter.'

'So you're on the rugby team?' I ask.

'Not yet, but I want to be.'

That's kind of surprising. Maybe I'm wrong, but I'd assumed rugby players were big, tough, muscly guys, who'd fight for the ball without considering the consequences. And not like Henry.

'There's an open training session on Friday,' he says. 'I might have a chance as a winger. They're the little fast ones who run and score points. So I have to improve.'

'We could run together often, if you like. Just let me know.' I say it without really thinking it through. 'If you want to, that is. I love running. I was in an athletics club at home.'

'Really?' Henry looks sidelong at me. It's a glance, but enough to send another shiver down the back of my neck. 'Grace is on the track team. I'm sure she'd take you along to training if you like. Shall I ask her?'

'Sure.' I tense. 'That would be cool.'

Grace is on the track team. So Henry can run with her.

Which would be way more natural. And doesn't bother me. Why should it?

I don't know what else we chatted about. Henry's pretty knackered by the time we get back to the courtyard a good fifteen minutes later, after a lap of the whole grounds. I wouldn't mind doing a couple of sprints now, to calm my circling thoughts, but there isn't time. Once I get back to my room, I shower and get dressed quickly. Sand-coloured trousers, white polo shirt and dark blue jumper.

At breakfast, I meet up with Tori and the others. Not much later, we head off to lessons. My day begins with tutor time, with Ms Barnett, followed by PE, with Ms Ventura. I don't see Henry again until later on, in maths. Part of me has spent the whole morning looking forward to it, while the rest of me would rather run away when Mr Ward enters the classroom. I only start to relax a little once I realize I'm ahead of the others on this course. Mr Ward calls me and a couple of others up to the board to solve some equations. Every classroom here seems to have these high-tech interactive whiteboards – not like my old school. At any rate, I haven't seen an ordinary chalkboard anywhere.

Mr Ward just gives a curt nod once I've solved the problem without difficulty, and he makes a note of something on his iPad as I sit down.

He leaves me in peace for the rest of the lesson. When the bell goes for lunch, and the others leave the room, I pack up my things extra slowly.

'Are you coming?' Henry asks in passing.

'Yes, in a minute. I just wanted to . . .'

He understands my hesitation. 'We'll be in the dining room. Just text me. Hold on.' I can't react in time as he reaches for my hand. He holds it firmly in one of his own, while the other grabs the felt-tip that's still lying on my desk. My heart skips a beat as he takes it into his mouth to pull off the lid. His hair falls into his eyes as he presses the cool tip of the pen against the sensitive skin of my palm. It tickles a bit as he writes, and it's only then that I see he's giving me his number. As if we could miss each other in the dining room – I mean, it's not like the canteen at my school in Germany where anyone can sit wherever they choose. Here, we have set tables and there aren't that many people, but apparently it matters to Henry that he immortalizes himself on my skin. And I . . . Well, I don't have a problem with that, let's put it that way. Who knows? I might need to ask him something about schoolwork sometime. Or check out his profile picture . . .

'That last number's meant to be a nine,' Henry mumbles, raising his head. His eyes are dark green as he puts the lid back on the pen and slips it into my pencil case. Have I mentioned that he has a very nice mouth? 'See you soon.'

'Yes.' I clear my throat a little as he turns away.

Help. Why was that so hot?

I run the thumb of my other hand over the black numbers. Once I'm sure the ink's dry, I clench my fingers into a fist and slip my bag onto my shoulder.

Mr Ward is just reaching for his stick and turning to the door as I approach him.

'Excuse me, sir,' I begin.

He gives an irritable sigh. 'I haven't got much time.'

'I just have a quick question,' I say hastily. *Oh, yeah, what is it then?* What's happened to all my prepared sentences?

Mr Ward looks impatiently at me. His eyes flit to the clock above the door. 'I'm busy,' he says, 'so if you could get to the point?'

My tongue has difficulty forming the words. Then I just say it. 'You mentioned my father yesterday morning.'

'Yes.' His hand tightens on the handle of his stick. 'I did.'

'Where did you know him from?' Mr Ward narrows his eyes. Suddenly I feel incredibly naïve. 'I just wanted to . . .' He still doesn't reply. 'I'm not in contact with him and I was hoping you could—'

'I said you look like him,' he interrupts me harshly. 'That doesn't mean I feel the need to speak about him.'

I freeze.

'Just be glad that he no longer plays any role in your life, Ms Wiley.' Mr Ward's voice is as cold as ice as he turns away. 'Was there anything else?'

He doesn't wait for my answer. My legs only remember how to walk once he's turned towards the door again. His lanyard clatters as he locks the door behind me.

Just be glad . . . Does that mean my father once played a

role in Mr Ward's life? Did he go to school here with him? How disrespectful would it be to ask a teacher his age?

I don't dare ask anything more. Mr Ward's expression is an impenetrable mask.

'I didn't mean to be rude,' I say instead.

Mr Ward doesn't answer right away. Then he says: 'Don't waste your energy on the past. As your teacher, I would suggest that you're better off investing it in your studies.'

My heart is numb, my mind blank. I nod before he walks away, then set off in the opposite direction. It's only after I've taken a few steps that I remember this isn't the way to the dining room. I stop and open my hand, with which I've been clutching my bag the whole time. I can just about see the black marks on the navy-blue fabric.

'Fuck . . .' I whisper.

Henry's number is smeared: my palms are sweaty.

I shut my eyes.

HENRY

I can't remember when it became a tradition that I have lunch with Grace and her family on Wednesdays. It feels like it's always been that way, yet today I almost forgot. If Grace hadn't been waiting for me at the foot of the stairs, I'd have turned left and headed for the dining room with the others.

Now I can't stop thinking that Emma might be looking for me. If I had her number, I could just let her know now.

'Are you expecting something?' Grace asks, as I glance at my phone to see, yet again, no message from her. Instead, Maeve has sent another of her weird memes to our family WhatsApp group. This one features a frog and, yet again, I don't get the joke. I've long since given up trying to understand them.

'Hm?' I look up. 'Oh, right, no. Sorry.' I put my phone away as Grace's mum sets a huge casserole dish on the table in front of us. Meanwhile, her dad reaches for my glass, to fill it with water. The thought of how much I'd rather be somewhere else makes me feel guilty.

Grace's parents, Diane and Marcus, know mine. They were at Dunbridge too, all at the same time, in the same year. Just like Grace and me. Since I've been at the school, I've seen Grace's parents way more often than my own. I used to spend almost every weekend with them. No wonder the Whitmores' house feels almost like a home from home to me.

I've spent less time here as we've got older, and this year my days will be so packed with lessons, school council meetings and prep supervision that it'll be hard for Grace and me to see much of each other either. But however full my diary is, Wednesday lunch with her family is a fixture.

'Oh, thanks.' I automatically reach for my plate as Grace's mum tries to keep piling shepherd's pie onto it. 'That's plenty.'

'Are you sure, Henry?' She eyes me carefully. 'There's no need to hold back.'

'Stop fattening the boy up, Diane,' says Grace's dad.

'I'll give you some to take back with you,' she announces, handing me my plate. 'We all know what an appetite boarding school works up.'

'That's what toast's for,' remarks Marcus, which earns him a reproachful look from his wife. 'Or that's how it was in our day. Toast between lunch and dinner, toast at half-midnight. The toaster in your father's room was worth its weight in gold. Apart from that time when he accidentally got one of his curtains—'

'We know the story, Dad,' says Grace, and I grin.

'I know, I know. Your old folks will keep telling the same old stories. It was such a long time ago now. I wish I could have my time at Dunbridge over again.'

'That's what my parents always say, too,' I put in.

'There, you see.' Marcus turns his attention to his lunch.

'So, how are they doing, Henry?' Diane asks, as she loads Grace's younger brothers' plates. Gregory and Augustus are day pupils, too. Greg's in the junior school and Gus is in the third form. I've known them since they were little. It's all kind of weird.

'Yeah, they're good. It's a lot of work but they're happy. They'll probably come over for a couple of weeks at Christmas.'

'Oh, that's nice.' Diane beams. 'Well, in that case, you

must all come over for a meal. Maeve and Theo too, of course, if they're around.'

'I'll pass that on,' I promise. 'I'm calling them later today. I haven't managed to get through to them yet.'

'Being school captain really is keeping you busy,' Grace remarks, with a grin.

'Oh, yes, your new role, Henry,' Diane says. 'You certainly are following in Theo's footsteps.'

My stomach tenses, but I keep smiling. That's just how it is. Whatever I do, it'll always be measured against what my big brother's already achieved. OK, so he wasn't *school* captain, but – let's be honest – at a Scottish boarding school rugby captain is definitely the more prestigious post.

And, right on cue, Grace mentions rugby, which gets her dad and brothers all fired up. Marcus played for the school, too, back in the day, and he's giving me all kinds of tips, while Greg and Gus tell me about their training on the junior teams.

'And you've got your own personal running coach in Grace, haven't you?' Marcus concludes. My smile is rather strained because I'm suddenly thinking of Emma again.

'Yeah, that's ideal, isn't it?'

To my surprise, Grace doesn't reply, just keeps her eyes fixed on her plate. I'm about to ask her if everything's OK when she looks up. 'Shall we help clear away?' she asks.

'Henry might like a little more?' Diane asks.

'No, thank you,' I say hastily. 'Honestly.' I'm sure that

Diane's already running her mind's eye over her Tupper-ware pots, picking out the biggest one to pack the leftovers into for me.

Once we've helped her parents take the dishes through to the kitchen, we head up to Grace's room. It's the first time we've had to ourselves, and after such a long time apart, I probably ought to have certain ideas on my mind. But instead I glance back at my phone, to check that Emma still hasn't messaged. I'm sure she found Tori and the others. I hope she did. I remember that I meant to ask Grace about the track team.

'I told Emma you're on the track team and that you might take her along to training,' I say, shutting the door behind me. 'She was in an athletics club at home.'

'Oh, cool,' says Grace.

'I hope that was OK,' I add.

'Of course it was. Why wouldn't it be?'

'I don't know . . . Maybe I should've asked you first.'

'I'm happy to take her along next week,' says Grace.

'I'm sure she'll be pleased . . . And what your dad said just now . . . Would you like to run with me now and then?'

Grace doesn't answer straight away, and I feel a sneaky sense of relief. She's busy: I shouldn't expect her to make more time for me. And I could take Emma up on her offer and run with her. Without having to feel bad about it.

'When you say, "now and then", what did you have in mind?'

'I don't know. Once or twice a week?'

'I'll have to see if I can squeeze it in,' she says. 'Between A levels, training and piano, it's pretty full-on at the moment.'

'It was just an idea.'

'I'm sorry, Henry.'

'No, it's fine. Don't worry about it.'

I wander over to her desk and idly pick up a book. As I do so, I spot a prospectus lying there. I recognize the logo at once.

'Still planning on Oxford, then?' I ask.

Grace turns to me. For a moment, as she sees what I'm looking at, she seems kind of overwhelmed. I take the brochure, perch on the bed and start to flick through it. Glossy photos of ancient buildings and perfectly manicured lawns. It looks like Dunbridge Academy, only brighter.

Grace has come closer now. 'I wanted to find the right moment to tell you,' she says, and I wait for my belly to clench. I feel nothing. Maybe it's because part of me had been prepared for this moment. 'Not on WhatsApp or on the phone. I'm sorry.'

I reach for her hands and draw them between my legs. 'There's no need to be sorry,' I mumble. When I raise my chin a little, Grace kisses me. 'You ought to go to Oxford if you want to.'

She doesn't say anything, but I know what she's thinking. *You too . . .*

It's what everyone thinks. That I'll work my arse off, get

straight A stars, so that I can take my pick of offers from Oxford or Cambridge colleges. But it's not like that.

'Olive and I went down there in the holidays and looked round St Hilda's. The college is dreamy, Henry.'

St Andrews is lovely too . . . But I don't say that. Because we've had this conversation too often already. Because I don't want Grace to take any decisions for my sake that'll make her unhappy. Even if I don't want to think about what that means for us.

'I really think I could get in,' she says, as I pull her onto my lap.

'Of course you will. Your grades are good and Ms Kelleher will write you a great reference.'

'Yes.' She swallows. 'But—'

'It's what you want,' I interrupt.

'And you're really set on St Andrews? I mean, you could put Oxford down too, keep your options open.'

'Grace,' I say quietly, but she's still talking.

'I get that you want to be near Maeve and Theo. But . . .' I know exactly what she wants to ask. Don't I want to be near her too? And of course I do. I really do. But maybe not quite enough. I don't even know. Because, yeah, Grace is part of my life, and I can't imagine not being with her, but at the same time, when I think about my future, I don't know if I see us both there. I just know that Grace wants to get away. From Ebrington, from Scotland. And I don't. I've been on the move long enough, and I've finally arrived here.

97

I raise my head and see it all in her amber eyes. Those few nights when I secretly slept over with her and we painted a picture of moving in together after school. She was going to study history and politics and I'd do English or biology. Everything would be weird and unfamiliar – leaving school, starting at uni – but we'd conquer this new world together.

I brush a hair off her face. 'We don't have to decide anything for ages yet.' I don't know why I say that. And I don't know why Grace nods. We've known each other six years. And we've been together for three. Three years, and sometimes I get the feeling we've kind of run out of things to say. After all, there's only so much you can talk about when your everyday lives are practically identical and you have all the same friends. But that's probably normal. Normal for things sometimes to feel more like a habit than a relationship. To keep having the same conversations and the same arguments too, these days. If we argue at all. Sometimes I'm afraid it's all gone too flat even for that. OK, I can't think about this any more. It's driving me crazy. But I can't admit that I'm not seriously considering Oxford, that I can't see myself changing my mind. We know each other through and through. We know when the other is lying. Grace knows that. I know that. And we ought to talk all this through, even if it's uncomfortable, and it's bound to hurt a lot. I really wish I could just change the subject now . . .

'Hey, did you see that Ms Buchanan's wearing a wedding ring, now?' Grace asks.

9

EMMA

I don't know where the time's gone as my first week at Dunbridge Academy draws to an end. It's Friday, my lessons are over for the week, and now it's considerably quieter in the corridors. The day pupils have gone home and a lot of the boarders seem to have left for the weekend, too.

'Have you made any friends?' Mum asks.

It's the first time we've Skyped since I arrived last Sunday. I nod and lean back against the wall beside my bed, as I place my laptop on my lap. 'I get on really well with Tori, in the room next door,' I tell her. 'We're in some of the same classes and she's shown me everything this week.'

'That's great, darling.' Mum smiles.

'Everyone else is really nice, too. Especially . . .' Especially Henry. Henry, who I spend more hours a day thinking about than is probably good for me. Will he be here over the weekend? Or will he spend the days with Grace?

'Uh-huh? So who's "everyone else", then?' Mum asks casually.

Obviously she's seen right through me. 'A few others in my tutor group. Tori, Olive, Henry, Sinclair . . .'

'Sinclair? Like the head teacher?' Mum asks.

'Yes, he's her son. Do you know her?'

'No, not really. She was a year or two older than me, but I spoke to her on the phone when they offered you a place. It's nice that she came back to the school.'

'Yes. I like her.'

'So, how are lessons? Is Mr Ringling still there?' Mum asks.

'Yes,' I say, in astonishment. 'Henry has biology with him, and I had him for PSHE yesterday.'

'How nice. Say hello to him for me – he might remember me. He was new to the school in my day.'

'I will,' I say.

I also make a mental note to ask Mr Ringling about my dad. If he taught Mum, he must have taught him too. And perhaps he'd be prepared to tell me more than Mr Ward was.

'Which other teachers do you have?' Mum asks.

'Ms Ventura for PE and Mr Ward for English and maths.'

'Ward?' Mum echoes. Her voice has changed and there's something about her tone that I don't like. 'Not Alaric Ward, surely?'

'Yes. Do you know him?'

'Not really,' she says. 'He was in my year. I didn't know he'd gone into teaching.'

I say nothing, hoping she'll tell me more. But it doesn't work.

'What's he like?' she asks.

'I don't think he's very popular with anybody,' I say. 'He seems kind of . . . bitter.'

Mum gives a cautious nod. 'Has he said anything to you?'

'Why do you ask?' I say. 'I mean, why would he say anything to me?'

'Nothing. I just wondered. Given your surname, he'd be bound to.'

'He did mention Dad,' I say, and see her expression harden. 'He said I look like him. But that was all.' And it's probably better if Mum doesn't know that I asked him about my dad. Or that he didn't want to talk to me.

'OK.' Mum's smiling, but it looks kind of strained. 'I'm sure Mr Ringling must be nicer, though. Is he?'

There's more to this, more to find out about Mr Ward and my parents, I'm sure of it. Otherwise Mum wouldn't have changed the subject so abruptly.

But I don't know what it is. Or why I'm not allowed to hear about it. But I know that if I'm going to find out, it'll be here, in this place.

HENRY

What was I thinking, showing up to this open training thing? Did I think it wouldn't be this bad? Wow. At least past-Henry had a sense of humour.

Jeez, this is awful. It was bad enough just turning up among all the other potential new team members. Everyone else who's come to the trials is way younger than me. No surprise there. Most boys here have played rugby since the juniors, and the junior teams are obviously the best way into the seniors. It's rare for anyone to want to start as late as this. Maybe I should spare myself the humiliation and walk away. But that would be just as embarrassing at this point.

I can feel the weight of Valentine Ward's and Mr Cormack's eyes on me as we warm up and pair off for the first drills. I'm partnered with Gideon, who's already on the team, and although I'm sure he's not putting his full strength into the throws, it's still brutal enough. We have to run half the length of the pitch, throwing and catching the ball as we go, and by the time I try to circle the cone to head back again, my knees are so weak that I fall flat on my face in the muddy grass. My hip hurts like hell, my thighs are burning as fiercely as my lungs, and I don't want to know how red my face is. I'd say I'm really giving it everything, but apparently that's not enough. I can see it in Val's mocking expression. He yells a few words of encouragement in our direction, then goes to stand next to Mr Cormack, who's making notes on the clipboard in his hand, his face inscrutable.

I want to stop. I *need* to stop. Or I'll throw up. Oh, God, no. I'm about to pretend that my bootlaces need retying when Mr Cormack blows his whistle, almost splitting my eardrums.

'Good. Everyone new, come to me!' he roars. The team carry on their training without him, while we trudge over. All I can see around me are red, sweaty faces and mud-smeared bodies. I look longingly in the direction of my water bottle, miles away in the stands. A moment later, I hold my breath as I notice the girl coming past all our jackets and kit bags.

It's Emma, running on the track that circles the pitch. The floodlights are on and the red-orange sunset has almost completely faded. I look up to the clock on the electronic scoreboard opposite. It's already half past nine ... Is she really training voluntarily at this time in the evening? I wonder if Grace did take her along to the track team?

'Bennington.' At that moment, I hear Mr Cormack's voice. 'A little less staring into space and a little more concentration, if you don't mind.'

I tear my eyes away. 'Yes, sir.'

He stares at me for a moment, then at his clipboard. 'Good. Baker, Valtersen, DiSanto, Hsuan, you're in. Training on Monday and Thursday evenings at seven thirty, and on Wednesdays at five. An hour's weights in the gym every

SARAH SPRINZ

Tuesday, and Fridays too, although that's optional. If you have any other questions, ask Valentine. Fifteen minutes' cool-down now, and you can go.'

I shiver as the others thank him and wander away. They're all third- and fourth-formers, and they were way better than me. There's no denying it.

I jump as I hear my name.

'Bennington, Stokes, Meskill.' Mr Cormack looks us in the eye and I have trouble meeting his gaze. 'You've got a month to show me you can do better. You were poor today. I expect you to do extra training so that you can get somewhere near the team's level. The rest of you can try again next year.'

Wait a moment . . . Does that mean I'm in? Subject to conditions, at least?

'That's all,' he says curtly. 'You too, cool-down, then get in the showers. Be back in your rooms by ten.'

I choke out a quiet thank you, then turn away with the rest. Gideon stretches out his thumb to me, turning it questioningly up and then down. I hold my thumb sideways to signal that it had gone mediocre at best.

You were poor today . . .

Wow. It had been all I was capable of. I couldn't have done more without puking my guts up onto the pitch. I haven't the faintest idea how I'm meant to raise my game enough inside a month for Mr Cormack to give me a real chance on the team. Let alone for me to play in a match. Because that's the point of all this. If I don't get anything to put on my

UCAS form, then why bother? Four sessions a week, and my own personal training on top of that.

Valentine looks at me, a self-satisfied smile on his lips, before twisting his face into a regretful grimace.

Don't flatter yourself, Bennington . . .

I give a quiet laugh as I jog sluggishly along the edge of the field. But maybe he's right. It would probably be wiser to throw in the towel now and admit that there are easier things to put in my uni application. I could do some volunteering. Or join the choir. This is so stupid. I'm wasting my time. I want to be a teacher, not a rugby player. But if I've set my mind to something, I put in the effort and the hours until I've achieved it. That's always worked until now. And I'm not prepared to let a guy like Valentine Ward get me down.

EMMA

Henry looks utterly shattered as he stumbles from the pitch towards the changing rooms. At first I'd thought maybe this wasn't rugby training at all, because I'd been expecting the players to be padded up as they wrestled for the ball. I'm embarrassed to admit that, until now, I'd thought that rugby and American football were basically the same game. But now I'm learning that the British version does without bulky shoulder pads and helmets. Which is kind of impressive because the whole thing looks just as brutal.

I hadn't been sure at first if I'd be allowed to run on the track while the training session was on, but Mr Cormack didn't send me away, just nodded to me and turned back to his clipboard.

Anyway, it was kind of nice not to be running on my own, and to hear the rugby guys yelling. Especially since that video call with Mum, after which I haven't been able to stop thinking about my dad and Mr Ward. I tried calling Isi to take my mind off it. Since I've been in Scotland, we've only messaged a couple of times. She declined my WhatsApp video call – she was out somewhere at the time. I'm probably reading too much into it, but it feels kind of weird that my best friend is being snippy. If I were her, I'd want to know every last detail, however tiny, about the new school. But I haven't had a chance to tell her anything – not about boarding-school life and not about Henry either. And I really wouldn't mind talking through this whole thing about him with someone. Not that there even is a thing, really, but . . . I'd still like to tell someone. And Tori doesn't seem the right person. I really like her a lot, but she's been friends with Grace, Olive and everyone for years.

So I do the only sensible thing. I don't talk, I run. After forty-five minutes of tempo runs, I can hardly feel my legs, but that's OK because it means I'm too dead for my brain to keep churning. It's a simple equation. If you run until you can't think straight, you can't stay moody either.

But it doesn't seem to have worked on Henry, even though

he was sprinting and catching that ball every time I happened to glance his way.

His chest is heaving and he drops onto the bench like a sack of potatoes, propping his elbows on his knees. I want to tell him he needs to keep moving, even if his body is demanding the exact opposite but, unfortunately, I'm on the wrong side of the track just now, doing my cool-down routine.

There are only a few players still on the pitch as I finally stop and pick up my stuff, which I left on the edge of the stands. Henry's gone, and I shouldn't be so disappointed about that. I wish I could ask him how the try-out went, though. It seems like he cares a lot about getting onto the team.

I'm still really warm, but I pull my hoodie on before I start stretching. I'm just straightening up from a hip flexor stretch when he's suddenly standing in front of me.

'Hi.' His cheeks are still red and I smile slightly as I straighten. 'Saw you running.'

'Yeah.' I don't know what else to say. My heart's pounding again. Does he think I was watching him? I hope not. 'I needed to clear my head a bit.' I can see exactly what Henry's thinking, but before he can ask I hurry on: 'How did it go?'

A shadow crosses his face and he shrugs his shoulders. 'Honestly? It was shit.' He laughs but I can hear his frustration. 'The idea of getting onto the team was clearly a bit over-ambitious.'

'It looked good to me,' I say, instantly regretting it. Great! Now he *knows* I was watching the whole thing.

But Henry just shrugs again. 'Mr Cormack doesn't think so. I've got a month to prove myself, but I might as well save myself the pain.'

'Hey, what kind of attitude is that?' Henry looks startled as I frown at him. 'Giving up before you've even really started? Is that the school captain spirit?'

He has to smile, but only for a moment. Then his face is serious again. 'I just really underestimated this whole thing. I'd have training four times a week, and I need to work on my fitness on top of that. And even then, there's no guarantee that I'd make it.'

'If you don't, you'd have had a month's fitness training,' I point out. There it is, that freaking smile again.

'I like the way you think,' he says, and my cheeks, which are still flushed from training, burn even hotter. I hurriedly bend down for my bag so that Henry won't see my face. We're practically the last off the field. As we walk back to school, all I can hear is the gravel crunching under our feet.

'Did Grace ask you about the track team, by the way?' Henry says at some point.

I raise my head. 'No, not yet. Why?'

'Oh, she said she would. Maybe she forgot.'

'Maybe,' I repeat. 'Will you be at hers over the weekend?'

God, Wiley. What the hell has that got to do with you?

Henry looks a little confused. 'No. Why d'you ask?'

'I was just wondering. Never mind. Forget it.'

'I'm here almost every weekend,' he says. 'I sometimes go

to my grandparents, but they live in Cheshire, which is a bit south of Manchester. We used to spend most of our summer holidays there too.'

Oh, is that where his accent is from? It's incredibly hot. Oh God, what's wrong with me?

'Do you visit them often?' I ask, just for something to say.

'Not as often as I should,' he admits. 'It's five hours by train. Sometimes my brother drives me – he's got a car.'

I'm about to ask him about his brother, but almost the moment we step through the gate, a man approaches us. He taps his watch with his index finger.

'Ten o'clock. Wing time,' he calls out.

'We're practically there,' Henry replies. He turns back to me. 'Are you here this weekend?'

'Yes.' I don't know where else I'd be.

He smiles. 'Good.' He leans forward. He hugs me. Breathe, *breathe*. 'See you around, then. Sleep well, Emma from Germany.'

10

EMMA

Jacob Wiley was born in Glasgow and is a Scottish singer-songwriter.

I stare at the letters until they blur as my eyes start swimming. Not that that matters – I know every line of his Wikipedia entry off by heart. I've read it often enough. Probably too often to be good for me, but what can I say? If your only source of information is a webpage that, in theory at least, any random person can edit however they like with just a few clicks, it's easy to get paranoid. There could be something new, so I have to look. Every day. Several times on some days. That's just how it is. Even long after I ought to be asleep. I'm *sooo* tired, but even after almost a week at Dunbridge, everything's so new and exciting that I can't get any rest at night, no matter how knackered I am. There's too much to think about. My dad, Mr Ward, Grace, Isi, Henry, especially Henry and his freaking smile. He's got dimples too and it's just not fair. I'd like to ask him what he meant by 'See you around, then.' I should have asked him for his number again. Or would that have been inappropriate? He only wanted to give it to me so that I could find him at lunchtime. Which still makes no sense, but obviously I haven't dared ask him about that either.

Whatever. Whatever . . . I have to think about something else. I have to get some sleep. But the bed still doesn't feel like it's mine, and it's too quiet here. All I hear is the occasional glugging from the old water pipes in the wall or some nocturnal animal outside.

Do the teachers stay at school over the weekend, too? Maybe I could look for Mr Ringling tomorrow and ask him subtle questions about my dad. Or should I try Ms Barnett first? She's sure to be here. But I don't even know what I want to know. To be honest, I know nothing at all. All I can do is lie here, next to my laptop, reading these sentences that I know off by heart.

Life

Jacob Wiley grew up in the Hillhead area of Glasgow. He began to play the guitar and piano at the age of five. Wiley attended Dunbridge Academy, where he was a member of the school choir. He left school at the age of seventeen, without completing his A levels, to tour as a support act for the band The Vagabonds.

It's all there. The title of his first single, the dates of his first solo tour. That he lived in Germany for a few years. As a support act to a different band. You can read it all on the internet.

> Wiley's second marriage was to the Puerto Rican singer Camila Soler and the couple lived together in Sacramento, California. After their divorce, he moved back to his homeland.

That may be true, but it's not the whole truth. Properly speaking it ought to say something like: *Prior to this, he had an on-off relationship with German lawyer Laura Beck. They have one daughter together, Emma Wiley, who barely knows her father and wonders to this day why he left.*

But it doesn't.

Those words have been in the Wikipedia edit pane a few times, typed by me, the blinking cursor mocking me. *You haven't got the guts, don't kid yourself. You're not part of his life. Deal with it. If he wanted you in his life, you'd know about it.*

Sometimes I hear his voice in my head. Promising to take me with him the next time he goes on tour. He sounds seriously euphoric. I must have been about seven at the time, and I didn't doubt him for a second. I still believe him to this day. Believe that one day Jacob Wiley, my dad who doesn't want anything to do with me, will turn up, stand there with his guitar slung casually over his shoulder and say: *Time to go, Emma. Come on, the tour starts tomorrow.*

You'd think at some point that would all stop. That you'd eventually forget someone's voice after you hadn't seen them for years.

But the problem is that if your dad's a singer, you can't forget his voice. It's all too easy to open Spotify or, on really bad days, YouTube. Then you can see him, too. And then you can start looking for similarities. Until your head aches and your eyes are burning, whether that's from the harsh light of the laptop in the darkness, or from the tears.

And then you google the boarding school he went to, and imagine what it would be like to go there and find out more. Because the Facebook messages and emails you sent him have gone unanswered. Because you don't want to make a fool of yourself by asking your mother. Does she still have his mobile number or anything?

Just leave it. That voice in the back of my mind is getting louder and louder. *You're running into trouble here.* And maybe that's true but, let's face it, running's the only thing I'm any good at.

There's a knock from somewhere, which makes me jump. My mouth is dry and my laptop screen has gone black. Seems like I did drop off after all. What's the time? It's not time to get up, is it? No, it's still dark outside and . . .

Another knock. Someone's at my door. I get goosebumps as I walk barefoot over to it. I've left the window on the latch, as I do every night, and the ancient wooden floorboards are freezing. They feel almost damp to the touch.

I've only opened the door a crack when a figure pushes its way into my room. It takes me a full three seconds to recognize Tori, who holds her index finger warningly to her lips and shuts it behind her.

'Phew.' She sighs. 'I was seriously scared that Ms Barnett would catch me.'

'Is something wrong?' I ask. My voice sounds rough and I clear my throat.

'I haven't got your phone number,' says Tori, to my surprise.

'So, you came knocking on my door in the middle of the night to get it?'

'Course not, but it means I can't WhatsApp you. I need to get Olive to add you to our group. She's the admin.'

'Tori, what the hell . . .?'

'Sorry, sorry. I know it's late. But you have to get dressed.' She smiles mysteriously. Before I can reply, she claps her hands quietly. 'Spur-of-the-moment midnight party, lovely lady!'

'What?'

'God, you're as dim as Sinclair when you've just woken up. Come on, we're meeting Olive on the stairs in five minutes. Put a warm jacket on. It's freezing out there.'

'You're not serious?' I say, even though Tori's face is so excited she clearly means every word of it. I run my eyes over her. Yep. She's wearing jeans and trainers, and has a jacket over her school hoodie. Her long coppery hair is tied up in a mad bun.

'The dress code only applies in the daytime,' she says, winking at me and pushing me over to my wardrobe. 'Come on, come on, hurry up.'

'Isn't this against the rules?' I ask, opening the cupboard.

'Course it is. But if anyone catches us, we'll just say that I was feeling ill and you were helping me get some fresh air.'

I can't help laughing. Tori sits on my bed, frantically messaging a WhatsApp group, while I slip into jeans, a jumper and my jacket. She's kind enough to leave me time to brush my teeth before shoving me out into the corridor.

I hold my breath as we walk down the hall. When we reach the staircase, she pulls me over to the right-hand side. She flattens herself against the wall, and I copy her when I spot the motion sensor above the door. It's only once we've got down the first few steps that Tori audibly exhales. Halfway down to the next floor, we bump into Olive and a couple of other girls in our year. I recognize Inés and Salome from my English class, Amara who's in my tutor group, and two other girls whose names I can't remember. Olive gives us a wave. Her eyes skim impatiently over me and I suddenly wonder if she minds Tori bringing me along. I decide not to worry about it, and just follow the others downwards.

We cross the small inner courtyard in the darkness, then go through two gateways. I've lost all sense of direction by the time we get outside the walls. It seems like we're out of sight from the school now, and earshot too, because the others start giggling and talking quietly. The night is chilly and I'm glad of my jacket. I'm about to ask Tori if this mid-night party is happening outdoors but then we head towards the greenhouses I'd seen earlier from the running track. There's a light on in the furthest of them, and soon I'm following the rest through the door.

It's warm, even though there are several broken panes. I guess this one is out of use, because instead of plants I see a muddle of odd chairs and a load of people partying. There doesn't seem to be any more risk of being overheard – the music is loud, and so's the laughter.

'We're far enough from the main buildings here,' Tori explains, as she catches my eye. 'We're miles from every-thing apart from the gardener's house, and Mr Carpenter's as deaf as a post.'

'That's not true,' says Salome, stroking one of her many tiny braids out of her face. 'I'm sure he knows exactly what goes on here. But he won't say anything so long as nothing gets broken. And the other greenhouses are strictly off limits.'

'So's alcohol,' remarks Sinclair, cheerfully. He's heading towards a boy who looks amazingly like Tori. His red hair is a touch darker than hers.

'William,' Tori informs me. 'My—'

'Little brother?' I suggest, and she nods.

'Did Lover Boy remember the wine?' Sinclair asks Will, nodding at a dark-haired guy in black boots and a biker jacket, who looks the exact opposite of a boarding-school pupil.

'You're so cringeworthy, Charles,' I hear William grumble, which makes me laugh. He's the first person, apart from the teachers, I've heard call Sinclair by his first name. The way they act around each other, you'd think he and Sinclair were brothers too. 'But, yeah, Kit brought something from the shop.'

'I love him,' declares Sinclair, reaching for the bottle that Will's clasping. His eyes keep flitting over to Kit, who seems older than the rest of us. But maybe that's just down to the cigarette, wedged oh-so casually behind his left ear. When he suddenly glances our way, William casts his eyes down, like he's been caught out.

'There are no glasses, I'm afraid,' says Sinclair, passing me another bottle.

I hesitate for a moment, then take it.

'You don't have to,' says Tori, at once. She doesn't make any move to drink any herself. Instead, she's watching sceptically as Sinclair lifts the bottle to his lips.

'Have you ever been caught?' I ask, remembering the school rules that Ms Barnett had listed the day I arrived. *No alcohol anywhere on the school grounds. That's non-negotiable.*

Sinclair and Tori exchange a brief glance. 'Yeah, once,' he admits. 'But that was three years ago. They're stricter when you're young. Don't worry.'

'I don't know.' Maybe they're stricter with everyone who isn't the head's son. Mind you, I can't imagine she'd let anyone give Sinclair special treatment on her account. 'I don't want to get into trouble in my first week.'

'Henry, have you been brainwashing her?' Sinclair sighs, handing the bottle on to Olive.

'Very funny.'

His voice . . . *Jeez, girl, cool it.*

I try to smile as I turn to face him. Friendly but not too friendly. Being-pleased-to-see-a-classmate friendly. No more. I fail the moment I realize Henry's already looking at me. A few strands of his dark hair are peeking out from under his hood.

'Did we wake you?' Tori asks. Henry glares sharply at her. On a closer look, he does seem kind of tired. Maybe it's still the jetlag that isn't jetlag. I hand the bottle on to Salome.

'Aye, and guess who had to climb in through the window to do it? Yours truly.' Sinclair flits past me and comes to stand next to Tori.

'Me too,' she says. Sinclair looks puzzled. 'To wake Emma, I mean.'

'Through the window?'

'No, I had to knock for her. Just as well Ms Barnett didn't hear.'

'Aren't you in the WhatsApp group?' Sinclair asks me, and I shake my head.

'Your number got smudged,' I tell Henry, not thinking, 'or I'd have texted you.'

Olive, Tori and Sinclair are all looking at him. The look Tori and Sinclair give each other speaks volumes, while Olive is eyeing Henry derisively.

'Oh, right,' he mumbles. 'I did wonder.'

'Anyway, tell me your number, and I'll share it in the group,' Tori announces, when the silence between us gets awkward. Soon after that, I'm a member of 'Midnight Memories' with its three moon emojis. There are fourteen in the group, and I can't shake off the feeling that not all of them want me. I feel Olive's eyes on me as I stand with Henry, Tori and Sinclair. She's sitting on one of the tatty old armchairs, tapping on her phone, as she watches me. It's only when Grace walks into the greenhouse with a couple of others that she stands up. Henry vanishes to say hi to them. I'm nervous, even though I have no reason to be.

'Hey, Emma.' I jump when Grace speaks to me. 'I've been meaning to ask you if you'd like to come along to the track team next week. Henry says you did athletics at home.'

I'm burning up. Is this a trap? Why's she being so friendly? Olive must have been telling her about the Henry's-number thing, right? Or wasn't she?

'Oh, yeah, I – I was in a club in Frankfurt,' I stutter.

'Cool,' she says, with a smile. 'We train three times a week, out in the grounds if possible. Monday at five, if you like.'

'Oh, that's . . . Thank you. I'd love to come.'

'We'd love to have you,' says Grace, turning away.

How can she be so nice? I don't get it, and it's not exactly helping me feel any better. Grace is stunning. She's kind, clever and dedicated. She's perfect for Henry, because he's all of those things too. And as for me, what am I even doing here? She's just perched on the arm of the chair that Henry's sitting in. He puts his arm around her, but they don't kiss. Maybe they're not the kind who have to advertise that they're a couple. Noah liked to do that. Making out in front of the others at parties, even if I didn't really feel comfortable. I hastily glance away as Henry looks towards me.

I spend a while chatting to Amara and Salome, who tell me about their families in India and the US. Out of the corner of my eye, I spot Grace and Henry standing up a while later. They're probably about to slip off together. I can't hear what they're saying, but I see Henry nod, then lay his hand on her cheek and kiss her. A bit later, Grace waves to everyone and slips out through the glass door. Is she off home again? When I pull out my phone, I see we've been here almost an hour and a half already.

'So, how's your first midnight party?'

Startled, I hurriedly stick my phone away. When I glance up again, it's right into Henry's face. His skin looks so soft. It's not fair.

'Very cool,' I say, feeling the heat rush to my cheeks. Wow, what an original answer, Emma. But Henry just smiles and digs his hands into his jacket pockets. He looks like he'd rather be back in bed than hanging around here. 'Just kind of late . . .'

He laughs. 'I know, right?'

'You're such wusses,' remarks Sinclair, as he pushes past us with a bottle and a bag of crisps.

'Just ignore him,' says Henry.

'Has Grace gone home?' I ask, regretting it that very second. God, what's that got to do with me?

Henry hesitates a moment. He's probably wondering the same thing. But then he nods. 'Yeah, she was tired. She's not really the type for midnight parties.'

'But you are?'

He grins. 'You just mustn't go to sleep beforehand, that's the trick.'

'That's where we both went wrong, I guess.'

'Looks like it.' He smiles. 'How's your week been?'

He has to ask that. He's school captain and a prefect and it's not like he's personally interested. I mustn't forget that.

'Stressful, but good,' I say. *Stay calm, Emma. It's perfectly simple.*

'Lots to take in, huh?'

Oh, God, OK, there's no way I can stay calm if he's going to look at me like that, the hint of a smile on his lips and his head slightly to one side.

'You could say that.'

The music goes off and we turn at the same time.

My blood runs cold. Did the teachers hear the noise of the party? Are they on their way? But the others are still chatting, unfazed.

'Who's going to take over the music?' Sinclair looks around. He catches Henry's eye. 'Not you.'

I laugh as he pulls a face. 'Why not him?' I ask.

Sinclair looks like he'd been waiting for that question. 'He listens to charts stuff.'

I frown. 'So? So do I sometimes . . .'

'No, not sometimes, Emma,' says Sinclair. 'Always. All fucking day.'

'You only listen to chart stuff?' I ask Henry.

'And the Top 100 on Spotify sometimes.'

'Which is basically the same thing,' murmurs Sinclair.

'But, why? I don't get it,' I say.

'I don't get it either,' says Sinclair. He turns to me. 'I'm telling you, count yourself lucky your room's in the other wing.'

'Hey, I practically always have headphones on,' Henry says.

'Yeah, but I still see it in your friend feed on Spotify. Minging.'

'But Emma can do that from the girls' wing too, if she adds me.'

'Oh, yeah, true. Whatever. Anyway, it's a disgrace.'

'Hey, that's taste-shaming.' Henry sounds genuinely insulted.

'The charts epitomize the absence of taste,' declares Sinclair. 'And the Top 100 is basically the same thing.'

Henry looks at me, offended, but I'm afraid I have to agree with Sinclair as he heads off towards the sound system.

'It's not my fault,' Henry says. 'There's so much music out there, I don't know where to start.'

I can't help laughing. 'There are ready-made playlists. Autumn Moods, Workout Songs, anything you like.'

'Yeah, but there are too many of them too.'

'Do you ever listen to your Discover Weekly?' I ask.

Henry frowns. 'What's that?'

I sigh. 'Oh, wow . . .'

'What?'

'Nothing, nothing. Do you listen to music while you run?'

'I don't know.' He shrugs his shoulders. 'I always avoided running until now.'

'Oh, yeah, right. I can put something together for you for training. With some charts stuff in it too, I promise. I even use my playlists to pace my runs. That's perfect for me – I can have slower songs for gentle runs and faster ones for tempo efforts. I'll share them with you. Although to start off with, it's better to run without music so you can concentrate on your breathing.'

Henry doesn't seem convinced.

'Are you going to train with Grace?' I ask. 'I bet she knows all the tricks too.'

'Maybe, we'll see. She's really busy.'

Before I can say anything, Tori wraps her arms around me and drags us off to play a kind of truth or dare. Except that the dares are all drinking, so for her, Henry, me and a few others who don't drink alcohol, there's only the truth option.

As a result, I learn that Sinclair would rather be able to talk to animals than speak loads of languages, and that a guy called Omar always cries at Disney films.

'Seriously?' Sinclair asks. 'Disney?'

'Totally, man. Haven't you ever seen *Brother Bear*?'

'I love *Brother Bear*.' Tori sighs.

'That's masochism, but OK.'

Tori rolls her eyes and leans round to me. 'Sinclair's the artsy type – he loves all those weird classics. *Dead Poets Society*, *The Dreamers*, you know the stuff . . .'

I nod, though I've never seen either film. Maybe I should watch them sometime.

'Enough of your cheek,' says Sinclair.

'Hey, I'm just telling it like it is.' Tori leans back again.

'OK, your turn.' Sinclair points at Henry with his wine bottle. He seems already to have decided on his question because he asks it without hesitation. 'Big spoon or little spoon?'

There's an expectant silence as Henry gives him a withering glare. Suddenly I'm pretty certain we're not talking about cutlery.

'And you have to tell the truth even if you're stone-cold sober?' Henry asks, but it's a feeble attempt.

'Especially then,' declares Sinclair.

'OK.' He sighs. 'Little spoon . . .'

The others sigh too and laugh quietly.

'Shame Grace isn't still here,' says Sinclair. 'I'd love to check this with her.'

I've never found it so hard to keep smiling.

'Hasn't anyone still got those photos from the Norway trip?' Olive asks. 'They definitely fell asleep like that back then.'

Henry seems pretty uncomfortable with this whole thing because he ignores her and just asks the next question. I'm hearing the words, but I'm not really paying attention. Tori asks me if I'd rather be able to eat anything, no matter how spicy, or never burn my tongue on hot food again, so I pick the second choice, obviously. I feel Henry's eyes on me as more questions are asked. He's gently biting his bottom lip as he gazes at me, and I force myself not to keep thinking about it. And not to look at his mouth. He breaks off eye-contact as soon as he notices I'm watching him, too.

I don't know how much later it is when the greenhouse eventually empties. Sinclair's sitting between Tori's knees on the floor next to one of the armchairs, and she's massaging his shoulders while deep in a heated discussion with Olive and a few others about the unannounced maths tests that Mr Ward apparently likes to dump on people.

When I look at the time, it's later than I'd thought. My head is pounding a bit, my eyes are burning, and I'm finding it increasingly difficult to keep up with everyone's rapid English.

It may be coincidence, or it may not, but at this exact moment, Henry looks at me. He eyes me, then nods questioningly at me.

I shrug, and even if I don't quite understand what this non-verbal communication really means, it seems to work.

Sinclair cranes his neck to blink upwards to Henry as he stands.

'I think I need to get some sleep,' Henry says. He glances at me, and I get up too.

'Me too.' I'm expecting some comment, someone to boo, or say, *Party-poopers*, like Noah or Isi would definitely have done, but nothing happens.

'Sleep well,' says Sinclair, leaning his head back against Tori's knees again.

The others say goodbye to us, too, and I avoid looking in Olive's direction as I walk out of the door ahead of Henry.

Suddenly, this feels out of bounds. Because we're alone out here and I'd forgotten how dark it was. Maybe it's just because I'm very tired, but it seems colder to me now. I shiver and dig my hands into my jacket pockets as we walk over the meadow. Damp grass tickles my ankles, the voices from the greenhouse growing quieter with every metre. By the time we've reached the path, I can't hear them at all.

This is all there is. The chirping crickets, Henry's footsteps and mine on the gravel. And my heart, which is thumping loudly. Why aren't we speaking? Do we have to keep quiet so that no one hears us?

'How tired are you?'

An owl hoots, cold air fills my lungs, and Henry really did just ask that.

'Why?' I can't see more than his silhouette beside me as I turn my head towards him.

'I was just wondering . . . If you're really tired, I'll walk you right back to your wing. But if you're not, we could take a little detour. There are some secret passages through the cellars under the school.' His eyes burn into me. 'It's really spooky, though.'

I hardly dare breathe. 'I like spooky.'

My eyes have gradually got used to the darkness and I can see his smile now. 'OK,' he says.

'OK,' I repeat. Then, 'Or are *you* too tired? You're really tired, right?'

'I'm not *that* tired. Besides, you're at a Scottish boarding school. We have to go on secret night-time wanders – it's part of the authentic experience.'

'Are you sure? We don't have to . . .'

'I'm sure,' he says, and I fall silent. 'It's through here.'

Henry takes my wrist and pulls me into an archway to our left. His touch is like a mini electric shock running through my whole body. I don't want him ever to let go – seriously, I mean it – but I'm afraid he doesn't realize that.

This doorway is so inconspicuous that I'd probably have walked right past it. I follow Henry down the steps. It's pitch black in here. Henry lets go and pulls out his phone.

127

The places where his skin touched mine are prickling in a way that feels like regret and desperately wanting more. A moment later, he's using the torch mode to light our way.

We come to a door in dark wood with solid metal fittings. It looks locked. Henry starts to rattle at the latch. Very loudly, to be honest. Automatically, I hold my breath and glance back over my shoulder. A moment later, I hear a squeak and Henry pushes the door open.

'Are you sure this isn't against the rules?' I whisper, before I follow him. It smells kind of musty down here, but not exactly unpleasant.

'Oh, it's obviously way out of bounds,' says Henry, 'but who's going to know?'

He shuts the door behind me and I wonder what we're doing here. Sandy gravel crunches under our feet. I raise my head as Henry shines the light over the walls and ceiling. We're in some kind of passage.

'There are tunnels under the whole school but most of them never get used.' He beckons me to follow him. 'They say that thirteen pupils went missing down here once.'

'Ha-ha,' I murmur.

'OK, there were only eleven of them. There's even a dungeon under the church.' He glances at me. 'I bet your old school never had anything like this.'

'You're right, it didn't,' I admit. 'Do you have a school ghost too?'

'Yeah, his name's Simon.'

'No, can't be, I'd have heard about it,' I say.

'Is that right?'

'My mum would have mentioned it for sure.'

'He's new,' he explains. 'My parents never met him either, and they went to school here, too.'

I prick up my ears. His parents were at Dunbridge Academy? At once, my head is full of questions. How old are they? Do they know my dad? Might Henry even know my dad? I'm just wondering about the subtlest way of finding that out when Henry points to our left, where the passage branches out into tunnels in several directions.

'So, what's the story?' he begins, and my stomach ties itself in knots. Don't ask. Don't ask about *that*. Please, just let it go. 'Were both your parents here at the school, or just your mum?'

Of course. But I can't really hold it against him – I'd be interested too if it were me.

So I nod. 'They met here.' I just keep staring ahead down the dark passage and don't look at Henry's attentive face. It's a bit easier to explain things if I don't have to make eye contact with him. 'My mum came here from Germany in the second form, and my dad's from Glasgow.'

'And you all live in Germany now?'

I gulp. 'Just Mum and me.'

Henry doesn't ask any more questions. But suddenly I'm telling him. 'He walked out when I was eleven, and I never heard from him again.'

129

I'm psyching myself up for some platitude. Something like, 'Oh, I'm sorry,' or 'Whoa, that's tough,' but Henry doesn't say anything. Small stones scrunch under the soles of our shoes and then there's his voice again.

'Do you often think about him?'

'No, not really.' Well, that's a flat-out lie. *Yes, every day. Way too often to be healthy.* That's what I ought to say. I swallow. 'Only sometimes.'

'It must be weird, being here,' says Henry. 'Where he used to be too.'

'It is weird.'

'Do you want to get in touch with him?' Henry asks, and that's the whole problem. Part of me wants to say, 'Yes.' Loud and clear. It's the part that can't watch those sappy dramas – the 'I'm going to find my dad and he's going to love me even though we barely know each other' kind without crying hot, angry tears. The other, bigger, part of me knows that it doesn't work like that in real life. That I'm way too let down and hurt. That I don't want to find him just so he can act like he actually has any interest in me. Because he can't do, or he wouldn't have left. I only want to find him so I can ask him questions. Fucked-up, uncomfortable questions. Why was everything else more important than Mum and me? Why did he choose to do it, and why doesn't he care about me?

'I want to find him,' I say, without considering whether or not it's wise to tell Henry that. Dark tunnels, echoing footsteps. And me wanting Henry to know everything. 'I can't ask my mum about him. She wants to make sure he can't let me down again. And I thought that here I might find out who he was. And where he is.'

These are things I've never told anybody. Not Noah, not Isi. Nobody. But I've told Henry and, in the end, I'm only doing this because I know that he's a stranger. Someone I'll spend a year in super-tiny classes with, ducking out early from secret midnight parties with to go on night-time walks in spooky tunnels with, and to tell the truth to. And then I'll never see him again.

'My parents were at Dunbridge too,' says Henry. 'I could ask them. They might know him.'

'What are their first names?' I ask.

'Catherine and Tom,' says Henry, and the tiny spark of hope inside me is blown out again. Their names mean nothing to me, and if my dad knew them, Mum would too. And she'd definitely have mentioned them to me.

I nod all the same, because that's easier than explaining why there's no point. 'Did they meet here too?' I ask.

'Yeah.' I hear the smile in Henry's voice. 'This school is like some kind of dating site. I know loads of couples who met here.'

'Like you and Grace,' I say.

He doesn't answer right away. 'Like me and Grace.' He stops and points his phone torch down another branching tunnel. 'We can go this way.'

'How come you know your way around down here so well?' I murmur.

'Years of practice. And a good memory.'

We reach a staircase and Henry lights up the broad steps ahead of us. Just before we get to the top, he switches off the torch. We're inside a building, and there's pale moonlight shining through the high windows.

'We have to keep quiet again now,' he whispers.

It feels totally surreal, walking beside Henry along the deserted corridors. I haven't the least idea which part of the school we're in, but this area seems vaguely familiar.

Henry puts his finger to his lips as we approach a large set of double doors in dark wood. He puts a hand on the latch and cautiously pushes it open. There's a long, drawn-out screech and Henry bites his bottom lip, waving to me to go ahead. I flit through the crack in the door and stop.

'Oops, sorry . . .' murmurs Henry, as he stumbles into me. His hand is on my side; he pulls it back and I hurriedly step forward. He shuts the door, switches his phone torch on again and then I recognize where he's brought me.

'Ta-da! The school library,' he says, as the tall shelves, laden with countless books swallow his voice. 'It doesn't get more clichéd than this.'

'That's a shame,' I murmur. The sound of his quiet laugh gives me goosebumps.

'I'll have to think of something to make your Scottish

boarding-school experience even more authentic,' he promises.

'It's already pretty good,' I say, holding my breath as Henry puts his hand on my shoulder. We shouldn't keep touching like this, and I don't know what's going on here, but it's driving me crazy. 'Except the phone light is really killing the atmosphere.'

'That's why I'm looking for the candles.'

I have to laugh. 'Seriously?'

'Yes, of course. Ah, here they are.' I stay still as Henry steps to one side and puts his phone down on a small shelf. Seconds later, there's a hiss and a little flame strikes up. He lights three candles and it's brighter now. The warm light throws flickering shadows onto all the books against the walls. Most of them look so old and valuable that I don't dare get them down.

Silently, I walk past one bookcase, running my fingers over the spines. Henry follows me.

'Does it ever get normal, living here?' I ask, after a while, not looking around.

'I don't think so, no,' he says.

At that moment, I spot a little plaque on one of the shelves: *Yearbooks 2015–2020*. They're chunky and they all look exactly the same, apart from the different years on the spines. My heart beats faster.

I glance at Henry; he's just pulled down a book and started flicking through it.

I hastily look up to the labels on the shelves.

Yearbooks 1995–2000

Yearbooks 1990–1995

1994. That must have been their year.

I'm about to reach out for the book when Henry joins me. 'What are you looking at?' he asks.

'Nothing,' I say hurriedly, turning away and pretending to study the display case full of trophies and photos that's standing right next to the bookcase.

I don't know why I don't just tell him the truth. Maybe because I have to be alone when I look in that book for clues to the man who couldn't care less about my existence. It's humiliating enough as it is.

'Rugby's the shit here, isn't it?' I ask instead. It's the first thing that comes to mind. Hardly surprising, considering all the cups and photos I can see behind the glass.

'Pretty much,' says Henry. There's a funny tone to his voice now. He holds the candlestick a little closer to the case, until the flickering light falls on the group pictures behind the trophies.

'That's Theo,' Henry says, at the very second that I think the guy in the middle looks so much like him. 'My brother. He was the rugby captain.'

'Wow,' I breathe, stepping a little closer to the trophy cabinet. 'Is that why you want to get onto the team?'

He laughs. It's probably meant to sound natural. But, if so, it's not working. 'God, no. Apparently it might help my uni application.'

'Is that so important?' I ask.

'Maybe,' he says curtly. 'I'm pretty good at all my subjects, so it might not make much difference, but they say it looks good to play for the school.'

'Where do you want to go to uni?' I ask.

I'd expected Henry to say Oxford or Cambridge, but he doesn't. 'St Andrews,' he replies.

I'm surprised.

'It's a bit north of—'

'Edinburgh, I know,' I say. 'My mum went there.'

Henry's face brightens. 'Really?'

'Yeah. Law.'

'Do you want to go there, too?'

'I don't know. I think I'll study somewhere in Germany. Maybe at the *Sporthochschule* in Cologne, if I pass the entrance exam.'

He pauses. 'I mean, now that you're here . . . you could finish your A levels at Dunbridge and study in Scotland, or in England . . .'

'I know that,' I reply, and it sounds a bit more snappy than really necessary. But I've had this conversation so often, with people who apparently know the right thing for me better than I do.

Henry doesn't speak again. He keeps looking into that display case, and I start to feel guilty.

'Do you really want to be a teacher?' I make an effort to sound friendlier.

'Yes.' His eyes wander over the shelves, to the end of the room. 'I really do. I dream of coming back and teaching here one day.'

'I don't think I've ever met anyone who dreams of going back to their school,' I blurt. 'Most of them want to get as far away as possible once they've done their exams.'

Henry is silent briefly. 'I know. But Dunbridge Academy was the first place that really taught me what home means. I didn't even know I was missing anything until I started here. I'd been to so many schools and lived in so many places. But it's different here. I belong here and I'd like to pass on the stuff I've learned here to others.' It's quiet for a moment, then Henry laughs. 'Wow, I sound like such a geek.'

I can't help grinning. 'But a very nice geek.'

'Hey . . .'

'Oh, sorry, should I have said something like "That's crap, Henry! You're a total rebel?"'

'Yeah, you really should.'

'Sorry, I'm just such a terrible liar.'

Now we're both silent, and my eyes stray, as if on auto-pilot, back to that trophy cabinet. 'So, the rugby team,' I murmur. It's a big deal to Henry. 'What's the time?'

'What?'

'What's the time, Henry?' I repeat.

He looks at me like I'm out of my mind. Then he glances down at his phone. 'Almost three.'

'OK.' I reach for the candlestick. Somehow I hadn't

136

realized that our fingers would touch. And there's something about those touches, something I'll never understand. Little bolts of lightning that turn into liquid heat. Henry's eyes darken as they wander down from mine to my mouth. The candlelight flickers in his eyes and I go weak at the knees. He's holding his breath; I can see it. 'We have to get to bed.'

'Why?' Henry asks, and my stomach leaps as I hear the quiet disappointment in his voice.

'Because tomorrow morning we're going for a run.'

11

HENRY

She's hard-core. She's even tougher than Mr Cormack, and I'd never have thought that was possible.

Running an extra four times a week – that's right, on top of the morning run. An hour at medium intensity at five thirty on Tuesday and Friday mornings with the morning run as our warm-down. Seriously. The actual warm-down. I want to cry. And throw up. And lie down and never get up again. Not necessarily in that order.

Wednesdays and Saturdays are for technique and coordination, followed by tempo runs on the track. Oh, yeah, and stretching exercises every day, using this foam roller thing that's definitely the work of the devil.

But I guess this is a good thing. I'm really having to work

at it. I remember Maeve's cheery messages to our WhatsApp group when I mentioned that I'd got onto the team on probation. *See! I knew you could do it!* And Theo's *Don't embarrass me now.*

'If it's not too much for you, we could add in strength training, once or twice a week,' says Emma. 'It's important to work on your core and explosive strength. But that's up to you to decide.'

How can she talk so much while she's running beside me? OK, so they say that you should keep your training at a level where you can still chat as you run, but that never seems to work out for me. We're only jogging slowly, but I still feel like my heart's going to burst out of my chest after three minutes tops.

'Yeah, sounds good,' I pant. She's really trying hard to hide it, but I know perfectly well that she's grinning at me being out of breath yet again.

It's only your second week of training, Henry. You have to give your body time to get used to this new workload. It'll take at least a month, if not two, for you to notice any improvement in your stamina. That's perfectly normal. I don't really believe that, but nobody asks me. So I just try to keep up. I'll never comprehend how Emma can be so fast. Or how she can actually enjoy this. Never, never, never.

'Watch your posture,' she says, and I force myself to tense my stomach again. I have to stay straight and not arch my back or I'll get backache. God, I always thought running was simple – I mean, it's as natural as walking – but nobody ever told me how wrongly you can do it.

'I went into the gym for the first time on Saturday,' she continues. 'The facilities here are amazing! We need to do loads with resistance bands and the roller. No more shin splints, Henry.'

'Could we train on the running machines sometimes?' I suggest.

Emma just laughs, so I wave goodbye to that idea.

'In impact terms, it just doesn't compare to outdoors. And you're training for the rugby pitch. Wet, muddy grass. We'll be much better off out in the grounds.'

I'd sigh, but I don't have the breath for it.

'We might use the machines sometimes in bad weather,' Emma concedes later.

'It's meant to rain next week.'

She laughs. Damn. 'Rain's no reason not to run. I meant more like hail and snow. Do you get much snow here?'

'Sometimes . . .' Not very often. Oh, man, I'm so screwed.

'You'll soon make progress, honestly.'

I doubt that, but what choice do I have? I need to get fitter, and even this shitty endurance training must be basically the same as anything else. If you keep working at a thing, and persevering, eventually you'll succeed. But I'd way rather spend hours cramming in the library than doing this much running.

I want to stop. I think it with every step.

I could stop.

Next step.

Got to stop.

Next step.

Just for a moment.

'Anyway, it's all in your head,' says Emma, at that exact second. Almost like she's in mine. 'Anytime you think you can't go on, you can actually go on at least that long again.'

'Doubtful,' I wheeze.

'Seriously, no doubt about it. You just have to take your mind off it. Do you like listening to podcasts? Or audiobooks?'

'Kind of.'

'Or I'll make you a playlist that's all charts songs. D'you think that would help?'

'I think stopping would help.'

'No, Henry.' She smiles, and now, after kilometre four, her cheeks are gradually flushing a pale pink. This is still no fun, but if I have to run four kilometres every morning to see that, it might just be worth it.

EMMA

'So, what's going on?' Tori begins casually, but there's something in her voice that gives me a clue about where she's heading. 'Are you and Bennington running together every day now?'

OK, fine. It was a predictable question, but did Tori really have to ask it almost as soon as we've left the school's thick walls behind this afternoon? Maybe the whole point of this trip to Ebrington was actually more to do with interrogating me than showing me around the village and cheering me up after the shitty English test that Mr Ward dumped on us with no warning.

'I don't think he's ever done the whole morning run of his own free will before,' Olive remarks, as she twists her still-damp hair up into a bun.

'I'm helping him train so he can get onto the rugby team.'

'Why isn't Grace training with him?' Olive eyes me.

'Presumably because she doesn't feel like getting here two hours before school starts every morning, and then having to go home again to shower?' Tori suggests.

'She could use Henry's bathroom,' Olive says curtly. Her words are like tiny daggers in my chest. 'And, anyway, why don't they train in the evening?'

'She hasn't got time,' I say. It feels like a lie, yet it's exactly what Henry told me.

'Or maybe Henry just prefers running with Emma.' Tori's eyes bore through me. 'Do *you* like running with Henry?'

'I, uh . . .' Olive is now staring at me too and I know that, whatever I say, there are only wrong answers here. 'It's nice?'

'Nice?' Tori laughs. 'Yeah, OK, Henry in his PE kit is

definitely a nice sight. He's got such a cute arse. So it's actually mean of him not to be interested in sport.'

'Apparently he is now,' Olive replies.

'Yeah, but you know what I mean.'

'Well, he's no Sinclair . . .'

'Emma's not into Sinclair.'

I open my mouth but Olive doesn't give me time to speak. 'No, but you are. And clearly Emma's not into Henry either, because he's with Grace.'

Ouch. Breathe. I daren't look in Olive's direction.

'I love him like a brother, Livy,' says Tori, in that deliberately casual voice. 'Like a brother.'

'Course you do,' murmurs Olive. 'Except when Sinclair wears those super-skinny jodhpurs, huh?'

I'd probably have been grinning if Olive's words weren't still echoing in my head. Why did she even come when she clearly can't stand me? This would have been way more fun with just Tori.

I stare intently at the dark stone walls and wonky gabled roofs of the houses lining the street.

'Whatever. We're here to show Emma around, anyway,' says Tori, pointing to a shop window on our left. 'That's the Blue Room Café. Their cake is the best, and the scones are to die for. Which is hardly surprising because they get them fresh from Sinclair's every day.'

'You mean Sinclair's dad's bakery?' I ask.

'Exactly. It's down there,' says Tori, pointing along the

cobbled street. 'Everything's half price after three o'clock. Sometimes Sinclair brings the leftovers into school too.'

'Is that where the bread for breakfast comes from?' I ask.

Tori nods. 'Handy, isn't it? This is the Second Chance, by the way. Sometimes they have amazing vintage stuff. Further along, there's a pub, a florist, a tiny cinema, and then there's the most important shop around here: Ebrington Tales bookshop! They don't have the hugest selection, but last year they finally added an LGBTQIA+ shelf. I only had to ask four times and show them the pictures of Waterstones in Edinburgh for them to get it.'

'Shall we head over there on Friday?' Olive asks.

She's looking at Tori, but Tori immediately glances at me. 'To Edinburgh? Want to come, Emma?'

I avoid Olive's gaze. 'Yeah, I'd love to, but my mum's coming for a visit.'

'Oh, that's nice,' Tori replies. 'Well, the weekend after then? We're flexible, aren't we, Livy?'

Olive just nods.

'We missed out Irvine's,' says Tori, pointing across the road. 'It's everything rolled into one: supermarket, deli, chemist and post office.'

'And they sell booze too,' adds Olive. 'At least when Kit's on the till.'

'Speak of the devil,' murmurs Tori, tugging me back by my jacket sleeve. It's not until I peek down a narrow alleyway between the buildings that I realize who she means.

It takes me a moment to recognize Tori's brother William and Kit.

'No way . . .' whispers Olive, in disbelief, while Tori presses a finger to her lips. Will has his back to the wall while Kit's arm is raised above his head, leaning on it too – and then Will pulls Kit to him and kisses him.

'William Belhaven-Wynford,' Tori breathes. 'What on earth are you up to?'

Olive laughs. 'How come they've got it together but you and Sinclair haven't?'

'Shut up,' Tori mumbles, as we walk on. 'I'm not interested in Sinclair.'

'Yeah, right.'

'So how's it going with Val?' I ask. Fortunately, Tori turns to me.

'Pretty good, I think. He's super-busy with study and training, so we haven't actually spoken yet.' Tori smiles, and perhaps I'm just imagining it, but I think she sounds a little disappointed.

'He's sure to have time soon,' I say.

She nods. 'I hope so.'

'Can we pop into Irvine's?' asks Olive. 'I need some toothpaste.'

I follow the pair of them into the shop, which really does seem to stock anything you can imagine. Tori piles a mountain of snacks into her basket, while Olive limits herself to a few toiletries. As we thread our way to the front of the shop, down the narrow aisles, we see a man at the counter. My pulse quickens as I spot the stick he's leaning on. Mr Ward . . . The bad feeling I had after that test today floods back into my mind. Has he started marking it already? He turns his head in our direction as the man behind the counter reaches into one of the pharmacy cabinets. Mr Ward whips the little white packet off the counter and stashes it away in the inside pocket of his coat.

I keep quiet as Tori and Olive say hello to him.

'Shouldn't you be in class?' Mr Ward asks, as he pays. I hold my breath as his eyes rake over me. 'Or out for a run?' The disdainful way he says the word makes me shiver. Has he seen me and Henry running together? What if he has? What's it to him anyway?

I can't answer him, but fortunately Tori speaks for all of us.

'No, sir, we've got a free afternoon,' she replies, sugar-sweetly.

Mr Ward's expression darkens. 'Well, make sure you're all back in time for study hour.' He nods curtly to the pharmacist and turns away.

'We've got almost two hours until then,' murmurs Olive, as he walks away. The bell jingles as the shop door closes behind him. Olive and Tori pay and, as I stand beside them, I can still feel Mr Ward's eyes on me. This morning in English, just now . . . Every time I see him, I remember the evasive way Mum answered me on the phone. Maybe I should have another go at asking her when she comes for the weekend.

Mr Ward is out of sight by the time we get back onto the street. Tori wants to drag me off to the café and Olive heads back towards the school. I can't say I'm upset about that. I feel much better when it's just me and Tori. And there's something I've had on my mind for ages that I'd really like to talk to her about. So, once I'm sitting opposite her in the tearoom a little later on, sipping my tea, I pluck up all my courage.

'Er, Tori . . .' she looks expectantly at me '. . . I don't know how to say this, without sounding totally dumb, but–'

'Whatever it is, I'm sure it won't sound dumb,' she interrupts, smiling at me.

'It's just . . . Do you know if I've done something wrong to make Olive kind of . . . pissed off with me?'

Tori's silence lasts a moment too long. 'Don't let it bother you if she's a bit off sometimes. Olive doesn't mean anything by it. It's the Scorpio in her that comes out now and then.' She pauses before she continues. 'Things have been kind of complicated between her and me for a while,' she says. 'We were this really close group for ages, and Olive . . . well, she doesn't deal so well with change.'

Change . . . So, with me crashing in between them.

'Oh, right,' I mumble, stirring my tea.

'I'm so glad you're here, Emma,' says Tori, impetuously, smiling at me. 'And, God, I don't think I'm the only one who is.'

12

HENRY

It's the way things always are at the start of a new school year. Everything happens at once, and at mega-high speed. The days fly by, and I love it. The feeling of having so much to do and being absolutely where I'm meant to be. Mind you, it doesn't feel quite the same on evenings like this, when I've got rugby training and two hours of death stares from Valentine Ward, but that's what I wanted, so hey.

I don't know if my training with Emma has had any effect yet, but at least it means I'm completely knackered by the time I drop into bed every night. Even now, I'm shutting my laptop on my Netflix series right at the start of wing time because I can't even keep up with the plot. Although, for once, that's not because I'm too tired. My thoughts keep wandering. To Emma and her fingers between my shoulder blades when she says: *Stand up straight, Henry.* To her slender neck and the sweat on her smooth skin. I didn't know that could be a turn-on, but what can I say? When I shower after a run and feel my own salty sweat on my tongue, I find myself imagining it's hers. I have to. There's no other option.

I push the laptop aside, turn off the light and roll onto my back. My head is heavy, but I don't shut my eyes. I stare into the darkness and think about her body. I imagine putting my hands on her waist and feeling that line of super-soft skin. Because her top's ridden up and she hasn't done anything about it. Like she's OK with it. I think about her pink lips and her cheeks, which flush the same colour once we've run for long enough. I wonder if that would also happen if she were lying underneath me, my mouth exploring her body. If her lips formed my name, which sounds so sweet the way she says it. If she put her head back and arched up towards me.

It's enough to make my breath come harder and my boxers tighten. I shut my eyes, as an imaginary Emma's fingers push downwards over my belly, then open them with a start.

'Hi,' whispers Grace, shutting my door behind her. 'I know it's wing time already but . . .' She stops as I sit up and fumble for the light switch. I blink and pull the duvet over my crotch. 'Oh, did I wake you?'

'No, I . . .' I cough, but my voice is still hoarse. 'I was just so tired after training.' There's a throbbing between my legs. Liar, liar, liar. 'Is everything OK? What are you doing here?'

Grace is still standing by the door. I'd get up and go over to her, but I've got this boner, and it's nothing to do with her. 'I was round with Olive, and I thought . . .'

She doesn't say it out loud, but she doesn't have to. I know what she wants to tell me. That nothing's happened between us since I got back, and things used to be the exact opposite of that when we hadn't seen each other for ages. Back when I spent the whole return flight thinking about how I'd kiss her and press her into the mattress. But that was then. Secret nights together, forbidden touches. Our first times in beds that were way too narrow, and I don't know exactly when all that stopped. It wasn't a conscious decision, more of a gradual process.

I should say something. Ask her if she wants to stay over, for example. I should do it, but it wouldn't be right. I don't want to admit it, but it's true.

'Anyway, sorry, I didn't mean to wake you,' says Grace.

'You didn't,' I answer, and that part's even true. I was still awake because I'm an arsehole who was thinking about another woman.

'I think I'd better get going, then.' She reaches for the door handle. And I say nothing. I just wait as she turns around. Slowly, as if she wants to give me a chance, an opportunity to use. But I don't take it. Her eyes come back to me again.

'Text me when you're home,' I say, and I hate myself for it. 'OK?'

'Yes.' Grace forces herself to smile. 'Sleep well, Henry.'

'You too,' I whisper.

Grace walks away. My girlfriend, I sent her away. I wait till she's closed the door behind her. I listen out in the silence. I let myself fall back; I press the pillow into my face so that nobody can hear the sound of frustration that escapes me.

EMMA

What am I doing here? I haven't the faintest idea. All I know is that it was somehow way nicer walking down these empty corridors in the middle of the night when Henry was by my side. I didn't notice then how dark and creepy it was. But maybe that's down to the rain that's now beating against the windowpanes and the wind whistling around the walls. Every time I hear some other weird noise, I jump and whirl around, praying that nobody will catch me. It isn't quite as late as last time, when I was out with Henry, but I doubt I'd get into any less trouble for that. It's long past wing time and I'm meant to be in my room, but my mind kept racing, always coming back to that shelf of yearbooks.

When I was in the school library this afternoon, I soon realized that flicking through those books in the daytime is not an option. Not while Mr Elling, the librarian, is wheeling his little trolley up and down the aisles and my fellow pupils are sitting at the tables, reading. You can't borrow the year-books, so I took out the three novels we're going to be reading in English over the next few weeks. And wondered when would be the best time to come back here, undisturbed.

I don't know what I think I'm going to get from this. It's quite likely that I'll find a photo of my parents in one of those books. But what good will that do me? I'd just torture myself looking for similarities, then have to remind myself that I'd be not one step further on in my pointless quest. But what can I say? My gut instinct is telling me that I have to do this, so I've got no choice.

When I make out the big double doors at the end of the hallway, I sigh with relief. They open with a quiet squeak.

I don't know what it is about rooms full of books, but somehow you feel safe inside them. My footsteps aren't echoing any more. The sound is swallowed. There's a different smell too, of wood and paper, dust and promises.

The candlestick is in the same place as last time, but I don't dare light the candles. Instead, I pull my phone out of the kangaroo pocket on my hoodie. The cold light of the torch doesn't fit the vibe, but I can't risk accidentally knocking into a candle and setting the whole school on fire. That's totally the kind of thing that would happen to me. So, I'd better not.

I walk along the shelves until I reach the yearbooks. My eyes hurriedly flick over the dates.

1994. My heart thumps when I find the right spine.

I reach out my hand, but hesitate as my fingertips touch the smooth binding. It's not like I'm expecting much from these yearbook photos. I've seen pictures of Mum and Dad at my age before. But, somehow, looking at them in our cellar is different from doing so here in the library of the boarding school whose walls could tell me the stories that no one else will.

I pull down the book. It's heavier than I expected. I put my phone on the shelf so that I can hold the yearbook with both hands and blow the thin sheet of dust off the top edge.

Class of 1994. I run my thumbs over the inscription, then open the book.

There are lots of pages. So many that at some point I sit down on the old wooden floorboards and use my phone torch to light them.

I go through the list of names and hold my breath when I finally find their names.

Laura Beck.

Jacob Wiley.

Laura and Jacob. Mum and the man who could've been a father to me, if he'd felt like it.

And then I read the name two lines above my father's.

Alaric Ward.

Is that him? Mr Ward? Were they in the same year group?

I flick on. There are group photos from the junior school. Ten or fifteen children at most per photo, and I have to analyse them all. Not to find Mum, no. She didn't start here until the second form, but my father must have been here from the start. And maybe Mr Ward was too.

I've gone through almost all the photos, and I'm just wondering whether to start again at the beginning, when I stop.

It's the eyes that make me think I'm looking at myself as a child. The pale blond hair, that eventually darkened on him. But not on me.

It's my dad, and he must be eleven, twelve at most. The tip of my nose is almost touching the paper, I'm leaning in so close to the book, but I can't tell whether or not Mr Ward is among the other pupils. It's not until I get to the second senior form that I'm sure. He's standing next to my dad and not looking anywhere near as bitter as he does these days. More like mischievous. Rather like that Valentine when he happens to be looking less arrogant than normal.

Then I spot Mum. Of course. Second form, her first year at Dunbridge Academy. She's standing on the back row, looking kind of uptight and shy. Not at all the way I know her. My dad's hair is a bit longer than everyone else's, and he looks sort of rebellious, even though he's wearing uniform. But school uniform doesn't suit him. He's staring into the camera and not smiling.

I turn the pages. Look at the photos from the third, fourth and fifth forms. In the lower sixth, they're standing together and my father's hand is somewhere behind Mum's back. She's not looking at the camera, she's gazing at him. He's acting like he hasn't noticed, but his smile tells a different story. He knows exactly what he's doing. It's the first photo where he and Mr Ward aren't side by side. Mr Ward is a row back, behind them, and glancing in their direction. He looks kind of jealous. My parents belong together in a strange way. My mum looks like a model pupil. My dad looks like an adventurer, bold, like someone who wants more from life than scoring points and playing by rules dreamed up by other people. He looks like the kind of person you can't pin down. The kind you can't really predict, who'll promise you the world one day and be off over the hills the next, because he comes and goes like the tide. He was like that then, and Mum still fell for him.

My throat feels tight as I flick further on. More pictures from the lower sixth and no Dad. No Mr Ward either. He doesn't reappear until photos from the upper sixth. Where did he get to in between? And why does he look so different now? As if all the light had gone out from his eyes. I stare at those photos, as if they could give me answers, but I can't find them. I just peer at pictures from the start of the academic year, and then from the leavers' ball. Fancy gowns, beaming faces, hats thrown into the air. Group photos. Mum holding her results and beaming. No trace of my dad. Maybe he was up on some tiny stage at that moment, thinking he'd made it. He'd struck lucky: he was living his dream; he'd beaten the system.

It was the first time he left her. I know that he did it again, lots of times after that. That he went back to Mum when she was at uni and he hadn't got a record deal in London. That they lived together for a few years, and he left again when she was pregnant. That he came back, just before I was born, that he moved to Germany with her, that there'd be times when things were good for a while, until they weren't again. That it seemed like everything suffocated him. Their flat, their relationship, his daughter. Me. I suffocated him, and now he hasn't the faintest idea that I'm sitting here, and that I want to find out who he was, who he is. I'm not a step further on. What did I expect?

A noise makes me jump.

I slam the book shut, jump up, stand motionless, my ears pricked in the silence.

My heart is racing.

But it was just the wind.

HENRY

It's torture getting out of bed while the rest of the school's asleep. The whole school apart from Emma and me. But maybe that's also why I kind of like pulling on my running clothes, brushing my teeth, bleary-eyed, while the first rays of the sun shine onto the school walls.

I drink half a bottle of water and pull on my running shoes, then walk downstairs.

I'm late. Emma's already waiting for me in the courtyard. When I step outside and walk towards her, she's got her left foot resting on one of the flower tubs as she stretches.

'Hi,' she says. I love it when her voice still sounds a bit rough and sleepy. 'I thought we could jog to the track, then do some interval training until it's time for the morning run. Is that OK?'

I groan, and follow Emma as she starts moving. 'Intervals, in the morning?'

'Yeah, it's super-effective, trust me.'

'I'm sure it is.'

She doesn't reply and her eyes flick up over the school walls. As I follow her gaze, I recognize the person standing up there at one of the windows. It's Mr Ward, and he's staring down so fiercely at us it's like we're doing something wrong. Emma seems thrown by it until she looks away.

'How did you sleep?' she asks hastily, as we run through the gateway side by side. The first birds are twittering and, as always in late summer, threads of mist are still hanging over the fields. I decide not to talk about Mr Ward. The morning run ought to be the time in the day when she can forget everything else and not have to worry about grumpy English teachers.

'Fine,' I say truthfully. 'I'm dead by the time I fall into bed these days.'

'Are you making sure you get at least seven hours' sleep?' she persists, and I have to smile.

'Is there any chance we could start a bit later if I'm not?'

Emma grins. 'Not really.'

'Bummer.'

'But I could come round in the evening and take your phone away at ten at the latest.'

'There's no need. I'm asleep by then.'

She laughs. 'OK, very good.'

'How about you?' I ask. 'Have you settled in a bit?'

'Yes, I think so.' The gravel crunches under our feet and I feel my pulse starting to quicken. Not long ago, I'd have been out of breath already, and now it feels like I'm just getting warmed up. 'My mum's coming to visit at the weekend.'

That makes me smile, because she says it so casually, yet I can hear in her voice how much she's looking forward to it. And that makes me happy, especially when I remember that nobody came with her on her first day here. 'That's nice.'

'Yes. I hope the weather's good. We want to go and see the Highlands.'

'It's more authentic in the rain, you know,' I say. 'But I think you'll be in luck.'

'So how are things with your parents?' she asks. 'Do you only see them in the holidays?'

'Basically, yes,' I say. 'Sometimes they come over to Edinburgh in between, but mostly we fly out to them. They save up their leave so that we can spend as much time together as possible.'

'You and your brother and sister?'

'Yes.' I nod. 'It used to be easier when Theo, Maeve and I had the same school holidays. It's got a bit more complicated since they've been at university. They usually have to do placements during the vacations.'

'In hospital?'

'Exactly,' I say.

'You're a real medical family, then,' remarks Emma.

'Yes, my grandparents worked in the NHS, too.' I shrug. 'I'm the first to break with tradition.'

'You have to do what you're passionate about,' she says. 'That's what matters.'

'Perhaps.'

'No, not "perhaps", Henry. Definitely.'

'Well, we'll see. I think they're all secretly hoping I'll change my mind. I mean . . . most people who go to school here study medicine, law or economics.'

'But do they enjoy it?' asks Emma. 'Or are they just doing it because it's expected of them?'

'That's the question . . .' I pause as she smiles. 'What?'

'I think I'll have to up the pace. You're managing more than three-word sentences.'

'Oh, no,' I say with a groan.

'Don't worry, when we do the intervals, we'll go to your maximum heart rate.'

'I can't think of anything more delightful.'

'Me neither,' says Emma, and sadly she doesn't sound the least bit ironic.

She's as good as her word, because we've barely reached the sports ground when she picks up the pace considerably.

The first rays of sunshine are falling over the rugby pitch, but that's not why the sweat's burning in my eyes a few minutes later.

Emma's idea of interval training is suicidal. And I don't think she's even running as fast as she can. It's nuts, and she makes it look so easy. I'm running flat out and she doesn't let me slow down until I feel like my heart's going to burst out of my chest any second.

'Make sure you keep your hips level,' she says, as we're running more slowly again after a couple of sprints.

You don't stand still when you're training with Emma. I soon figured that much out. There's only full speed and easy jogging. Her cheeks are flushed and a few strands have worked loose from her plait as she comes alongside me. She puts her hands on my hips and my heart skips a beat. 'You mustn't let them tip forward. Imagine you're carrying a full glass of water inside you and it has to stay upright so that nothing spills over.'

'Weird image,' I pant.

'I know, but it helps, right?'

It would help if she took her hands away. But as soon as she does, I wish she hadn't. My skin is burning where she touched me. Suddenly I think about last night, when I didn't ask Grace to stay. Her eyes, all those things that went unsaid between us. I have to push it down – there's no other way. Otherwise I'd have to face the fact that I spend too many hours a day thinking about Emma, and I owe it to Grace to be honest with her. But I know what that would mean. And I can't do it. I can't do that to her.

'Three more intervals and that's enough for today,' Emma decides.

'Three more?' I banish those thoughts to the furthest corner of my brain. 'You're insane.'

'No, but we need to get into the anaerobic zone,' she explains, as if she were the one doing A-level biology, not me. At this moment, I twig that this is the thing she was born to do. Study sport science at that specialist college in Germany. And that I don't want her to leave in a year's time. I really don't.

'I've been in the anaerobic zone for the last hour,' I say.

'I doubt that.' She glances at her running watch. 'OK, in fifteen seconds back to full intensity.'

I groan, but what can I do? When Emma runs, I run.

'How . . .' I gasp, as she relaxes the speed after a minute and a half '. . . the hell can you be so fast?'

There it is again, the shadow that crosses her face. 'It's all just a matter of technique and fitness,' she says, and I guess that's probably true, but I don't believe it's the whole truth. There's something else there, but I'm not the guy she wants to talk to about it. And that's OK. I just hope there's someone else for her so she can talk about anything, even about the things she's thinking of when her eyes glaze over in class and she gets that worried expression on her face.

'OK, no, actually that's not all,' she says, to my surprise. 'Has anyone ever properly hurt you?'

Suddenly I feel kind of shitty. Because, if I'm honest, I don't know. Of course it hurts when I have to say goodbye to my parents at the airport. When I remember that I won't be able to be at this school with my friends for ever. Or when Grace and I argue. Not that we do argue. Our last fight was months ago and I can't even remember what it was about. In fact, we don't actually talk any more, even though there's so much to say. But we both know what would happen. We'd have to face up to the fact that there's nothing left. That you can argue only if you feel something. And I've stopped feeling anything.

'You have to think about the pain,' says Emma, and I ban myself from thinking about Grace again. Because I get the feeling that Emma's telling me something she never tells anyone. 'About the feeling when the person you love just goes away and abandons you. You have to imagine yourself running after that train and not being quick enough. It's getting faster and faster, and sitting inside it is the person whose fucking attention you want. But he's being carried away. So you run, as fast as you can, because it's all you can do. That's what you have to think about and, if you're lucky, you might reach the point where your head is just empty and you don't care so much about all of that any more.'

She's talking about her dad, I'm sure, but I daren't ask her.

For a couple of seconds, the silence hangs between us, as

oppressive as a thunderstorm. Emma avoids my gaze. I realize we're standing still only when she claps her hands.

'Whatever. Forget it. OK, next interval, come on.' She's running again and all I can do is follow her, my mind whirling.

Why didn't I say anything? Something like, *I'm sorry you had to go through that. If you want to talk about it, I'll be here.* Instead, I'm silent, watching as she argues it out with herself. As she runs. And suddenly I understand. When she takes her body to the limit, her thoughts stop. When she's so focused on breathing and keeping on running, there's no room left for emotions.

I pick up my pace as Emma announces the next sprint.

You have to think about the pain.

The fact that it isn't Grace's face in my mind's eye should probably make me think. Instead, I remember the heavy feeling when Mum and Dad give me one last hug at the airport. All those stupid goodbyes that have got so normal they shouldn't hurt any more. But it'll never stop being unbearable when they leave me on my own somewhere, and I have to be so fucking independent. I think about Maeve, getting on the train after a visit here and heading back to St Andrews. About me, standing at the station and having to hold myself back so I don't run after her. Now I don't hold back.

My shins and thighs are burning, my lungs on fire. My pulse is racing, and once the last interval is finally over, I'm pretty sure I'm about to throw up.

I stop, and as my stomach lurches, I crumple. The blood is rushing in my ears, and my eyes are flickering. I can't breathe fast enough to take in the oxygen my lungs are painfully demanding.

'No, stand up, Henry!' I feel Emma's hand on my shoulder as I fall to my knees. The grass is cold and wet under my palms. I choke down the gagging. 'Arms above your head, come on. You'll soon feel better.'

I hear her as if through a thick layer of cotton wool, but somehow, my body does what she says. 'Breathe into your belly. You have to keep moving or your blood pressure will drop off. And tell me if you need to be sick.'

'You're crazy,' I somehow croak out. The roaring in my ears is gradually fading. Her hand is between my shoulder blades. Even though my T-shirt is dripping with sweat. God knows what made me think of that right now.

'Better?' she asks, as I rub my face and put my head back.

'I need to sit down,' I mumble.

'In a moment,' she promises. 'Looks like we really did work you to the max this time,' she remarks.

I glare darkly at her. 'I almost died.'

She smiles. 'Yeah, almost.'

'And it's not even breakfast time yet . . .'

'That was so good, Henry. I'm proud of you.'

'That I almost threw up?'

'Yeah.' She shrugs. 'You went to the limit.'

'You can say that again.' My pulse is slowly starting to ease.

'It's an important part of making progress in your training. Honestly. Tell me when you're ready and we can jog slowly back. The others must be about to start the morning run.'

'Can't we walk?' I suggest feebly, but Emma shakes her head.

'No chance, sorry. But we'll go super-slow. Cool-down tempo.'

'You have no heart.'

'Just as well I do, or I couldn't run this fast.' When she points enquiringly towards the school buildings, I nod. She really is running slowly, but my stomach is still grumbling.

My dripping top is clinging to my body, the sweat is burning my eyes, but all I can think about is Emma's words as we get closer to the school. At some distance away, I see the other pupils doing their morning run. Some of them aren't quite as half-hearted as the rest.

I turn my head to Emma. 'You really want to find him, don't you?'

I'm sure she knows who I mean. Her father. The man who gave her a reason to run until she can't go on.

'I think so.'

I nod. And at that moment I know I'd do anything to help her.

13

EMMA

It's amazing how quickly a new routine becomes a habit. I've been at this school less than three weeks, but I don't have to keep checking my timetable now. I just know when I've got English or maths. The anxious tummy-ache I get before every lesson with Mr Ward is a reliable reminder of that. I'm doing fine in maths and can keep up well, but in English he's still making me feel I'm behind. I don't even want to think about when he might hand back our papers from that unannounced test on our current reading – the one where I was basically guessing. I don't have any problems with PE either, but that's not much consolation. And this isn't even the only thing that's messing with my head. I'm always feeling Grace's eyes on me in the hallways. Sometimes I almost wish she'd just be mean to me. Then at least I'd know where

I stood. But she's friendly and kind, which makes everything so much harder. On Monday I actually went to athletics training with her, but it made me feel bad. Because it was only a few days after I'd been in that darkened library with Henry, since when I've constantly been fantasizing about what it would be like to kiss him.

You'd think I wouldn't have much time for that kind of thing. My days are planned, and run like clockwork. Each starts with registration at eight thirty and then there are lessons until lunch, from one to two. After that, I have more classes, training or enrichment. I also had to choose a duty, like helping the younger kids with their prep, or working in the sick bay, the library or the garden. I picked gardening. So, one afternoon a week, I'm part of a group helping Mr Carpenter and Mr Ringling in the school's huge grounds.

I have to admit that I'm not sorry Olive does lifeguard duty at the school pool. This way, I'm on my own with Tori while we help Mr Carpenter outside. By now, I'm pretty sure that she only picked this option because Valentine Ward does garden duty, too. It's none of my business, but I have to confess that I don't like him much – which has less to do with him being Mr Ward's nephew, and more to do with him generally ghosting Tori. I like her a lot, but we've known each other such a short time that I don't feel in a position to tell her she deserves better than someone who plays with her emotions. It seems to me she's a lot happier in Sinclair's company, even though she doesn't seem to

SARAH SPRINZ

notice it. But, sadly, he doesn't do gardening with us – he does stable duty and helps out with the riding lessons. And Henry does prep supervision, which makes sense given his career ambitions.

I'm pretty sure this community-service thing would never have worked at my old school. Nobody wanted to spend any more time at Heinrich Heine than was strictly necessary. Voluntarily staying on to sweep up leaves in the playground or help little kids with their homework? No way. So it's all the more amazing how seriously these duties are taken at Dunbridge Academy. And somehow it feels nice to work with the others making sure the school can be the best possible home for us all.

'Make sure you don't snip too far down, Emma.' I raise my head as Mr Ringling leans over the roses I'm cutting. I hadn't even noticed him coming over to us. 'Just here is fine. At the moment we're just dead-heading them.'

'I'm sorry,' I mumble.

'Not a problem. This all looks like you're doing a fantastic job.' Mr Ringling smiles and I relax a little, until I realize he's still watching me. 'It's daft, but every time I look at you, I see your father. He must be very proud of you.'

Fortunately, Tori and the others aren't around just now. 'I have no contact with him,' I say. 'My parents split up.'

Mr Ringling raises his eyebrows in surprise. 'I didn't know that.'

168

'Doesn't matter.' I force myself to smile. 'Did you know him well?'

'It was a long time ago, but I remember him and your mother very well. It was a shame that he left the school after—'

Mr Ringling breaks off as Tori, Salome and a couple of younger girls jump up, screaming.

'Get it away, get it away!' Salome's braids fly out as she shakes out her hands and grimaces with disgust.

'What's the matter?' Mr Ringling straightens up.

'Eew, a snake! There was a snake.' Tori shivers.

'Are you blind?' Valentine calls from the other side of the flowerbed. 'It was just a slowworm, and it was tiny.'

'It was massive!'

'And it was definitely more scared of you than you were of it.' Mr Ringling brushes some mud off his hands and turns towards them. 'Slowworms aren't snakes, they're legless lizards, and they're perfectly harmless.'

I'm not listening any more. It's what he said about my dad. *It was a shame that he left the school after—* Yes, but after *what*? How can I ask him more about it without the others hearing?

There's only another fifteen minutes until we have to put down our gloves and secateurs to make it back to school for study time, so I don't get another chance.

I'm about to go into my room when Tori calls, 'Tea?'

By now I know that almost everyone in the sixth form has

169

their own kettle in their room and at least one packet of teabags. I'll have to remember to ask Mum if she can get a kettle for me when she comes at the weekend. Until then, I'll rely on Tori's generosity – I'll have to pay her back with a huge box of teabags soon.

'I'd love one, if you don't mind,' I say.

Tori rolls her eyes as she fishes about for her key. 'Will you stop being so bloody polite? We're neighbours and you can have anything you like from me.' She pushes open the door and I follow her inside. 'OK, maybe not that iconic Harry Styles *Vogue* cover. It cost a bomb, but what can you do?'

She puts her key on the desk, every last centimetre of which is, as ever, covered with books, tarot cards and the camera equipment she uses to film videos for her social media. And there's that very same famous cover on the wall next to it, along with a few Polaroids and postcards. There are more books piled on Tori's chest of drawers and the shelf above her desk. I recognize some from her recent Books of the Month video. She showed me the other day, by way of explaining just what BookTube means. But Tori doesn't just have heaps of YouTube subscribers. She posts on Instagram and TikTok almost every day, and she's built up a huge community there too. It doesn't surprise me because her book recommendations and photos with Dunbridge in the background are like something straight out of a Dark Academia Pinterest board.

'Wasn't I going to give you some more fairy lights?' Tori

asks, as she disappears into her tiny bathroom with the kettle.

'It's OK,' I call. 'My mum's bringing me some at the weekend. But thanks for the offer.'

'Have you got any plans?' Tori comes back into the room.

'We want to go and see the Highlands. How about you? Are you and Olive going into Edinburgh?'

'No. I'd totally forgotten that Will and I have to go home. My cousin's getting married.' Tori sighs. 'It's going to be a total pain in the arse.'

'Don't you get on?' I ask.

'No, no, we do, but my family gets kind of carried away.'

'It's going to be big, then?'

'You have no idea,' says Tori. 'They've rented a castle.'

'Oh.'

'Yeah,' Tori says. 'If your surname's Belhaven, I guess you have to live up to it.' She takes two mugs off her shelf as the water starts to boil. She hands me the dark blue one with the school crest on it. 'But that doesn't mean anything to you, does it?' she asks. 'Belhaven-Wynford?'

I shake my head. 'Not really. Sorry.'

'Oh, God, don't apologize – I love you for it.' Tori sighs. 'It's just that anyone who grew up round here has almost certainly heard of our family.'

'Oh, I didn't know . . .' I pause.

'I didn't mean it like that. It's nice just being Tori,' she says, smiling at me. 'Not the Belhaven-Wynford lass.'

'Well, you'll always just be Tori to me,' I say. 'And I'm sure it's the same for Olive, Henry and Sinclair.'

'That's true,' she says, reaching for the huge metal canister where she keeps her pyramid-shaped teabags. 'And Val gets how tricky it can be sometimes.'

'Does he?' I ask.

Tori nods. 'My mum sometimes works with his. You just know people when you move in the same circles.'

'So you knew Val before coming here?'

'A bit, but we never really spoke. Not till now.' Tori lifts her head. 'He looked over my way fairly often, didn't he?'

To be honest, I hadn't noticed. 'Yeah, sure,' I say hastily, as Tori looks expectantly at me.

'I knew I wasn't imagining it. I think he doesn't want his friends to notice, but, well . . .' Tori tails off as someone knocks at the door. 'Hell-ooo?' she calls, throwing the teabags into our mugs and filling them with hot water, as the door opens.

'Four o'clock. Study time, you two,' says Ms Barnett, popping her head in.

'I know. Emma just needs some tea,' Tori declares. I glance apologetically at our houseparent, but she just nods.

'The tea thing works every time,' Tori says, once she's shut the door behind her. 'Whatever it is, you can always say you were just making a cup of tea.'

I have to smile. 'I'll remember that.'

'Still no milk or sugar?' asks Tori.

I shake my head. 'Thank you.'

'Happy study hour, then,' she says, as I walk to the door. 'I so can't be arsed. I'll probably spend my whole time scrolling on TikTok.'

I laugh. 'Can you tag me in some more of those book videos, please?'

'I knew you'd get hooked on BookTok.'

'It's the best.'

Tori giggles and waves to me as I leave her room with my mug. The corridor is almost empty, as always at this time of day. Ms Barnett is coming out of a room at the other end, and nods to me as I slip into mine.

I put my mug on my desk, and my bed really does look inviting. I've been here long enough by now to know that, with a bit of luck, Ms Barnett won't look in again and I can just spend an hour reading or watching YouTube. According to Tori, it's only the juniors and younger years who have to show their houseparents that they've really been working. They also have to hand in their phones first. Pretty strict when I think that at my old school nobody cared when or how you did your homework. But although I could get away with not working, I sit down at my desk. I'd rather focus on reading for English, so that next time, I can prove to Mr Ward that I'm capable of keeping up with the A-level course.

I've just got out my folder and I'm about to put my phone away when I see the Instagram notification. I've been meaning to switch those off for ages now. I don't want to be informed every time Isi or anyone else posts a story.

It was Isi, and now I'm going to have to find out what she shared or I won't be able to concentrate on my work. I'll just tap on the app for a moment, then switch off notifications.

Isi's reposted a story that Betil – a girl in the other class – shared yesterday evening. They seem to be at someone's home – at least, the room and its orange lights remind me of the party cellar in Eros's parents' house. The photo, a selfie of Betil and Nikola, makes my heart stand still. Not because of the two of them, but because they're pointing their fingers at a couple wrapped around each other on the sofa in the background.

It's Isi and Noah, and they're kissing. Betil's holding her phone higher, they're laughing, and Isi and Noah are looking at them.

I feel numb, yet my thoughts are whirling.

Isi's kissing Noah. Noah's kissing Isi. Isi and Noah are kissing. And it doesn't look like drunken snogging at a party, no way. It looks like the reason why Isi's been so quiet on WhatsApp. She's got together with Noah. Even though she didn't have a good word to say about him when I was with him. She ripped him to shreds, and when he dumped me, she said I should think myself lucky because I was too good for him. And now she's kissing him at some party, in front of people I thought were my friends. While I'm in Scotland.

Why did she share a thing like that? She must know I'd see it.

My blood runs cold.

Maybe she wanted me to see it . . .

Because everyone's the same. Because nobody gives a fuck if they hurt other people.

Noah, who dumps people by WhatsApp, like a fucking coward.

Isi, who pretends one thing, then gets together with him.

My father, who records 'For Emma' and disappears off the face of the earth.

I don't get it. What did I do to these people and why does it always have to hurt so much? It shouldn't be a surprise any more.

I can't cry, I'm calm. I exit Isi's story, and deactivate all notifications. I shut the stupid app and put my phone to one side.

And then I sit there, staring at my practically empty pinboard, wondering what the hell is going on.

14

EMMA

Emma love, could you give me a call at lunchtime?

Every time I read Mum's message, I hear her voice in my mind. She sounds worryingly serious – after all, why should she want me to phone in the middle of the day? We generally speak in the evenings, and it's always spontaneous. Mum calls me, or I call her, and either the other person answers or they don't. But this is weird. I immediately find myself thinking about the time she rang to tell me she was stuck in Nice and wouldn't be able to fly to Edinburgh with me.

All the way through maths and history, it's like I'm sitting on hot coals, and I wish I could fast-forward through time. I tell Tori and Olive I'll catch up with them at lunch, and sigh with relief as they head for the dining room without asking any questions.

I pull my phone out of my bag and head in the opposite direction, outside. I sit on a bench in the little inner courtyard and dial Mum's number.

She answers in two rings. 'Emmi-Mouse?'

'Hi,' I say.

'Where are you right now?' she asks.

I blink up at the sun, high above me in the sky. 'Out in the courtyard.'

'Oh, that's nice. Is the weather good? I saw—'

'Mum,' I say, and she falls silent. 'Why did you want me to call you?'

I hear her sigh. 'I'm so, so sorry, Emma, but I had to fly to Madrid at short notice,' she says, and my body goes numb. Not all at once, but slowly. Like the meaning of her words has to work its way through me. From my fingers, gripping the phone, to my wrists, to my shoulders . . .

I don't speak. I just wait for her to carry on. *And then I'll get a flight from there to Edinburgh tomorrow evening. I just wanted to tell you that I'm going to be a bit later than we originally planned.* But she doesn't. What she actually says is: 'It's an important client. And, unfortunately, I'm going to have to work through the weekend here.'

'So you're not coming?' I ask, even though that's exactly what she just said.

'I can't make it, Emma. I really am sorry. One of my colleagues was meant to be here instead, but he's in hospital, rushed in for an emergency operation. And nobody else knows the case as well as I do. But I can probably wangle the weekend after next off instead and . . .'

Mum's still talking, but I've stopped listening to her.

It's perfectly clear. She's not coming. She has to work and I can't even be pissed off about it because some guy's in hospital and that would be heartless. And I'm not heartless. Quite the opposite. I've never felt my heart as clearly as I do in this moment. Because it's aching.

'Emmi?' Mum says. 'I get that you're cross . . .'

'I'm not cross,' I manage. *Just disappointed . . . And confused and alone, and Isi was kissing Noah.* Normally I'd tell her about it, but what's the good of that when Mum won't be with me this weekend now, and I don't want to cry down the phone? I can do that on my own in my room.

'I'm really, really sad about it too,' Mum says. 'I was so looking forward to it. The weather's meant to be great.'

Pull yourself together.

Say something.

Anything.

'But then it wouldn't be the authentic Scottish experience.' I don't know why Henry's words should be the first that come to mind. They're just there.

'Yes, that's true,' Mum says. I can hear the smile in her voice and suddenly my eyes start to sting. This is the problem with people, and with looking forward to the things they promise you. It just makes for unnecessary pain if you believe them. I know that, yet I still keep falling for it.

'I feel awful,' Mum says. 'Everything happened so fast this morning. Sometimes I hate this job.'

'Yeah, but you love it too,' I remind her. 'And it's not as bad as all that. You can just come another time instead.'

'Will you do something nice this weekend anyway?' asks Mum. 'With your new friends, maybe?'

I think about Tori, who's going home, and Olive, who definitely won't have time for me. 'Sure,' I say, all the same. 'We might go into Edinburgh.'

'Oh, yes, do that, definitely. I'm sure they know their way around much better than I do these days, but the café in Waterstones always used to be one of my favourites.'

'I'll suggest it.' I clear my throat. 'I have to go to lunch.'

'OK. Shall we speak later this evening? Or how about a *Grey's Anatomy* watch party?'

Despite myself, I can't help smiling. 'Yeah, let's see. I'll message you, OK?'

'Fine, Emmi.'

We say goodbye, and once I've hung up it really is hard not to burst into tears. Mum isn't coming to visit. It's not the end of the world, but I'd been looking forward to it. A lot.

'Hey, Emma!'

I close my eyes for a moment, then look around.

'Have you had lunch?' Grace asks. She was walking with a small group, but she's stopped while the others walk on.

'No, not yet.'

'Come on, then!' She beckons me over. When I hesitate, she adds, 'Is everything OK?'

'Yeah, fine,' I say hastily, grabbing my bag. I hope she can't see that I was on the edge of tears. I have to keep acting like nothing's wrong. Distraction. Talk to people. It's really not hard. 'I was just on the phone to my mum.'

Grace and I talk, but I don't really know what about. Our next training session, school stuff. She's nice, the way she's always nice, but today I don't even have the headspace to feel guilty around her.

The dining room is full of voices, laughter and the quiet clatter of cutlery. Most people are already sitting down, so we don't have to queue for long at the hatch. I've lost my appetite, but I force myself at least to take a sandwich. If necessary, I can wrap it up and eat it later.

Grace is chatting to a friend, and I follow her in silence to our table, from which Tori's waving to me. She pats the chair beside her, making me smile.

Henry's on the other side, and he looks up as we come closer. Grace drops a kiss on his cheek then sits down with her friends a little way off. I listen to the other conversations.

'Are you sure you don't want to try a bit?' Tori asks me, for the third time. 'We only get waffle day every other week.'

I eye my untouched sandwich. 'Maybe next time. Thanks, though.'

'Aren't you feeling well?' she asks, and Henry raises his

head. He's a few places down and it's pretty noisy around here, but his eyes rest enquiringly on me.

'No, don't worry. It's just . . . I'm still so full from breakfast,' I say.

'But there's always room for a tiny wee waffle,' Tori replies. I'm sure she means well but it's hard to maintain my smile. 'You can get one for later, if you want.'

'Not fair, I never get one from you,' Sinclair complains, and Tori rolls her eyes.

'You had your own waffles.'

'But they don't fill you up. Just as well I brought some bread from the bakery yesterday.'

The others keep chattering. Henry's still looking at me. When I glance his way, he wrinkles his forehead. His lips form a silent 'What's wrong?' but I shake my head.

Nothing's wrong. Or at least nothing that I want to tell him about. Or even ought to . . . Now I look away to the side and realize that Grace is watching us. My blood runs ice cold.

I don't know whether Henry noticed. I stop glancing in his direction because it's desperately hard not to burst into tears when he's looking at me like that. It's easier just to eat half of my sandwich in silence and listen to Tori and Olive's conversation. To laugh now and again so they don't get suspicious. To concentrate on the things I have to do here. To put my tray back, to reach for my bag and follow the others back to the classrooms for the afternoon lessons.

'Hey.' I feel someone touch my shoulder, and stop still. Henry pulls me gently aside in the corridor. Why is it that every time he stands facing me I notice how much taller he is than me?

'What's up?' I say cautiously.

'Are you sure everything's OK?' he asks, and, God, he has to stop this.

In the end, even I don't really know. I totally shouldn't care what Noah gets up to. We split up. He can kiss whoever he likes. But I do care because she's my best friend. Isi, who doesn't tell me anything now. Who gave Noah such a hard time for what he did to me. And now she's kissing him. I don't get it. She was the one standing on my doorstep with chocolate and my favourite ice cream when he dumped me. Who handed me one tissue after another when I couldn't stop crying. Who told me he wasn't worth it. That no man in the whole damn world was worth this. And I believed her. Because I really thought she meant it.

Was she in love with him even then? Did they just wait until I'd gone away to get it together? It's so shit, and I can't tell anyone, not even Mum because she's not going to be here this weekend.

My eyes are stinging. Henry's hand is still on my shoulder. Fortunately, I don't have to come up with an answer.

'Do you think Mr Ward's got the tests today?' Tori asks, turning back to us, and Henry moves away at once. My heart skips. He's still close to me, but not *that* close any more. It's a just-friends-and-nothing-more kind of distance.

I step past him. 'I don't know. Is he a fast marker?' I work at keeping my tone light, and it's ridiculous how well I succeed.

''Fraid so,' says Tori.

I don't look back to Henry as I follow her to the classroom. I lay my phone on the shelf beside the door and we head to our seats in the second row.

'Oh, no,' Tori mutters, as Mr Ward enters the room as punctually as ever, the moment the bell rings. Henry slips in, only seconds later. 'See that bag?' she continues, and I glance up to where Mr Ward is putting a bright red carrier in the middle of his desk.

'The tests?' I ask, and Tori nods.

'They'll just sit there for the whole class, and he won't mention them. Then he'll hand them out five minutes before the end. He loves to torture us,' she says, still in a low voice, as we stand up respectfully.

'Hello, everyone.' Mr Ward nods to us, and we sit down. And, indeed, he doesn't utter a word about the bag, which sits there in plain sight, like a threat, distracting me for the entire forty-five minutes.

But at least it doesn't seem like anybody else can concentrate any better. Whether I glance left or right, I see only anxious faces. The hands on the wall clock seem to crawl today, and even when the bell goes, Mr Ward still hasn't mentioned the tests.

'Before you all leap up and run away, you may collect your test papers,' he says coolly, as the first chair legs scrape and books rustle. At once there's silence again. Mr Ward pulls the pile of papers out of the bag. 'The results in general leave something to be desired. In some cases, I find myself seriously wondering whether you've actually read the novel. But, well, they're your grades, aren't they? I did my A levels long ago.' He picks up the first booklet. 'Attwell,' he says, and Gideon stands up. 'Bennington.'

And so it goes on. My fingers are icy cold, my heart is pounding as the others are called up one at a time. Tori walks back, sits down beside me and turns over her booklet.

'Emma Wiley,' says Mr Ward, tauntingly slowly. I stand up and walk forwards. 'You really do take after your father.' He hands me the paper. 'There is still just about time to change subjects.'

I say nothing as I return to my place.

'So?' Tori glances anxiously at me.

The lump in my throat grows to the size of a tennis ball as I turn the booklet over.

'Oh, no . . .' she murmurs. 'But it really was super-hard. Don't let it get you down, Emma.'

I nod silently, unable to speak. It's just a crappy mark. An

F. *Failed*. My first mark at this stupid school that I should never have come to.

HENRY

I stand up and pack away my things while Emma's still sitting in her seat like she's been struck by lightning. Her test paper is in front of her and I can't shake off an uneasy feeling that it didn't go too well for her.

But that can't be the only thing. At lunch earlier, she looked on the edge of tears. She hardly touched her sandwich, when she normally eats like a horse, which is hardly surprising given the incredible efforts she demands of her body pretty much every day. Something must have happened.

I hurriedly stuff my iPad into my bag, and Emma stands up too.

'Henry, did you have a chance to speak to Mrs Sinclair about the New Year ball?' asks Inés, who has suddenly appeared beside me.

'No, not yet, sorry,' I say, glancing in Emma's direction.

'Do you think we could . . .?' she continues, but I've stopped listening as Emma reaches for her bag and rubs her eyes with the back of her hand. Only for a moment, but it's enough to make my heart lurch. She's crying.

'Inés, I'm really sorry, I have to see Mr Ringling now,' I lie. 'But I'll speak to Mrs Sinclair. Promise.'

'That would be great,' says Inés.

I force myself to smile, then abandon her, only just remembering to get my phone from the pigeonhole. Emma's forgotten hers. It's the one with the grey-blue case. I know because it's almost the colour of her eyes.

Without further ado, I pick it up and leave the room. I look around the corridor, but I can't see Emma anywhere. Where did she go? I can't even text her now.

After only a few feet, I spot Emma in one of the alcoves down the corridor. She's got her back to me, and if I hadn't just seen her crying, I'd think she was just waiting for some-one there. When I tap her shoulder, she jumps. Her eyes are slightly red.

'Hi.' She gulps, and it breaks my heart to see how hard she's trying to keep control of herself.

'You forgot your phone,' I say, but there are so many things I want to say instead.

What's wrong?

Talk to me.

What can I do to make it better?

Emma looks from my face to my hand. 'Oh. Thanks.'

'That test was so hard,' I blurt. 'There was no need for Mr Ward to dump a thing like that on us right at the start of term.'

'Did it go badly for you too?' she asks.

I think of the red A that Mr Ward had written – probably only with great reluctance – at the bottom of the page. When I still don't reply, Emma seems to understand. She shakes her head, almost imperceptibly. 'Henry, you really don't have to try to cheer me up.'

'I do,' I say. 'I'm your school captain so I have to do that.' *And I just can't bear seeing you sad.*

Her eyes are still glittering as her gaze travels across my face, and I wish I could just give her a hug. Because I can imagine that none of this is easy for her. Being new, maybe homesick, and getting a teacher like Mr Ward, who isn't exactly encouraging, to put it mildly. And there's probably something else. The stuff with her dad. And Emma looks as if she could really do with someone who just listens to her while she pours out her troubles. I want to be that person. I want it so badly that it hurts.

'Henry.' I resist the urge to shut my eyes as I hear Grace's voice. 'Are you coming?'

Where? Then I remember. Enrichment with Ms Barnett. I don't want to go.

'I'll be there in a minute,' I say.

'You go. I've got PSHE.' Emma smiles, but she looks tense. It's so fleeting, just a matter of seconds, but it gives me a stomach-ache. 'See you later.'

Grace gives me a piercing, reproachful look. I feel everything within me putting up barriers, even before she's said a word. And the problem is that when you were together for so long, you know each other. Grace can see through me. She doesn't say a word. Her eyes bore into me. Then she turns away.

Hot rage and desperation boil in my chest. It's rage at myself. Because I'm running into a brick wall. I force myself to take a deep breath, then another, before I follow her.

Grace is walking quickly and I drop back. The distance between us is getting bigger, and then she's swallowed by a gaggle of fourth-formers and I can't see her any more.

It's only then that it hits me.

When you were together for so long, I thought. *Were*.

Not *when you've been*.

When you were.

15

HENRY

'Bennington, wake up!' Mr Cormack's voice echoes over the pitch to me. 'Was that meant to be a pass, for God's sake? Twenty push-ups for everyone if that ball touches the ground one more time.'

His whistle makes me jump, and I get back into position. The others pass the ball to each other, I run into a space, put my palms up to make a target, and Omar throws me the ball, so hard that it slips through my hands.

I hear Mr Cormack's whistle again, followed by the sounds of him cursing and the others groaning in annoyance. The next thing I notice is the damp grass beneath my palms as I drop to the ground to do the push-ups.

Why am I putting myself through this?

And why is my mind all over the place, everywhere except here on the pitch?

I know why. The explanation has pale blonde hair and hasn't answered the text I sent her earlier. Emma wasn't at dinner, and neither Tori nor Olive knew where she'd got to. Judging by what I know of Emma, she was probably outside, running her heart out.

My upper arms are burning as I finish the last press-ups and drop back to my knees. Valentine Ward is glaring at me – if looks could kill – but I haven't got the energy to care what he thinks of me. Not today.

Mr Cormack doesn't leave us time to catch our breath. We go on as if we'd never stopped, and I've never found it harder to concentrate on the drills.

I was crap today, I'm sure of that, as Valentine rants in the changing room while I pull off my sweat-sodden shirt. I don't let myself listen, because I really have got other things to worry about right now.

I have a quick hot shower, but even so, it's almost ten by the time I finally get back to our wing. As ever just before wing time, it's like rush-hour on our corridor – everyone suddenly remembers some vital reason why they have to knock on someone else's door, or hurry to the shared kitchen.

Sinclair emerges from it, heading to his room; he's wearing joggers and has a slice of toast and Nutella in each hand. His hair's still damp; he probably just got in from riding. Or somewhere.

'Want some?' he asks, holding out a slice to me as he passes. I shake my head. He waits a millisecond, then walks on, biting into the toast.

'You been with Tori?' I ask, when he's almost reached his door.

Sinclair stops. 'Why d'you ask?' he mumbles through a mouthful, turning towards me. He sounds kind of like I've caught him out.

'Just wondered. She might have heard from Emma.'

'You mean cos Emma wasn't at dinner?' He waits for me to nod. 'No idea. Tori didn't mention it.'

'Oh, OK,' I say, before he can ask why I'm so bothered. If Tori didn't say anything, I'm sure Emma's fine. Or else she hadn't seen her ... I find that hard to imagine, though. Tori likes Emma. She took her under her wing on her first day here.

'Why?' asks Sinclair. His pale eyes bore into mine, and when it comes down to it, I know it's no use lying to my best friend. He knows me too well. But there are some things you have to work out for yourself before you can tell anyone else about them. And this thing with Emma is one of those.

'Quiet time in ten minutes, lads!' Mr Acevedo's voice rings down the hallway. 'That includes you two,' he adds, pointing towards Sinclair and me and clattering his lanyard.

'Yes, sir!' Sinclair salutes with his toast, then gives me a challenging look.

'Let's talk tomorrow,' I say evasively. He takes another bite and I reach for my key. There's something in his expression I don't like. But he just unlocks his door.

'Sleep well, Bennington,' he mumbles.

'You too.'

I press the light switch, walk into my room, and the noises die away as my door clicks shut. For a moment, I stand still, indecisive, then toss my rucksack onto the chair and let myself fall onto the bed.

Somehow the quiet is driving me nuts. And so's the silence from Grace. She sat next to me in enrichment and we didn't say a word to each other. After that, she had Italian and I was busy with prep supervision. Everything's shit and I don't even know what there is to say to her, so I don't say anything. Maybe that's because part of me is hoping she'll take the decision for the two of us. Right now, I don't feel that I can. I don't want to lose her, not as a good friend. That's the only thing I'm certain of. And I would if I ended things between us. It would be over. For ever. I'd give anything to be able to creep over to the west wing, like in the old days, and pour my heart out to Maeve. She always had some kind of answer. I could email her, or even call her. Maeve will definitely still be up, but I'm not in the mood to explain this whole mess over the phone. So I just lie on my bed, staring at the ceiling.

I find myself thinking about Emma again. Hopefully Tori's with her to comfort her.

I shut my eyes.

Why is it so important to me to know how she's doing? If I worried constantly about the wellbeing of all four hundred and thirty-two pupils at this school, it would keep me seriously busy. But Emma's in my head. Emma's everywhere I want to be. What am I thinking?

I blink as my hoodie pocket vibrates. I sit bolt upright and grab my phone.

E: No, it's all fine, honest. I just wasn't hungry

No matter how often I read the words, I don't believe her. Meanwhile, the fact that she replied has set my heart beating faster.

H: Want to talk about it?

She doesn't answer straight away, but she's still online. She starts typing.

I reach for a cushion, jam it between the wall and my back, and settle in for a long night.

EMMA

I don't know why, but it's kind of a relief to send Henry lots of little messages, telling him the things that are making my belly ache right now. It's long after ten, everything's gone quiet outside and we ought to have been asleep ages ago. The Wi-Fi is switched off at wing time, so this is really hammering my data.

It's a mix of texts and short voice notes, and I already feel like I've known Henry all my life. I should probably be scared by how much I want to tell him. But, for some reason, I'm certain that all this stuff is safe with him.

How much it hurts, seeing Isi with Noah. That my best friend's ghosting me and that I'm suddenly no longer part of what used to be my life.

I tell Henry everything. Even how scared I get when I think that my dad might not want anything to do with me if I ever do find him.

That I feel guilty about keeping secrets from Mum. That I feel like I'm getting carried away with this plan and forgetting how to stop. And how disappointed I was that Mum's work took priority over me yet again.

I message him with it all, as I'm lying in bed, then I eventually get up and go to the bathroom to brush my teeth and pull on my sleepshirt. My head aches, my eyes are sore from crying, but I can't stop. It's 11.48, and Henry's not online any more.

I resist the temptation to switch back to Instagram and put myself through more humiliation in the shape of Isi's story. But she's probably not posting that stuff now. She's with Noah. In his room, in his bed. Stop it, stop it, stop it.

I click on Henry's profile photo instead. OK, so you can't

see much of his face, which is half hidden under his hood, but I can't help smiling. Because seeing how happy he looks makes me happy. Because I know that that smile is even more attractive in real life. Even if I'm not the person it's aimed at. And that's the next issue. Grace, who wasn't quite as nice as usual today, and for good reason. Because I like Henry. A bit more than just like him, actually. And I don't even want to like him – I've had enough of guys who play with my emotions, then vanish out of my life. Seriously, I've had it up to here.

I sink back into my pillows and shut my eyes. But if I've had enough, why do I keep thinking about the next one? Why do I have to be this person who can't just switch off her stupid emotions? It feels wrong to think about Henry in that way. He doesn't feel like *the next one*. He feels like the one where everything's a bit different. And that's exactly what scares me. I didn't come to this school to make friends, let alone fall in love. Way too much else in my life is a work in progress right now for me to get involved with anybody. I have to find out who I am. I have to be independent and unapproachable. But it just feels so nice to be looked at by Henry. And I can't even think about what that means. God, he's got a girlfriend. Why would he want *me*? This broken, bitter person who'll be gone again in a year. It makes no sense.

Nothing that's happened in the last week makes any sense. But at the same time, it feels like this thing between Henry and me was meant to be, exactly as it is. As if, no matter how hard I fight, the next step has been obvious for ages.

Maybe Noah had to dump me. Maybe I had to rush into deciding to spend a year abroad. Maybe I had to dash for the airport just in the nick of time, and maybe I had to run bang into Henry. Maybe.

I don't believe in Fate – everything that happens to me hurts too much for that. Everything happens for a reason? But what reason should there be for my best friend getting off with my ex, and my dad being long gone? What the hell kind of stupid deeper meaning can there be in him not giving a crap about me? I don't want to know. I just want to look him in the eye and find out if there's anything left. Or if he feels bad about it, at least. Or if I don't matter enough to him even for that.

I have to get some sleep.

I'm just putting my phone aside when the screen lights up.

H: Open your door

For a moment, I stare at the message.
Typo? Autocorrect? Did he mean that?
Before I can ask, he messages again.

H: Seriously, Emma. If Ms Barnett catches me on your corridor, I'm dead!

I jump up. I hope he's not being serious.

I glance down at myself. Before I have time to wonder if my shorts and baggy sleepshirt are excruciatingly cringy, there's a barely audible knock on the door.

Oh, for God's sake, he was being serious.

I chuck my phone onto my bed and flit over to the door. I've barely opened it a crack when Henry's pushed his way into my room. He presses his finger warningly to his lips, at least until I've shut the door again. Now he finally exhales.

'Hi.'

God, what's he doing here? And why is he so gorgeous? Why are his eyes kind of sleepy and his hair even more messed up than normal? Why? It's just not fair of him.

'Hello,' I whisper, and a tiny smile plucks at the corners of his lips. 'What are you doing here?'

'Fulfilling my responsibilities,' he says.

'Breaking all the rules and putting us at risk of major stress?'

'Whatever,' he declares, as if it really doesn't matter. 'You're sad and I'm your school captain.'

Suddenly I can't move. I should've pretended that everything was fine earlier. But what did I do instead? WhatsApped him for so long that he clearly felt the need to come and check on me.

'I'm not . . .' I begin.

But Henry takes a step towards me and I fall silent. 'Emma.'

'What?' I whisper.

'Want to go for a night-time walk and tell me everything without having to look at me?' he asks, and, in fact that's exactly what I want. Apart from the not-looking-at-him part. Because that's exactly what I'm doing, and it doesn't feel like I'll be able to stop any time soon. Not when he's standing in front of me like this and the warm light of my bedside lamp is shining on his face.

I shake my head.

'Are you sure?'

'No, you're too tired,' I say.

For a fraction of a second, something flickers in his eyes. 'I'm not—' he begins.

'Don't lie to me,' I whisper. 'You need sleep, Henry.' *And you have to go. You can't be in my room, looking at me like this.* But I don't say that. I just stand there facing him, wanting to do so many things that I'd hate myself for tomorrow.

'Yes,' he says, but neither of us moves.

My heart skips a beat as Henry's gaze flickers to my mouth. Only for a second – I blink and he's looking me in the eyes again. Then he glances past me to the bed and, oh, God, I want that so much. I don't want to go to sleep alone. It's not fair on him, but maybe that's the part I miss the most since Noah and I broke up. Those fleeting moments as you're falling asleep, when you come round again and sense that there really is somebody there.

'I could . . .' Henry begins, and I nod before he's even finished his sentence.

I'm so weak.

He takes my hand, and what is it about warm skin? What? I don't understand it, but when I feel it, I don't care about anything else. Henry gives me a hug and all I can think about is how long it's been since anyone did that.

'Tell me what I can do,' he whispers, and my throat tightens a little

'I don't know,' I mumble. 'I don't know what's wrong with me.'

He lets go of me, and when I look up at him, there's that tiny smile again.

'What?' I ask.

'I think you might be homesick,' he says.

I want to deny it, but then I remember Mum's voice and her hugs, and suddenly the tears well in my eyes.

I'm not sure if Henry's noticed I'm crying. Until suddenly his hand is on the back of my head, pressing me to him. That's the moment when a hoarse sound fights free of my throat. I can't stop it, and the more annoyed I am with myself, the worse it gets.

'I'm sorry,' I say. 'This is so stupid, I–'

'Stop that,' Henry whispers. 'It's OK, Em.'

God, how can he call me that?'

How can he do that? Henry's intelligent. I know that. Not just in a doing-mental-arithmetic-and-joining-the-dots kind of way. He's smart when it comes to words and reading faces, the times when I say one thing and actually mean another.

He gets all that, and because he does, I'm sure that he also understands what all this means, here and now. That we're too close to each other. That from now on, I'll always know the smell of him. That I really like this blend of cinnamony shower gel, warm vanilla and black tea. That his fingers are so warm and gentle, and that he's just the perfect height to rest his chin on my hair parting while I cry helpless, hot tears into his jumper.

It's like there'd been a plug holding in everything that had built up since I got the taxi to the airport on my own and had to act like I was coping, and now Henry's pulled it out. I played the part so well I even convinced myself. But the truth is, I'm not coping. Not at all. I'm asking myself what I'm doing here and why my life's been such a mess since I left home. If the whole thing was a mistake.

But then there's Henry's warm body against mine and, deep within me, I sense it wasn't. That there's some kind of connection between us that I've never felt with any other person in my life. Not this intensely, and not after such a short time. That it can't just be chance that he's standing in my room right now, holding me like this. No, it's his own conscious decision. He could be anywhere, but he's here, with me.

I rarely cry in front of other people, but I know what it feels like when I've overloaded them. It's different with Henry. He's just standing there, holding me and waiting for just as long as it takes, for the moment when I'm all cried out. When it eventually comes, he lets go of me slightly.

I shut my eyes because I can't believe this is really happening. That Henry's laying one hand on my chin and lifting it gently, so that he can wipe away my tears before pushing me over to my bed.

I feel the mattress at the backs of my knees, and that urgent feeling in my belly. I hope he'll stay. Even if we both know that he shouldn't.

Outside, the clock strikes midnight. Henry nods to me to budge over.

Boarding-school beds are narrow. I'm lying so close to the wall that the tip of my nose is almost touching it. My heart beats faster. We don't say a word as Henry switches off the lamp. I feel him slide up behind me. When he puts an arm around me and pulls me to him, my heart stands still.

I stare at the wall and don't dare to breathe. Henry doesn't take his arm away. My back is against his chest, which is slowly rising and falling.

I don't know what it is, maybe just his presence, but somehow everything's a little more bearable. Maybe it really is just his warm body against mine that means my mind can no longer believe so firmly that everything totally sucks. Maybe it's his fingers, which are gently stroking my arm, ever more slowly, until his hand eventually comes to a stop.

When Henry falls asleep, he sinks into me. His arm grows heavier, but it's not unpleasant, not at all. It's the exact opposite, as I feel his breath against my shoulder.

I wait a while until I dare to move. The duvet rustles,

SARAH SPRINZ

Henry twitches, but his eyes stay shut. When I turn onto my back, his face sinks onto my shoulder.

He looks way younger when he's sleeping, and I can't help it, I have to run my fingertips over his cheek. His skin is as soft as I thought it would be. His arm weighs heavily on my belly, his breathing is slow and even, and tiny waves of peace wash from his body over mine.

My eyes are still stinging, and my throat is dry. I'd like to get up, have a drink, blow my nose, but Henry's sleeping and that means I mustn't move now. I can only roll back onto my side as cautiously as possible, and curl up, because that's the only position in which I can fall asleep. And which puts at least a hand's breadth of distance between our bodies.

My curtains aren't completely shut and a little light is falling into my room. Normally, at this time of night, everything's quiet, but now there's Henry's quiet breathing, and with every breath it's harder not just to shut my eyes.

I must have done so, because when Henry moves, I open them, blinking and startled. He slides a little closer behind me – I'm the little spoon – pulls me closer, and then his hands relax again.

This whole evening feels like a crazy fever dream. I'm exhausted from crying, from feeling. But none of that matters now. It's warm, it's lovely, it doesn't matter where I am because Henry's lying next to me, holding me, like everything is definitely, definitely going to turn out OK.

16

HENRY

No. *No* . . .

Not yet, please. It can't be morning already, I've hardly slept twelve seconds and I hate my alarm. I hate it. I hate it for going off, because it's so lovely and warm in this bed and my body feels as heavy as lead. I hate the fact that I'm going to have to get up in a moment, brush my teeth and put on my PE kit. Maybe it'll rain and the morning run will be called off, maybe . . .

I realize too late that the alarm has stopped and that something's moving beside me. I really couldn't care less. My head empties again, the quiet, it's all so nice, and I jump as I hear someone knocking. Much harder than normal, and it's not Mr Acevedo's voice. It's a woman. I open my eyes fully and my blood runs cold.

'Time to get up, Emma.'

Shit . . . A strip of light falls into the room around the door. A moment later, it goes dark again as Emma pulls the duvet over me.

'Morning run in twenty minutes.' Ms Barnett's voice reaches me, muffled by the layers of fabric, and I daren't breathe. I feel Emma beside me, pushing herself up onto her elbows and nodding.

'Yes.' Her voice sounds rough, her warm, soft body is touching mine, her sleepshirt's ridden up a little over her hips, and I bite my bottom lip, hard enough for it to hurt, but none of that's any use as all my blood rushes between my legs.

Fuck, fuck, fuck . . . *Think about the morning run, Bennington. Cold, drizzle, fog. Misery.* Although not when Emma's running beside me, getting those red cheeks, and her hair all frizzed up by the rain and . . . Fucking shit.

The door is shut again and at that moment Emma exhales audibly. I slide a little away from her and pray she didn't feel anything. She pulls the duvet back slightly, and her eyes are still small and tired, but now there's a hint of panic in them.

'Hi,' she whispers, and I want to kiss her. Her soft pink lips. That's really all I want to do at this moment, and I can't for so many different reasons.

'I should—' I begin.

Emma nods. 'Yes,' she says at the same time, without looking away. I want to run my hand through her pale blonde hair, while she grabs hold of mine – and, God, what have we

ANYWHERE

done? Why did I forget I was here and that I'd been intending to slip back to my own room before half past six if at all possible? So that nobody would notice where I was. In the girls' wing. In Emma's bed. While Grace is at home, in her own bed, and holy shit, I'm so dead.

I straighten and something flickers in Emma's eyes as I get to my feet. Her gaze runs over my body. She looks so little and vulnerable, and I have to go.

'Sorry,' I mumble, and turn away.

My pulse is racing and I'm in luck that I don't bump into anyone. The sky is overcast and grey. I just about make it across the courtyard to our wing before the first raindrops fall. So much for the morning run. In a matter of seconds, the light drizzle turns into hammering rain, which drowns out my hurried footsteps on the stairs. The noise of it still hasn't stopped by the time I get up to our floor. Just four more doors to my room. Just three, just two . . .

'Henry?'

I freeze.

No.

Shit.

I shut my eyes, take a deep breath and then, in slow motion, I turn around.

Mr Acevedo's floor-length dressing-gown trails behind him as he comes towards me. He pulls it around himself and eyes me critically. I can't think of anyone who is less of a fan of early rising than our houseparent seems to be.

205

'Morning run's off. Go back to bed,' he says, and relief floods through me.

'Yes, sir,' I mumble hastily. I'm about to turn away when he continues.

'Hold on a moment . . .' He comes a step closer. 'Have you come from outside? Have you already been out running with your little friend from the west wing?'

I thank myself for having had the sense to put on running shoes, hoodie and joggers before I went over to Emma's yesterday. I clear my throat. 'Yes. It wasn't raining till just now.'

'Got in just in time, then,' says Mr Acevedo, pointing to my room. 'Better go and have a shower.'

I nod and turn away.

Phew . . . I hardly dare breathe as I walk to my room. I'm just fishing my key out of my trouser pocket when the door next to mine opens.

Sinclair's hair is sticking up all over the place. 'Morning run's cancelled, isn't it?' he asks hopefully, blinking at me. 'Man, Henry,' he murmurs, and I eye him warningly. I don't know why, but he's seen right through me. His eyes are gleaming with a mixture of amusement and curiosity.

'Just don't say a thing,' I hiss. Sinclair grins and I stick my key into the lock. 'And, yes, the morning run's off.'

'Alleluia,' he mumbles, and as I step into my room, I'm a different person from the Henry who left it last night. One who does crazy things without thinking. Breaks the rules and cheats on his girlfriend. Because that's what it was, wasn't it? I slept in the same bed as Emma. I was closer to her than I've ever been to anyone apart from Grace. I didn't kiss her, and nothing went any further, but I knew it wasn't right.

I'm totally screwed, and as I have a hot shower, rage boils up inside me. I'm angry with myself. Why did I do that? I shouldn't have slept at Emma's. I shouldn't even have gone to hers. Why do I constantly feel the need to be with her? I'm spending way too much time with her. And I don't want to change that.

I groan with frustration, and that's got nothing to do with the water having suddenly gone cold.

EMMA

Henry cancels our next training session, and in the end, I'm grateful to him for that. On Friday, I only see him at meal-times and in lessons, with enough other people around us that I don't have to speak to him. There are only stolen glances and hasty looking away when the other person notices. And I hate that I let things get so complicated between us.

Although I have to admit that they were complicated right from the start. From the moment I stepped into the arrivals hall in Edinburgh and realized that Grace was his girlfriend. I saw him and knew that this thing would blow up around my ears. Because I wanted him. Because I wanted Henry Harold Bennington, regardless of what that meant.

Ha, and here we are now, and I still want him. But I'm not allowed to want him. Even after he got a hard-on lying next to me half asleep and I couldn't think about anything else all the next day. But apparently we're acting like that never happened. Like I didn't feel it or something. The weight of his warm body, the heat of him, right next to my skin, and – No. I have to stop this. Maybe I just imagined it. And even if I didn't men sometimes just get them. It had nothing to do with me. I mustn't read anything into this. There won't be any Henry and Emma. There's only Henry and Grace.

He can't skive off the regular morning run now it's Tuesday. I spent the weekend alone. On Monday we only saw each other in class, and avoided each other the rest of the time. I expect him to join Tori and Sinclair and take the shortcut, but he doesn't. Henry's eyes flick back and forward between me and the others a few times, and then he jogs through the gate beside me. We don't speak to each other. I run faster than normal, at a pace that tires even me after a few minutes, but Henry keeps up. I don't know if I should be irritated or proud. Only a few weeks ago, I'd have shaken him off a long way back.

The ground is muddy, the sky heavy with clouds. Henry's chest is rising rapidly and laboriously, and I want to tell him to clench his fingers into loose fists, not to be so tense in the shoulders. But I don't.

'I'm sorry,' I say eventually, once we've overtaken a small

group of people and we're on our own. 'Last week . . . I didn't mean to bother you.'

'You didn't bother me,' Henry replies. 'It was just . . . I don't think I should have come round so late.'

He shouldn't come round at all.

'It wasn't fair on Grace,' he says, and I wish we could go back to his fitness level when we first started training and he could barely string three sentences together. It would save me from having to have this conversation. But I can't always run away every time anything gets complicated. 'And the walls in this place have ears – eyes too. There's so much gossip. I wouldn't want her to hear rumours.'

'Me either,' I say, at once.

I hate this conversation. It's the opposite of how we've spoken to each other before.

'We should stop this.' The words are out before I've even thought them through. Henry opens his mouth but I don't let him speak. 'Running together. I don't think it was a good idea. Besides, you're in much better shape now.'

'It was rugby yesterday,' says Henry, and I wonder if he was even listening to me. Then I remember. It must have been the deadline to earn a place on the team.

'I'm in.'

'Really?' I blurt. I can't help the pleasure in my voice. 'That's—' My tone is much more detached as I go on: 'I'm glad for you, congratulations.'

'Yes . . .' Henry hesitates. 'Thank you.'

'All this training is over anyway, then.' I hate that there's this tiny edge to my voice. The slight disappointment, which Henry can hear, I'm sure of that.

'No,' he says. 'Mr Cormack says he'll give me a chance, but I have to keep working at it, to be better by the time of the first match. He won't play me until then, he says.'

I understand. It's only if Henry actually gets onto the pitch in person for an important match, if he's not just on the bench, that this will all have paid off for him.

'Oh.' I give him a little sideways glance. At that moment, he looks at me too, and I notice, yet again, how different the green of his eyes can be. Outside, in daylight, it's so pale that it's almost blue. Last week, in the dim light of my room, it was much darker. Forest green, moss green, dark-almost-black green.

'Do you think we could keep on running together?' he asks straight out.

I have one job. Turn him down, keep it friendly but firm. But ... Just now he hinted in a roundabout way that we shouldn't be seen together so much. This latest question sounds like the exact opposite. 'Are you sure that would be a good idea?'

Henry pauses. 'Yes, I mean ... we're just good friends, aren't we?'

Tch, and here I make my mistake. I nod. Even though we both know that that's ridiculous.

Because *just friends* don't wake up with a throbbing

between their legs when they've had another dream about the other person holding them in their sleep.

But if we can't be just friends, we can't be anything. We'd be classmates who avoid each other. And I couldn't bear that. Besides, it would be pretty difficult. This isn't just school, it's where I live. I see him from morning to evening. In class, at meals, just after getting up and at some midnight party. It's impossible, so I've got to pull myself together. We can act like adults around each other. Like friends. And friends help each other out. Without ulterior motives.

'We are,' I tell him.

211

17

HENRY

'God, this place really hasn't changed.' Maeve spins on her heel before we leave the rear courtyard through one of the large gateways in the north wing. Her pale green dress flies out around her calves as she does so; her hair's shorter than the last time I saw her.

'It's not that long since you left,' I say.

'True.' She looks up once we're out on the gravel path that circles the buildings. Above the school's dark brick façade and pointed turrets, the sun is shining in a cloudless blue sky. 'A year and bit, but it feels like half a lifetime.'

I nod, because it feels like that to me too. It seems ages since I started the fifth form, on the first day when it wasn't just Theo who'd left but Maeve too. I was no longer the youngest Bennington – I was the only Bennington. Maeve's well into her medicine degree now, while Theo is a year ahead of her.

I can barely remember what it was like when I saw my brother and sister here every day, around the school or in the dining room at mealtimes. I knew I could go to them any time I needed them. I didn't realize how privileged that made me until later. And I miss it. Because even if everything goes to plan and I get into St Andrews, too, I know it won't be the same, that things will never be the way they were when we were all at Dunbridge Academy together. Theo often talks about doing a semester in Canada, and Maeve's hinted that she wants to travel. They won't stay in Scotland for ever. In that respect, they're completely different from me. Even though I'm sure that they'll look back on their time here with happy memories, they found it restricting to spend so long in one place.

I guess those are the logical outcomes of travelling more in your childhood than other people do in their whole lives. Either you long to arrive somewhere, or you're constantly pulled to explore, to see the whole world. Theo and Maeve are definitely the second type.

'Do you miss it? Boarding-school life?'

'I miss being close to you,' she says, and I'm sure it's still there, the invisible connection that meant we always knew what the other was thinking. I'd been scared it might get lost if I spent such a long time apart from my big sister, but fortunately that doesn't seem to be the case. 'And I miss

213

boarding-school life too,' she continues. 'Everything's more anonymous somehow at uni. I don't even know my neighbours' names, they change so fast. And I miss the morning runs.' Maeve laughs. 'Who'd have thought I'd ever say that?'

'I can believe it,' I say, and her eyes rest suspiciously on me. 'I'm actually quite enjoying them, these days.'

'What have they done to you?'

'I had to put some effort into getting onto the rugby team.'

'Well, that's nuts too,' Maeve says. 'So, did you make it?' She smiles. 'Of course you did. You always manage anything you set your mind to.'

I walk next to her in silence.

'How's Grace?' Maeve asks.

'Fine,' I say. 'She sends her love.'

When Maeve doesn't answer, I turn my head towards her. She's a few steps away from me now, sitting on the wide wooden swing that hangs from a thick branch on one of the old lime trees that line the path to the stables.

'What?' I ask, as she just looks at me.

'Nothing.' She pushes off and swings towards me. 'No, there is something, isn't there?'

'Maeve . . .' I groan.

'Have you two had a row?'

'No,' I say. We don't see enough of each other for that. We only meet in lessons and in the dining room. Or for lunch with her family, which I feel worse about every time.

Especially now when all I can think about is Emma's sleeping body next to mine. That and her warm, soft skin.

'What is it, then?'

'Nothing,' I snap. 'Everything's fine, OK?'

Maeve doesn't bat an eyelid, which makes me even angrier. There's never been any point in trying to lie to my sister. I don't know how she does it, but somehow, she always seems to know how I'm feeling better than I do myself.

'OK.' Maeve looks up into the branches as she swings forward again. She sounds utterly unimpressed. And she isn't even trying to get me to talk. She doesn't say a thing. Not a word. Not one single . . .

'When you and Eliza . . .' I can't stop myself. 'Did you ever wonder if you were just still together out of habit?'

'Yeah, I'm afraid so.'

I gulp.

'Pretty shitty feeling, isn't it?' Maeve lets the soles of her shoes scrape over the ground until the swing stops.

'Yeah.' Why's my throat so dry?

'But I don't think there's anything wrong with thinking that kind of stuff.' Maeve looks at me. 'It means you're developing as a person.'

'It *feels* like there's something wrong with it.'

'Why?'

I could roll my eyes. Because that's how she always asks. It forces me to be brutally honest with myself, which I'd normally prefer to avoid.

There's a small, dishonest *I don't know* on the tip of my tongue. But I bite it back because I know we won't get anywhere like that. So I just talk. No filters, no over-thinking. Maeve's the only person in the world I can do this with.

'Because we've grown apart from each other.'

'Why could that be?'

I think about Emma. I'm thinking about her and nothing else.

'What's her name?' Maeve asks, and my first instinct is to deny everything. But suddenly I'm sick of it. Of lying to myself, lying to my friends. Lying to Emma. Because I don't want to be *just friends* with her. I want more, I want everything, and I want it with her. 'Or him?'

I shake my head. 'Her.' My voice sounds suddenly rough. 'Emma.'

'Is she new?'

I nod. 'She's German, just here for a year. We met at the airport when I changed in Frankfurt.'

Maeve smiles. 'Cute, Henny.'

Henny . . . She's the only person who still sometimes calls me that, from back when I couldn't pronounce my name properly.

'Stop it, Maeve, it's horrible, all of it.' I groan. 'What am I even doing? None of this makes any sense . . .'

'You fancy her, of course it doesn't.' Maeve says it like a totally self-explanatory fact.

But it's not true. I know what a crush feels like. And this

with Emma is more than that. It's so much more than having a crush on her, and that scares me.

'I can't do this. I can't fall in love. I'm with Grace.' I swallow hard and I don't want to be this guy. Grace has always done everything right. She's important to me and I don't want to lose her. If I listened to my feelings, instead of my mind, that would definitely happen.

'That's true, but are you happy with her? Are you two happy together?' Maeve doesn't take her eyes off me, and I just can't speak.

I'm thinking about everything and nothing. About weekends with Grace and her family, about our conversations, talking whole nights away, laughing till we can't breathe, knowing there's always someone there for me. But then I think about rows over tiny things and silence about the stuff that's so crucial and so big that it scares me. About this feeling of having got used to Grace. It's almost like indifference, and I'm the worst human being in the whole world, but it's true. I like Grace, her presence, her sense of humour, our relationship. I respect her. I want the very best for her. But since that day a few weeks ago when I ran into this German girl at the airport, and sat in an aeroplane feeling grey-blue eyes burning into the back of my neck, I haven't been able to forget it. Because nothing with Emma is enough. Because I want more. And because I think I could have it with her.

I only remember Maeve's question when I feel her eyes on me.

'We're not unhappy,' I begin. 'But . . . I think we're not properly happy any more either.'

'As happy as you are when you spend time with Emma?'

Why do I feel so guilty? I really wish it wasn't this way, but whenever I'm with Emma, it seems like I feel everything twice as intensely. And that's dangerous.

'There's no point. She's only here for a year. She'll leave, and then I'll have given Grace up. The whole year with her, it's . . . How can I explain it to her when I don't understand it myself?'

'Who says she'll only stay a year?' asks Maeve, and I resist the urge to shut my eyes in despair.

'Emma says so, and she means it. She's here to find out more about her dad. Her parents met at Dunbridge and she has no contact with him.' I pause. These are Emma's secrets. Things she told me in confidence, and only me. But I promised to do whatever I could to help her in her search. So I have to get Maeve involved. 'His name is Jacob Wiley. He's a musician and he was born in Scotland.' I tell her everything I've found about him on the internet. 'Do you know if Mum or Dad ever mentioned them? They must have been only a couple of years apart.'

'Hm, I see.' Maeve rests her index finger against the tip of her nose, the way she always does when she's thinking. 'No, I don't think I've ever heard of him, sorry.'

'No worries. It was a long shot.'

'If he was at school here, there's bound to be someone who knew him.'

'Mr Ward did. He's made a few remarks.'

'Oh, God, he's probably the only teacher I don't miss.'

'He's getting worse,' I say. I glance around unobtrusively. Luckily, there's no one nearby who could have heard us.

'I think it annoys him to this day that I got an A star for A level,' Maeve muses cheerily.

'I bet it does. I really don't know why he went into teaching. It really doesn't seem like he wants anyone ever to learn anything.'

'You'll make a way better teacher.'

I have to smile. 'I hope so.'

'Have you started thinking about universities yet?'

I nod slowly. 'Yeah, but I don't have to decide anything for certain just now.'

'True. Well, you've got plenty of time. Does Grace have any plans for where she wants to go?'

'Oxford.'

'OK,' Maeve says, and I'm sure she knows what that means. She doesn't bother with pointless clichés. That long-distance relationships and weekend visits can work out, can keep it going. It didn't work for her and Eliza, and they were only an hour and a half apart, in St Andrews and Edinburgh. So why would it work out for me and Grace if there was four hundred miles or so between our universities?

'When did you know you were going to have to split up?'
I ask the question as if it were about no more than the weather. How can I sound so casual?

'I didn't want to face up to it for ages,' she says. 'But, really,
I knew back when we started applying to universities. We
spent the whole of the upper sixth pretending that everything wasn't about to change between us.' Maeve doesn't
look at me as she continues. 'I sometimes wish we'd ended it
before we left school. It might have been easier to settle in at
St Andrews if I hadn't spent the whole time wondering how
we could patch things up.'

I sigh. 'Sometimes I wonder how Theo and Harriett manage.'

'That's Theo for you,' Maeve says. 'He says hi, by the way.
He's still pretty much living in the library even though it's
still the vacation. He's decided to revise last year's work
before next semester.'

'That's Theo for you,' I repeat.

'He's wondering if he can take a semester out next spring
and do some volunteering with Mum and Dad on their
project.'

'Oh. Seriously?'

Maeve just nods.

'When's your flight?' I ask.

'Next week. I'll be back just before term starts again.'

'Then I guess we won't see each other before that?'

Maeve shakes her head with a smile. 'But that's why we're
seeing each other now.'

'You'll be careful, though, won't you?'

'I'm always careful, Henny.'

'Just saying,' I mumble.

'And when I get back, you can come and visit me again. Uni's not so stressful at the start of term.'

'That would be nice,' I say.

'After all, you need a look around if you're going to study there. And I've signed up as a volunteer for your open day after half-term. We'll see each other then.' Maeve smiles. 'And bring Emma. I'm just saying . . .'

I've just opened my mouth when I hear a voice.

'Maeve Bennington?' Ms Barnett is walking towards us, and she smiles as we turn around. 'I thought as much. How nice to see you! You look so grown-up.'

18

It's horrible. I've screwed up with Emma, there's no denying it. Why else would she be avoiding me like this? Because she is, I can feel it. Now whenever we run together, all our conversation is really superficial, and the rest of the time, it's basically never just the two of us.

Emma's avoiding me, and I'm avoiding Grace. For the first time in two years, I bail on our Wednesday lunch with Grace's family. I can't just go and sit there like nothing's happened. I'm a pathetic coward, but I can't do it. Not while I'm feeling like a lousy cheat.

The last time I didn't go it was because I was in the sick bay with a fever, and Grace brought me homemade soup that Diane had sent. I don't really remember much about it because I pretty much slept for a week, but Grace came as often as she could. This time, my excuse for cancelling is an essay. A lousy essay. Which I could write absolutely any other time, but I've come up with assorted reasons why I totally have to do it over Wednesday lunchtime. I'd forgotten it was due; there's rugby training this evening. Really lame excuses, but Grace saves me the humiliation. She doesn't even question it when I send her a WhatsApp. She just messages *That's a shame* and *Everything OK?* And I answer *Yeah* and *I'm really sorry.*

I hate myself.

To match my mood, the friendly late-summer days have given way to a grey wall of cloud and rain. The morning run is cancelled three days in a row, and I toy with the idea of running on the treadmill in the gym instead. The only reason I don't is that I'm afraid of bumping into Emma.

Rugby training is a suitable punishment for me, too. Mr Cormack is hardcore, even when it's pissing down and the pitch has turned into a mud pit. This evening, I fall flat on my face more often than ever before – much to Valentine Ward's amusement. But at least I succeed in turning my frustration into energy so that, when we finish the drills and play a game, I manage to break some tackles and to score the odd try. It's the first time Mr Cormack's praised me. My first thought is that I have to tell Emma, but then I remember I shouldn't. OK, so we're friends but apparently we're friends who don't speak to each other; and can no longer look each other in the eye.

This evening I use the team showers in the new sports

complex, instead of going straight back to my room. Here, the whole floor is tiled so it doesn't matter that huge lumps of mud dissolve off my kit, turning the water brown.

I want to get some sleep and not have to talk to anyone, but at the same time, I want to go to Emma and force her to speak to me again. I want to go on night-time walks with her, during which I can forget that there can never be anything between us. I want to be the person she can tell anything – I want that so much. And I don't even understand why. If I had any idea, maybe things wouldn't be such a mess.

It's dark, I'm running late – by the time I get back to the east wing, it's already fifteen minutes into quiet time. I'm on the stairs when my phone buzzes in the pocket of my joggers. That means someone's calling me. And nobody ever calls me. Unless something's happened.

I stop, pull it out and frown as I read the name on my screen.

'Maeve?' I say, instead of hello. 'Is everything OK?'

'Yes, sure, everything's fine, Henny.' She sounds kind of excited. 'Is this a bad time? Or have you got a moment?' she asks. 'I think I've found out something interesting.'

EMMA

It's not easy to avoid Henry, but I manage. When we're with the others, nobody notices that we hardly talk to each other.

Luckily we don't sit next to each other for anything except chemistry and Ms Ventura hardly ever sets work to be done in pairs. There are plenty of other people around in the dining room too, so we don't have to interact with each other there. As a result, our training sessions are the only tricky part of the day. But we're just friends, aren't we? We can deal with that, even if it's just the two of us.

I've increased our pace so much that it's almost impossible to chat as we run. I guess that's OK by Henry as he hasn't complained. He complains less in general than he did at the beginning. He does what I say, makes an effort, and he's improving all the time. What more do I want?

I've been asking myself that question for a few days now, but I can't answer it. Not even when, just after wing time, I'm lying on my bed, curled up in a tight ball. All I know is that I'm in a chronically bad mood and that Henry doesn't seem to have mentioned our little sleepover to Grace. If he had, there's no way she'd still be as friendly to me. Or else she knows she doesn't need to worry. After all, they're perfect together. Everybody knows that. God, I hate it all so much.

Although I have to say that this afternoon, at athletics, things were a bit tense between us. Grace didn't look at me. Most of the time, she and Olive had their heads together. I felt awful, and at first I kind of hated Henry, and then I hated myself.

Meanwhile, Isi seems to have blocked me from seeing her

stories because I don't get shown them any more. Of course it's possible that she's too busy to post anything, but I know my best friend. Barely a day goes by without her sharing something.

I suppose it ought to be doing my head in, making me sad, but surprisingly I really don't care. I'm busy enough loathing myself over Henry, for God's sake.

Our corridor's gone quiet now, the tower clock has struck ten, and I'm mentally bargaining with myself over how long I get to lie here before I finally drag myself to the bathroom to brush my teeth, when there's a knock at the door.

Is it Tori? It seems a bit early for a spur-of-the-moment midnight party, and to be honest, I don't know that I'm in the mood for one. Besides, I didn't see anything in the Midnight Memories WhatsApp group. Unless I've been kicked out of it. Who knows? Wow, even I'm getting sick of my negativity at this point, but everything really is utterly crap.

I groan with irritation as whoever it is knocks again, I stand up, open the door, and freeze.

Am I seeing things? Did I actually fall asleep, and now I'm dreaming, or is that actually Henry standing outside my door, his hair still damp, wearing joggers and his blue school hoodie?

He's sending me urgent messages with his eyes, holding his finger to his lips and nodding to one side. Down the empty corridor.

I open my mouth, but don't say anything.

'Not for long,' he whispers and, sadly for me, his voice is still out of this world.

It takes me a few seconds to come back to life, slip my bare feet into my trainers, pull on a jumper and reach for my key. Before I know it, I'm walking beside Henry away from my room. By now, I've got the motion-sensor business down pat, along with the fact that once we get out to the stairway, we're pretty much safe to talk. But Henry doesn't say anything, so I don't either.

We reach a darkened corridor and switch on our phone torches at the same time. Our place for night-time strolls and, oh, God, I've missed it. I didn't know how much I'd missed it.

'What's going on?' I ask eventually, when things are getting silly. There must be some reason he's picked me up out of the blue for a late-night walk, even though we're avoiding each other. Or I'm avoiding him. Whichever. We both know it's not working.

'Henry,' I repeat, when he doesn't reply. 'Is everything OK?'

His eyes glance nervously over my face. Even in this dim light, I can see how keyed-up he is. He clears his throat quietly. 'Yes. I just wanted to ... I have to tell you something.'

'And it couldn't wait till morning?'

'No, Emma.' He sounds so insistent that I hold my breath. 'It couldn't.'

'OK.' I stop. 'What is it?'

Henry looks as though he's working out his next words very precisely while not taking his eyes off me. 'Well, so . . . I know you told me everything in confidence and I promise I haven't breathed a word to anyone else, but the other day, when my sister was here for a visit, we talked about your dad.'

Everything within me goes numb as Henry continues.

'I'm really sorry. I hope you're not pissed off with me. I thought she might know something. That Mum and Dad might have mentioned his name or something. But Maeve says they never did—'

'Henry,' I interrupt him. There's this suppressed trembling in my voice, and within a fraction of a second, it's spread to my entire body. 'Why are you telling me this?'

'Because Maeve called me today.' He coughs, and I forget to breathe. 'A friend of hers had heard of him. She's from Glasgow, and she says he's doing a gig. It's not being advertised online anywhere, but she'd seen a poster.'

'When is it?' I whisper. My pulse is racing.

'On Friday.' Henry pauses. 'In a tiny pub, but, yeah . . . I guess he'll be there.'

I'm trying to get my thoughts together. My dad. In Glasgow.

'How – how far is it from here to . . .?'

'An hour and a half,' says Henry. 'If we left before dinner, we could get the train to Glasgow from Edinburgh. The last bus back here goes at midnight. I looked it up just now.'

'That . . . that's not allowed, is it? Being out so late . . .'

'No. But I can ask Tori and Sinclair if they'll cover for us. Nobody will notice.'

I swallow. 'Us? You mean . . .?'

'I'm coming with you.' Henry's eyes are dark green as he stares at me hard. 'Well, if you want me to, that is.'

19

HENRY

It's a dingy pub in the north-east of Glasgow, and I don't know what I'd been expecting – long queues at the door, endless arguments with bouncers to persuade them to let us in even though the place was rammed and the concert was sold out?

But when Emma and I reach Cowcaddens, none of that is the case. A couple of guys are hanging around outside the pub for a smoke; they eye us, then pay us no more attention. A few flyers are stuck to the dark wooden door, but none of them mentions anything about a Jacob Wiley concert this evening. If Maeve hadn't forwarded me that photo her friend took, I'd have been convinced we were in the wrong place. But I can hear muffled music coming from inside the pub.

Emma gives me a quick sideways glance. We've barely

spoken a word to each other since we met at the bus stop outside the gates after study hour. I can feel how tense she is, as if her nerves were my own, and I can't bear it. The way she sat next to me on the bus to Edinburgh, then the train to Glasgow, shoulders hunched. I wish we'd come to the city for some other reason. One that didn't cause her to sink into helpless silence, or make my stomach ache.

'Want me to wait here somewhere?' I ask, as Emma's eyes dart from me to the pub.

'No.' She turns back to me straight away. 'I mean ... unless you'd rather.'

I shake my head and reach for her hand. I do it simply because I think it's what she needs. I'm sure of that as her ice-cold fingers wrap around mine.

It's only a moment or two. Then she pulls her hand away and walks up the couple of steps to the entrance.

We step inside the gloomy pub. The first thing I notice is the stale air. This isn't one of the fancy bars you find in posh parts of town. This is all dark wood, sticky floorboards and the smell of old smoke and beer. Beside the bar is a stage, so small it's not really worthy of the name. It's more of a small platform in the corner, slightly raised and with just enough room for a couple of speakers, lights and the microphone. The space in front of it is practically empty. There are just a few people standing there, mostly with drinks in hand, leaning against the bar or a stand-up table. The music is loud, but you can still hear people's voices as they chat.

I almost stumble into Emma as she stops abruptly in front of me. Her eyes freeze on the man with the guitar, standing behind the microphone. He's got his eyes shut as he sings and plays along to the backing track. I know nothing about music – maybe this is some kind of amazing indie rock, but all I can say is that I'd probably have skipped it on Spotify. There's no 'skip' button here, though. There's just Emma and me in the pub, and this guy who's apparently her father.

It's dark and I can't see much, but immediately I'm looking for a resemblance. He's tall, slim, and his hair, which he's got tied up in a messy man bun, is strikingly blond. Not as pale as Emma's, but maybe that's just the bad light in here.

He must be about the same age as my parents but looks like he's lived way harder. His face is kind of sunken. He's like my image of an artist – kind of obsessed, and out of touch with reality.

His voice through the speakers is deep and smoky, and when the song ends, I notice an unlit cigarette jammed into the mic stand. Emma crosses her arms, still staring straight ahead. I want to ask her if everything's OK. I want to know what she's thinking, if he's the way she remembered him, what all this is doing to her. But I can't, because the next song's starting. So I stand beside her because it's the only thing I can do.

I've no idea how long this performance goes on. A few people leave the pub, a few more come in, but they seem less interested in the music than in cheap drinks. It's kind of sad that some of them don't even clap after the songs. In each brief gap between numbers, he turns away to grab a glass. My stomach clenches. I don't like any of this.

I've entirely lost track of time by the time he announces his final song. Emma hasn't moved from her spot the entire time. We clap when the others clap, he puts down his guitar, the bar staff switch the recorded music back on again. It's all so sad and none of it's anything special. And Emma's still transfixed, still staring in his direction.

EMMA

He climbs off that stage. It's pretty dark in here but I'm afraid that isn't the only reason why he misses his footing. Glass shatters, he catches himself on the bar and sways.

Nobody seems to have noticed; most people are deep in conversation again. I hear the voices, the laughter, then take a step in his direction.

I feel Henry's hand on my shoulder. 'Are you sure this is a good idea?' he asks quietly. He looks worried, and somehow that makes me furious. Because I'm worried. Because it hadn't occurred to me that my dad might be this much of a drunken wreck. But I didn't come all this way for nothing.

'I have to speak to him,' I mutter. And find out if there's anything left. 'Can you . . .?'

'I'll wait outside, OK? You can call me if . . . if you need me.'

Why should I need you? The words are on the tip of my tongue, but I bite them back. Because I'm angry and scared. Scared of being disappointed and regretting all this. And none of that is Henry's fault. Quite the reverse. He's here with me when he didn't have to come.

So I say, 'OK,' and for a split second I feel the crappy emotions trying to overwhelm me, my suppressed shivering rising inside me, and I want to ask Henry if he'd give me a hug. Like he did in my room the other night. But I don't because that would make me cry and I don't want my dad to see me like that.

'See you in a bit,' Henry says quietly, turning away. It's surprisingly painful when he lets go of my shoulder. He glances back at me, then digs his hands into his jacket pockets and walks out of the pub.

And I'm alone. I'm in a strange country, in a strange city, in a grotty pub with a drunken stranger, who's no father to me. I'm reasonably certain that Mum wouldn't approve. She doesn't have the faintest idea that I'm doing this. The realization hits me like an electric shock, and for a moment I regret not discussing it with her first. Ask her if she thought it was a good idea to go to Glasgow to meet him. But I know what she'd have said. And then I'd have had to do this in secret.

My dad lifts his head as two women walk towards him. I'm too far away to hear what they're saying. But I see one pull out her phone. When she looks around, her eyes meet mine. She waves to me and my blood runs cold.

'Would you mind taking a photo of us?' she asks, and I nod my head, on autopilot.

I take her phone and my dad glances in my direction. I don't know what I'd been expecting. For something to happen in his face? For his eyes to widen in surprise, for him to come over and put his arms around me? But he doesn't. He doesn't look at me. He looks at the phone, and I remember what I'm meant to be doing with it.

I take three photos. My fingers are trembling, but there's nothing I can do about that. Fortunately, the women seem too drunk to notice. I give them back the phone, force myself to smile as they say thanks and turn away. My dad is still standing at the bar and now his eyes wander over to me.

'Want a selfie too?' he asks.

He doesn't recognize me. I can see it in his eyes. There's nothing. And I hadn't thought about what I'd do in this situation. I just didn't think this through at all.

'I wanted to ask you if you'd have time for us to talk somewhere quiet,' I stammer. It's not a polished English sentence, I'm just too overwhelmed. And then his eyes light up with surprise.

'Aren't you a little young for that?' he asks, and for a moment I don't know what he means. Then I freeze. Does he take me for some groupie who wants to get into his hotel room?

I open my mouth, but can't get a single word out.

'Are you even eighteen? Anyway, I need another whisky.' He leans against the bar. 'Make it a double,' he calls to the barman, who nods curtly. His voice doesn't sound at all as I remember it. His eyes wander over me and I want to get out of here. I don't want him to be my father. I don't want him to be drinking in a filthy pub, playing for a handful of people who look just as fucked up as him. This isn't the Jacob Wiley I've been imagining, the one who played me lullabies on his guitar and promised that I could come with him on his next big tour.

Then he looks me over and I feel my stomach clench.

'Dad . . .' I mumble, and I hate the pleading note in my voice. 'It's me.'

I have no idea if he even heard me. At least not until something in his expression changes. He leans forward slightly.

'Emma?' he asks, so incredulous that I want to cry. 'Fuck, it is you, isn't it?'

I just nod in silence.

'God, why didn't you say something right away? I didn't even recognize you. You're so fuckin' grown-up, Biscuit.'

Biscuit. It's just a nickname, and a really crappy one at that, but the casual way he says it gives me goosebumps. Because I'd forgotten he used to call me that.

I don't know what's happening as he pushes himself away from the bar and comes towards me. I don't know if I want him to hug me. I did want that just now, but I'm not sure any more. I force myself not to flinch as he puts his arms around me. I can smell a mixture of alcohol, cigarettes and sweat, but I can't smell him. He doesn't smell the way I remember.

'What're ye doing here? Fuck, you're tall.' I can hear the slur in his speech.

'I was in the area,' I manage to answer him. 'And I hoped we'd be able to talk.'

He laughs. 'Course we can. But not here. This isn't the kind of place my daughter oughta hang around in. I know somewhere nearby. We can get something to eat. You hungry? It's on me, Biscuit.'

I'm not hungry. My stomach is a tiny ball of fear and it shrinks even more as my dad turns to one of the women in a group a few metres away. 'Lou, I'll be back later to clear up.'

All she says is 'Aye, right . . .' with a dismissive wave. Her eyes run over me, and I feel kind of dirty.

I stand there in silence as my dad grabs his jacket and points to the door.

'What d'ye think of the gig?' he asks, once we're outside. There are still a few people standing around by the doors, but nobody pays any attention to us.

'It was great,' I say, because I have to say something.

My dad laughs. 'Loada fuckin' bores. But, hey, this is Glasgow. Lousy shitehole.'

I say nothing. Why doesn't he ask what I'm even doing here? Why I'm not at home. In Frankfurt. With Mum. There's

no way he can know that I'm at school here. Isn't he
interested?

I spot Henry across the road, leaning on a wall. Our eyes
meet and I feel him scanning my face for signs that everything's OK. So I give a slight nod. I'd like to tell him where
we're going but I don't even know. I can only hope that
Henry will follow us. I seriously hope so.

'Oh, fuck,' says my father. 'Got a light?'

'No, I . . . I don't smoke.'

His eyes slide over to me. 'What a good girl! You really are
Laura's daughter, aren't you?'

I don't know if he's expecting an answer. He sounds more
American than I remember him. I suppose that's not surprising seeing how long he lived in California. Somehow he
sounded friendlier with a Scottish accent, but maybe that's
just my imagination.

I wait as he talks to a group coming towards us. Two
young men just give him a sceptical look and walk on without a word, but a woman stops, gives him a light and a
cigarette too.

My dad mumbles his thanks as we move on again. He
drags on the filter and blows the smoke out into the night.
'So where's the wee friend who was with you just now?'

So he did notice us come in, then. We were the youngest
people in that pub by a long way so maybe that was why we
stood out to him, even if he didn't recognize his own daughter standing right in front of him.

'He's waiting nearby.' And then I decide just to tell him about Henry and my life. 'His name's Henry and we know each other from school. I'm on a year abroad at Dunbridge Academy.'

I think it's the first time he's properly looked at me. 'You're at that posh dump?' He laughs a deep, droning laugh and I want to put my hands over my ears. 'God, did she actually send you there? Your mother's insane.'

'I wanted to come here.' *To find you. Which is turning out to have been the biggest mistake of my life.*

'Aye, sure, wanted to.' He grins and nods to one side. I follow him towards the little bar, which looks a bit more welcoming than the pub earlier, at least. My dad drops the cigarette onto the street and I suddenly remember Mr Ringling had once mentioned during garden duty how many litres of groundwater are polluted by a single dropped cigarette butt. I say nothing as he stubs it out with the sole of his worn-out leather boot, then we walk in. It's brighter in here than in the pub, and the air smells of greasy food instead of beer and sweat.

'Hey, Joe,' he says, to the man behind the bar as he orders something to eat, which I don't follow. I don't understand anything any more. What's going on. Why I'm here and not at the school. With Henry. Anywhere I can carry on living with the illusion that my dad is the man I remember.

'How did you even find me?' he asks, as he sits down opposite me at one of the little round tables.

'From a friend.' I get the sense that he's not really bothered how I came by the information. 'She's from Glasgow and heard that you were performing.'

'Intriguing,' he says, leaning back a little way as the landlord brings over two beers. I hesitate as he puts them down in front of us. Two thoughts are running through my head. The alcohol ban at school and the question of why he didn't ask what I'd like to drink. But I don't have the nerve to say anything when he raises his glass invitingly.

So I follow suit. I clink glasses with my dad, but I want to run. My legs are tingling the way they always tingle when I can hardly bear to sit still. I want to run, as fast and as far away as possible. But I'm here now. I'm sitting with him. None of this makes any sense.

'So, what did you want to talk about, then?'

For a moment, I'm not sure that I've heard properly. Does he really mean that? We haven't seen each other for years and he asks what I want to talk about. There's so much I'd like to say to him. Can't he guess? Doesn't he think he owes me an explanation? Not even an apology – no, I'm not expecting that, but an explanation would be in order, wouldn't it? A reason, something that will let me stop making assumptions and over-thinking everything.

'Why did you go?' My voice is quiet and I hate how uncertain I sound. You can hear my hurt. How much I'm longing for him to look at me and say he's sorry. That he's missed me every day. Even if he's lying.

But he just sighs, deep and long, before he leans forward and plants his elbows on the table. 'Emma, I'm sure you're a clever lass,' he says, 'but grown-up stuff is complicated, you know? I had to get out of there, out of everything in Germany. Nothing was working out. Your mother and me, we just kept fighting. I needed a break from everything. Back then, I thought it would just be a break, but then I got the chance of a deal with this record company in the States. Didn't come to anything – the arseholes backed out at the last second and I didn't have the money for a flight home. I'd been counting on the advance so, well, there I was and I had to make the best of it. New music, new inspiration, you know the kind of thing.'

'But you could have got in touch,' I hear myself say. 'I wrote to you. A little while ago.'

'Oh, those Facebook messages,' he exclaims. 'Shit, I read them, yeah. Made me happy, seriously, Biscuit.'

I can't move.

He read them. He read them himself, it wasn't just some social-media guy, someone from his management who didn't tell him about them, the way I'd always kidded myself so as to be less disappointed. He'd got them, and it still didn't seem worth the effort of answering me. Suddenly I wish I'd never mentioned it.

'You could have answered.' My voice is quiet, and so's his sigh. I'm getting on his nerves. Me. I'm his daughter and I'm *getting on his nerves*. I can see it in his face. He takes another swig of beer without looking at me. 'I know, I know. I screwed up. All of it. But it wasn't because of you. I really wanted to come back but . . . What can I say? Maybe you'll understand when you're older.'

What can I say?

That he's sorry. He could say that. But I just sit there in silence.

'Hey, don't look at me like that, OK?' he says, and I jump. 'You look so much like your mother. God, is she still the same?'

I don't answer. I don't want to ask him what he means by that.

'What does she do? Still the high-powered lawyer, God's gift to the world? I bet you want to be like her one day, don't you?'

He has to stop this. He can't talk about Mum like that. He has no fucking right.

'She's always busy,' I mutter woodenly. But she never left me in the lurch like you did.

'Busy. Of course she is.' He studies me more intently. I want to look away. 'What about you? What are you into? D'you still play the piano?'

'I gave up.' *When you left. Because there was no one to practise with me any more.*

'What? Really? Shit, that's sad. You had real talent. Did your mother talk you out of it?'

'No,' I snap. 'She didn't.'

242

'Well, anyway. You could always start again. How old are you now? Fifteen?'

'Eighteen,' I whisper.

'Hm, OK, that's a bit too late, really. But school's more important, am I right?'

I say nothing, but he doesn't seem to expect an answer.

'Wow, eighteen,' he murmurs, as he reaches for his glass again. 'I was around that age when I dropped out of school.'

'Why did you do that?' I ask, because I have to ask something. I can't just sit here in silence the whole time. I've been waiting for this opportunity for too long.

'Why did I chuck it? Dunno. I couldn't be arsed with the whole thing. That school, it's a ridiculous place. I had a deal with this band, I could play for people. It was what I wanted.'

'Don't you regret it?' I ask. 'Not getting your A levels?'

Walking out on Mum?

Barely knowing me?

Turning into this?

'A levels, everyone always wants A levels . . . To do what? Go to university? God, no. I don't regret it. There's more to life than that, Biscuit.'

My fingers grip the cold, full glass and feel the condensation trickle beneath them.

'But tell me something about yourself. What kind of stuff d'you listen to?'

'Music, you mean?' I ask.

He laughs. 'Yeah, what else?'

'I listen to pretty much anything.' I swallow. 'I like indie and alternative, and more mainstream stuff too. Harry Styles, Taylor Swift, you know . . .'

He's not even listening. I'm sure of that when he starts humming a tune. I fall silent as he shuts his eyes and his head sways to and fro.

'Sorry, I'm sorry, but can you feel that?' He digs his phone out of his jacket pocket apparently to record what he's been humming. 'This city does something to me,' he declares, pocketing the mobile again. 'I reckon my next record's going to be my big break, I can feel it. God knows where it's coming from, but I've never written this many songs this fast. You have to give them a listen. I can give you my number, then I'll send you stuff, just let me know.'

My chest seems laced up, but I nod. His number. I don't know if I want it. Fortunately, I don't have to answer because the landlord puts two plates of fish and chips in front of us. My dad starts eating.

I have absolutely zero appetite, but I force myself to take a chip.

'Seriously, though,' he continues, looking up at me. 'What are you doing at that school? Morning assembly and study hour.' He laughs out loud. 'Is that still a thing?'

I nod.

'Such a heap of conservative bullshit. Just obey the rules and keep your mouth shut. You won't learn anything you need for real life there. Oh, God, your mother will kill me.

Don't listen to your old man, don't do what I did. I mean, look at me. I've got nothing, no proper job, nothing but the wrong women . . . But I have to make music. I have no other option. The fucking States did me over. Godawful country – everything's superficial, everything's fake, but maybe it has to be that way. My next album's gonna be about that. The songs are more honest than anything I've written before.'

He's just talking about himself, Emma.

I want to scream at the voice in my head to shut up. But I can't because it's right. He hardly asks any questions, and when he does, it's apparently only to dump on everything. Mum, Dunbridge Academy. It makes me so angry.

I just interrupt him. 'Do you remember that song you wrote for me?'

My father actually falls quiet, and when he looks at me, I know he's got no idea what I'm talking about.

'"For Emma",' I say. 'I found this tape. It was in a box, in the cellar.'

'"For Emma",' he repeats slowly. 'Yeah, yeah, I do, now you mention it. Shit, that was a long time ago. Back then I thought the song would make it onto the album. But somehow . . . It didn't fit. An album has to tell a story, you know. But it might work on the new one. Aye, I remember. It really could . . .'

'You'd do it again, wouldn't you?' I interrupt him a second time. 'You'd leave Mum again and just walk out, right? You'd promise me that you'd come back and take me on tour with you, and then I'd never hear from you again.'

'Emma, you just don't get it. Laura suffocated me – she drove me crazy. You just don't know your mother. She's totally obsessed . . .'

I stand up and he tails off.

It's not a conscious decision, it just happens. My mind is racing, yet my head is empty. I have to get out of here. I have to go. Get away from this man who's badmouthing my mum and doesn't even register that he's hurt other people. He doesn't care. There's only him and his music. Jacob Wiley, still just a guy with a guitar and no conscience.

And he doesn't even try to stop me when I turn away.

I think this is when I understand. That he doesn't give a shit. That it was a mistake to come here. That I'm not his daughter. Because he never wanted a daughter.

He might be saying something. I can't be certain because the blood is roaring in my ears. I step through the door into the darkness and don't feel a thing. I feel nothing. Not my racing heart and not the bitter feeling of knowing that this was a mistake.

I go weak at the knees as I recognize the figure who emerges from the darkness on the other side of the street. Henry's here. I'd almost forgotten him. He was here the whole time and now he's coming towards me.

'Everything OK?' he asks, as he stands in front of me, even though I'm sure he's known for ages that it's not. 'Emma, how did it go?'

I feel his hands on my arms and I can't bear them. I walk

down the pavement, I feel the tears in my eyes and I can't cry now.

I can't.

I. Just. Can't.

So I run.

HENRY

I'm glad he's taken her to this little place where I can see them through the window, sitting at a table, and not to some flat. He may be her father, but I've got a bad feeling about this whole thing. So has Emma. I can tell by the tension in her body. She's barely moving as she sits in front of him.

They seem to be eating something and I don't care that I'm stuck out here in the freezing cold. I have to be here when she comes out.

When she suddenly gets up, I think she's going to the loo. But she's not. She turns away and heads for the door. Her dad watches her, but stays sitting there.

My heart's going at double speed as she appears. Her face is controlled, but her clenched fists show me that nothing's OK.

She seems not to have seen me. Her eyes don't look at me until I walk over the road towards her. For a moment, I see the quiet panic on her face and I'm afraid Emma might burst into tears at any second, but before I've reached her, she's banished all emotion again.

'Everything OK?' I ask, as I stand there with her. Why isn't she saying anything? 'Emma, how did it go?'

She stares at me and I want to hug her tight, promise her everything will turn out OK, whatever it is. When I lay my hands on her arms I realize it was a mistake.

She flinches, tears glittering in her eyes. I stop as Emma steps a few feet to one side, ties back her hair and starts running.

I hesitate way too long. But it's obvious what she's doing. Running so as not to have to feel anything. Because she feels driven and helpless.

My legs start moving even before I've made up my mind. I run through Glasgow in the middle of the night, wondering what the hell happened. All I see are streetlights, headlights and bright shop signs. Emma's fast, but I'm fast too, these days. She took care of that. My heart is racing, my lungs are burning, but the adrenaline keeps my mind off them.

I catch up with Emma when she stops at a pedestrian crossing on a busy junction. I don't think about it for a second, just grab her arm,

'Stop this,' I gasp. 'Emma, please. Stop and talk to me.'

She wants to tear herself away when the lights change, but I won't let her. I hate having to hold her back, but I mustn't lose her in a strange city in the middle of the night.

248

'Talk to me,' I repeat, more insistently.

'I can't, OK?' Her chest is pumping, and I can feel her suppressed trembling. 'It was horrible. It was so bad. Is that enough for you?'

'Emma, I–'

'He was an arsehole. He didn't give a shit. Mum was right. She was right all those fucking years. But I didn't want to believe her. He didn't have an explanation, Henry! He had nothing. He said he'd do it again, walk out again and . . .'

'I'm sorry,' I whisper. 'I'm so bloody sorry, but that means he's not worth it. Nobody who just walks out on you is worth it. He's a lousy arsehole and you deserve so much better than a person like that in your life.'

Her eyes dart around restlessly and I can see the tear-stains on her cheeks.

My eyes are on her mouth, and, God, I have to. I have to kiss her – I have to, I have to, I have to. I can feel her pain and I can't bear it. I'm still holding her tight. We're so close to each other that our jackets are touching. I'd just have to bend over slightly and our lips would be too.

Emma's stopped breathing. I know because I'm holding my breath, too. Her mouth is slightly open, and her eyes flit over my face. She digs her hands into my jacket pockets, maybe by accident, maybe on purpose. In the end, it's hard to say which of us leans in. Maybe we both do, at the same time. Because we can't help it. Because I want her

SARAH SPRINZ

closer – because I need her closer. Because it's pointless trying to convince myself otherwise.

There's only about an inch between our mouths.

But I can't. It's not right.

I remember Grace. Oh, hell, I remember Grace.

And I pull back.

250

20

EMMA

We catch the last train back to Edinburgh and don't speak another word to each other. We sit side by side, but with a safe distance between us, and I feel dirty. This whole stupid evening, my pathetic father, cold smoke, stale air. And Henry so close to me that I couldn't help myself and just leaned in at the exact moment he did too.

We didn't kiss because he stopped us. Just as well, because I wouldn't have done. I don't think I would. No, I know I wouldn't. There's no way I'd have stopped him because I'm weak, a failure. God, what was I thinking?

Henry pulled back at the last second and it was a slap in the face. Because for a tiny moment I thought he actually wanted it.

He should never have come. It's ridiculous. Just friends . . .

251

He said that and I nodded. And I'd have let him kiss me. Because I'm a stupid arsehole.

There are too many thoughts, and they're all driving me mad.

That crappy pub, my dad, that horrible conversation with him: all of it seems a lifetime ago by the time we reach Edinburgh. We're the only passengers on the bus to Ebrington, and I want to cry. If Henry weren't here, I would. But he is here. He's sitting next to me and I can't look him in the eye.

Not even when we get off the bus, walk down the lane and slip through the gate. Almost all the windows are dark now.

'You can go through here. Nobody will see you this way,' says Henry, pointing to our left.

I nod. He doesn't say, 'I'll walk you to your wing,' like he normally does. Of course he doesn't.

And I don't say anything. I don't thank him for coming with me. I don't say sorry for almost kissing him. Which I should. I have to: we can't part like this, for God's sake!

Henry stops as I turn back.

'Henry, I'm sor—'

'No,' he says quietly. 'Emma, please . . .'

He looks at me, I see the pleading in his eyes and I understand. We'll never speak of it again. Because it never happened.

I'm not sure if anything has ever hurt as much as it does when I turn away again. No, that's not true. I'm pretty sure it hasn't. This evening's in a class of its own. Because I've lost hope twice.

I don't cry until I'm lying in my bed. Nobody caught me, and if they had I wouldn't have cared. Because, let's be honest, what's the point of me being at this school now?

HENRY

My head is empty when I ring the Whitmores' doorbell the next day. I should have planned exactly what I'm going to say to Grace. She deserves that. A proper conversation. Not this. Not this absolute panic reaction. This feels like impulsive damage limitation when actually it's way too late.

I've fallen in love with Emma. I've known that since she was standing in front of me in Glasgow and I couldn't kiss her. I've known that since I slept beside her, since when I haven't been able to forget the scent of her. I've known it since she gave me that mildly sceptical Emma-look and my heart skipped a beat.

I've fallen in love with Emma and I have to split up with Grace and there's no way of doing that without hurting her. And Grace deserves better than to be hurt. She's always done everything right. But she deserves better and it's breaking my heart that I can't be the guy to give it to her.

I shiver as the door opens. Grace is wearing jeans and a yellow T-shirt.

I wait for her to say, 'Oh, hi,' and kiss me, then step aside for me to walk in. But she just looks at me and I'm sure she understands what all this means. She looks me in the face and something flickers in her eyes. A tiny emotion, a tiny spark of fear that tells me she's been waiting for this. That Grace knew that eventually I'd be standing at her door looking at her like this. We both knew it. We've spoken less to each other in the last few weeks than ever before. The end was in sight. It was just a matter of time. But neither of us expected it to happen. Not yet anyway.

'Can I come in?' I ask, and Grace wakes up from her trance.

'Yes, sure.' She steps aside. No hello kiss. 'Is everything OK?'

I nod, even though nothing's OK. Absolutely nothing, and it's all my own fault.

I step through the doorway into this house, which has felt for ages like my second home. But it isn't any more. It's Grace's home and I was merely allowed to be a guest here for a while.

'Aren't your parents here?' I ask, when I notice how quiet it is.

'No. It's just me.'

'Oh, right.' That's probably a good thing. We can talk in peace, which means I'm really going to have to do this. No more excuses or apologies. Just the truth. Painful, unpleasant truth.

I raise my head as Grace shuts the door, and I shove my hands into my trouser pockets. Should I ask her if we can go to her room? Or sit on the sofa? Where's the best place for this kind of conversation? I didn't think this through at all.

And then I just start babbling. 'I was in Glasgow with Emma yesterday,' I say, even before Grace has turned to face me. There's confusion in her face. 'She met her dad there. It didn't go very well. I think he's a bit of an arsehole and—'

'Henry,' she interrupts, 'why are you telling me this?'

'Because then I almost kissed her.'

It's a bomb in word form and it goes off silently between us. Grace looks stunned, but she gets herself back under control amazingly quickly. At that moment I see she knew everything. She just never said. Not once. She was nice to Emma, didn't utter a bad word about her or doubt me. But she saw everything, of course she did, and I'm the shittiest human being in the entire world. I want to say something but I can't. Not until she's said something.

Grace nods slowly. 'OK.' It sounds more like a question.

'Grace, I'm sorry, I – I didn't mean to . . .'

'Stop it.' Her voice is quiet but clear. 'Stop saying things you don't mean.'

I open my mouth but she doesn't let me speak.

'You're not sorry. You wanted to kiss her. I've seen the way you look at her, Henry.'

I say nothing and it's cowardly. I know that. It's my bloody job to have this conversation and I can't do it.

'This is the end, isn't it?' Grace asks, and when she smiles uncertainly and looks at me with glittering eyes, the tears start to sting mine too.

'I think so.' My voice sounds croaky.

Grace shuts her eyes briefly. A tear runs down her cheek. She takes a deep breath, then looks at me again.

'It's not true that I don't mean what I just said,' I say. 'I am sorry, Grace. I'm so sorry for hurting you. I didn't want to. And you don't deserve it. You deserve someone who'll go to Oxford with you and want the same things you want. And that – that's not me.'

It's crazy how quiet we're being. How silently Grace cries and how hollow my head feels. It's like a crash in slow motion, one we'd seen coming. For weeks. We've been mentally preparing ourselves for this but that doesn't make it hurt any less.

'We're not Henry and Grace from the first form any more, and that's OK,' says Grace. I hear the tremor in her voice and hear her trying to suppress it. 'We're older, we've both grown up.' She pauses. 'But, sadly, we've grown in different directions.'

I nod, against my will. I see Grace with the plaits she had in the first form and remember how she used to cheer me up when Mum and Dad had to go back to the airport. I see her beaming with joy at good exam results, and the two of us during never-ending summer nights, but now it *is* coming to an end.

'It feels like I cheated on you.' The tears choke off my voice, but I can't stop them. Because it *really* feels like that. Because Grace was loyal, always, and I wasn't. I'm leaving her. I'm splitting up with her. For a girl I've known just a few weeks. Which is nothing compared to the time I've spent with Grace. But it was enough to show me how much more could be possible. That time with Grace is nice and time with Emma is indescribable.

Grace stands facing me in silence as I cry, and doesn't look at me. '*Did* you cheat on me?' she asks, and there's no hint of accusation in her voice. I know that if I had, I'd admit it now. Because Grace deserves the truth. No matter how much it hurts.

'No,' I say.

'OK.' She nods without a second's hesitation because she trusts me.

'But I slept at hers,' I blurt out. 'A while ago, she was upset, I just went round to hers to talk and then . . . I slept there. In her bed. We were both dressed, and nothing–'

'Henry, it's OK,' she interrupts. Calmly. We aren't fighting, we aren't hurting each other. Not intentionally at any rate. We're so fricking mature and grown-up, and there it is. The proof that I like Grace, admire her, respect her, but I don't love her. Because if I did, we'd never be able to speak about all this so calmly.

'I hate hurting you like this,' I whisper.

'I know. I hate it too. But I want you to be happy. I want

that because you mean so bloody much to me, Henry. And, yes, it hurts, but sometimes change does hurt.'

'I want you to be happy too. And we don't make each other happy any more.'

'No, we don't.'

'Can I give you a hug?' I ask her quietly, but don't move. I just wait for her to nod. But Grace doesn't. The tears glisten in her eyes, and then she slowly shakes her head.

No . . . This is the moment when I realize what's just happened. That it's over. Irreversibly over.

'OK.' My body trembles. It feels like all this is just a dream. 'I'm sor—'

'Go . . . please,' says Grace, her voice breaking on the second word.

I turn away without touching her. I've hugged her a thousand times. I've done it light-heartedly. I've done it thinking that this will be for ever. But the truth is that nothing is for ever. And I'd have held her for longer if I'd known it would be the last time.

I don't feel a thing.

There's nothing. Nothing at all. I'm simply empty, and something about that scares me.

I've been so composed since I walked down the Whitmores' front steps and Grace shut the door behind me. It felt so surreal to walk back to school in glorious sunshine, the way I've done so often in the last few years.

It must be the last scrap of common sense within me that carries me to the door at the end of our corridor. I know. I don't know what I'll do if he isn't there, I haven't thought ahead beyond this moment. Seconds tick away, then the door flies open.

Sinclair looks like he's only just pulled on his hoodie and I'm bracing myself for some remark. But he just looks at my face. 'What happened?'

Fuck, coming here was a mistake. I can't speak. Not even to my best friend. I just want to cry until I'm so tired that I fall asleep, so that I won't have to feel all this any more.

'Shit, Henry, what's wrong?' Sinclair repeats, glancing past me. The corridor's empty. I'm empty. There's no point to anything. 'Is something up with Grace?' he asks, and I don't get how he does that. How he always knows just what my problem is.

My throat is still choked up as I nod.

'What's wrong? Is she not well? Come on, say something! What's—'

'Nothing's wrong with her.' I get some words out, and my voice has never sounded so weird. Sinclair stares at me and then I just say it. 'It's over.'

He opens his mouth. 'What?'

'We split up. I split up with her. Over. Finished.' I'm raising my voice with every word, my eyes are burning again, and Sinclair understands. He takes my wrist and pulls me into his room, past the wall by the door, which is plastered layers deep with the Polaroids he started taking in the second form – one of everyone who entered our shared room for the first time. There's a picture of me right at the top, next to the ones of Gideon, Omar and Sinclair. The door shuts and I just want to cry.

'Oh, boy. OK, come here, sit down.' Sinclair pushes me onto his unmade bed, and I wipe my eyes with the sleeve of my hoodie as he turns away. He digs around in a drawer, pushes aside a tea caddy with the school logo on it, and reaches behind it. Before I can ask what the hell he's looking for, he's straightened up again. In one hand, he's got a packet of Tunnock's teacakes and there's a bottle of gin in the other. He raises his eyebrows enquiringly and I make a grab for both.

I've never cared less about breaking the rules. The gin burns my throat. It has to stop. This terrible pain, I can't bear it any longer.

I split up with Grace. It's really true.

'OK.' Sinclair sits down next to me, takes the bottle away from me and puts it on the desk. Then he hugs me. That's the moment when I really start blubbing. Not in a cool way. Not cool at all. It's the exact opposite of cool.

Sinclair doesn't comment. He just waits till I've calmed down a bit. 'So, you split up with Grace,' he says slowly. 'And the reason for that is called Emma.'

I shut my eyes because there's no point in denying it. 'It's that obvious, is it?'

'Nope,' he contradicts me. 'But I'm not your best friend for nothing.'

'I screwed up,' I whisper. 'Shit, Sinclair, I've—'

'Henry,' he interrupts harshly. 'Stop that shit. You haven't screwed anything up. You're smart. You'll have done the right thing.'

'I split up,' I repeat slowly. 'With Grace.' And it's almost as though I hadn't taken it in until this moment. I had that conversation. I didn't just think the words, I said them out loud. Words that I can never take back.

'Does Emma know?'

'No,' I say hastily. 'Course not. She's . . . I dunno, but she doesn't know about it.'

'You have to go to her,' says Sinclair. 'It's important for you guys to talk.'

'I can't yet. It would look like I was just hooking up with her on the rebound. And don't you dare say that's just what I'm doing.'

'Well, in theory . . .' he begins, but he laughs as I glare at him. 'I'm joking, Henry.'

'I'm not in the mood.'

'I noticed.' He hands me the bottle. 'Well, have a drink if you're not going to talk to Emma today.'

I take it in silence and stare at the *Dead Poets Society* poster by his bookcase.

Today . . . Right now I don't feel like I'll ever be able to speak to Emma again without it coming across in the wrong way. I split up with Grace and a naïve part of me thought that would solve all my problems. But that's not true. I don't feel even a tiny bit better.

The gin burns in my throat, but what do I care?

'Whoa, whoa, whoa, Henry, enough.' Sinclair takes the bottle away again. 'Or you'll be steaming in ten minutes.'

'That was the idea.'

'We have to go down to dinner.'

'No way am I going down to dinner.'

Sinclair rolls his eyes. 'You always were a drama queen,' he murmurs. 'Well, at least eat one of these. Here. And now talk about how you're feeling.'

'I can't talk about how I'm feeling.'

'Henry, that's my bit. *You* can, and we both know it.'

I peel the foil off one of the teacakes. 'No, you're right. Talking about feelings stinks.'

'But you feel better afterwards.'

'It was a mistake, wasn't it?' I blurt. 'It was a mistake, right?'

Sinclair leans back against the wall and hands me the bottle again. 'Does it feel like a mistake?'

'I don't know.'

'I think you do.'

'No.' I sigh. 'Stop it. Not that . . .'

'Henry, answer my question.'

'I don't know, OK? I don't know a single thing any more.'

I gulp. 'I had everything. Fuck, why am I like this? Everything was perfect the way it was, wasn't it?'

Sinclair shrugs his shoulders. 'Was it?'

'Stop asking all my questions back at me.'

'Why?'

'Cos it's driving me nuts.'

'Because you have to face the truth,' he corrects me. 'And that hurts. It's OK, Henry, that's what the gin's for.'

I drink because it's all pointless. 'It was perfect,' I say in the end. 'For a long time it really was perfect, but it wasn't enough. It was good, it was nice, and I had no idea that that isn't everything. D'you understand? It was like driving down the motorway with the handbrake on.'

'Not good for the gears,' he remarks.

'What's that got to do with the gears?'

'Well, the engine then, whatever. Either way, it wasn't good.'

'It really wasn't good,' I mumble, taking another swig. 'Or, yes, it was good. But underwhelming-good.'

'And Emma's overwhelming-good?'

'Emma is . . . No idea.'

'She's hot, that's for sure.'

'She's not hot, she's beautiful,' I say.

'Henry, stop drinking, you're getting sentimental.' Sinclair goes to grab the bottle, but I pull it away in time.

'It's true,' I insist. 'Have you ever looked at her, Sinclair?'

'You're in lust with her.'

'I'm afraid it's more than that.'

'Have you shagged her?'

'God, no,' I retort hastily. 'I'd never . . .'

'OK, fine, you have principles, got it.'

'Think of Grace,' I mumble, letting him take the bottle this time. 'How shitty would that have been of me?'

I don't know if I'm imagining the bitter twist to his lips as he drinks. 'Pretty shitty.' When I don't say anything, he raises his head. 'What? Don't look at me like that.'

'Are you thinking about Tori? She's dating Valentine, these days, right?'

'The guy's a weapon, but I guess she knows that,' he says curtly. 'And stop changing the subject. We're talking about you and Emma.'

About me and Emma. I don't know why, but at that second, I allow myself to think it for the first time. Emma and me. The two of us. I want that so badly.

'You have to go to her,' Sinclair says, at the same moment I think I have to go to her.

'I can't,' I mumble. 'Not now. I have to get this right, you know?'

'You're Henry, you get everything right.'

I laugh miserably and reach for the bottle.

'No, no, I get it,' he says. 'So wait a while, then.'

I want to go to Emma right now. More than anything. I want to be rash and impulsive. I want to kiss her and . . .

264

Shit. I really do want to shag her. But with feeling. Hard but with feeling. God, Sinclair's got to take that gin off me. How is it possible that the bottle's almost half empty?

'We almost kissed,' I say. 'Me and Emma. Yesterday, when we were in Glasgow. She met someone important to her there and afterwards ... It almost happened but I pulled away at the last moment. Not because I didn't want to. Because of Grace. But Emma ... I think she took it totally the wrong way.'

'Man, of course she did. How else would you have taken it?'

As a brush-off. Obviously. I pushed her away.

'I'm such an arsehole,' I mumble, as I think about the hurt expression in Emma's eyes.

'A super-sensible arsehole.' Sinclair shrugs his shoulders.

'I have to talk to her,' I announce, and I'm about to stand up but Sinclair pulls me back down to the bed.

'You're drunk, Henry.'

'Don't care.'

'I do, though. And so do you. You want to be sober when you tell Emma you love her.'

I groan. And I'd like to press pause. I'd like to stop being so confused. I'd just like to do the right thing. But instead I'm leaving Grace – because I can't see any future with her – for Emma. And I don't have any future with her either because she's leaving in a year. What's the point?

At that moment I understand. There is no point in love.

There was just the heat in my belly and the fluttering in my chest the very first moment I saw her. At the airport, when I didn't know who she was but was sure I wanted to find out. And I tried not to let myself get involved with her, I really tried, but the truth is that I want to kiss Emma Wiley. I want her in my bed. I want to be the guy she tells everything to, whose arms she falls asleep in. And I'm not prepared to deny that any longer.

21

EMMA

All I can think of is Henry and that horrible moment when he pulled back. We don't meet all weekend, which is fine by me. I skip the dining room and go to Irvine's for pasta and tomato sauce, which I cook in the kitchen for our wing. Anything's better than bumping into Henry. Or Olive, who keeps giving me the kind of look I'd give anyone who wanted to pinch my best friend's boyfriend.

And it's not even true. I didn't want to. I didn't want to fall in love with Henry. I wanted a quiet life, but he had to go and turn up, and be drop-dead gorgeous, like I'd been begging for it. I don't want to see Henry or Grace, Olive or anyone else. But I don't want to think about Glasgow or my dad either. I have to push it all down, so I run. Two and a half hours on Saturday, cross-country, until I end up in some forest, with no idea where I am and get scared that I'll never find my way back to school.

I do get back though, by which time I can't feel my feet, and I have a long, hot shower. And then I lie motionless on my bed. Henry and I almost kissed. And I wanted to. I wanted him to. I didn't want him to pull away. I wanted him to put his hand behind my head and push me up against a wall, with his whole sinewy body and the unrestrained desire that was in his eyes for just one second. He can't sleep next to me and wake up with a hard-on, then expect me not to think stuff like this. He can't ask me how I am, listen to everything, always, go to Glasgow with me and follow me through the city. It's not OK. I hate him. I hate Henry Bennington. I hate Noah Friedrich. I hate Jacob Wiley. I hate every fucking man on this planet. And, most of all, I hate myself.

I press the balls of my thumbs against my closed eyes as the tears sting them.

It's not fair. I thought I'd feel better if I came here. But I feel worse. I've found my dad and I wish I could have my naïve ignorance back.

I can't think about it. All of it is driving me crazy. I should be studying, reading the set novel for English, doing my prep, using my time here wisely, but I'm not doing any of it. I'm lying motionless on this mattress, hoping that eventually I'll fall asleep.

*

I don't see Henry on Monday either. Not at morning assembly or in the dining room as he seems to be skipping breakfast.

I only feel Sinclair's eyes resting heavily on me, then Olive's as I pass her and Grace on the way to lessons. Grace's eyes are red and swollen, and I can't breathe. Has he told her everything? Did they fight? Over me? Did she find out for herself? Has she forgiven him?

I don't know, and it's none of my business. I can't concentrate on PSHE. Not with Olive and Grace staring at my back. I want to get out of here.

I have a free period now before English, but instead of going to the library, like normal, I'm heading for my room. Or that's the plan as I make for the west wing after class. I'm probably imagining it, but it feels like every pupil in this entire school is watching me. And that's not possible.

All the same, I keep my head down. At least until I pass a little group of people and hear someone say: 'No, they split up, seriously. Come on, you could see she'd been crying.'

My first impulse is to stop, turn back and ask who they're talking about. It could be any random couple, but somehow, I'm absolutely certain.

'That's wild,' says one of the girls. 'Grace and Henry were so perfect together.'

My heart starts racing, and the thoughts are whirling in my mind.

They split up?

They fucking split up?

Are they mad?

I force myself to walk on when I feel them staring at me. Whispers behind hands. Nods in my direction.

'Congratulations.' I jump as I hear Olive's voice. 'Satisfied now?'

My blood runs cold as she walks past me.

'Livy,' murmurs Grace. 'Stop it.'

'Does she think she can come here and just push her way in between everybody? First Tori, then you and Henry. I'm sick of it. Everything's changed since she started.'

'Well, that's down to you.' I don't know where Tori sprang from, but her voice has never sounded as chilly as it does now, as she steps to my side. 'I am quite capable of deciding for myself whom I want to spend time with, and I guess Henry is too.'

Olive exhales, and Grace tries to pull her away.

'And, yeah, break-ups are shit, but there wouldn't be the tiniest problem between us two if you didn't keep turning everything into one.'

'Wow, good to know it's all my fault,' Olive hisses, vanishing into the crowd. Grace follows her after a brief glance in our direction.

'Sorry.' Tori sighs. 'But you shouldn't take it personally.'

'I didn't want this,' I blurt. 'I didn't want to come between you and I didn't want Henry and Grace to . . .'

'Emma, there are two sides to everything.' Tori glares warningly at assorted younger kids, who actually walk away

270

now. Even so, I still feel like the entire corridor's looking at me. 'Come on.'

She takes my wrist and pulls me after her. I want to cry as I follow her into the inner courtyard, despite the drizzle. The air is chilly and heavy with rain, and I force myself to take some deep breaths as I stand with Tori under the narrow eaves, which shelter us from the wet.

'So it's true then?' I ask her. 'They broke up?'

Tori nods. 'Henry finished with her. On Saturday. Sinclair told me so.'

Saturday . . . So, the day after we were in Glasgow. I shiver. Henry's face right next to mine, his warm breath on my lips: I can still feel it.

'You went out together on Friday, didn't you?' says Tori.

I don't answer, stare into space. The dark cobbles are damp and glistening. A couple of hyperactive juniors run through the rain in their blue Dunbridge jackets. 'Yes,' I admit. 'We were in Glasgow. We almost kissed.'

To my surprise, I don't hear a shocked intake of breath from Tori. In fact, I don't hear anything. When I turn to her, there's just a slight smile on her lips.

'But he pulled away before anything could happen.' Everything in me is fighting not to say the words out loud. Because it's so damn humiliating.

'He's Henry. He always has to do everything right,' Tori remarks, as if it was the most natural thing in the world. 'He's the most Cancery Cancer I've ever met.'

'No, you don't understand,' I mutter. 'It was horrible. We didn't say a word to each other after that. I know he regrets it.'

'Emma, the guy's crazy about you. Sinclair says the same. And we've known him for ever, so trust me.'

All the same, I don't dare believe what she's saying. I can't allow myself to hope. It would hurt too much.

'Have you seen each other since?' Tori asks.

I shake my head. 'No.'

'Maybe you should talk.'

I say nothing, but just the idea almost turns my stomach. I can't talk to Henry. I smashed up his relationship. I came to this school and caused nothing but chaos.

'You have to talk,' Tori repeats.

I nod, to keep her happy, because what have I got to say to Henry? That he's made the wrong choice and ought to ask Grace to take him back. They're made for each other. They're the perfect couple, everybody knows that.

But my heart keeps racing. I'm weak at the knees. Henry and Grace have split up.

The bell goes for the next lesson. I follow Tori back inside, dodge running juniors, and pray not to bump into Henry.

HENRY

The news got round quicker than I'd have liked but I'm not surprised. Gossip in this school travels at a speed that would be the envy of any news agency. I could spend time puzzling over who leaked the information that we've split up, but I don't care. Everyone was sure to hear about it sooner or later. And I haven't the energy to worry about it.

I'm empty. Since being at Grace's on Saturday, then waking up with a pounding skull after my evening with Sinclair, I've been empty. I couldn't cry any more or speak to anyone, it wasn't possible. I might have called Maeve if she weren't in Kenya right now, where she's sure to have more important things to do than listen to her kid brother's love woes. So I spent the whole of Sunday in my room, only leaving my bed to go to the bathroom or get the minimum of nutrition into my body.

Sinclair came round – without alcohol this time – and we watched some Netflix series that I can't remember anything about, and I guess I must have fallen asleep, because suddenly he was gone.

And then Monday came and I couldn't hide any longer. It was awful to walk down the corridors this morning and pass little whispering gaggles. Yet that's nothing to the pain I feel when I remember Grace's red eyes, which show me that it must be way harder still for her.

We didn't blank each other, we gave each other tense smiles and said hello. We're so fucking sensible and grown-up, and I hate it. Because it hurts all the same.

No idea if Emma's got wind of our break-up, but I'd be surprised if she hasn't. But what was I expecting? That she'd come to me and we'd be able to pick up where we left off with that almost-kiss last week? That's bollocks.

I see her again for the first time in English. Head down, no eye contact as I pass her desk. She's staring at a blank page in her diary, and I don't have the guts to say anything to her. Not here, in front of everybody else, let alone Mr Ward, who appears on the dot, as always.

I can't concentrate on anything and I'm sure Emma's the same. Mr Ward's still got it in for her. And today his questions catch me out too because obviously I spent the whole weekend doing anything but my damn prep.

I don't know how I dragged myself down to rugby training and I have even less idea how I'm going to get through the next hour and a half on the pitch in the drizzle. Mr Cormack's in a bad mood, Valentine's not holding back with the dumb wisecracks, but I don't care. I just want to get back to my room, to my bed, to sleep and not think about anything until the chaos that's my life lately has miraculously sorted itself out again.

Running with Emma seems to be over for good. We haven't discussed it, but it's obvious. At the Tuesday-morning run, we each do our own thing. I still haven't spoken to her. And the longer I leave it, the more wrong it feels to go up to her and say, *Hey, I dumped Grace, how about us getting together now?* I know what that would look like. Like the kind of heartless bastard who just hops from one girl to the next.

But it's not like that. OK, if I'm brutally honest with myself, I guess Emma is the reason I split up with Grace. But she's not the *only* reason. It was already inevitable that we'd break up. Emma wasn't the cause, she was the final straw. She showed me that there is more. That majorly intense emotions like these can be terrifying. And I want majorly intense emotions. But not this crappy despair. Although maybe that's just part of it. At least it proves I'm still alive, doesn't it?

Mind you, I didn't think about what would happen next. What comes after I've done the thing I was most afraid of? Not relief, that's for sure. It's shit. I want to say so much to Emma, but I don't dare. Maybe we both need time to understand what happened in Glasgow on Friday. What that means for us. Yet at the same time all I want is to go to Emma and ask her how she's doing. How she's coping now that she knows who her father is. I think back to that moment when we walked into the pub and she saw him. I remember Emma's frozen expression and motionless body, the disappointment and pain in her face when she walked out of that restaurant without him and he let her go.

But I don't ask Emma how she is. I watch her from a distance, pissed off with myself that she's avoiding me. But I have to accept that she doesn't want to talk to me. Because that's obvious. Even though it's driving me crazy.

After chemistry, I'm putting away Sinclair's and my kit when suddenly she's standing right next to me. Emma, in a white lab coat that's way too big for her, Bunsen burner still in hand.

I can't move. Apparently neither can she. My head is suddenly full of words, but my tongue's been struck dumb. I can hear voices, scraping chair legs, the usual end-of-lesson sounds. I can feel my heart pounding in my throat.

I only come back to life as Emma's eyes wander past me. To the cupboards, which I'm blocking.

'Can I . . .?' she begins, and I immediately step aside.

'Yeah, sorry.' My heart racing again, I stay beside her. I've got this nervous dizziness because I know I'm going to have to say something. More than *sorry* or even *I apologize*, although those are the only things that feel right. *How are you? Could we talk?* Something like that would be appropriate.

'Emma?' My voice sounds rough and it has some effect on her. I can see that and, no, I'm not so desperate that I'm imagining it. Emma jumps. The beakers rattle as she puts the burner into the cupboard.

'Be careful with the equipment,' Ms Ventura says sharply, but I don't think Emma even hears her. Her whole body is tense as she turns away again.

'Could we maybe—'

'What? What, Henry?' She cuts me off.

It's the first time she's looked me properly in the eye. And I can see all her pain. Eyes like fire, burning with reproach. Because I'm not doing anything, just staying so bloody passive. At this moment I wonder if I've waited too long. Or if

I should have kissed her, regardless of Grace. And in the same second, I hate myself for thinking that.

It's just a heartbeat. A missed chance, then Emma turns away. I want to grab her arm but my hands are like lead.

She walks back to her place.

EMMA

No way he'll be there, Emma.

Why did I know that wouldn't be true when I let Tori convince me to come to the midnight party? Did she and Sinclair take it upon themselves to lure Henry and me to this place, to force us to have a conversation? If so, it was a seriously crappy idea. I see him the moment I follow Tori into the old greenhouse, and my first impulse is to turn on my heel and leave.

I stop in the doorway and Salome crashes into me. Tori looks apologetically at me over her shoulder. I ought to make a run for it, but I stay put when Henry glances in our direction. He looks knackered, but he's still gorgeous, and I hate it. I hate that I instantly forget everyone else in the room when his eyes rest as heavily on me as they're doing now. I hate that I'm boiling hot despite the pissing rain outside. I hate that I can't help thinking about Glasgow. About Henry, who spent so long waiting for me. His hands on my arms, his face so close to mine. I don't know why I keep subjecting myself to this humiliation in memory form, but I can't wipe away the images. I have to get away from here.

'Oops, I didn't know . . .' Tori begins, as I catch her eye. She really does look sorry, but I just shake my head.

'Nice one, Tori,' I mumble, before I turn away.

HENRY

Gideon cracked some joke, Sinclair's laughing loudly, and I'm swigging out of this bottle again because everything's pointless. I don't want to be here, but of course I came anyway because I kind of hoped Emma might be.

She isn't. I look towards the door every time anyone walks into the greenhouse, but it's never Emma. And if it was, I don't know what I'd do. Ask her if we can talk? Here, at this party? Great idea. She's sure to be in the mood for that.

'Hey.' I feel Sinclair's hand on my shoulder and raise my head. He gestures towards the door.

It's her. I stand up, and the ground sways beneath me. I put the bottle down, not looking. I only have eyes for Emma. Her ash blonde hair, fallen across her face and slightly damp from the rain. Her eyes flick over the greenhouse and she spots me right away. I jump as we gaze at each other. I know I mustn't wait a second longer. We have to talk. I have to apologize, explain everything to her and find out how she's doing.

Sinclair steps aside, unasked, to let me through and says nothing when I have to grip his shoulder. Maybe the alcohol wasn't such a good idea, but I can't change that now.

Emma's outside again, and I wonder if I imagined things just now. Tori's expression is hard to read as she stares at me, while Olive glares murderously as I leave the greenhouse. My eyes take a moment to adjust to the darkness. Then I make out Emma's silhouette a few feet away. She's wrapped her arms around her body and is on her way back to the school buildings.

I start to run.

'Wait!' The crunch of my feet on the gravel is the only sound in the night. I'm afraid she might start running, too, but Emma just walks steadily on. Which might mean she'll hear me out. I dare to hope a tiny bit. 'Emma.'

She whirls around as I touch her shoulder. 'What?' she snarls.

'Emma, I'm so –'

'Have you been drinking? Henry, are you kidding me? What's going on here?'

'I hoped we could talk,' I begin, but Emma laughs at that.

'Talk? What about? Grace?' She shakes her head. 'So it's true?' She stares at me, and suddenly it's like I can't move my tongue. I can't speak, yet she deserves an explanation.

'Shit, Henry, is it true? Did you break up with Grace?'

Her eyes bore through me and, suddenly, I'm livid. With Emma, with Grace, but above all with myself.

'What if I did?' I snap back.

'Did you break up with Grace?' she repeats, even though she's apparently known for ages.

'Yes, yes, for God's sake!' I blurt out. 'I broke up with her. You heard right.'

'Why?'

'Why what?'

'Why did you do that?'

'I don't know,' I snarl.

'Don't lie to me!'

'Being with Grace wasn't enough any more. It was just better this way.'

'Are you out of your mind, Henry? God, you two were perfect! You'll regret this, you'll–'

'You have no idea!' Suddenly, we're both yelling. 'You want to know why I broke up with her? You really want to know, huh?' I'm drunk, I have to stop this. But Emma doesn't flinch as I take a step towards her. 'Why do you think I did it?'

'Because you're an arsehole,' she whispers, and I get it. Because I'm no better than her shitty ex-boyfriend or her disappointment of a father. The men in her life who play with her and drop her as soon as things get tough.

'Do you think it was fun for me?' I snap. 'Do you really think I wanted to be that guy? The guy who hurts Grace and throws away what we have? Shit, Emma, three years, three shitting years. I hate being the arsehole, but you gave me no choice.'

'No.' Her index finger jabs my chest. 'Oh, no, Henry Bennington. You take that back. I've got nothing to do with this. You chose, not me. I never fucking asked you!'

'Didn't you? Didn't you? So, you didn't look at me like that, and tell me all that stuff, and think it wouldn't bother me? For God's sake, I didn't want this! I thought things were perfect with Grace but I had no idea that that wasn't love. That there's more than that. I didn't plan to fall in love with you, Emma Wiley, but I'm only human. And you know it. So don't ask me why I did it. We both know.' I take the last step towards her. 'I did it so that I could finally do *this*.'

EMMA

I've never been kissed like this before, by Henry in the shelter of the darkness. Hands in hair, furious and desperate. Whole body, pressing me back against this cold wall.

His lips are as soft as I'd hoped. His hands are strong and skilful. It takes me a whole four seconds to be more than frozen, taken unawares, for me to be able to dig my fingers into his hair. I pull him closer because I *need* him closer. His hips press against mine, his body so hungry for me. I have to lean my head back slightly as he pushes his knee between my legs and pulls me up onto his thigh with hot hands on my bum, until my body consists of nothing but heat and throbbing. I'm dizzy because I can't breathe and I don't want him to stop. Noses crashing together, his lips on my teeth, his tongue in my mouth. I hadn't expected Henry to be able to kiss like this. To be able to hold me so tightly and press me against this wall, almost rough, but actually gentle. It's better than anything.

And then he just stops.

The night is quiet and there is only our heavy breathing as he suddenly pulls back. His eyes are on me, heavy as ton-weights, almost startled, as I dig my fingers harder into his forearm, wanting to pull him back.

'Sorry,' he murmurs, his eyes gliding over me, lips glistening, and he has to carry on. He can't just stop now, he has to keep kissing me or I'll die. 'I . . . May I, actually?'

'Yes,' I gasp, because his voice sounds so deep and raw, and the throbbing between my legs is unbearable.

'I didn't ask you if you . . .' He falls silent as I lean forwards. Kissing Henry feels like the most intimate act of my entire life and I don't want it ever to end. It's a flowing movement, his mouth is open, his tongue hot.

'How about you?' I breathe, as he shoves his fingers into my hair again. His thumbs run over my cheeks, he pulls me closer, so close, until my brow is against his. 'Do you want to?'

'Emma, I've wanted you since we got on that plane,' he murmurs, and I have to shut my eyes. 'It's been driving me crazy, every day that I've seen you and haven't been able to kiss you.'

'Now you can kiss me,' I say, and he finally does what I want him to do.

It's more than just kissing. I know that as Henry moves his hips against me and I wish that he'd touch me through the thin fabric of my leggings. I want his fingers between my legs, his scent in my nose, his heat on my skin. I want all of that right now. I've wanted it for so long.

So I grab his hands and pull them downwards. He immediately shoves them inside my jacket and under my jumper. His fingertips are cool, and I'd happily have us believe that that's why I get goosebumps and they're not from Henry's lips on my throat. A muffled yearning sound escapes me as he strokes upwards over my sides. Henry shudders as he hears it. I don't know if I've ever found anything such a turn-on as the certainty that I can cause this reaction in him. It's indescribable, and I feel beautiful.

We're moving in a rhythm that's part of something bigger than ourselves. I don't know what it is, only that I have to have it. My knees are weak, my head is full of fog, and I'm not even drunk. Henry gently tugs my lower lip between his teeth and my face towards him as I let my head drop back. He whispers my name and it's over. I simply dissolve. I go numb, then light, and I notice too late that Henry's frozen in front of me. Then I hear it.

'Is somebody there?'

We whirl around simultaneously and look into this harsh torchlight.

'Fuck,' whispers Henry. He grabs me by the wrist and I can't do anything but stumble after him. It's a mystery to me how my legs even carry me, but somehow they're still functioning as we walk over the gravel. The fine rain settles ice-cold on my face and steams where it hits the places that Henry's lips touched. He pulls me into a corner, pushes me into an alcove and presses two fingers against my lips. His chest rises heavily against mine as we stand pressed motionless together.

I can smell wet wood, the cinnamon scent of Henry, and the whisky on his breath. The ball of light runs across the ground a few metres away from us, then moves on. I hold my breath as Henry presses up against me.

'Whoever it is, show yourself now or there'll be consequences.'

'Mr Ward?' I whisper.

Henry presses the flat of his hand against my mouth and nods before glancing over his shoulder. He exhales slowly as the light moves on and disappears out of our field of vision. 'He'll report any rule-breaking to our houseparents right away,' he says, taking his hand from my lips. He gently runs his knuckles over my mouth, then reaches into his trouser pocket. 'We have to warn the others. If he sees the light in the greenhouse, they're busted.'

I try to breathe normally as he lowers his eyes to his phone and starts typing. I only notice that I've raised my hand to touch my lips when Henry looks distractedly back from his phone to me. The corners of his lips twitch and it's so endlessly attractive. He puts his phone away and steps aside. Soon afterwards, the light in the greenhouse goes off.

'Come on.' Henry reaches for my hand. 'We should go back so that we're in our rooms if the houseparents check up.'

I hesitate for just a moment, but it's enough for Henry to understand.

'Mr Acevedo will only glance in. After that, I can come to you.'

22

EMMA

When I reach my room, the whole corridor is still quiet. A few minutes later, I hear noises next door, so Tori must be back too. A moment later, my door is opened. I pretend to sleep as Ms Barnett looks in, and only dare to breathe again when the door closes.

My phone lights up. It's a message from Tori.

T: Where are you??? Ms Barnett's checking rooms

I roll onto my side and start to type.

E: I know, I'm here
T: Oh, OK. Phew!
E: Did you get caught?

T: *I think everyone ran in time. Henry warned us. He went to look for you*

I type back.

E: *I know. He found me*

Tori sends an emoji of a moon with a knowing grin, but I don't reply because I hear a sound at my door. I immediately jump up and open it. Henry slips into my room. I hold back until he's shut the door, then wrap my arms around him and kiss him.

'Everything OK?' he murmurs into my lips.

I nod. He kisses me again. 'God, that was close.'

Stop talking . . .

I press my body against his and it works. Henry puts a hand on my head. He's got the wall against his back, and as he pulls me to him, a floorboard creaks under our feet. He leans forward slightly, wraps himself around my thighs and I wrap my legs around his hips as he lifts me up. As he carries me through the darkened room, we kiss more slowly because he has to watch where he's putting his feet.

He lays me on the bed and lingers over me. I know we won't go any further tonight as a tiny smile twitches his lips and he presses a kiss on my nose.

'We kissed,' I say, as he pulls off his shoes and I slide under the duvet.

'Yes, I think we did.'

I raise the covers slightly so that he can come to me. It feels so familiar and yet so new, as we lie on our sides next to each other, looking at each other. It's still a squeeze – our knees bump into each other. Henry lifts his leg so that I can wrap mine around it.

'And you split up,' I repeat.

Because of me. So now I'm the arsehole who stole Grace's way-too-perfect school captain boyfriend.

'Things hadn't been good between us for ages, Emma,' says Henry, as if he could read my mind.

'So why didn't you split up ages ago, then?'

'Because there was no reason to.'

'But now there suddenly was?'

Silence.

'I don't want to be the reason,' I whisper.

'I know. But there are two separate things. The break-up, which is between me and Grace, and this . . . This is only between us.'

'Are you sure you'll still see it the same way by daylight tomorrow?' I wonder. 'When you're sober again and everyone's talking?'

'I don't give a shit if the others talk.'

Henry's choice of words surprises me a little, but I kind of like it too. So he isn't always polite and correct. This evening is the living proof that he can also kiss me furiously and press me, full of desire, up against some random wall. I need more of this Henry.

'Did he ever text you back?' he asks, out of the blue.

'Who?' I reply, but then I realize he must mean my dad. 'No. He hasn't got my number. I've only got his.'

Henry says nothing, and somehow it still works: I keep talking. His presence is still like some kind of truth spray that I breathe in, then want to tell him everything.

'It was horrible, Henry. He only talked about himself, the whole time.' My throat tightens in that grim way, like any time you might cry. But I'm not going to shed any more tears over Jacob Wiley.

'I'm sorry,' he whispers, 'that it didn't go well and that I wasn't there after that.'

'You were.'

He shakes his head ever so slightly. 'You know what I mean.'

I keep quiet, but then I raise my chin a little. It's enough, Henry understands. I recognize the question in his eyes and put an answer into mine. He holds my cheeks and kisses me. It's different this time. So damn gentle that the tears sting in my eyes.

This must be a dream. Henry in my bed. Henry's lips on my mouth, his thumbs running over my temples. He puts his hand on my back, between my shoulder blades, and pulls me to him until my head is on his chest and I can't look at him any more. Maybe that's intentional because he gets that it's easier for me to talk that way. For a while, I just lie there. Breathe in his scent and feel his fingers, which are drawing little patterns on my back.

'He just dumped on everything,' I whisper into Henry's T-shirt. 'Badmouthed the school, Mum. And I didn't say anything.'

'I think that says more about him than about you.'

I feel the slight buzz of his chest as he speaks. I love it. I have to shut my eyes as he presses his fingers into the back of my neck.

'He really isn't the way I thought, Henry.'

'And he really had no answer as to why he left back then?'

'He said Mum suffocated him. He couldn't stand things in Germany with us. And he said he'd do it again. He'd leave again.' Henry looks at me as I raise my head and budge back a little way. 'I think I understand now what Mum always meant. Why she was so cautious and wanted to stop me getting my hopes up. He'd leave and come back as it suited him. He promised me things and just forgot them. I bet it was the same for her. And she had me and her job. I thought she was bitter and broken and trying to make up for it all through work. But I was wrong. She's way stronger than him.'

Henry doesn't take his eyes off me.

'She wasn't building a career for anybody else but herself. Because the only life you can control is your own.'

I swallow. It's strange the way everything suddenly makes

sense the moment I've said it aloud. How could I seriously have thought that Mum was the one in that broken relationship who needed pity? Why did I have to see how lost my dad is before I could understand that he doesn't live some exciting rock-star life but is trapped in a dream that will never come true? Why did I think Mum was forcing her values on me when all she wanted was to offer me opportunities? Suddenly I understand it. That she didn't want me to learn and grow for her sake. That it was all for mine.

I only notice how deep I am in thought when Henry tucks a strand of hair behind my ear. His very dark green eyes are warm as I look at him.

'What are you thinking?' he asks quietly. 'I want to know.'

'What is this between us?' I ask, without a second's thought.

And Henry answers without hesitation. 'I think it's serious.'

'Yes.' I swallow. 'I think it is too.'

'Even if you're leaving in a year.'

'Maybe I won't leave,' I say. Henry raises his eyebrows and I keep talking. 'Maybe I'll finish my A levels at Dunbridge Academy.'

I don't know if I've ever seen anything as cute as Henry trying to suppress a smile.

'You could apply to Oxford or Cambridge if you were here . . .'

'Or St Andrews,' I add.

'Or St Andrews,' he repeats. 'If you wanted. They do sport science now – I saw that the other day.' Henry rests his head in the crook of his arm. 'It kind of made me think of you.'

My stomach hops slightly.

'There's an open day at St Andrews after half-term. You could come and look around. Maeve is one of the student guides, doing tours of the uni and answering questions.'

'Then I could meet her too,' I say, and Henry looks so happy.

'Tori and Sinclair are coming,' he says.

I laugh. 'Why don't any of you want to go to Oxford?'

Henry shrugs his shoulders. 'No idea. Maybe we're all weird.'

'Then I must be too.'

'I knew from the start you'd fit in.'

I find myself smiling. 'It feels nice having friends who are always there. I think I like this whole boarding-school thing in general.'

'That's nice.'

I lean forwards slightly. My lips brush Henry's. I can feel that he's smiling.

'We're kissing, Emma,' he says, as if he can't quite believe it.

'We're kissing, Henry,' I repeat, and I don't want us ever to stop. These are different kisses from back then in the drizzle, up against that wall. Slower kisses. Still very perfect kisses.

Henry's eyes are tired when he eventually lets go of me and looks at me.

'You ought to go back, oughtn't you?'

'Maybe,' he murmurs. 'Should I go back?'

'You should sleep here,' I whisper, and the crazy thing is that it doesn't feel weak to ask him not to leave me on my own. It feels right. 'Little spoon?'

Henry smiles, first in surprise and then in real happiness. My belly feels warm as he kisses me again, then rolls cautiously onto his other side. He reaches for my hand as I slide up behind him and interlaces his fingers with mine.

'You have to tell me everything,' he says, as he runs his thumb over my wrist.

'OK,' I whisper, because I sense he's about to fall asleep anyway. It's unfair, I wish I could do that too, but it's also kind of nice to lie next to Henry as his breathing evens and my thoughts slow.

We kissed for the first time; it was a really intense moment. I don't know what it means, I only know that I've arrived at Dunbridge Academy.

23

HENRY

It's a mystery to me that I made it back to my wing on time. Emma and I woke up early, just before the sun came up, but we still had a lot of kissing to do before I made it out of bed.

My lips feel sore. They're throbbing as I see Emma again in the dining room after the morning run. I'd like to be the cup she's sipping from. She glances at me over the rim and I feel warm again. She looks tired, but it seems to me that she's kind of radiant too. Maybe only I can see that, no idea. Either way, I love it.

Sitting in English, spending the whole lesson looking at the back of her neck is torture. I didn't know that a body and skin could take up such a vast amount of space in my thoughts, but everything's a bit different with Emma. During biology I'm thinking about where I could kiss her later. I don't mean where we'd go, I mean where on her body. There are so many places left for me to kiss. It's overwhelming. I can't think about it all without my trousers getting too tight, so I force my attention back to meiosis and mitosis. I'm not in very good shape for Ms Barnett's test, which is coming up, but there we are.

Sinclair shakes his head as he sits down beside me in Latin.

'What?' I ask.

'Congrats,' is all he says.

'What?' I repeat.

'Henry, it's obvious. D'you two think nobody's noticed the way you're looking at each other?'

I just smile.

'God, he's in love,' says Sinclair with a sigh.

Fortunately, he doesn't have the chance to ask any tricky questions. Ms Barnett shuts the door and hands out the test papers. Somehow, there's still quite a lot of information in my head and I hand mine in before anyone else.

As I wait outside for Sinclair, I look at my phone and see a message from Maeve.

M: Sorry! I've only just got Wi-Fi again. Everything OK?
H: Yes, how's it going?

She's online and starts typing back right away. My intention of not dumping my love troubles on her failed a few days ago when she sent me a couple of memes and asked how I was doing. I dropped a few hints and asked her if she'd have time for a chat, but Maeve wouldn't be Maeve if she hadn't immediately figured out that something was up.

> **M:** *Yeah, fine, all good. Why's it so hot in Kenya?*
> **H:** *Dunno, I always forget that part too. Say hi to Mum and Dad*
> **M:** *Will do, and hi back! Henry, what did you want to talk about?*
> **H:** *Nothing urgent*
> **M:** *Grace?*

I type on because it's no use trying to hide anything from Maeve.

> **H:** *We split up.*
> **M:** *Oh, no :(Have some big-sister hearts . . . Sorry I didn't answer. Want to speak now?? I could call you in 5 minutes but not for long, sorry, got to head back to the hospital in a bit.*
> **H:** *No, it's all good! Honest, I'm fine.*
> **M:** *Are you sure?*
> **H:** *Emma and I kissed*
> **M:** *I see . . . Want to Skype at the weekend? You have to tell me everything.*
> **H:** *Sure*
> **M:** *Unless you're in Loveland with Emma. In which case, don't let me disturb you*

H: *Ha ha*

M: *I want to meet her, got that?*

H: *As soon as you're back. She's coming on the open day*

M: *Perfect. Are you happy, Henny?*

I have to smile.

H: *Yeah, pretty much*

M: *Excellent. I have to go*

H: *Take care*

M: *Always do*

I pocket my phone as I hear the first footsteps in the corridor. Soon after that, the bell goes for the end of the lesson. The classroom doors open, we all flood out and it's ridiculous how happy I am. Emma and Tori emerge from a room at the end of the hall, Tori's chattering on, Emma nods a couple of times. Her eyes scan the hall and find me right away.

'How did it go?' she asks, as the two of them come to join me.

'Not bad.'

'Which means very good,' remarks Tori.

I just shrug and can't help watching Emma's lips. Would she mind me kissing her now? Here in front of everyone else? I don't know if I'm the one who ought to decide, but perhaps she'd find it hot too if I just . . .

Her gaze slips from my eyes to my mouth and, yeah, why am I even still thinking about this? She only looks surprised for the first moment as I take a step towards her and kiss her. She seems OK with it. I'm OK with it, too. Very much OK. This is no lame hi-how-are-you-fine-how-are-you kiss. Somehow, it's impossible to kiss Emma like that. I always have to kiss her *properly*.

'Er, guys, what did I miss?'

Emma just rolls her eyes as Tori starts squealing beside us.

'Oi, stop that right now, or I'll have to inform my mother that there is improper physical contact going on here,' says Sinclair, but he's grinning.

Emma laughs and it's the most beautiful sound on this whole bloody planet. Help, I need a bucket of cold water. A slap in the face would work too, I think.

Which I get as I look over Emma's shoulder. Right into Grace's eyes. It feels like all my blood has drained down into my legs.

It's only for a very brief moment as her gaze rests on us, but it's enough, and I feel terrible. Her fingers tighten around the strap on her bag, she forces a smile to her lips and turns away. She disappears between small groups of pupils, who are nodding discreetly in our direction and whispering. It doesn't surprise me. We'll be the main topic of conversation at this school for a few days more, then Valentine Ward will start dating someone else and nobody will still be talking about Emma and me. All the same, part of me wants to go after Grace and apologize to her. But we're not a couple now.

'Henry?' I jump as Emma takes my hand. She seems not to have spotted Grace.

'Hm?' I look at her. 'Sorry, I . . . What were you saying?'

'I was asking if you want to go for a run later. You don't have training today, do you?'

'Not till tomorrow.'

'OK.' Emma's smiling but her eyes are sceptical. 'Or aren't you in the mood?'

'Sure,' I say at once, forcing myself to banish all thoughts of Grace.

'Sinclair!' Gideon yells down the corridor. 'Is your mum coming to the parents' evening next week?'

'Piss off, Attwell.' He sticks his middle finger up at him, at least until Ms Barnett walks out of the classroom with her pile of test papers.

'Is your mum coming?' I ask Emma. Maybe she'll take the chance to make up for the missed visit.

And Emma's nodding. 'Yeah, and she's staying for the weekend.'

'Oh, nice.'

'Your parents won't be coming though, right?'

'No, definitely not. It's way too far. But they'll have a video appointment – there are loads of parents who can't come in person.'

'Don't tell my mum that or she might change her mind again.'

Although that was clearly meant to sound ironic, I can

hear the pain and hint of fear in her voice. I don't like it. I'm angry with the people who've let her down. She doesn't deserve that. She doesn't deserve to be made to feel like a burden. Which Emma believes she is. She really does. Why wouldn't she after her shithead father just walked out, then made such a dick of himself when they met up again?

At the same time, I know it wouldn't do any good for me to try to convince her otherwise. She has to realize for herself before she can believe it. But maybe I can at least help with that part a bit.

EMMA

I only knew how much I'd missed Mum when I cried for sheer relief as she stepped out of the taxi onto the courtyard and I could finally hug her again. The part of me that's been confronted with a whole bunch of disappointment lately had been refusing to look forward too much to her visit. Pure self-preservation in case it didn't work out, I guess. But it did.

Although she's only staying a couple of days, Mum's got a massive suitcase with her. It's filled with the things I've asked her for in the last few weeks. Now, all at once, I've got a kettle, my own bedding and a new string of lights.

Mum's constantly darting around here and there, all bright eyes. I can feel how pleased she is to be back at Dunbridge Academy.

'Who are we seeing first?' she asks, as we head back downstairs, a little later.

'Mr Ward.' Mum flinches almost imperceptibly, but I see it. 'Maths and English.'

'OK.' She clears her throat quietly. 'Mr Ward. Who else?'

'Ms Ventura, Ms Kelleher and Mr Ringling.'

As we walk towards the classrooms, we meet other parents. It's just a parents' evening, but it's almost like a special occasion. But maybe that's only because we're all in school uniform. Including Henry, of course, who's standing at the foot of the stairs in his role as school captain, next to Mr Harper, the secretary, looking outrageously good.

Henry glances at us as we come closer. He smiles his school-captain smile, looks away, then right back at us again.

His lips form a soundless *Hi*. I wonder how inappropriate it would be to kiss him now and decide on *very*. So I just stop and turn to my mum.

'Mum, this is Henry.'

'Nice to meet you, Ms Beck,' he says at once, holding out his hand.

He remembered. I'd mentioned it once, but of course he remembered that my mum has a different surname from me.

'Oh, Henry,' Mum exclaims. 'You're *Henry*! How nice! It's lovely to meet you too.'

It's weird hearing Mum speak English again. Like she used to with my dad. I know that she still has to speak

SARAH SPRINZ

English for work almost every day, but I only hear it now and then on holiday. And it's the first time I've really taken in that Henry and I don't speak German to each other. English is just so normal now that I simply forget.

'Did you have a good journey?'

I'm sure it's not the first time Henry's asked that question today but, somehow, he manages to sound genuinely interested.

'Yes, thank you. It's a little bit like coming home.'

'Oh, yes, you were at school here too, weren't you?' His eyes meet mine. 'Emma told me that. We're doing two of the same A levels.'

Henry's immediately snared her with that unfair charm of his. She laughs and throws a sneaking glance in my direction once we're walking on again. Luckily, I can avoid any further questions. It's time for our first appointment. Mr Ward is sitting at his desk, sorting through various files.

Mum stops as we approach the open door. She puts her shoulders back a fraction as we walk in. He raises his head and, suddenly, there's something in his expression I've never seen before. Emotion. Pain, fury, contempt. They vanish as soon as he stands up.

'Laura,' he says. I only realize when Mum calls him by his first name too.

'Alaric,' she replies. It's her lawyer voice. I only know it from when she's on the phone. She doesn't say, *Nice to see you.*

They shake hands. Mr Ward gives me a curt nod, then indicates the two chairs in front of his desk.

'I presume we're not waiting for Jacob?'

Mum doesn't flinch, but my throat feels tight. At this moment, I understand there must be more to this. More things that Mum won't talk about with me. More secrets and tangled links.

'No, we're not.' Mum's voice is chilly. She's sitting very straight. 'Let's talk about my daughter.'

I don't want to be here. Why do pupils have to come to parents' evening conversations here at Dunbridge? It can only be awkward.

'Yes, we should do that.' Mr Ward finds a page in his notebook. His eyes pass over me and I find myself holding my breath. 'Emma is very ambitious, you have to give her that. I teach her mathematics and English. She is putting in a solid performance in maths, but in English there is room for improvement, to put it mildly. She didn't pass the first test of the school year. Currently, she's averaging a C grade in her written work, while I would put her spoken proficiency at B minus. We don't make allowances for non-native speakers here, of course. It's clear from her accent that you only speak German to her. It's a great shame.'

'Could we please stick to the point?' Mum's voice sounds calm, but her expression is adamant.

'Of course. Well, Emma will only be here a year, so as far as that goes none of this is a particular disaster.'

I glance at Mum. I haven't told her my idea of maybe staying at the school for the whole of sixth form.

'We'll see,' is all she says. 'I'm sure there are plenty of other ways that she can work on catching up with the others, aren't there?'

'Indeed there are. Emma would always be very welcome to ask me for advice.'

'Then I'm sure she will.'

Why am I even here? The two of them are talking about me like I'm not in the room. Mum isn't usually like this. I'm on the verge of saying something when Mr Ward starts talking about the next set of exams. He seems different from normal. Slower. It's weird. I don't know if I'm imagining it. Maybe he didn't get enough sleep. Mum makes the occasional note and I nod, as if in a trance. My thoughts keep wandering. It's these little moments when their eyes meet and Mum's expression hardens. When she looks at Mr Ward's stick, which is leaning against the edge of the desk, her eyes go kind of faraway.

I find myself thinking about the yearbook photos. About the fact that Mr Ward suddenly wasn't there. About what Mr Ringling said in the garden. What happened back then, and is it possible that my parents had anything to do with it? I wish I could just ask. Right now. While I'm here with them. But I don't dare.

I have no idea what else Mr Ward said. Mum seems strangely composed as we walk to the next room. It's not until we talk to Ms Ventura and Mr Ringling that I start to relax. Unlike Mr Ward, they're practically heaping praise on me, it's almost embarrassing. All the same, as Mum and I step outside again, I can think about only one thing.

'Phew, we made it.' Mum smiles. 'Mr Ringling is still as nice as ever.'

'I didn't know you knew Mr Ward so well.' It's a lie: of course I knew it. But Mum doesn't know that.

Maybe I'm imagining things, but her smile is more strained now. 'He was in our year.'

'Didn't you get on?'

Mum hesitates, and I know she's not going to tell me the truth. 'Things were a bit complicated,' she says. 'There was no love lost between him and your father.'

'Why?'

'Oh, Emmi-Mouse, it was all so long ago. I can't even remember exactly.'

Mum turns away and lets her eyes wander over the ancient walls.

'I met him,' I say. She turns back to me. 'Dad.'

'You did what?' she blurts.

'Yes.'

'When? Did he come here?'

'No. I went to see him.' Suddenly I feel guilty. 'I'm sorry I didn't tell you but I didn't want you to worry. And I had to do it alone. You wouldn't have approved.' Mum opens her mouth but I don't let her speak. 'You totally wouldn't, believe me.'

She sighs quietly. 'OK, you're right. Maybe I really wouldn't have approved.'

'You see.'

'OK, so you met him. And, how was it?'

'It was . . . difficult. He was drunk. Maybe it wasn't the best time.'

'He was *what*?' Mum's eyes bore through me. 'Where did you meet him?'

'In Glasgow,' I tell her. 'He was doing a concert in a pub.'

'In Glasgow? Emma Charlotte Wiley, I hope you're not telling me that you went to Glasgow on your own to meet your father in some pub?'

'I wasn't on my own,' I say hastily. 'Henry came with me. He was there the whole time.'

Well . . . almost the whole time.

'I can't believe it.' Mum rubs her temples. 'But fine. So you met him. Maybe that was important.'

'I think it really was.'

'And could he believe his eyes? What did you talk about?' asks Mum, and I can feel how much effort she's making not to sound reproachful.

'He didn't even recognize me at first. And then it was . . . disillusioning. He mainly talked about himself . . . Somehow, I'd hoped for more.'

'I'm sorry, Emmi.' She sounds genuinely upset. 'I really am so very sorry that your father isn't here for you. I wish things were different. And I hope you aren't blaming yourself for it.'

My throat tightens. 'I hope you aren't either.'

When Mum smiles at me, her eyes are sparkling, but maybe I'm imagining that too.

'Aren't you angry with him?' I ask. 'I'm only asking because I'm angry. I'm so angry, and it's tiring.'

'I know, Emmi. It's exhausting. But you can let it go and make better use of your energies.'

'How did you let it go?'

'I don't know. It took a long time, and I still haven't completely. I'm angry with him for doing this to you. But nowadays I mainly feel sorry for him because he threw away the chance to see you grow up.'

Mum looks at me and I know it's the truth. That she's stopped hating him. Because it doesn't do any good. And I really wish I could too.

It's true that I've done more than my fair share of crying in the last little while, but I think I have my reasons. This is just a super-intense phase. But this time it feels different. These aren't hot, furious tears, they're lighter. I'd got myself so invested in this idea of finding my dad that I couldn't see I have Mum. That she's always been there and working her arse off to give me every opportunity. I just took it all and I wasn't satisfied. It wasn't enough for me. But in these few seconds it's like everything just slides into place.

24

HENRY

Emma's been different since her mum came to visit. More together, and more kind of unbuttoned. Or, at least, it seems that way to me when she gets back to school on Sunday evening after spending the day in Edinburgh with her mum. We spend hours kissing in her room, the only reason I don't spend the night with her is that Ms Barnett catches us just before wing time and is sure to pop back later to check that I've definitely left.

It's a surreal time. Lately, I've been asking myself if I'd ever really been in love before, because nothing compares to this. I never felt so fluttery and light when Grace looked at me. I never spent minutes at a time not paying attention in lessons because all I could think of was how soft her mouth was. I never wanted so badly to know everything going on inside her head, every single thought – it feels almost like I can't survive without knowing. I even look forward to the training sessions that Emma and I have started again. I missed them during our little break. Seriously. This is what things have come to.

It's like we're living in a transparent bubble, and I wish it could never burst. I'm actually physically addicted to being close to Emma. Maybe I ought to be worried by this crazy magnetic attraction. Sometimes it scares me when I think how much we still have to tell each other. How many things I don't yet know about her and urgently need to find out. I only know the Dunbridge version of Emma and I forget way too easily that there's a completely different Emma out there. One who speaks German and had a life before she switched schools. A life that she'd been intending to go back to next summer. There's a long time to go until then but it still makes me nervous. I suppose I ought to be a neutral non-toxic boyfriend, who supports her every decision, whatever it looks like, but the fact is that all I want now is for her to stay here. There's no point in denying it. She means way too much to me for that. We haven't spoken about it again and I haven't got the guts to raise the subject. Not while everything's so pink and perfect.

These days, we're not just running in the mornings: we sometimes go out in the evenings too. Like this Saturday, for instance. At around halfway, we stop in the woods because we have to kiss. It really is a matter of considerable urgency.

My heart-rate doesn't drop the whole time, so I'm sure we can count it as part of my training, though Emma would probably disagree. It doesn't really faze me that we're dripping with sweat – it's actually kind of hot. My knees are soft and there's no way it's a coincidence that her mouth fits mine so perfectly. Emma's way of moving is almost more than I can stand. I can feel everything through this thin sports kit. Her warm body, every movement – I can't get enough of it because Emma was always so far away and now she's here.

I'm too distracted to pay any attention to the weather but I guess I should be grateful when at some point the sky chucks an ice-cold shower over us. We run back, we laugh, it's unreal, and it eventually gets unbelievably cold, so I pull Emma towards the sports centre. She's shivering as we run through the empty corridors – the whole place seems dead, the boys' changing rooms are deserted, and we keep kissing as we pull off our shoes.

My head switches off as Emma pulls me to her by the waistband of my shorts. It's a fluid, self-confident motion that takes my breath away. Her hips meet mine. I'm hard right away and I have to bury my hands in her hair. It's damp on my fingers, I pull her head back slightly and forget my own name as a stifled groan escapes her. She pulls her hands back from my waistband and runs them over my belly up to my chest.

Our eyes meet. Her pupils are wide, her cheeks red and, God, I have to kiss her. I have to kiss her right now.

She raises her hands to my head as I run my thumbs over

her cheeks. I don't know who's pulling who closer. Maybe we both are, simultaneously, equally desperate, equally relieved when it happens.

This is no gentle kiss. It's hungry and greedy. It's everything I could ever imagine and more. It's this weightless feeling in my stomach as I pull her towards the showers.

I can taste her sweat, salty and damp. My fingers slip over her skin. I can't stop. It's a kiss that has only a beginning, no end. Breathing through the nose so we don't have to stop, her hot tongue in my mouth and nothing else matters now.

I stumble backwards against some wall in the team showers and I can't breathe as Emma's warm body presses against mine. She gasps, right in front of me, as she feels my erection. She hesitates very briefly. Then, tantalizingly slowly, she moves her hips against mine. My eyelids flutter closed, she kisses me more, my head sinks back against this cold tiled wall, and Emma lets her fingers wander over my jaw. Over my throat to my collarbone. When her hands reach my chest, I lay mine on her bum. I press her against me, but it isn't enough. There are too many clothes, there's too much fabric. We gasp all the same. I blink. It's only a tiny glance as she looks at me, and I understand. My hands slide lower, I grab her and lift her up. I turn with her, Emma wraps her legs around my hips and then I press her back against the wall as I move against her.

'God, Henry.' She groans, and I can't stand it. It's just too much. There's too much heat, too much attraction, as she presses her legs more firmly against me and lifts her hips.

311

Her hands run through my hair as we keep on kissing, and then she grabs the neckline of my running top. She hesitates for a tiny moment and it drives me out of my mind.

My eyes find hers, we look at each other, and for a second we freeze motionless, facing each other.

'Have you got . . .?' she begins, her voice hoarse.

'No, but Sinclair has. Wait.'

Reluctantly, I leave her on the floor. I feel dizzy. We're going to do this. I know the combination to Sinclair's locker but the damn thing doesn't open until I give it a thump with my fist. Emma's standing in the doorway to the showers wearing nothing but her skin-tight leggings and a blue sports bra that hugs her figure perfectly. My tongue tingles as I think about what's beneath it.

I dig through Sinclair's crap. I have to fight back a groan of relief when I finally find his condoms.

Emma wraps her arms around my neck as I get back to her.

'Are you sure?' I whisper. It's hard to breathe.

'Yes,' she breathes. 'Are you?'

'I'm sure too.'

Her eyes flit from mine to my lips and back again. Then she carries on. I plant kisses on her cheek, her throat and her left collarbone as she grabs the hem of my shirt. It's all taking way too long. I lean away slightly and pull it off, then let my fingers wander over her belly and her leggings. She slips out of her sports bra and drops it on the floor by her feet.

312

My mouth dries as my eyes take her in. Her throat, beaded with sweat, her slender shoulders, her small, full breasts, down to her flat belly. Emma takes a step forwards. When our bare chests meet, it's perfect. Hot skin, smooth, soft skin, and all this stupid clothing that has to go. We keep on kissing, and Emma's hands reach for my shorts. I never knew undressing each other could be such a turn-on.

We let each other go briefly to undress, and then we're standing face to face in this communal shower, wearing nothing but underwear, and I've never felt so complete. When Emma grabs her knickers, I have to gulp. We strip off our pants at the same time, watching each other. I'm trying to control my heavy breathing but it's impossible. She looks me straight in the eyes and we face each other, stark naked. Then we take a step forwards.

Emma's hands reach for the back of my neck, mine find her face. We pause, an inch or so apart. I feel her hot breath on my lips, her eyes roam over my face, and I kiss her. It's different this time. Long and deep. Without otherwise moving, at least until Emma pulls me closer and lets her warm hands run over my back. We gasp for breath in unison as my throbbing meets the heat of her. And then Emma moves her hands between us.

My eyelids close as I feel her fingers around my erection. My forehead sinks into hers as our hands meet.

'Wait,' I murmur, thinking of the condom. The plastic crackles, it's all taking too long.

Emma waits until I'm looking at her again. Her fingers tremble as I feel her on my skin. But I can't carry on until I've checked something.

'Have you ever . . .?' I begin hesitantly, because there's no way of asking that isn't problematic. But I have to know if she's a virgin. Not because it matters to me but because I want everything to happen at her pace. That she knows we can stop. Even now.

'Yes,' she says. 'With Noah.'

I can't say I'm relieved, but in a way I kind of am.

'How about you?' she asks, yet I'm sure that she knows. 'Grace?'

I nod silently.

'OK.'

'We don't have to . . .' I say, but Emma shakes her head.

'Yes, we do, Henry,' she says, and something flickers in her eyes in the darkness as she reduces the gap between us.

OK, yes, she's right. We have to. It's just good to know that she sees it the same way.

I feel her hold her breath as I guide my erection towards her with my hand. When I move inside her, it feels like time's falling apart. My hand hits the cold tiles behind her, her brow moves away from mine as she puts back her head. I feel her hands on my shoulders and suppress a gasp as she starts moving.

I force myself to hold still as Emma moves her hips gently forwards and back, cautiously at first and then more determinedly. We pant at the same time as I bring my hips towards her. She groans quietly and I do it again. And then again. Until her legs are trembling and her breath is going as fast as mine. They're not movements any more, they're thrusts. Emma, who's guiding my hands to her thighs and wrapping her legs around me as I lift her up again. My fingers slip over her skin, hers dig like claws into my shoulders as we pick up speed. It's more intense than anything I've ever experienced.

It's hard in the gentlest way, it's deep and thrilling, and as she starts to throb around me, and the pressure builds within me, I can no longer hold back my groan. The panting sounds she's making, her legs pulling me closer, her fingers on my skin, her hot breath on my neck, and then the pressure gets too much. I have to shut my eyes as the tremor rolls through my body.

My breath is still heavy. Her hands are roaming through my hair. I know she didn't come when she pulls me closer and holds on tight. Her fingers stroke the nape of my neck, and her lips are gleaming red, as I raise my head again. She's looking at me with that smile in her eyes.

'Sorry,' I whisper, kissing her. Slowly and carefully.

'What for?'

'You didn't come.' I look at her. 'Or did you?'

She shakes her head ever so slightly. 'It's not so bad. It was still lovely.'

'We could . . .'

She kisses me and I forget what I'd been going to say. Nothing else matters, and there's something so beautiful about that.

Emma closes her eyes as I pull myself out of her and lower her carefully to the floor. She draws me closer but stops in mid-movement as I push my hand between her legs. Her pupils widen almost imperceptibly as I look at her. She bites herself gently on the bottom lip and I feel her twitch as I touch her with two fingers. I kiss her mouth and move my hand.

'Tell me if it's good like this,' I whisper into her side, and feel her get goosebumps.

'You don't have to,' she murmurs, and falls silent as I stop.

'I don't have to or I shouldn't?'

There's just a look, then Emma's hand on mine. She increases the pressure and I understand. We kiss as I touch her. I only relax when she gives that quiet groan again, and I drop to my knees in front of her.

EMMA

Henry on his knees in front of me and with his mouth between my legs is more than I would ever have thought possible. It was incredible enough feeling him inside me, but this is something else. It's throbbing heat in my belly and the certainty that I could come like this. My knees start to tremble, I feel his hands on the backs of my thighs and I have the feeling my legs might give way beneath me at any moment . . . It's ridiculous that I'm thinking about that of all things. I have to tense my stomach muscles because it's too much but the trembling doesn't stop. Henry doesn't stop and it's almost more than I can bear. He finds the right position, the right pressure, he stays there until I fall apart under his hands and his mouth and, oh, God, his tongue.

I claw my fingers into his hair, he digs his fingers into my skin. I've never been so hot. Maybe I'll burn up into nothing right here and now, beneath his hands, but at least it would've been worth it.

My head falls back, my eyes close. A sound escapes me, one I've never heard myself make before, and it makes Henry shiver. It's a wave flowing through my body from the parting of my hair to the tips of my toes, until my legs won't hold me any more and I fall to my knees in front of Henry. My body is soft, my muscles have stopped working. They've simply dissolved into thin air, but it's OK.

Henry pulls me to him, I sink onto the tiles in front of him. He kisses me. I can taste myself and him and it's incredible. My head is empty, I can't think. Only Henry. Henry everywhere. Henry in my head, Henry in my mouth, my stomach, on my skin.

He pulls himself up a little, to turn on the water. I keep

SARAH SPRINZ

my eyes closed and lean back my head. The warm droplets fall onto my face. The tiled floor is cold – I'm only just noticing that again. We're in the male showers, it was our first time, and it's perfect. It really is pretty perfect.

Once we've showered, Henry pulls a change of clothes from his locker for each of us. I may never understand what it is about wearing a sweatshirt that belongs to someone you like. It's soft and way too big. It smells a little of laundry detergent and a lot of Henry. On the way to his wing, I'm relatively certain that I'll never be able to take it off, but then I'm lying next to him in his bed and everything is so cuddly and warm. Henry pulls the hood of his sweatshirt up round my face and ties the drawstrings under my chin. I let him because he's smiling so much as he does it, and then he bends down to kiss me. I'm seriously smitten with him. Shit.

I don't think a thing like this with Henry happens that often. It doesn't compare with anything. When Noah and I got together, it just kind of happened. We didn't talk all that much. At some stage Isi started making jokes until everyone knew we fancied each other. There was this theme party put on by that year's *Abitur* class, and it was the first time I'd drunk alcohol, and Noah kissed me. And then it was kind of a thing, Emma and Noah, for quite a while. It feels like a lifetime away, but I remember how much it hurt when it was suddenly over. I look at Henry and wonder what it must be like for something old to come to an end and something new to begin. All in such a short time. I guess it's exhausting.

'What's up?' he asks quietly.

'Do you miss Grace?' I ask.

'Em . . .' Henry hesitates.

Maybe it's inappropriate to bring up the subject of his ex-girlfriend right after we've first had sex. I don't know.

'I'm just wondering,' I mumble. 'I want us to be able to talk about anything.'

Henry's eyes soften. 'I want that too.'

'You see.'

'And yes. I do miss her somehow.'

'You were together a long time.'

Henry nods. 'Although I don't know if "miss" is the right word. But I think about her a lot and hope she's OK. I never wanted to hurt her.'

'I'm sure she knows that.'

'Probably. But it doesn't change anything about what I did.'

'So long as you didn't break up with her over WhatsApp, I'm sure it's OK,' I murmur, and maybe that's mean of me, but I can't help my cynical side taking over when I remember how that felt.

'Is that what Noah did?' asks Henry.

'Yeah, it was pretty shitty.'

'Have you seen anything else of him and your friend?'

I shake my head. 'I muted them.'

'On Instagram?'

'Yeah.'

'That's good.' Henry picks at the hoodie-string bow until it undoes. 'Don't let it get to you.'

I really don't have to let it get to me. Of course it does a bit, but I'm trying.

'I think Olive hates me,' I say, out of nowhere.

Henry frowns. 'Why would she?'

'Because I arrived here and, first, I came between her and Tori and then I stole Grace's boyfriend.' And now he's lying here with me. 'She said so herself.'

Henry stays silent for a while. 'If she has to hate anyone, she ought to hate me.'

'Henry . . .'

'No, seriously, I mean it. You didn't come between anyone. Tori likes you, you get on well, and if Olive has a problem with that, it's between her and Tori. The same goes for Grace and me. You're not the cause of the problem. Don't let anyone tell you you are.'

'So, you wouldn't say that none of these problems even existed before I got here?'

'That's rubbish and you know it. They were just simmering under the surface. Like a dormant volcano. It was clear that it wouldn't work out in the long run. And I'm glad you're here.' Henry smiles. 'Don't you dare go anywhere else now.'

'Apart from St Andrews with you?' I say it half ironically,

but his eyes gleam in the hopeful way that gives me stomach-ache. What if I don't get in? I curl up beside him. 'Do you honestly think I could do it?'

'Of course you can do it.' He says it without a second's hesitation. 'You can do anything you put your mind to.'

'My grades aren't good enough.'

'But you've got almost two whole years here.'

'Have I?'

'I hope so.'

'I talked to Mum about it last weekend,' I say.

Henry looks at me. 'And?'

'She was pleased, said it would be nice for me.'

'I think it would be nice for you, too. And for me, of course.'

'I thought as much.'

'But it's your life, Em,' says Henry, to my surprise. 'You shouldn't take this kind of decision for her sake, and certainly not for mine. The most important thing is for you to be happy, and if that means you're living back in Germany next year while I'm here, we'll manage. There are phones and FaceTime and aeroplanes.'

I hadn't known until now how much I needed to hear those words. It's as if a weight I hadn't even been aware of has been lifted off my shoulders. There's warmth in my belly, and I'm feeling so many things for Henry all at once. Affection, gratitude, admiration, respect. He really means all of that. Being with him is a whole different level of lovely. Because he's self-aware enough to tell me he'd like to have me here with him, while at the same time he'll have my back unconditionally, if my plans for the future don't match his. It feels so healthy.

'I don't want phones and FaceTime, though, I want this,' I say. 'With you.'

He smiles.

'Can you picture us going to St Andrews together?' I ask, rolling onto my back and looking up at the ceiling.

'I can definitely picture that,' he says. 'I bet there are some great night-time walks there.'

'Not as good as the ones here, of course.'

'We'll have to find out.'

'We could live together,' I say, without thinking. 'Without wing time and the fear of getting caught.'

'And you don't think it would take the fun out of things?'

'I'm pretty sure it wouldn't.'

Henry leans over me. 'But until then, we can make the most of the thrill of secrecy.'

I can't answer because his mouth is on mine. My lips open for his tongue, as his warm, heavy body presses me deeper into the mattress. I slide my hands over his shoulders into the sleeves of his T-shirt until there's no more room for me there with his firm upper arms.

Shall we do it again, Henry? I'd be so up for that, but what if someone hears us? There's no way it's a good thing for me to be so blasé about it. I'm too deep in love. I want Henry and I get him, his mouth, his weight and his scent.

It's a little less greedy than in the showers earlier, but I don't feel any less tingly or full of anticipation when Henry stands up to fetch a condom. He has to move faster. *Please.*

I slip off the joggers he lent me and then his hoodie, under which I'm not wearing anything.

Henry's hands are trembling slightly as he raises my arms above my head and crosses my wrists on the pillow, before pushing another one under my hips. It's quiet. All I can hear is the rustle of the duvet and our heavy breathing. Henry's careful as he enters me. He's careful as he starts to move, until I stretch my pelvis to meet him, and then he's not careful any more.

He leans down to me, his hair falls into his face. He kisses me again. He thrusts gently, he thrusts harder and my head falls back. His hips find a new angle, one at which everything's a bit different somehow from what I knew before. Henry does it again, thrusts again, gasps as I gasp. All I can do is to move with him, deeper, faster, trembling hands, empty head. He's making a big effort to keep quiet, but I can still hear them, his non-noises. They push me a little way over the edge, and when he has to shut his eyes and press his lips together, it's over. It's simply over.

I fall into Henry's arms and I love it. When he runs his lips over my collarbone, it's perfect. I just lie there like I'm on a tiny cloud, a ninety-centimetre mattress, smooth, hot skin and his scent. I can't leave here. I'll never again be able to go anywhere that Henry isn't. Every day has to be like today. Every kiss like the one where he just strokes my lips very gently with his and pauses directly over my mouth. Until I, with a huge effort, raise my head and kiss him. It's the height of happiness. I understand that now.

Later, I'll sometimes ask myself if I shouldn't have guessed at this point that it couldn't stay this way because it was too perfect. Too pink, too light, too beautiful. Because the cloud was a patch of turbulence and we're falling. Hand in hand, but very fast. There's nothing to be done.

25

HENRY

'So, which phase of cell division can we see here?' Mr Ringling's gaze roams around the classroom. 'Inés?'

The helpless expression in her eyes is enough to tell me she doesn't have the faintest idea.

'Which image shows mitotic figures? Come on, people, it's nearly lunchtime for me too.' Mr Ringling looks at me. 'Henry, please, have *you* at least understood this, or is it just me who's incapable of explaining it properly?'

I look at the images on the screen. 'Top left?'

Mr Ringling sighs. 'OK, it really is my fault apparently. Fine. Shall we listen to the mitosis song again? Would that help?'

'Oh, please, no,' mumbles Omar.

I suppress a laugh, but can't prevent the irritating little jingle from starting to play in my head. Mr Ringling is looking positively baffled, when there's a sudden knock at the door.

I frown as Mr Harper pops his head in.

'Excuse the disturbance, but it's urgent,' he murmurs. 'Could you just . . .?'

'Er, yes, of course.' Mr Ringling turns to us. 'Have another look at the last chapter, please. I'll be right back.'

I reach for my book, but it's kind of hard to concentrate – Mr Harper looked at me in such a weird way. Why is he here? Normally the school secretary just summons people over the loudspeaker system if there's anything important. It's not unheard of for Mrs Sinclair to call me into her office to discuss something relating to the school council. Sometimes even during lessons. So there's no reason for me to be particularly worried when Mr Ringling reappears in the classroom after a brief while.

'Henry? Would you go with Mr Harper, please?' He seems weirdly anxious.

'Oh.' I stand up. 'All right.'

Mr Ringling glances at my desk. 'I think you should take your things.'

That's the moment I get an ache in my belly. I'm wondering desperately what this could be about as I follow Mr Harper down the corridors. Normally, he likes to chat and ask you how things are going, but this time he doesn't say a word, which is making me kind of edgy. I'm on the point of asking what's going on when we reach the offices.

'After you. Mrs Sinclair is expecting you.'

I feel his hand on my shoulder before I open the door. There's something about the expression in his eyes that scares me.

'Thanks,' I mumble, entering the room.

I've stepped through this doorway loads of times, but this time it's different. I can sense it: there's this tense feeling making it hard to breathe.

Mrs Sinclair isn't sitting at her desk as she usually is. She's standing by the window. There's a young man beside her.

They both turn to face me.

It's Theo . . .

What's he doing here? Has he come for a visit? Why didn't anyone tell me?

Mrs Sinclair's face is grave. Theo's is pale. I can't move.

'What's happened?' I blurt.

Mrs Sinclair looks at Theo. His Adam's apple bobs as he gulps.

All he says is 'Maeve,' and my blood runs cold.

EMMA

'Thank you for listening. If you have any questions, please, ask them now.' I exhale soundlessly as the others in the room start to clap.

'Wonderful, thank you, Emma.' Ms Kelleher smiles at me,

standing up. 'Very well done.' She glances at the clock. 'OK, we're pretty much out of time for today. The rest of you can head off to lunch break early so that I can give Emma my feedback on her presentation.'

I wipe my sweaty palms on my trousers, and pull my USB stick out of the laptop at the speaker's lectern. Giving a talk on the Industrial Revolution in Britain had cost me some sleepless nights. I'm so bad at speaking in front of other people, but at least it's over and done with now. Tori and Sinclair give me two thumbs up as they pass me on their way out.

Ms Kelleher waits until everyone's left the room, then glances at her notes.

'How do you think that went, Emma?' she asks.

'It was OK,' I begin. 'I was very nervous.'

'It didn't show.' She smiles at me. 'You spoke fluently, your English is excellent, and the content more than fulfilled the brief.'

I daren't move.

'I'm giving you an A star.'

'Oh.' I'm taken aback. 'Thank you.'

'You earned it. Keep up the good work, Emma. And now off to lunch with you.'

I stand up, still with butterflies in my stomach. 'Thank you,' I repeat, reaching for my bag.

'I'll see you again on Friday,' says Ms Kelleher, as I leave the room.

In the hallway, I look around for Tori and Sinclair, but they've disappeared. Maybe they've already gone to the dining room for lunch. I'm about to glance at my phone when I hear my name.

'Emma?' Grace is walking towards me. For a moment, I panic. But then I see her worried face. 'I wanted to let you know.'

'What's the matter?' I ask.

'Henry was called out of biology just now. He had to go to the head's office and he didn't come back.'

'What? Why? What's happened, Grace?'

'I don't know, but apparently his brother's here. I saw Theo's car in the courtyard.'

She doesn't continue, but she doesn't have to. 'So that means . . . something to do with his parents?'

Grace gives a helpless shrug. 'No idea. I heard that he's in his room, packing. I just thought you should know.'

'Thanks, Grace,' I manage to say.

My body feels weirdly numb as I turn away. As I go, I reach for my phone, but there's no message from Henry. Of course there isn't. If something's happened, no way will he have room in his head to message me. Shit, don't let it be anything bad.

I start running, without consciously thinking. My steps echo in the hallways. The closer I come to the east wing, the emptier they are. My heart is pounding in my throat as I reach Henry's floor and hurry down the empty corridor.

His door is open and a young man is standing there, his phone pressed to his ear. He's tall, sporty and slim in a Henry-like way. He's the guy from the old rugby-team photos. Theo Bennington. An older version of Henry, and as white as a sheet. His eyes flit over me as he makes his call, I can't take in what he's saying, none of it matters. I have to get to Henry.

I mumble a quiet hello as I step past Theo into the room. I don't think he even sees me.

Henry's stuffing things at random into a bag.

'Henry?'

He turns.

As I look into his face, I know this is bad. He's not crying. It's pure shock. Compressed lips and a blank gaze.

I drop my bag onto the floor and walk over to him. 'What's—'

He interrupts me. 'She's dead.' His voice has never been as dull, and his eyes just kind of look through me. 'Maeve. They're saying she's dead . . .'

'What?' It's like a punch in the guts. 'Henry, what's happened?'

He jumps, and at that moment he looks at me properly for the first time. His shoulders twitch as I lay both hands on his arms.

'I don't know, it's . . . They found her in the camp and took her to hospital in Nairobi. She was tired yesterday evening, wanted an early night because she had a headache. They think it was cerebral malaria. They found her too late,

330

this morning, in her tent. But I don't know, I . . .' Henry's slurring, mumbling, speaking too fast and when he falls silent, I pull him to me. His whole body is trembling and I want to do something – I *have* to do something – but I don't know what.

Malaria. I know what it is, but at the same time I don't. A fever, something to do with mosquitoes, and you can die from it. I've heard of it. But so suddenly? How is it possible? How can his sister be dead? It has to be some kind of mistake.

But then his brother wouldn't be here to pick him up, would he? I don't understand a thing. I want to say so much, but I can't speak. I can only hold Henry tightly and wonder what I should do.

Are you sure? Could it be some kind of mix-up? What do your parents say? Holy shit, maybe this is all a really horrible nightmare.

It's not a dream. It's reality, in which Henry's brother turns to us and I let Henry go.

'They were able to book us onto the flight,' he says, and I get it. They're flying to Kenya. Theo's eyes flit over me. 'We have to hurry, Henry. The plane to London goes in an hour and a half.'

26

HENRY

Nothing bad has ever happened to me before. I've grown up in countries where I don't speak the language, and which are dangerous enough that travel warnings advise against going there. I've lived in areas where there are tropical diseases and other health risks.

I've never worried about it. After all, things have always turned out fine. I never had a pet that died. My grandparents are all still alive. I've only experienced grief and shock in books and films. I could relate to them. Sometimes they made me cry if they were super-emotional, but I never really related them. I turned the TV off, shut the book, and forgot what they felt like. There was no room for them in my life. Everything was light-heartedness.

Naïvety.

Peace of mind.

This isn't a film. It's real life, and I'm getting off the plane beside Theo. Nine hours in cramped seats with this oppressive fear in my guts. Nine hours with no internet, nine hours in which I imagined Mum calling and saying, 'False alarm.' That it wasn't Maeve. Or that she woke up, that she's tired and confused but she's going to get better. That she got lucky. That we all got lucky. Nine hours when I wanted to cry but couldn't.

I'm dizzy. I haven't been able to eat. I'd like to go to sleep and kid myself that this isn't really happening. Nairobi is busy, loud and hot, even now, in the middle of the night. I can't breathe, it's all too much, but Theo is calm and composed, so I am too. I have to be like him, and it isn't even all that hard.

I don't cry until Mum and Dad walk towards us on the hospital corridor. Tears of exhaustion and helplessness. Hot tears into Mum's top – they're both wearing regular clothes: she's no longer a paediatric surgeon, he's no longer an anaesthetist, they're a mother and father, and their daughter is brain-dead. None of it makes any sense. Not when they silently shake their heads and Theo starts asking questions. Loud, furious questions – how is it possible when she was taking anti-malarials? Why did nobody notice? Didn't the headache and cramps give them a hint? Wasn't there anything that would have shown she was infected? I want to put my hands over my ears. I want him to stop because I want quiet. I want Maeve to join us and laugh because nothing's as bad as all that, but it is bad. It could have happened at any time, and it's happened. The thing Mum and Dad discussed with us from the start so that, even as little kids, we understood why we had to use slimy insect repellent and sleep under mosquito nets. Why we shouldn't go near standing water at dusk, why we should always have long trousers and sleeves, even in the heat.

Maeve knew all that. She learned it at an early age, and it was still no use.

I cry, I can't stop, even when we're eventually allowed to go to her. She doesn't look like she's only sleeping – there's too much equipment in this room for that, ventilators, syringe pumps, and so on – but on the other hand, she doesn't look like she'll never wake up either. I can't take it in. Her skin is warm. None of it makes any sense.

It feels like we're only allowed to stay with her a few minutes, but the sun's come up outside when we leave the hospital. They've switched off the machines. I can't feel a thing.

The streets are teeming. There's noise and people everywhere.

And Maeve is dead.

She's dead.

My sister . . .

And I don't understand.

I just don't understand.

EMMA

I feel like the main character in a film, where everyone except me has read the script. Everything just happens, and as I try to pull myself together, I just let it. Let's be honest, what else could I do?

Henry's come back to England with his family and right now they're with his grandparents in Cheshire, where the funeral's going to be. We've spoken on the phone. I asked him if I should come but he said no and I accept that, even though I'm worried about him. But he needs to be with his family.

Henry misses the last two and a half weeks of school before half-term. It's all so trivial in the grand scheme of things, but Tori, Sinclair, Olive, Grace and I divide up Henry's lessons and take notes for him. Omar and Gideon help too, so we can cover everything. I guess schoolwork is the last thing on his mind but it's all we can do. Mrs Sinclair called us into her office the day after Henry left, and asked us to do it.

By that first evening, everyone had heard the terrible news. My throat clenched even more the next morning when everything went silent as we walked into the dining room. I dread to think what it'll be like when Henry's back. But it's clear to me now that pupils at Dunbridge Academy are more than just names on a list. Ms Barnett was stunned, and so was Mrs Sinclair. Mr Cormack, Mr Ringling. Everyone seems upset. Even Mr Ward bites his tongue as he hands me a list of the course material for the next little while so that I can structure my notes for Henry.

The lower- and upper-sixth-formers, who remember Maeve, seem to freeze on the Monday of the funeral, when Mrs Sinclair talks about what happened. Tori stands silently beside me when the head teacher calls for a minute's silence, and grips Sinclair's hand; he wipes his eyes with the other. Even Valentine Ward is unusually quiet. And all I can think of is Henry.

I fly home for half-term. Mum's waiting for me at the airport and hugs me as I cry.

I write to Henry every day, but try not to intrude. I'm aiming to be sympathetic and supportive, nothing more, because Henry's still in total shock. When he wants to, we talk on the phone. He doesn't cry, but he doesn't say much either. He doesn't have the words because he's numb and overwhelmed. Sometimes I tell him stuff, sometimes we just sit in silence together until Henry falls asleep and I hang up.

It doesn't feel like three weeks have passed since Henry drove to the airport with his brother. My time in Frankfurt is surreal. I feel kind of uprooted, because I'm missing Henry and boarding school, and Isi doesn't get in touch and neither do any of my other old friends here, even though they've seen my Insta story and know I'm back. To be fair, I have to admit that I haven't contacted any of them either. All my thoughts are with Henry, so much so that I even forget to ask Mum for more details about Mr Ward and my dad.

Mum drops me back at the airport at the end of the holiday, so I'm on time. My lips are numb, my fingertips cold as I walk through the hallways until I reach the point between two moving travelators where I ran into Henry. I stop for a moment, then go on to the gate. Maybe I'm subconsciously spending the whole forty-five minutes till boarding starts waiting for Henry to turn up, out of breath, his hair all over the place. But he doesn't, obviously. He's not here, he's in Cheshire. Or maybe that's not true – he ought to be on the way to Dunbridge Academy now because he'll be back in lessons from tomorrow. We'll see each other again and I don't know why that scares me. Maybe because I get the feeling I'll be facing a completely different Henry from the one of a few weeks ago. Although we've been in touch, I haven't the least idea of how he's really doing.

I remember the way he said *Welcome home, Emma from Germany*, that time as we sat in the bus from the airport to the school, and it's kind of true. This journey still feels like an adventure, but also like coming home. Familiar faces on the coach, although not so many today because the only flight got in so late that I won't get back until after wing time.

When I get back, our corridor is quiet, but there's a light on in Ms Barnett's room. I knock on her door, as agreed, to let her know that I'm in, and to my surprise, she gives me a big hug before sending me off to my room. I put down my suitcase without opening it, grab my phone, and start to message Sinclair:

E: *Are you with him?*

He answers in a matter of seconds.

S: *I was. He's asleep now.*

Sinclair's still typing so I wait.

S: *Mr Acevedo's light's off so the coast is clear.*

It takes me a moment to understand that Sinclair's long been aware of what I'm really thinking. I send him a quick thanks, then stand up. Of course I know the boys' wing is strictly out of bounds at this time of night, but I don't care. I can't believe Mr Acevedo would be totally unsympathetic if he caught me with Henry tonight.

All the same, my heart's beating faster as I walk down the dark corridors. I know my way to Henry's room like the back of my hand now. Every corner, every step, I could find him with my eyes shut.

The lower-sixth corridor is completely silent. Mr Acevedo's room is indeed dark. But I still try to keep quiet as I walk to the end. I reach Henry's room, and the door's open a tiny crack. I silently thank Sinclair, because he must have been the last person there with him, and deliberately didn't quite shut it.

It's dark in there, but the moonlight outside is enough for me to make out Henry's silhouette. He's curled up on his side in bed, and his head jerks up as I shut the door behind me. I put my finger to my lips as I come closer. Suddenly I remember the way he came into my room like this at the start of term. That all seems so far away now.

Henry doesn't put the light on, just sinks back onto the mattress. I slip off my shoes and budge up next to him. His body is warm, but I can feel a suppressed trembling as I pull the duvet over us. We don't speak, don't say a word. I just put my arms round him and press my face gently into his shoulder blade.

I don't know exactly when Henry starts crying. I only know that once I've noticed it, it makes it hard to breathe. He's crying almost without a sound. His shoulders are shaking and his pain becomes mine, because, eventually, he bursts into hoarse sobbing.

He's never cried in front of me. And I've never felt anything like this before. I never knew that anything could hurt as much as someone else's pain when everything you wish for in the whole world is for them not to have to experience anything like it. And I can't make it better. I can only lie next to Henry and hold him tightly, stroke his face and keep whispering to him that I'm here. He may not even be able to hear me, but I can't help thinking about the time he lay next to me like this and him just being there was enough to make everything a tiny bit more bearable. But I also know that the reason I was crying then isn't remotely comparable to why he is now.

I don't know how long it takes Henry to calm himself. Thirty minutes, an hour, three? I only know that my heart is still hurting as his hoarse sobs dry and he is lying in silence beside me. My shoulder aches, and I'd like to roll over but I can't. Instead I go on stroking Henry's arm, his wrist. When I push my fingers between his and he doesn't respond, I know he's asleep.

I shut my eyes, listening in the darkness. My heart is heavy with overload and pain. But I'm here with him, and I hope he knows he doesn't have to cope with all this alone. I press my nose gently into his shoulder blade. His scent hasn't changed. Perhaps that's the only thing that's remained the same.

I don't let him go. Not even when I feel he's deeply asleep. Crying the way Henry cried is tiring. It's late, I can feel his exhaustion, and I want to stay awake, to keep watch in case he has a bad dream, so that I can wake him in time, but I can't. I fall asleep. I'm scared.

27

HENRY

Maeve has been dead for four weeks and I still can't take it in. Time stopped in the moment I walked into the head's office and saw Theo. And since then, it's never really got going again.

I've missed three weeks of school. And I don't give a damn. I can't even think about it: there's too much other stuff filling my head.

There's an impenetrable veil over the days in Nairobi before Maeve's funeral. It feels like I wasn't even really there. It's scary how little of it I can remember. The return flight, our time with Gran and Gramp in Cheshire, it's all fuzzy and out of focus. I felt like I'd lost all contact with the real world, and if it hadn't been for Emma, who texted or called every day, I'm certain that that would have been the case.

She and the others have made it as easy as possible for me to come back to school. They're there round the clock. They listen to me, they sit in silence with me or take my mind off things, whichever I need at the time.

When I walk into the dining room between Emma and Tori on Monday morning, I feel all eyes on me. Of course, everyone knows what's happened.

I follow Emma to our table, voices hush, conversations tail off. It's unbearable. Emma turns to me as I stop halfway. I don't have to explain. I just barely perceptibly shake my head, mumble, 'Sorry,' turn and leave the room.

Emma comes to stand beside me in the small inner courtyard. The sky is almost ridiculously blue. It makes me angry. I feel an overwhelming urge to kick one of the huge planters, but I pull myself together because that would be silly. Instead I clench my fists, then walk on.

Emma stays with me. She doesn't speak, doesn't ask me where I'm going, just walks beside me.

'Sorry for being like this,' I say at some point, coming to a stop.

'Listen, Henry,' she replies at once. 'You can be however you like. You can cry, be angry, irritated, I don't care. I'm not going anywhere. Unless you genuinely want to be on your own . . . Do you want to be on your own?'

My throat is tight. 'No.'

'OK, then.' She lowers her gaze, straightens her skirt and

looks up to the sky. She's not even trying to get me to talk. She's just there.

What did I do to deserve you?

I shut my eyes for a moment, seriously asking myself that question. And I'd like to say something but it's not possible. It's too exhausting. The journey here was exhausting, last night was exhausting. The conversation with Mrs Sinclair and Mr Ward, who told me not to worry about schoolwork or grades, that they'd be glad to see me back in lessons, but that if I give any teacher a signal, I can just leave the class at any time without explanation. That I don't have to do the next lot of tests if I don't feel up to it. That I can speak to Ms Vail, the school psychologist, any time I want to. I guess I ought to have cried because everyone is so concerned for me, but the truth is that I didn't feel a thing. I didn't feel touched or grateful. I sat facing Mrs Sinclair's desk and nodded silently. None of it is any use. Maeve won't come back if I walk out of lessons or dodge the tests. She's never coming back because her dead body is in a wooden box five feet underground, and I just can't take it in.

My only goal is to make it through the day. Every day, that's my goal. To hang in there when the darkness won't let me out of its clutches. Even making it through the day is too much sometimes. At those times, it's just about getting through the next hour, the next minute, even just the next breath.

I know why I can't talk. Because I'd go mad and find myself pleading with heaven just to let me through to Maeve. I suppose it's despair, grief, this overwhelming dark emotion. The kind of pain that nobody prepares you for.

They say it'll get more bearable eventually. But I'm not convinced of that right now.

EMMA

Henry's been back at school for almost two weeks. He's struggling, and every day, I'm waiting to see if things are going to be any better. But they aren't. I keep glancing at him during our English test. He looks so desperately tired, can hardly keep his eyes open. I'm not sure if he's showered. He's sitting motionless over his paper, pen in hand, but I don't see him write anything.

'Keep your eyes on your own work,' Mr Ward warns.

I look hastily away again.

The test is challenging, but fair. Now I've caught up with the others, I can answer the questions surprisingly easily. It ought to be no problem at all for Henry, but when I hand in my paper just before time, he's sitting motionless in his place, both elbows on the desk and his head in his hands. As I pass, I catch a glimpse of his paper. It's blank, and my stomach lurches. Mrs Sinclair said he didn't have to do the test, and I don't get why he didn't take her up on that.

I walk out, not even happy that I think I did OK, seeing that Henry's apparently handing in a blank sheet of paper. Maybe Mr Ward will let him off. I could ask Ms Barnett for advice. Or Mrs Sinclair. Henry can't keep sitting there doing nothing when we get to the mocks, can he? He got a D in Latin yesterday, and I'm pretty sure Ms Barnett marked it generously so as not to fail him altogether.

Henry's clever enough that he'll get good predicted grades, but he won't be able to keep on like this without putting his A levels at risk. And then it'll all be for nothing. Then we won't have a future together at St Andrews, like we were planning just before the world came to a stop around us.

Maybe I ought to think less about the future. Maybe instead I should be thinking about what I can do to help Henry, but I'm stumped. I've never lost anyone, not like this, anyway. It's different from the way things were after my dad walked out. I was eleven, I didn't understand, but I thought he'd be back before too long. After all, he'd promised. It was a different kind of loss. And it's not like I've found a way of making the pain any easier since then.

I can only try to be there for Henry and not pressurize him. Not resort to tactless clichés. *She had a great life. I'm sure she's happy where she is now. She wouldn't want you to let yourself wallow like this.* That's bollocks. Nobody knows what Maeve would want. She's dead. And Henry has to grieve. It's just so painful and exhausting to be at his side and unable to do a bloody thing.

It drives me crazy to remember the way he cried on his first night back at school. And that he hasn't since then. Not once. Mostly he's just apathetic and blank. He laughs with the others sometimes, and when he sits with Gideon and Sinclair in the dining room, there seem to be plenty of times when he forgets what's happened for a second. Maybe it's self-protection. I don't know. I can only say that he's different when we're together. He's pricklier, thinner-skinned. Maybe that's better than indifference, because it means he still has feelings, despite everything. But I'm worried. I might not have known Henry long, but I know him well enough to be sure that it's bad for him to bottle up his emotions and not let them out. That eventually he'll burst. I can only hope that he's not alone when it happens.

I'm standing in front of the mirror in my tiny bathroom, in leggings and hoodie, brushing my teeth, when there's a knock at the door way after wing time. It's not Henry's knock. It sounds more like Tori. Toothbrush in mouth, I open the door. It is indeed Tori.

'You have to get dressed,' she says. 'Sinclair texted, they're drinking and Henry . . . He's overdone it a bit.'

'He's what?' I blurt. Toothpaste foam runs down my chin. I wipe it away with my hand and head back to the bathroom. Once I've rinsed my mouth, I head back to Tori.

'We should go and check on them. Henry doesn't usually drink much. I don't like this at all.' Tori is unusually anxious: her eyes keep darting from me to the door and back again. When I don't answer, she throws me my jacket. 'Put this on.'

I catch it. 'But isn't this—' I gesture towards my hoodie.

'They're on the roof, Emma.'

Someone could have told me sooner that there's this secret door near the boys' wing, which leads to a narrow spiral staircase that goes up to a tiny platform between the spires on the school roof. It's pretty well hidden from view up there. I don't feel entirely comfortable as I reach the top with Tori. The night is fresh: there's an icy wind blowing around the turrets and rooftops. Four people are crouched on the platform, Sinclair, Henry, Omar and Gideon, circled by glass bottles.

Sinclair jumps up when he sees us. Although it's dark, I can see his despair as he comes towards us.

'He just won't stop,' he whispers.

Tori seems dangerously calm. 'Then take the fucking bottle off him.'

'You don't understand, he . . .'

I leave them there and walk over to him. Henry lifts his head. I can see at a glance that he's wrecked. He's slumped with his back to a low parapet, his eyelids are half shut. I put the water bottle I brought from my room in front of him, and sit down.

'What the hell?' I ask.

He just shrugs. He goes to lift his own bottle to his lips but I grab his wrist.

'I think you've had enough Henry.' I hold the water out to him. 'Drink.'

'Could you just—'

'Drink this,' I say, a notch more sharply.

As he turns his head to me, I recognize the pain in his green eyes. I immediately understand why he's doing this. There's no need for it, it's toxic, this 'I'm drinking my emotions away and hoping it's the answer' stuff. He knows better. I'm worried for him, but it's making me angry too.

'Emma, you can have a drink too or you can piss off.' His tongue is heavy, and he's slurring. I know he's drunk and I shouldn't take his words to heart, but that doesn't make them hurt any the less. He's never tried to get rid of me before.

'I'm not going anywhere,' I hiss. 'Because you're not going anywhere either.'

'You don't know what I'm gonna do,' he mumbles.

'I'm very sorry, but that's just not true.'

'Yeah, it is. God, you're clueless! You don't know what it's like. But, hey, it's been a coupla weeks now, time for him to start pulling himself together, huh?' Henry's raising his voice more with each word. Omar and Gideon are acting like they're not listening. Tori and Sinclair stand rooted to the spot.

When Henry gets up and has to clutch onto the wall, my stomach lurches. I pull myself up too, grabbing him by the sleeve as he sways. My eyes take in the edge, which is only a few steps away.

Henry tries to pull himself free.

'Henry.' You can hear the effort I'm making to keep my voice calm. 'Stop this shit.'

'I just wanna be left in peace, OK?' he snaps at me.

I want to say something. Henry tries to sidestep. His foot connects with one of the bottles, glass clinking on glass. Sinclair has the presence of mind to take a step towards us and grab Henry by his jacket collar.

'Time for bed, Bennington.'

All I can do is watch the bottle as it rolls in slow motion over the edge and disappears into the darkness. A moment later, we hear the crash. From up here, it was fairly quiet, but I still hold my breath.

The others stand thunderstruck beside me. I've only just dared to breathe again when a light goes on down in the courtyard.

'Fuck,' mumbles Tori, ducking down. 'You lads are so stupid, you know that?'

I'm in total agreement with her, but I bite my tongue as I help her and Omar to gather up the bottles at lightning speed. Sinclair's already pushing Henry towards the stairs. I'm sure Henry knows the way better than I do, but it would be easy enough to miss one of the narrow steps in the darkness stone cold sober. I only uncross my fingers once he's made it to the bottom.

Gideon shuts the door behind us and I stand there. Our rooms are in opposite directions, and it would definitely be better for me and Tori to be in bed if Ms Barnett's going to be checking up on us at any minute. And I'm pissed off with Henry. But all the same, I'd rather turn to the left and make sure he gets safely back to his room.

Sinclair glances over his shoulder like he's read my mind. He opens his mouth, but before he gets a chance to say anything, the light goes on.

'Nobody move.'

I close my eyes.

28

HENRY

It must have been humiliating to have to blow into that breathalyser in front of Mr Acevedo and Ms Barnett, as if they were the police. So I suppose it's lucky that I can't remember much about it. To be precise, I don't even remember how I got down off that roof. The only thing that's burned onto my memory is the moment when Mr Ward suddenly came round the corner. He caught us red-handed.

Ms Barnett was cross. Mr Acevedo was disappointed, which is actually way worse, although there was so much alcohol in my bloodstream that I didn't really take it in. Mr Acevedo forced me to spend the night in the sick bay, where I puked up my soul a few hours later. My guilty conscience didn't strike until this morning, hand in hand with the droning headache that's making me only too aware of how badly I overdid things last night. I don't even know what I was thinking when I forced Sinclair to come and drink with me. I just wanted not to feel anything, and this time it actually worked. For a few hours at least. But it's turned into an utter catastrophe.

Emma, Tori, Sinclair, Omar, Gideon and I have been summoned to Mrs Sinclair's office instead of lessons. My whole body is fighting against stepping through the door and lining up with the others. Standing upright is enough of an effort, and the light is too bright. Mrs Sinclair is standing in front of her desk. She's as mad as hell, you can see that. She's trying to keep calm, but her eyes are spraying sparks as she walks up and down in front of us. Because we broke three school rules in one. We were drinking, we were out after wing time, and we were up on the roof, which is totally out of bounds. So, yeah, we've genuinely screwed up.

'You can count yourselves lucky that nobody was injured by that bottle.' Mrs Sinclair eyes each of us in turn. 'Such large quantities of alcohol, I really would have thought you'd have more sense.'

'It's my fault,' I say. My head aches. 'I talked Sinclair – uh, Charles – and Gideon into it. It was me who started it all. And Omar, Tori and Emma didn't drink anything.'

'That may well be so, Henry, but they were still caught out of their rooms after quiet time.' I open my mouth, but she doesn't let me speak. Sinclair glances warningly at me,

Emma's standing stock still beside me. 'And you all know what that means.'

'Mum,' Sinclair breathes, barely audibly, but she shakes her head.

'And I'm sorry, but there are rules at this school, and you have broken them. You will have to take the consequences of that. So I'm giving all of you a warning. You are all aware of what that means?'

I swallow hard. Breaking the rules again this term will mean big trouble. I'd never have dreamed that those words would ever be said to me. And, even so, it doesn't bother me half as much as I suppose it ought to.

'On top of which, each of you is to take on an extra cleaning or kitchen duty from now until the end of the month. Report to your houseparents at break time and they will allocate them.'

I ought to be punished harder than the others. I drank the most and I'm aware that Mrs Sinclair is only going easy on me because she can see that I wasn't boozing for fun.

'Very well. That will be all.' She straightens her shoulders. 'Go back to class now.' I'm about to turn away when she continues. 'Apart from Henry.'

I don't want anything more. I just want peace and quiet, I want to sleep and never wake up again.

Emma's eyes meet mine. She looks worried but I just nod towards the door.

'Sit down,' says Mrs Sinclair, as Omar shuts the door. She takes a seat, behind her desk, and studies me for a moment. 'I think we both know what a warning means for you as school captain.'

I shiver. Well, that's that, then. Job over. Shit. I hadn't even thought of that.

There's a tiny moment of panic before it's replaced by indifference. The same way that I've been indifferent to everything in recent weeks. So what? I'll resign. That'd probably be better for everyone.

'Henry?'

I don't know if Mrs Sinclair can see inside my head, but she seems to have been expecting something else. For me to beg her not to do it. What do I know?

'I should resign,' I say. That's all.

Mrs Sinclair gives me a long look. 'And you're really telling me that that means nothing to you?'

'It does mean something,' I lie. 'I made a mistake, and I'm truly sorry. Especially because I didn't want the others to get into trouble because of me.'

'I know that, Henry. And because I understand how very difficult this situation is for you, I won't insist on any further consequences. That, and because I value you a great deal as school captain.'

Now I should probably feel flattered. It's almost a shame.

'Thanks,' I say. It's ridiculous.

'But that isn't why I asked you to stay behind,' she

continues. I'm fearing the worst, which proves correct. 'How are you doing?'

For a brief moment, I feel that horrible pressure behind my eyeballs. But I don't cry. 'I'm OK. Thank you.'

Mrs Sinclair is still giving me a look. 'That is not entirely the impression I'm getting.'

What does she expect? Maeve's dead. Of course I'm not OK, but if I say it out loud, it'll make it real.

'In your last English test, you handed in a blank sheet of paper.'

I just shrug my shoulders.

'Why didn't you speak to Mr Ward?'

'What could he have done?'

'He could have let you off the test altogether and given you more time to catch up, as you know.'

I say nothing.

'Henry, we all want to do whatever we can so as not to make things harder for you, but you have to work with us on that. You need to speak to us, so that we can help you.'

I don't have to do anything and I don't need help, I think.

And then I say, 'I know. I'm sorry.'

'It wasn't intended as a telling-off. I understand that things aren't easy for you. You know that Ms Vail's door is always open to you?'

I nod. If I speak, I'll burst into tears. So I don't speak.

'And if it all gets too much for you, we can give you permission to go home for a while.'

Go home . . . Which home? Mum and Dad are back on the project, Theo's busy at uni and we're barely in touch. I could go to my grandparents in Cheshire, but what would I do there? Visit Maeve's grave? Fantastic.

'I spoke to Mr Ward. Ideally, you'd need to take part in the maths exam next week. He's planning on running a two-hour mock A level. Do you feel up to it?'

'Yes.' The word slips out. 'Totally. In English I had . . . some kind of blackout, I don't know.'

Mrs Sinclair doesn't believe a word of it. I can see that in her eyes. But I can't do anything else.

'Fine, Henry. That'll be all.' She looks at me. 'I'm here anytime if you want to talk to me. About anything at all.'

EMMA

I still can't believe we got caught last night and had to line up in Mrs Sinclair's office this morning. Since then, Henry and I haven't had a chance to talk. I'd thought we'd have time after the bollocking, but Mrs Sinclair asked him to stay behind. I can only guess at what she wanted to talk to him about.

I say goodbye to Tori, who has French now, while I head towards the science block for chemistry. I knock and open the door, but instead of Ms Ventura, Mr Ward is sitting behind the desk. I hesitate, but as I look around the class and see everyone who ought to be there, I pull myself together and realize he must be filling in for her.

'Sorry I'm late. I was with Mrs Sinclair,' I mumble, setting my phone down in an empty pigeonhole.

'I suspected as much.' Mr Ward looks down at the books he's marking. The others are doing prep or other work.

'Ms Ventura's not well,' Salome whispers, as I sit down.

I unpack my things. I'm longing to text Henry and ask him what Mrs Sinclair wanted. But that'll have to wait for the end of the period when I've got my phone back.

I pull out my history prep, but my attention keeps wandering. When the bell goes for break, I haven't made much progress. I put my books away again and follow the others outside. As always, a little traffic jam builds because everyone wants to start sending snaps right away, or else check to see what earth-shattering news has come in over the last hour, just as if all their friends hadn't been phoneless for the same length of time, and thus unable to message them. But I'm no better because my first move is to see if Henry's texted. He hasn't. Does that mean he's still pissed off with me? I'm not sure if he remembers everything. After all, he was wasted. Either way, I want to talk to him, ask him what last night was all about. He wasn't himself, evidently, but we can't go on like this. Since Maeve died, it's like he's slipping further and further away from me.

'Ms Wiley.' I jump as I hear Mr Ward's voice. He's emerging from the classroom and nodding to one side with his head. I follow him. 'I've been making appointments for the feedback sessions. Kindly come to my office next Wednesday at five.'

I relax slightly as he doesn't broach the subject of last night. 'OK.'

'Do you know where that is?' he asks.

'No.'

'Room 2350 in the old building.'

'2350?' I repeat, resisting the urge to dig out my planner and write it down. *Wednesday, 5 o'clock. 2350. Don't forget.*

'Yes. You'll find the self-assessment form online, on the student portal. Please fill it in and bring it with you. And be on time.'

He turns away before I can nod. I look back at my phone, then enter the appointment and room number in my calendar app. Just before I finish, a message from Henry pings in at the top of the screen.

H: *Are you free?*

My heart skips a beat, but then I catch sight of the clock. It's break, after the first double period, but I've got PE after that and I have to change.

E: *I have to get to PE. After that?*

Henry replies at once.

H: OK. I'll come and meet you. Got a free period

And there Henry is, waiting for me. We're on the running track, doing athletics assessments. I spot him sitting on a bench as I line up with Grace, Olive and Salome for a sprint race, almost at the end of the session. I bend down and position my feet on the blocks.

Ms Ventura counts us down, I make a good start. Grace is about level with me, the others are dropping back, but I hold on and cross the line first.

'Very good!' Ms Ventura's voice rings out across the track.

My chest is heaving, I have my hands on my sides, only letting go for a moment to high-five Grace. Her eyes meet mine, then wander over to Henry on the bench.

'Grace?' I hesitate, but I've been putting this off way too long already. 'I wanted to thank you.'

She looks surprised. 'What for?'

'For telling me. About Maeve. It was really kind of you.'

I can see that she's fighting to keep her smile relaxed and not to look hurt. 'There's no need for thanks.'

'Yes, there is,' I say. 'And I'm sorry. I didn't mean to come between you.'

'You didn't, Emma,' she says quietly. 'Truly not. And I'm not angry with you. I miss Henry but I want the best for us

SARAH SPRINZ

both. We weren't the best for each other. That's nothing to do with you. I'm sorry if I ever made you feel it was.'

'No, it's OK,' I say. 'I understand that.'

'We're women,' Grace says, to my surprise. 'It's our job to stick together, not to chase after men and see each other as rivals.'

I've had nothing but respect for Grace ever since we met, but now it's off the charts. Because she's so right, and it feels like an invisible weight's been lifted off my chest.

Ms Ventura whistles and waves us over, as she always does just before the end of class. Grace smiles and I follow her to join the others. Olive looks sceptically at us, but at least she no longer seems to feel the need to throw accusations at my head.

Henry stands up as we finish and the others vanish into the changing rooms. He shoves his hands into his trouser pockets as I approach.

'Hi,' I murmur, bending down to retrieve my water bottle.

'I wanted to apologize,' he says, so abruptly that I pause in mid-movement. 'I think I acted like a dick to you yesterday.'

I straighten up again. 'You were drunk.'

OK, he remembers. I can see it in his eyes.

'I'm sorry,' he repeats. 'I didn't mean any of what I said.'

'I know, Henry.'

'And I'm sorry for being like this,' he bursts out. 'I wish it was different, but I can't help it. I don't know, I'm furious and powerless and . . . I didn't mean to take it out on you.'

'Henry.' He falls silent as I reach for his hand. 'It's OK. These are exceptional circumstances.'

Eventually he shrugs his shoulders. 'I didn't want you to get into trouble for my sake, either.'

'It was my own decision to go up onto that roof.'

'But you wouldn't have done it if I hadn't been there.'

I study him. 'Just promise me you won't do it again in future.'

Henry's jaw muscles tense but then he nods.

'Do you want to go for a run?' I ask, and not all that long ago, I'd have bet my life he'd say no. But I think he gets how it works now, that running can help when nothing else does any good.

'Yes, I . . . I think so.'

HENRY

There's a smell of rain as we set off after our last lesson that afternoon. The sky is grey and heavy with clouds, but that couldn't interest me less.

Emma and I don't speak. She lets me set our route and our pace, so I just run at random. Past the sports grounds and greenhouses, down the path that winds along the edge of the woods for a while, then I turn off among the trees. It's tiring, my legs are heavy, I still have a headache, but I can't stop. I have to run until I hit the state where everything gets a little more bearable. I don't know what I'll do if it doesn't work. This is the final straw I'm clinging to, and I'm praying it won't snap.

There's so much I ought to talk to Emma about. About last night, about my jumbled thoughts and the paralysing fear that she won't go along with it for ever. That this thing between us is too new and fresh to stand up to me . That I'm afraid of it. That I can't lose her too. But I say nothing.

The sweat stings my eyes and mingles with the first rain-drops as they land on us. Emma doesn't ask if we should turn back. My lungs are burning. Past-Henry would want to stop now. But I can't, any more than I can go back to the time when I never had any real problems. To the way I blubbed after I split up with Grace and thought that that was real, horrible pain. It was horrible, yes, but it was fun and games compared to what I've been feeling lately.

I stumble over a root and bite back a curse. It makes me angry. Everything's making me angry, and I hate it. I hate Maeve being dead and that you can't yell at people who're dead because you're pissed off with them for not being around any more. I want to go back in time and cancel Maeve's flight. I want to drag her singlehanded off that plane and chain her up somewhere so she can't go anywhere she might die. I want to scream at her, ask her why she wanted to be the saviour of the world, but forgot to look after her-self. Why she's doing this to me. Huh, Maeve?

My heart's pumping.

Why. Weren't. You. More. Careful?

Just a little.

I want it to stop. I don't want to feel like this. The constant cycling between this endless emptiness and the hot seething in my chest. I want my old life back. I want it so badly, but I'm gradually starting to fear that I'm never going to get it.

I had no idea how much energy it took to gather yourself up every day and pull yourself out of the darkness. Every bloody day. Every bloody second. Every time I think of some new thing I'd like to tell her about. Like the stuff with Grace, which we never even got to Skype about. Because she was too busy and I plain forgot. Because I was so happy with Emma. Because I thought we had so much time.

Maeve, it's not fair, do you get that? You wanted to go off on an adventure and help people and then you died because of some fucking little mosquito and I can't take it in.

I feel guilty if I forget it for a moment. I think about you all and every bloody day and it feels like someone's crushing my ribcage. And all night too. When I dream about that hospital, about Nairobi, and wake up dripping with sweat, that's when it's worst of all. The moment when they switched the machines off repeats itself in my head. I've lost a person I thought would be in my life for ever. I was so bloody sure. I never even dreamed that one day I might be on my own. The hole that Maeve's left behind seems massive to me. She was the bridge between Theo and me. I don't know how we're meant to manage without her.

They say it'll get easier with time, but I'm not sure that's true. I feel worse than I did at the very beginning. I cry more often, but only in secret. I feel alone more often, even though Emma and the others are there and do so much for me. I'm afraid I'm getting on their nerves. That I just bring the mood down, that I'm no longer the Henry they want to be friends with, even though I know that's nonsense. I know they're worried for me and want to help.

It feels like everything's shifted.

The ground is muddy from the rain. I slip slightly, but I keep running. If I go fast enough, maybe my heart will just stop beating. I hear Emma's voice, I notice her dropping back behind me but I don't care. Her shitty theory doesn't work. It's not getting better: everything's just getting more intense. I'm running. I'm feeling the rain like pinpricks on my face. I can't take in as much air as I need. I'm running. I'm slipping. I land on my knees. The ground is muddy and wet. My fists pound on the sodding mud. A sound escapes me, one I've never heard myself make before, and then everything bursts out of me.

EMMA

'Henry!' I call his name but I don't tell him to stop because I know he can't. I just run and ignore the cold rain on my face. I'm running, and this time I'm having trouble keeping up. Henry is faster, I'm breathing wrongly, and after just a couple of lousy kilometres, I feel a stabbing in my chest. Maybe it's also because I can see Henry's clenched jaw when I finally catch up. His clenched fists, his face fixed grimly ahead. His curls are plastered damply to his brow. He's not listening to me.

The path through the trees is more reminiscent of a slide after all the rain over the last few days. Henry trips, lands on his knees. For a second he's frozen there. Has he hurt himself? I hope not, but then I see him punch the ground with his fists. Once, twice. Henry's back shakes, rises and falls as he breathes rapidly. I get goosebumps as a hoarse sob escapes him. He curls up and I kneel beside him.

He's crying differently this time. It's louder and more desperate. Furious, involving his whole body. I wrap both arms around him and hold him tighter than I've ever held anyone before. I shut my eyes and press my face into his shoulder because I can feel his pain as if it were my own. It's unbearable, but I can't do a thing.

I don't know if I've ever cried like Henry's crying. I've never had reason to. The business with my dad is a different pain. A slow, dull pain that's crept into my heart and made a nest there. I've learned to live with it. But Henry's been knocked off his feet without any warning, and since then, he's been falling. Deeper and deeper. I think we might have hit the bottom.

29

EMMA

We're frozen to the bone by the time we get back to school. Wet through and caked with mud. Dark brown water disappears down the drain as I rinse our running clothes in my shower. Then I stay under the hot water for several minutes.

Henry's eyes are still red as we lie in my bed with wet hair, but for the first time, it feels like he's really here again. Something must have happened in the wood just now, and even if I don't completely understand it, I'm happy that he's let emotions in again. And he's talking. Especially that.

When he speaks, between minutes of a not-uncomfortable silence, his words are so genuine it hurts.

'I don't know what I should do,' he whispers, his head on my belly. 'It feels like nothing exists any more.'

'I understand it feels like that.' His hair is almost dry as I run my fingers through his dark curls. 'It's not true, though. There's still so much, even if you can't see it right now.'

'You'll never get to meet.' Henry gulps. 'It's not fair, Em.'

'No. It's not.'

Henry says nothing. The raindrops still rattling against my window are the only sound as he runs his index finger over my knee.

'Do you think we'd have got on?' I ask.

Henry nods without a second's hesitation. 'You might have found her a bit overpowering, but Maeve would have loved you. And then she'd have spent the whole time sending you these weird memes that no one but her really finds funny.' Henry pauses, but there's something else he wants to say. I can sense it, so I say nothing. 'Nobody messages our family group any more,' he says in the end. 'It's horrible. Mum and Dad only text me individually. And Theo . . .' He doesn't need to spell it out, I get the idea. Theo doesn't message at all.

I roll onto my side so that I can put both arms around Henry. 'I'm sorry,' I whisper into his hoodie. It's the one I might just have stolen from him and hidden in my wardrobe. 'But I'm sure it has nothing to do with you.'

Henry doesn't answer straight away. 'I know,' he mumbles in the end.

'Next week is the open day at St Andrews.' Henry tenses almost imperceptibly. 'Are you coming?' I feel him shrug.

'I'm sure Mrs Sinclair would understand if we asked not to go,' I say.

'Yeah. Maybe. I don't know.'

I sense that I'm overburdening him, so I don't ask again. It's not a decision he has to take right now.

'But you have to go,' Henry says.

'I don't want to go if you don't go.'

'OK. Well, we'll see.' He's trying to sound light-hearted and it's tugging at my heart a bit.

'Just decide on the day, if you like.'

'Thanks, Em,' he says, some time later.

'Stop that,' I reply at once.

'No, really. Thank you. For being so understanding, even when I was being a jerk. It – it's just all so bloody hard.'

'It won't be the same for ever,' I say. 'Some day it'll be better. A tiny bit. And then another tiny bit.'

Henry doesn't say anything, but at least he doesn't contradict me.

'I'm scared I'll screw up in maths too,' he says eventually. 'In English that was ... I just couldn't think straight. I couldn't do it.'

My stomach clenches but I try not to let it show. 'Maths will be different. I'm sure of it. We can revise together, if you like.'

Henry nods vaguely, and I know that right now revising for some mock exam is the last thing he ought to be doing. But he still has to pass his A levels and get into uni.

Henry needs good predicted grades. Even if he doesn't want to study at St Andrews, given what's happened. Not many good universities are going to have lower entry requirements. But it definitely isn't the time to talk about that to Henry. All that matters now is for him to find himself again.

HENRY

They said I don't have to come to the St Andrews open day. I'm already regretting having turned down the offer to stay at school when we step off the bus after a ninety-minute drive. My stomach knots. Maybe I'll throw up on the university's perfectly manicured lawn, or maybe I just won't allow any emotions to stir. It's bad enough feeling Emma, Sinclair and Tori looking anxiously at me as Mr Ringling, who's in charge today, introduces us to the students who will show us around. There are three girls and three boys, and I can hardly look them in the face. When they introduce themselves, I don't recognize their names, so it's unlikely they were friends of Maeve's. This isn't Dunbridge Academy, it's bigger, more impersonal. They might have heard that a fellow student had died, they might have felt sad, but they'd have been too busy to dwell on it, with the new semester and catching up with their friends. I hate how bitter I am. And I hate that my throat's tight and my mouth's dry as we're divided into three groups, each of which is allocated two student guides. Mr Ringling likes me and feels sorry for me, so I'm sure it's no coincidence that I'm in a group with Emma, Tori and Sinclair. Liam and Felicity are second-year undergraduates, studying psychology and economics. They're nice, making jokes and answering questions as they show us a lecture theatre followed by the halls of residence. The building we're walking into isn't the one where Maeve lived, but being close to it is enough to stop me feeling anything. I'm simply numb. My head is dizzy, my fingers are cold. I jump when I feel Emma's hand on my arm. She looks at me, and an almost uncontrollable urge to shake off her hand rises inside me. Because I'm afraid of what would happen if I told her how I'm really feeling.

The others follow Felicity into the flat she shares with two other students. I stay in the hallway because I know what these rooms look like. 'Don't you want to . . .' I begin, as Emma waits beside me.

'Did she live here too?' she asks, instead of answering. There's no sympathy in her voice, just empathy. Until recently, I hadn't really known the difference.

'No. She was in the next building.' I have to clear my throat because my voice suddenly sounds husky.

'Have you been back since?'

I don't want to think about it. I almost stayed in Cheshire because I was too scared to clear out her flat with Theo,

Mum and Dad. It took us a whole day and I cried the whole time. But I suppose it was important. A way of at least starting to get to grips, to grasp what's happened. Because 'grasp' and 'grip' have to do with touching things. Holding things with your own hands, handling them. Maeve's clothes, her uni hoodie, which I wore in Cheshire until it stopped smelling of her. Her books, her pens. Her cold hand, before the coffin was shut.

'Henry?'

I jump. Emma's gazing at me. 'Hm?'

'Want to go somewhere else?'

I nod.

'OK.' Emma walks over to Liam, who's in the middle of chatting to Omar and Inés about his first semester here. 'Excuse me, is there a toilet here somewhere?'

'Yeah, sure,' he says at once, pointing. 'At the end of the hall, on the right.'

'Super, thanks.' Emma smiles and glances at me.

Liam doesn't notice that we move away from the group. Emma waits until we're out of sight, then takes my hand. It's only a small gesture, but it says it all. *I'm here, you don't have to do this alone.*

We don't speak as we leave the building. The air is cool – there's no denying that winter's on its way. We follow a group of students down the cobbled path. Their voices mingle with the squawking of the gulls as they sail over our heads.

'Did you often visit her here?' Emma asks, as we walk side by side.

'Only a couple of times. She came to see me at school more often.'

'The atmosphere's similar to school,' Emma says. 'I see why people want to study here.'

'St Andrews is much smaller than Oxford or Cambridge but there's everything you need here. And we're right by the sea.' I stop, but then I carry on. 'There's this tradition called the May Dip. On the first of May, hundreds of students run into the cold sea at sunrise. It's supposed to bring you luck in your exams and cleanse you from your academic sins.'

Emma smiles. 'Sounds like we need something like that at Dunbridge.'

'The first time Maeve heard about it, she immediately went and suggested it to Mrs Sinclair.'

'Wasn't she keen?'

'She pointed out that there wasn't any sea nearby. Maeve said she ought to run coaches to take us to the coast.'

'I love it!'

I have to smile. 'I could ask her about it again.'

'You really should. Turn on your school-captain charm – it's bound to work. And Maeve's prepared the ground for you.'

'She really has. She was full of ideas like that. In the upper sixth, she organized a strike in protest against the rule about wearing uniform on Mondays.'

'Didn't she like the uniform?' Emma asks.

'Sure. But she thought it was unfair that girls have to wear skirts and boys have to wear trousers.'

'Well, she's right there. Everyone should be able to wear what they like,' says Emma.

She's not talking about Maeve in the past tense, and I don't suppose she has any idea how much that means to me right now.

'So, did Mrs Sinclair see things differently?' she persists.

'I think she'd have been ready to listen, but somehow the plan never came to anything. It was just before the summer holidays, and after that, everyone had other issues, and Maeve was at St Andrews.'

'Well, we ought to take it up again. Does Tori know? I bet she'd be in.' Emma pulls her phone from her jacket pocket. 'Oh, there's a text from Sinclair. They're heading over to the library. Should we . . .?'

'Do you think anyone would notice if we didn't?'

'Probably not,' says Emma, as she puts her phone away again. She slips her hand into mine inside my coat pocket as we walk on and asks: 'Can you picture it?'

'What?'

'Us, studying here together.'

Lately it's been hard for me to imagine anything to do with the future. It's hard enough to bear the present. 'It would be lovely,' I say, all the same.

'Are you meeting Theo today?'

I fight back the urge to shut my eyes as I shrug. 'Probably not. He's in seminars all day.'

Emma doesn't speak.

'We don't talk that much.'

'Would you like to talk to him?'

'I don't know what I'd have to say to him.'

Emma kicks away a pebble with the tip of her shoe. 'Maybe the stuff you'd have talked to Maeve about.'

'I don't know. I think it would be weird.'

'You're not as close to him as to her,' says Emma, but it sounds more like a question.

'Maybe it's the age difference,' I say, although I know that's not the reason. Theo's only a year older than Maeve. It's not the age difference: it's the character difference. I'm not like Theo, and I've never tried to be. As the third child, it's hard to establish an identity of your own that's not based on copying the others. Theo and I have nothing to say to each other. And that used to be OK, because there was always Maeve to act as a go-between when I had the impression, yet again, that we were speaking different languages.

'I'm sometimes scared that I haven't just lost Maeve,' I say, 'but Theo too. We were never that close, but now . . . I always thought something like this would bring you closer together but apparently the opposite is possible too.'

'Maybe you need more time just the two of you, so you can get close again.'

More time, just the two of us. It's a shame we don't have

any. Because we're always busy – Theo's learning to be a doctor and I'm working on not going out of my mind.

'Sometimes I think he's not half as bothered as me that she's gone.'

They're words I never wanted to say out loud. Because they're so awful I'm immediately ashamed of even having thought them. I can't tell if things are less bad for Theo. And even if they are, who am I to judge whether the way he's grieving for Maeve is right or wrong?

'Maybe he just has a different way of dealing with it,' says Emma. I don't answer as we walk on. 'Maybe you have very similar emotions but they show up differently. You could find out if you talked to each other.'

Maybe Emma's right. I should try, at least. Even if that isn't the case and it turns out that Theo and I are just too different, at least I'd have tried. And that probably couldn't feel any worse than the fear that I've lost both my siblings.

30

EMMA

The next morning Henry comes down to breakfast for the first time in ages, and eats. I don't know if seeing that as a good sign is me being naïve, but it makes me happy. Even though it reminds me that even in biology he only got a C, and it's his best subject. It's making my stomach ache because I'm sure it means he needs to do well in our maths exam to keep his grades on track for uni. I decide to ask him later if he'd like to go through some past papers together in the next few days.

He's got rugby training as I head to my appointment with Mr Ward in the afternoon. It would be the understatement of the century to say I'm not looking forward to it. I did surprisingly well in the English test, but Mr Ward still doesn't miss any opportunity to put me down. At least the last few weeks haven't given me much time to wonder what might have happened between him and my dad. There were more important things to worry about.

I tuck an unruly strand of hair behind my ear and knock on the dark wood of Mr Ward's office door. Nobody answers and I strain to hear any sound behind it. Maybe the door is too thick for me to be able to hear him in there. All the same, I knock again, then press down on the handle.

It's a small room with a north-facing window. Filing cabinets, and a desk in the centre. No sign of Mr Ward.

'Hello?' I take a step into the office and look again. Did I get the wrong room? 2350: that's what Mr Ward said. I walk out into the corridor to check the little plaque next to the door. No, I'm in the right place. Maybe he'll be here in a minute. I turn and glance inside again. When I catch sight of the pile of papers on the desk, neatly stacked beside books, exercise books and a water bottle, I freeze. Then I step closer.

Lower 6th mathematics: mock A level examination

Hold on . . .

This is our exam. The paper we're going to sit on Friday.

I immediately retreat to the doorway. Why has Mr Ward left them just lying around like that? I glance hastily over my shoulder but the corridor is empty.

Shit . . . If he sees I was on my own in this room, he's bound to assume I read the exam papers. I break out in a cold sweat. Could you be chucked out for that? I have to get out of here and shut the door and wait a few metres down the hall as if I'd . . .

Or I could . . .

No.

No, no, no. No way. It's just a single thought but it's getting louder in my head. *C'mon, Emma. Now or never. There's nobody here. Think of Henry. Think of the way he's screwed up one exam after another. Think of his future, think of your future. St Andrews, the two of you, but only if Henry doesn't get even further behind.*

Look left, look right. Empty hall, three steps into the room. I pull out my phone, photograph the first page, turn over, take the next photo. I'm calm, I'm quick, it just happens. When I've almost finished, my elbow nudges the water bottle standing on the desk. It's made of glass, it tips as if in slow motion. My heart skips a beat as I just manage to grab it before it falls. But in the process, a couple of exercise books slip aside, revealing an open packet of pills. Is Mr Ward taking painkillers for his leg? Whatever, concentrate, Wiley.

It takes me less than thirty seconds to put everything back the way it was and get back outside. There's still nobody in sight, and instead, the thoughts crowd in. *Are you sure you put everything back the way it was before? Did nobody really see you? Holy shit, now the evidence is right there on your phone.*

I'm just about to step back into the room to check that I really didn't leave a trace when someone comes around the corner.

It's Mr Ward. I jump so violently that he's bound to have seen it.

'Here you are.' His eyes go from me to the door and back again. *Don't attract suspicion. Breathe normally.* 'I've been waiting for you.'

'What? I thought you said room 2350 . . .'

'2150,' says Mr Ward. I shiver. 'Round the corner.'

'Oh, right. I'm sorry.'

Did he see me? Shit, am I really that stupid?

My heart is thumping so loudly that I feel sure he must be able to hear it.

He eyes me sharply, then walks past me and reaches for the handle. His head twitches towards me as the door opens.

'Were you inside?'

'No,' I gasp. *Breathe. Shit.* 'Why?'

Mr Ward glares at me, pulls out a monstrous keyring and locks the door. He gives it a rattle to check, then turns and starts walking away.

'Are you planning to take root here?' he asks, when I don't move. 'I haven't got all day.'

HENRY

I've never been so shattered, but all the same I feel like the visit to St Andrews changed something. It's almost like the time after my run with Emma a few days ago. Things haven't got better, just different. I'm still embarrassed whenever I remember the way I lost control in the wood, even if I know there's no need to be. I've never felt as powerless as I did in those minutes when I sat on the ground, unable to breathe. And even if I could wish she hadn't seen me like that, I'm glad Emma was there. I don't know how long she sat beside me in the rain, just holding me. I only remember her voice once I'd cried myself empty. She didn't tell me to get up and pull myself together. She didn't say any of the things I'd been afraid of.

You can always tell me about her if you want. But if you don't want to, and you just need to cry, then I'll sit here with you, OK? You are allowed to feel this way. You don't have to get over it.

I hadn't known how much I needed to hear that.

I wonder where she is as I walk back to school after rugby. It went OK today. Maybe even OK-verging-on-good. For a while I was able to forget how sad I am. Mr Cormack announced the final squad for our game on Friday. OK, so I'm not going to start, much to Valentine Ward's joy, but I'll be on the bench and I think Mr Cormack will give me a chance and bring me on as a sub. I really hope so, because it's one of the biggest matches of the season. We're playing Alkmounton College, who are kind of local rivals an hour or so down the road. They're good, but we've generally thrashed them. We'll see.

I say goodbye to Omar and Gideon, who are heading down to Ebrington before dinner to get some stuff from Irvine's, and pop up to my room. The corridor is empty, most people aren't back yet, but I pause as I spot Emma sitting outside my door. She's leaning her back against the wall, has her arms wrapped around her legs and is staring so absently at the wooden floorboards that she doesn't even notice me.

'Emma?'

She raises her eyes and jumps up. 'We have to talk.'

'Is everything OK?'

'No.' Her voice sounds muffled, and she glances uncertainly over my shoulder. Then she looks at me again. 'It's important, Henry.'

'OK.' I reach for my key.

'I've fucked up,' she says, almost as soon as we're in my room.

I remember that she just had that appointment with Mr Ward. Was he mean to her again? 'What's happened?' I ask. She steps past me. I follow her. 'Emma.'

'I wasn't going to. Shit, it was just for a second and . . . I'm totally screwed.'

'Emma,' I repeat, but more firmly this time. She stops. When she slowly turns to me, there's panic flickering in her pale eyes. 'Talk to me.'

In slow motion, she reaches for her phone. I can't take my eyes off her face even as my own mobile buzzes in my trouser pocket. I pull it out and see that she's sent me some photos.

Four photographs of pages of text. I bring my phone closer to my face and then I understand.

'What the—'

'I'm sorry, I—'

'Where did you get these?' I blurt.

Emma's gone as white as chalk. 'I went to Mr Ward's office to look for him. I thought . . . I must have been in the wrong room. There was nobody there.'

'And it wasn't locked?'

'No, I didn't realize at first, but then . . .'

'That's our bloody maths exam.' I stress every individual word. With every second, Emma's looking more desperate. 'Why did you take the photos?'

She doesn't speak, just looks at me. Her jaw muscles tense.

'Emma, for God's sake! You're not serious, are you? This is cheating, you—'

'I know,' she bursts out. 'I know, Henry. I . . . Shit, I wasn't thinking. I was about to leave, but then I saw what they were and . . . I thought it would be useful for you, for Friday.'

'Useful for me to what? To look at the questions in advance? God, no, no way. If anyone saw you there'll be hell to pay. Do you know that?'

Tears shine in her eyes.

'*Did* anyone see you?'

'No! No one. I think . . . There was nobody there.'

'You think?'

'Fuck it, no. I got straight out of there. I didn't take anything. Mr Ward didn't come around the corner till afterwards.'

'Please, you cannot be serious about this,' I say slowly.

'Hell, Henry! Don't you understand? I didn't plan this. I'd never do a thing like this, but I – I did it for you.'

'It's not like I asked you to!'

'No, because apparently you don't give a shit about anything. I'm sorry, Henry, for thinking about your future and wanting to help you!'

'I can do without help like this, thank you very much.'

We're standing face to face. We're screaming. I feel panic trying to well up inside me but I suppress every feeling. We can't afford any mistakes now.

'Delete them,' I order her. 'Do it now, right now.'

Emma flinches and lowers her gaze. I can see her select the photos and delete them, as I follow suit.

'And empty your trash too. God, I can't believe this.'

When she raises her head and gives me a startled look, I know she hadn't thought of the trash. Nobody must find these pictures on her phone.

She swallows once she's finished. We look at each other for several seconds, until she turns away. She doesn't speak another word. I hear the door bang, throw my phone onto the bed, run both hands through my hair and turn to face the window.

31

EMMA

I was wrong. Seeing Henry collapsed in the woods wasn't the worst experience of my life. Fighting with him over those photos was worse. We don't speak to each other at dinner and carry on ignoring each other the next day. And then it's Friday, the day of the maths exam.

I didn't look at any of the questions before I deleted the pictures. A small, cowardly voice in my head is trying to persuade me that I therefore don't need to feel guilty. I didn't cheat, didn't gain any unfair advantage, but I photographed the papers. There's no getting around that.

I'm icy cold as I enter the classroom and sit down. Henry doesn't look in my direction even once. When Mr Ward comes in, I hold my breath. He puts down his bag and pulls out the test papers. As he hands them out, my palms are super-sweaty. His eyes sweep over me as he gives me mine.

I reach for my pen. My hands are shaking as Mr Ward walks back to the front, reminds us what time the exam finishes and wishes us good luck.

I don't remember any of the questions by the time I hand in my work an eternity later. My head is empty. I look at Henry but he doesn't pay me any attention as we walk out. Still, at least I saw him writing during the exam.

I don't stop with Inés and the others who are, as always, anxiously talking over their answers. I can hardly bear it at the best of times, least of all today. Instead, I follow Henry, who's already heading off down the corridor.

'Henry.' I catch his sleeve. He whirls around. 'I'm sorry, could we maybe . . .'

All he answers is, 'I have to get to rugby.' His voice is so cold that it hurts.

The match this afternoon, I remember now. I never even asked if he'll get to play.

Henry walks on. I let him go. I feel dreadful.

'Good luck,' I whisper, as he walks away.

HENRY

Emma photographed those exam papers for me and I'm still wondering what the actual hell she was thinking. OK, so my results haven't been amazing lately, but if I'd had any idea that she'd get herself into that kind of trouble for my sake, I'd have pulled my bloody finger out a bit. It scares even me how blasé I am about everything, but a little voice in the back of my mind is screaming at me that I ought to have seen it coming. That Emma would never just stand by and watch me let myself go like this. But to do a thing like that for me . . . It's just nuts.

Nuts and maybe also the warning shot I needed. I felt like throwing up before the exam, and not because I was so unprepared for it. No, I've spent the last few days imagining all the ways Mr Ward would have a go at Emma if he saw her photographing the papers. But he didn't, so I can relax. Nobody knows a thing. Emma deleted those photos before my very eyes. At least she didn't try to steal one . . . And, hey, it gave me something else to freak out over, apart from Maeve. I'm getting cynical but I don't care. I don't care about anything. It ought to bother me, but I don't care about that either.

I pull on my rugby jersey and line up with the others while Mr Cormack gives us his mildly aggressive motivational speech. I don't even care whether he brings me on or not.

It's freezing cold but the whole school has still turned out to line the pitch and fill the stands. There's a relaxed buzz, and everything's the same as ever. I spend the first half of the game on the bench, during which time I spot Emma.

She's sitting with Tori and Sinclair, following the match with that sceptical Emma-look. My heart twinges a little. It's so stupid that we're fighting. But it was so stupid of her to risk so much for an unimportant maths test. Hell, she could get expelled. She's already had a warning, and that was my fault too. All the same, I'm pretty sure that attempted cheating would get you thrown out on the spot. Mrs Sinclair is unforgiving of things like that. Quite rightly. But for Emma it would be a bit different. She'd never have done a thing like that for herself and for her own grades. Maybe the end doesn't justify the means – it's all so complicated. But then she got lucky. We got lucky.

I raise my head as Mr Cormack comes over.

'Ready, Bennington?' he asks.

I'm on the point of asking *What for?* but I force myself to nod because that's definitely what he wants to see. I stand up.

'You're going on for Gideon.' Mr Cormack pulls me slightly aside. 'Unless it's too much for you today.'

I swallow hard. Why should it be too much for me? 'No,' I say. 'I'm ready. I want to play.'

'That's the spirit.' I struggle to keep on my feet as Mr Cormack slaps me heartily around the shoulders. 'Get warmed back up, then, and you'll be on after half-time.'

'Thanks, sir,' I say, starting to jog.

The crowd cheers as we score a try just before the whistle. At half-time, Alkmounton are only two points ahead.

I'm actually a bit pleased that Mr Cormack's sending me on even though we're behind. But maybe he wants to rest Gideon so he can be fresh for the next big match.

Half-time is over. I'm warmed up and super-excited as I finally run onto the pitch with the others. The ref blows the whistle and my body goes through the moves I've been training for all these weeks. I stop thinking. I'm just running, catching, running faster, trying to score, but Alkmounton are crafty as well as fast and strong. I feel like my running lines are too predictable when their defence repeatedly bottles me up.

My pulse is racing, my muscles are burning. I have to be faster. I have to give them the unexpected – that's what everyone always says. Alkmounton increase their lead, Valentine Ward is smeared with mud, dripping with sweat and staring fiercely in my direction. I take up my position again. The front row secures the ball, and I glance at the crowd.

There are people yelling and cheering. I can see Emma sitting there and, in my mind's eye, she turns into Maeve. Maeve, jumping up beside me, throwing her arms into the air and cheering on Theo as he races down the pitch. I see myself in my first school uniform, I see myself walking through the corridors, almost bursting with pride because Maeve's not talking to her cool new friends but to me. I see myself standing on the courtyard as her taxi drives out through the gate and over the bridge. *Just a few weeks, Henny, until you come and visit me in St Andrews.* Her smile, her warm eyes. Theo's pale face as he turns towards me in the school office not saying a word. Because she's dead. Because I'll never see her again . . .

'Bennington!' I jump. Valentine's throwing the ball to me. 'Catch it!'

Instinctively I do, and I ought to run. I know that but my legs won't move. I hear Mr Cormack roaring something to me, Gideon, Valentine and Omar, gesticulating wildly, yelling too. Because I have to run. But I can't. I just can't.

I didn't see where he came from. Their flanker cleans me out. He takes my legs out – it's a seriously good tackle. Fast, hard, effective. I land on my back and the impact squashes all the air from my lungs. A second later and another body lands on top of us.

There's a dull ache in my head and pain shooting through my shoulder too.

I can't breathe. It can't be done.

Shit, it hurts. And it's dark.

Hold on.

Why is it dark?

And then I don't think anything more.

EMMA

I've been underestimating this rugby stuff. I realize that for definite when I see the entire school lining the pitch and in the stands, even though it's been drizzling slightly all afternoon. It's anything but comfortable. Tori, Sinclair and the others don't seem to mind, though. They're sitting next to me; Omar and Gideon are on the pitch with Henry. The team are warming up on the grass, and I can hear the voice of Louis in the upper sixth coming through the loudspeakers. This is a real event, and I grasp that as I notice the spectators wearing blue-and-white school rugby jumpers and scarves, Dunbridge hoodies and school caps. I see the school flag, hear people's laughter and sense the cheerful atmosphere.

The teachers are sitting in the front row, too. Even Mrs Sinclair is here. She's wearing some kind of Dunbridge beanie over her blonde hair and shaking hands with an older man who seems to be the head of the other school.

If things weren't an endless pile of crap, I might even be properly enjoying this. I love any kind of sporting event and suddenly I'm really missing our athletics competitions from home. But as it is, I just sip the lemonade that Sinclair brought down for us and try to plead with Henry with my eyes. I haven't wished him luck – there was no way he heard me after maths just now – and this is his first major game. He and Gideon are running up and down the edge of the pitch, warming up, sprinting, throwing and catching, stretching again.

Yet again, I realize how little I know about rugby as the teams come onto the pitch. Valentine shakes hands with the other captain and the referee, and then they take up their positions.

My eyes wander over the watching crowd. By some coincidence, I just happen to spot Tori's brother William, who is standing a little to one side with Kit, whose hair is trailing into his face. The two of them have grown closer than ever over the last few weeks. 'Young love,' Tori said once, with a knowing smile. Will strokes Kit's hair out of his face – he's talking insistently to him. They're way too far away for me to hear what he's saying, but he seems kind of upset. When Kit turns his head away, I see the dark purple bruise around his left eye. I'm about to turn to Tori and point it out to her when the whistle goes for the start of the match. When I look back again, there's no sign of William or Kit anywhere.

I forget about them as the cheering and shouts of encouragement grow louder around me. There are fifteen men on each team, and Henry isn't one of them. I'm almost glad: it looks brutal. I knew that – I've watched them train a couple of times – but it's different with the whole school there, freaking out and screaming at the players. Louis is commentating, but despite the loudspeaker, I can hardly hear him. All I can make out are numbers and words that mean nothing to me.

I follow the tussles. I cheer when Tori and Sinclair cheer and keep quiet if they boo or groan with frustration.

At the end of the first half, Dunbridge are slightly behind. I've figured that much out. Every player is coated with mud. It looks utterly exhausting, and when I see Henry warming up again just before the end of the break, I'm scared that he's going to be subbed on.

'Go get 'em, Bennington!' Sinclair yells, as they line up again. Henry looks towards us and I cross my arms over my chest. They start, and I can't breathe. It's kind of different with Henry running around down there with them. I *think* he's good, but my heart skips a beat every time he's got the ball and the opposing team are throwing themselves on top of him. He nearly scores a couple of times but never quite manages to dodge their defence. He seems kind of distracted. I don't know what he's thinking about when he looks over to the stand. Maybe Theo, who used to play here, maybe Maeve, who used to stand there, as she and Henry cheered on their big brother.

Whatever it is, he shouldn't be on the pitch today. I'm sure of that when Dunbridge get the ball.

'Bennington!' roars Valentine, hurling it in his direction. Tori's hopping anxiously up and down beside me. 'Catch it!'

The crowd roars. Henry flinches. He catches the ball but he doesn't move.

I jump up with everyone else.

Why isn't he running? Why the hell isn't he running?

Sinclair and Tori are screaming, the Alkmounton defence are running towards Henry. I hear yells and whistles, roaring, then a murmur that runs through the crowd. The guy launching himself at Henry must be about twice his size. He knocks him off his feet, and they hit the ground only seconds before another Alkmounton player throws himself at them.

I can't breathe. Henry no longer has the ball. But he's not getting up.

He's not getting up.

Why isn't he getting up?

The blood rushes in my ears as the other two pick themselves up. Tori claps her hands to her mouth, Sinclair mumbles, 'Fuck.' Henry's still not getting up. More to the point, he's not moving.

I don't know what I'm doing as I step to the side while the referee blows his whistle. I run down the stand, can't think clearly any more. The first of the boys are bending over Henry. Mr Cormack and Dr Henderson, the school doctor, are hurrying onto the pitch.

'Sorry, excuse me . . .' I mutter, as I push my way through. Past my fellow pupils, boys and girls, who were cheering a moment ago and are now staring at the pitch in shock.

My heart is hammering as I fight my way through as fast as possible.

Shit, Henry . . . Why did he hesitate? Why didn't he just run when he caught the ball?

I know why. Because his sister's dead and we had a fight and everything's just shit. Because I saw his face go rigid as he looked into the crowd. Because he's knackered, for God's sake, and shouldn't have been on the pitch. Not in that state.

I reach the pitch. The grass is slippery, my chest is tight, and the teams make way as I come closer to him.

'Henry?' asks Dr Henderson, who's kneeling on the grass

393

beside him, alongside Mr Cormack. Henry doesn't respond and I feel sick.

'Shit,' somebody mumbles. The roar of the crowd has given way to shocked silence. Louis's voice comes through the loudspeaker, saying something about an accident and a short delay for injury, as if we couldn't all see that for ourselves.

'Henry? Can you hear me?' I hold my breath as Dr Henderson reaches out to him. 'Look at me.'

The groan of pain from Henry's lips cuts me to the bone. He clutches his left shoulder.

'Fuck you, Bennington. That was the perfect pass!'

My blood runs cold as I hear Valentine Ward approach, livid with anger.

'Val,' someone says, but he shakes his head.

'He doesn't belong on this team. He ought to be back on the bloody bench.'

'That's enough, Val.' Mr Cormack's voice will tolerate no argument. Their eyes wrestle for a moment, then Valentine stamps away. I'm not sure if Henry even heard him. Dr Henderson stays perfectly calm. It's undoubtedly not his first rugby accident, but Mr Cormack looks worryingly serious. He has a hand on Henry's arm and is talking quietly to him while Dr Henderson investigates his shoulder.

'Definitely dislocated,' I hear someone say. Henry's eyes are shut, but I can see him pressing his lips together in pain. Dr Henderson says something about the hospital and A and

E, needing an X-ray before his shoulder can be reset, avoiding ligament and nerve damage.

I want to go to Henry and tell him I'm sorry for everything. But I can't. I just stand there as he first sits and later stands up. And he walks away, supported by Dr Henderson and Mr Cormack.

'Emma.' I feel a hand on my arm and look into Sinclair's face. He steers me gently towards the edge of the pitch, where Tori's standing. 'They'll take care of him.'

'I have to . . .' I begin, and I want to pull away, but Tori's holding me tight. 'They said they have to get him to hospital.'

'I'm sure it's just a precaution,' she says.

Sinclair nods. 'Let's wait here, OK? If nothing's broken, he'll definitely be coming back to school. And then they'll let you see him.'

'We had a fight,' I blurt. 'The day before yesterday, it was so stupid. I didn't get the chance to say sorry. I . . .'

'Emma,' says Tori. Her voice is gentle. 'Come on. I'm sure it looked worse than it was. Later, you'll be able to talk in peace and everything will be OK again.'

I want to contradict her, because absolutely nothing is OK, but there's no point. So I follow her and Sinclair past the stand as the referee blows his whistle behind us to restart the match.

We won. Just. By twenty-five to twenty-three. Another victory to open the season for Dunbridge Academy. After the match, dinner in the dining hall is like a festive banquet, but I haven't the least appetite. Henry's seat is empty and I like to think that the mood in general is a little subdued.

I messaged him but he hasn't replied. Probably his phone didn't get to the hospital with him and it's lying around somewhere in the changing rooms.

Dr Henderson went with him to Edinburgh as there's no hospital in Ebrington. That was over four hours ago. I know Henry will have a long time to wait, but all the same, I feel close to a nervous breakdown when I still have no news of him after dinner.

We're just clearing our plates away when I get a message. It's from Olive, who's never texted me outside the Midnight Memories group chat before.

O: *My dad and Henry are back, if it interests you. He's in the sick bay.*

'Was that Henry?'

I look up, right into Tori's face. 'No,' I murmur. 'It was Olive. They're back.'

'Henry too?'

I nod.

'OK.' Tori points at the tray in my hands. 'Give me that. You have to go to him.'

'Thanks, Tori.' I leave the dining room and run to the sick bay. My throat tightens a little with every step, even though I ought to be calmer now that I know they're not keeping

him in hospital overnight. Or even longer if they'd had to
operate on him. But I'm scared because I don't know if he'll
even want to see me.

That might be the least of my worries, though I don't know
that until I see Petra, the school nurse, through the door to
the sick bay. She's sitting at her desk and raising her head.

'Can I help you?' she asks.

'I wanted to see Henry,' I begin. 'I've been told he's here.'

She hesitates. Are there visiting hours? I've never been to
the sick bay before.

Nurse Petra gives me a searching look. 'He needs rest, and
he's asleep at the moment. But I can tell him you were here.'

I open my mouth as I realize she's not going to let me in.
'Please, I . . . Just five minutes?'

'I'm sorry.'

'My dad said she can see him.' I turn. Olive's standing in
the doorway. 'Shall I ask him if he can pop back?' She doesn't
bat an eyelid as she looks at Petra, holding up her phone
enquiringly.

Is she lying? I can't tell. If so, Olive has the perfect poker
face. There's certainly no one better at intimidating stares.
All the same, I'm pretty certain that's not why the nurse
nods – she just wants to get rid of us.

'Fine.' She looks back at me. 'But only five minutes. He's
on strong painkillers and has to rest.'

'Thank you.' I look at Olive. She turns away before I get
the chance to speak.

'Just head through the back there,' says Nurse Petra, indicating a door. I step into a dimly lit room with several beds, curtained off from each other. Henry's in the first on the left, but nobody else seems to be here.

When I approach his bed, I see that his eyes are shut. His left arm is bandaged and resting on a pile of pillows.

I don't know what I was expecting. For him to wake up as I sat down beside him? But he doesn't. His face is scarily pale. The worried frown I've seen between his eyebrows so often lately has vanished. His forehead is smooth, his mouth relaxed, but he still looks utterly exhausted. I should let him sleep, but I have to apologize. I have to tell him how sorry I am about everything.

His head twitches in my direction as I take his right hand. His fingers are cold, his eyes disoriented, roaming around the room, and then he sees me.

He's clearly drugged up to his eyeballs. He can't even open his eyes properly. My stomach lurches, and then he gently squeezes my hand.

'Hello,' I whisper, as Henry shuts his eyes again.

His lips form an almost soundless 'Hi,' but he's gripping my hand.

The lump in my throat grows, I have so many things to tell him, but suddenly everything seems way too trivial.

'Everything OK?'

I laugh joylessly when it's actually him who asks that question. Henry opens his eyes again when I don't reply.

There's only a bedside lamp on, but the light seems too bright for him. He squints as he studies me.

'How are you?' I ask quietly.

'Been better,' he mumbles.

'What did the doctors say?'

'No idea. Dr Henderson talked to them. They knocked me out to put my shoulder back in. Don't remember the rest.'

'OK. But there's nothing broken?'

'No, thank God. Just the dislocated shoulder and concussion.' He blinks hard. 'I think I need sleep . . .'

'Yes.' I should leave him in peace. He clearly can't take much in. But I can't go back to my room and lie down without having got a few things off my chest. 'I'm sorry, Henry,' I say quietly. 'For everything. For . . . for what I did. I hate us fighting. Please can we stop? We have to. I'm so sorry and I didn't mean for any of it to happen.'

'Stop,' he whispers. 'I'm sorry too.'

'I was so scared. I thought . . .'

'It's all OK, Em,' he murmurs.

I start to cry. 'So, we're not fighting any more?'

'I don't think so, no.'

'I wish I could take it all back,' I blurt. 'I wasn't thinking.'

'It's all forgotten.' He blinks. 'And not just because I'm all doped up.'

I can't help laughing. 'True. You've had a head injury.'

He shuts his eyes, but his lips form a smile. He doesn't

399

let go of my hand. 'Anyway, we won.' He blinks. 'We did, didn't we?'

'You did.'

'No thanks to me, but OK.'

I don't reply. It's silent for a few seconds, but then Henry looks at me again. 'Why did you stop?' I ask, quietly.

He exhales slowly. 'I don't know. I wasn't paying attention.'

'It was about Maeve. Wasn't it?'

Henry doesn't speak, but he doesn't have to. When he finally rolls his eyes and looks up to the ceiling, his eyes fill with tears.

I could kid myself that it's been a tiring day and the drugs are making Henry oversensitive and emotional. But the truth is, every day's been tiring for a long time now. And that's OK. Somehow I'm glad that he's crying and not swallowing it, bottling it up.

I stroke my thumb over the back of his hand as he closes his eyes, and the silent tears roll down his cheeks.

'I couldn't.' His eyes are red when he opens them. 'I was standing there, and all I could think of was how we used to sit in that stand together. When Theo was playing. It was so surreal. And then . . . no idea, I felt the thud as the guy tackled me, and two seconds later, everything went black.'

My stomach clenches. 'I'm glad nothing worse happened,' I say quietly.

Henry nods silently. I can practically feel how tired he is. When he blinks again, it's like his eyelids weigh a ton.

'Are you in pain?' I whisper. 'Do you need anything?'

He shakes his head. 'I'm OK.'

'I could stay until they throw me out,' I say.

'Is it wing time?'

'There's two hours yet.'

Henry smiles. 'Oh, right.'

'Try to sleep,' I whisper.

He does shut his eyes. 'No little spoon today?'

I have to laugh. 'I think your shoulder would have something to say about that.'

Henry doesn't reply. I sit beside him for a while, quietly watching as his chest rises and slowly falls again.

'Emma?' he whispers, at some point when I'd have sworn he was fast asleep.

'Yes?'

'That night on the roof.' He looks back at me. 'I shouldn't have told you to piss off.'

'Henry, it's—'

He cuts me off. 'I should have said, *Thank you for being here* . . . That, and I love you.'

32

HENRY

I had to stay in the sick bay until after the weekend. Not because of my shoulder, which the painkillers were helping me deal with to some extent, but because of the concussion – Dr Henderson said that meant I had to stay put, however daft I thought it.

Mrs Sinclair informed my parents, and I spoke to them from the hospital while I was waiting for my X-ray and convinced them there was no need for them to get on the next plane. Mum suggested sending Theo over, but I turned that down too. There was no need and, if I'm honest, I'm scared of meeting him. He'd find the fact that I finished my first rugby match in A and E hilarious.

In the end, Mum did believe me that everything was OK. I reckon Sinclair's been sending her regular updates on my state, because even after I slept for fourteen hours straight on my first night in the sick bay, I didn't wake up to any anxious messages on my phone.

OK, so that match was undeniably sub-optimal for me, but I know I was lucky. In the time I've been at Dunbridge, more than one ambulance has been called to rugby injuries. There's been everything from broken ribs and collarbones to torn cruciate ligaments and fractured ankles. My dislocated shoulder wasn't exactly a first for the team either.

But I can forget being able to play for weeks, and I'm not even allowed to run with Emma or train with the team. I suppose I needn't mind too much about the latter – after all, I've played for the school now, which I can put on my UCAS form, but I'm surprisingly disappointed. I'd never have expected to enjoy training so much. I *could* throw in the towel now and quit the team, but the fact is that, only a week after my accident, I'm missing it. Somehow I've got used to standing on the pitch three times a week, whatever the weather, rolling in the mud and chasing after the ball. But I won't be able to get back to it for two months at the earliest, and that's if I make good progress in my physio. Dr Henderson is optimistic, seeing that I'm young and my shoulder wasn't more seriously injured. I see him again at the start of the week and he tapes my shoulder but is not open to negotiations on the subject of this inconvenient bandage that I have to wear day and night for the time being.

I hadn't realized how limited you are with only one

functional arm. Starting with having a shower and getting dressed. I couldn't get into my school uniform without Sinclair's help, which was pretty humiliating. I'm lucky that I landed on my left shoulder and therefore have my right hand to write with. But in the dining hall, I always have to ask someone if I can add my stuff to their tray.

I don't want to complain, though – things really could have been much worse. At least they didn't have to operate, which would have meant no rugby for the next six months.

I don't know if it was down to the concussion or the anaesthetic from when they reset my shoulder, but for the first few days after the accident, I felt like I'd been run over by a lorry. I had to nap after lessons because everything was such hard work, and would wake up some time before dinner when my shoulder was starting to throb from my having lain in the same position for too long.

Things only start to improve a little over the course of the week. Emma doesn't want to run on her own, so we go for long walks across the whole school grounds, right up to the edge of the woods. The trees are bare, Maeve has been dead for more than two months, and even now, in early December, I can't think about her without wanting to cry. Those times when I hear some exciting piece of news my first thought is that I have to tell her about it. Those times when I look at Emma and remember that Maeve never got to meet her.

Nothing is getting any easier, but it seems like I've got

used to the fact that it hurts. I don't fight it any more, I try to feel it, even when it's hard.

After biology, I pick up my phone from the pigeonhole and, as I step outside, I see the message from Sinclair. He's got an unexpected free period and what time do I want to eat? What he actually means is should he wait for me so that I've got someone to carry my tray. I can't manage to answer him because I can feel my bag slowly slipping off my shoulder. I hate it. Before I can perform some awkward manoeuvre to stop it falling, someone comes alongside me and catches it.

'Hey.' Grace shoves the strap back up over my shoulder. 'That looks tricky with one hand.'

'Oh, thanks.' I clear my throat. 'Yeah, it is.'

'Thought as much.' She takes a step back. I can't help noticing the way she's looking at me. 'How are you?' I hear a hint of concern in her voice. Evidently she doesn't hate me: she still cares in some way like I care for her.

'OK, could have been worse,' I say. I can count on the fingers of one hand the number of times Grace and I have spoken since we broke up. We see each other in the corridors, in class, at lunch, but mostly only with the others around too. I've refrained from speaking to her because I can imagine that things are hard enough for her as it is, always seeing me with Emma.

Now she's smiling, but she doesn't look happy. Her smile looks forced, and her eyes are dull. I don't like that.

'Good, that's good,' Grace says. 'I'm glad nothing worse happened.'

I wonder if things will ever stop being so weirdly tense between us. We don't hate each other, we don't badmouth each other, but I think Grace is at least as scared of doing something wrong as I am. I've really been wondering how people manage to stay friends after a break-up.

'So, how are you?' I ask.

Grace hesitates. 'Fine. I . . . Yeah, everything's OK. I didn't mean to hold you up.'

'You're not,' I say. 'Seriously, Grace. Thanks for asking. I'm proud of us. I was scared that we'd ignore each other and . . . you know. I'm glad it's not like that.'

Her smile is a bit like the old days. It makes me happy, but not in the way that Emma's smile makes me happy. And that's OK.

'I'm glad too,' she says.

EMMA

Henry said he loves me, and I said I love him, too. That same evening, in the sick bay, and even if that wasn't the place I'd have picked for it, it just felt right. It's the first time I've said those words. I never told Noah that. But with Henry it was so easy. It was the truth.

On the Monday after his accident, he was back in lessons.

Another week's passed since then, and I'm glad he's getting better. He still has to take painkillers because of his shoulder, but that bandage pinning his arm at the correct angle to his body is the only reminder of his fall.

There's no EPQ today, which gives us both a free period. I go back with Henry to his room, in theory to read ahead in our set text for English. We don't even unpack our books, just start kissing the moment the door shuts behind us. Only kissing, nothing more is going to happen – after all, he has to take care of his shoulder – but that's dangerously easy to forget when Henry slips his right hand under my blouse.

He hasn't done that for a long time. But, then, we haven't kissed like this for a long time either. The last time we slept together, his sister was still alive. I'm sure that Henry is just as aware of that as I am. And I don't want to force anything. I pull back slightly as I feel the throbbing between my legs growing increasingly urgent.

But Henry puts his hand on my back and holds me to him. His pupils are wider than normal, a sure sign that the things we're doing right now excite him at least as much as they do me. He licks his lips and I want to feel his tongue in my mouth again. Or somewhere else. I can't think about that – he might not be up to it yet, which would be more than OK by me. After all, I'm a considerate girlfriend.

But not if he's going to kiss me like that. God, he knows what he's doing. But he's got a busted shoulder. We can't do this. He's not allowed to exercise. Or doesn't sex count as exercise? No way he asked Dr Henderson straight out! When Henry wants to roll on top of me on his bed, I press him back down beside me until he's lying with his back on the mattress. There's desire flickering in his eyes and I know he wants what I do.

'We've got another half-hour,' he says huskily.

'Henry.' I look at his shoulder. 'You have to be careful.'

'I *am* being careful.'

I study him for a moment, then sit up. I see the disappointment in his face, then the astonishment as I position my knees either side of his hips. Suddenly, I'm glad this is a Monday so I'm wearing uniform, and therefore my pleated skirt. Henry holds his breath as I slowly lower myself onto him. I feel the fabric of his trousers and the cold metal of his belt through my thin tights and knickers. I'm not prepared for it when Henry lifts his hips towards me. We're moving slowly and carefully, we're rubbing and touching each other through layers of material that have to go. I bend down to him again. We keep kissing, we keep moving. Henry reaches for the back of my head and pulls out my hair elastic. My hair falls into my face, and he strokes it back with his right hand. His eyes dart from my eyes to my mouth.

We get up again so that I can fetch a condom and he can lock the door. Then we undress. Hastily and impatiently. I'm faster, because Henry has to get rid of that bandage before he can slip out of his shirt. I face him, wearing only my underwear, so that I can undo his buttons and run my fingers over his bare chest. He shivers and I get goosebumps. I reach for his belt buckle and pull him to me with a slight jerk. Henry groans, he actually groans, and I want to do it again. There's a huge amount of pent-up energy in my belly when Henry puts a hand on my bum and presses me against him. I can feel him, I can smell him. When he grabs his belt, I hold onto his wrist. He exhales, a quiet sound, as I slip my finger under his waistband, only a little way, then pull it out again. There's this pleading in Henry's eyes, which makes me a little dizzy.

I undo his belt, he reaches for the zip. We keep kissing as I push him to the bed. Finally, he's lying beneath me again, in boxers and his unbuttoned shirt, as I kneel over him and undo my bra.

Beneath his shirt I can see the blue strips of tape, running from the nape of his neck to his shoulder, reminding me that I have to be careful. Henry seems to have forgotten. Pain twitches in his face as he raises his arms. I immediately take his wrists and push them back to the mattress. I hold them there as I slowly sink down onto him. He clenches his hands into fists beneath my fingers. As I press myself against his erection, he shuts his eyes. I can feel that he wants to move, and not just his hips. It must be a bittersweet torture not to do so. His arms are tense, his muscles rock hard, as I run my hands over them.

'Tell me if I hurt you,' I whisper, and stroke my fingertip over Henry's chest. I wait till he nods then sink my mouth onto his belly. His muscles tense beneath my lips. His skin is warm and smooth. It trembles as I run my tongue over it.

His arms quiver as I reach the waistband of his boxer shorts. I put my fingers on his hip bones and raise my head to look at him. Henry's mouth is open, his lips are red. I don't look away as I wrap my hand around him.

The groan that escapes Henry shoots directly to my core. His head falls back as I move my hand and finally slip it under the fabric. I feel him throbbing. I hear his quiet panting, which grows louder as I carry on.

'Emma,' he begs, feeling for my knees. I bend over him, reach for the condom and only roll off him to slip off my knickers. Henry's jaw is tense as he pulls down his boxers, which looks laborious with only one hand. I reach for his arm.

'Shall I . . .?'

He immediately nods. I jam the condom packet between my lips as I pull down his boxers. Then I rip it open and look him in the eye.

'Do you want this?' Henry asks, the way he does every time.

I nod. 'Do you?'

'Yes, I do.'

My fingertips tingle as I slip the condom onto him. It's different from normal, when Henry's heavy body pushes me into the pillows. It's slower and less greedy, cautious and deliberate, but I don't find it any less thrilling. Quite the reverse.

We both hold our breath as I guide Henry's erection to my

centre. I let myself sink onto him, I've almost forgotten how indescribable this feels. The pressure, the sweet pain, which only disappears when I force my muscles to relax. I try not to close my eyes: I want to see his face. I want to be able to stop if I'm hurting him. Henry closes his fingers around my knee as I raise my hips and sink down lower again. His grip tightens and I do it again. His eyelids flutter closed, he opens his mouth. He fills me completely. I move faster. I don't know if he's in pain or on the edge of it when this furrow appears between his eyebrows. He moves his hips, comes towards me, thrusts into me so deeply that I throw my head back and bite my bottom lip so I don't make any sound.

Our breathing is deeper, and there's a fine film of sweat on his skin as I trace my fingers over his groin. A shiver runs through Henry's body and he arches his back. I tense my muscles and feel him grown rigid beneath me. It's only a few seconds until his body relaxes again.

The heat of him pulsates in my belly. I don't mind that I didn't come. It's not always like it is in films and that's OK.

It's incredible lying next to him and kissing him until it's time to get dressed because Henry's got Latin and I've got history. His gaze rests heavily on me as he sits on his bed and I pull my tights and skirt back on. His hair's messed up, his lips are warm as we kiss again before leaving his room. Outside, Henry takes my hand as we walk downstairs. He smiles and I've never felt as beautiful.

*

411

At first I was afraid that anyone would be able to tell at a glance what Henry and I had just been doing, that we'd been having sex while the others were in class. I was particularly careful about redoing my hair in Henry's mirror, but the look Tori gives me and her tell-tale grin as I sit down leaves me in little doubt that she has some idea of where I spent the last hour. Fortunately, she doesn't comment.

'Has Henry asked you to the New Year Ball?' she whispers, while Ms Barnett writes on the board.

This is the first I've heard of there even being one. 'No.'

'Well, there's plenty of time,' she says. 'But you'll never guess who asked me.'

'Sinclair?' I suggest.

Tori looks at me as if I'm out of my mind. 'God, no.'

'Quiet, please,' says Ms Barnett, as she turns towards us.

'Valentine asked me,' Tori whispers, staring at the board. She bites her bottom lip.

'Valentine?' I whisper back.

'Yes.' Tori beams.

I'm on the point of asking what Sinclair thinks about that, but I hold my tongue. 'That's – that's great, Tori.'

'He's so gorgeous.' She sighs, and I can't help thinking about the way he spoke to Henry after his accident. Whether or not you like someone, it was downright unnecessary of him. Especially as I still don't quite get what Tori sees in Val. But maybe he's different when it's just the two of them. I suppose their family backgrounds and the expectations bound up with them help to bring them together. And I'm glad for Tori if she's got someone she can talk to about stuff like the responsibility and social pressure her surname puts on her.

'I'm sure Henry will ask you soon,' Tori whispers. 'What will you wear?'

'I didn't even know there was a ball,' I admit.

'Then we'll have to go dress shopping together.' She sounds properly excited.

'Victoria, Emma, if what you have to tell each other is so interesting, perhaps you could share it with everyone else.'

Tori goes red and lowers her head in embarrassment. Before I get a chance to apologize, the gong goes and there's a sudden announcement over the loudspeakers.

'Would Emma Wiley please come to the school office. That's Emma Wiley, to the school office.'

I freeze, feeling everyone look at me. I've never been summoned to the head's office in my whole school career. Never. I've never done anything to get into trouble. Until I got the idea of taking photos of the maths exam paper. But nobody saw that. Or did they? My heart starts to race.

Tori looks enquiringly at me, but I ignore her.

Ms Barnett appears equally confused as she nods to me, so I'm sure this must be about something else. Maybe Mrs Sinclair wants to talk to me about Henry. Yes. Yes, that's what it'll be. No reason to panic. God, I have to slow my breathing.

My thoughts continue to circle as I walk through the

hallways to the office. Maybe I'm driving myself insane for no reason at all. My knees are trembling as I reach the secretary's office. Mr Harper is sitting at his desk. He lifts his head. 'Go straight through, Emma.'

He sounds friendly. So this has to be something harmless. Or else he doesn't know what I did.

My panicked heart is pounding right in my throat as I knock and open the door. All my blood rushes to my feet as I see Mr Ward. And I'm sure of it. I'm busted.

'Emma, thank you for coming.' Mrs Sinclair isn't smiling. I feel numb as I shut the door. 'Sit down.'

It's so humiliating. Have they already phoned Mum?

'Emma, do you have any idea why we want to speak to you?' Mrs Sinclair asks. She sounds calm. Mr Ward's face is unreadable.

I don't know what to do? Deny it? 'Fess up, in the hope that it will make things better?

Will I be expelled?

I don't want to be expelled. I did it to help Henry. For his future, and now . . . It was so stupid of me.

'No.' The word is out, so there's nothing to do. I sit stock still as Mr Ward laughs scornfully. He crosses his arms over his chest.

'I saw you in my office, where the maths exam papers were kept. I didn't want to suspect you of anything, but on marking your exam, it was clear that you were familiar with the questions. You didn't make a single mistake.'

414

'What?' I blurt. 'I didn't . . .' *Fuck, think before you speak.* 'I didn't see the questions.'

'So it was pure chance that you were in an office where you had no business to be?'

'You told me to meet you there!'

'I told you to see me in the meeting room, 2150,' he says to Mrs Sinclair. 'I always lock my office, but that afternoon, I must have forgotten. But how could I have guessed that a pupil here would do such a thing?'

'I didn't . . .' I try again.

'Can you prove it?'

'That will do. I'm leading this conversation.' Mrs Sinclair exchanges glances with Mr Ward, then looks at me. 'Emma, I have to take Mr Ward's accusation seriously. But I want to hear your version of events. Were you in his office or not?'

My mouth is dry, my lips are numb.

Tell the truth, tell the truth.

The deeper you get in lies, the worse it will be.

'Emma?'

I swallow with an effort. 'Yes.'

My voice is quiet, but they heard. There's a hint of triumph flickering in Mr Ward's face. Mrs Sinclair looks stunned. 'But I came out again the moment I saw that nobody was there.'

'She must have taken photos,' Mr Ward interrupts me. 'She must have had her phone with her. All you have to do is check . . .'

'That's enough, Mr Ward.' Mrs Sinclair's voice is sharp.

415

When she continues, her words sound gentler. 'Emma, we can't check your phone without your permission. But if you allow us to, it might prove you innocent.'

The pictures were deleted. There's no chat to prove I sent them to Henry. There nothing. Bluetooth doesn't leave a trail, does it? If they don't find anything on my phone, Mr Ward has no proof.

Slowly, I nod. I reach for my phone, which I'd picked up again as I was leaving the classroom. The display immediately shows a series of messages from Mum. I just glance at them, but it's enough to reveal that Mrs Sinclair has already told her.

I'm about to give it to her when there's a knock at the door. Before Mrs Sinclair can say anything, it's opening.

It's Henry, his face expressionless. His eyes meet mine, my heart skips a beat. He seems to have put two and two together as he sees Mr Ward and the phone in my hand.

'It was me,' he says.

What is he doing?

I jump up as Henry closes the door and comes in. He's walking tall, his shoulders tense.

'Henry, you can't just—'

'No, you don't understand,' he interrupts Mrs Sinclair. 'I heard the announcement. This is about the maths mock, right?'

'We're talking to Ms Wiley here,' snarls Mr Ward, but Henry doesn't bat an eyelid. I try to implore him with my eyes, but he just stares past me.

'Emma saw me in Mr Ward's office. She was on her way to her appointment with him. I was worried about the exam and I made a mistake. I'm sorry.'

'He's lying!' I turn to Mrs Sinclair. 'It's not true, he didn't do anything. It was me who photographed the papers. I was in the room, and the papers were on the desk. I didn't mean to, I really didn't mean to, but I was thinking about Henry, and I wanted to do something to help him. I only wanted to help. It was wrong, I regret it, but he didn't do anything.' I don't know when I start crying. All I know is that I can't contain myself any more.

'It was her,' repeats Mr Ward.

'Quiet!' Mrs Sinclair rubs her temples. 'Oh, God, this can't be true.' She looks from Henry to me.

My blood runs cold as Henry pulls his phone out of his bag, unlocks it and lays it on the desk. I whirl round to him as I see the photos. Why does he still have them? Is he out of his mind?

He shakes his head as Mrs Sinclair and Mr Ward bend over his phone.

'I'm sorry,' he repeats, and I can't breathe.

HENRY

I knew what had happened as I sat there in Latin, hearing Emma summoned to the head. It was like I was on autopilot.

I stopped thinking. I stood up and Ms Barnett let me leave early.

I couldn't run because my bloody shoulder still hurts, but I can't feel a thing now anyway. There's just blankness, as Emma just stared at me aghast, when I put my phone on the desk. My phone with the photos, which I'd deleted but left in the trash. Because I'd had a hunch that we might still need them. They're proof, but teachers aren't allowed to go through my phone without my permission. Everyone's known it since there was that business a couple of years ago with Colette in the second form, and Mr Ward who ignored the rule.

But now they're looking because I want them to. Because I've been at this school for so many years now and never been in any trouble. Because I'm school captain and I've just lost my sister, for fuck's sake. Because if they're going to go easy on anyone, it'll be me. But not Emma who's only been here a couple of months. She wouldn't understand that, and maybe I didn't completely think this through, but I had to do it. The way she did something for me even though I didn't ask her to.

Her lips are soundlessly forming my name, but I shake my head mutely.

'I'm sorry,' I say, as Mrs Sinclair looks from my phone to me.

I see the disappointment in her eyes and I know that it's worked. She believes me.

'Henry,' she says slowly.

'It's not true,' Emma insists again. She has to stop crying, I can't bear it. 'Please, I . . . It wasn't like he says.'

'Emma, your phone please,' insists Mrs Sinclair calmly.

Emma bites her lip as she hands it to them. Her eyes are desperate and I can't look at them.

'Nothing,' murmurs Mrs Sinclair to Mr Ward.

'She put him up to it then, for all I know.' His eyes are blazing.

'I thought you saw Emma coming out of your office?'

'She was standing outside it,' says Mr Ward.

'And Henry? Was he there too?'

'No . . .' Mr Ward hesitates.

'I got out in time,' I say. I never knew I was such a good liar. 'I heard your voice just as I got around the corner. I was relieved that nobody had seen me but . . . It was wrong.'

'Henry,' Emma pleads quietly.

I suppress the urge to clench my fists. Don't show any emotion.

'OK.' Mrs Sinclair hands Emma her phone. 'Emma, please go back to class.'

'What?' she blurts. 'No, I . . .'

Mrs Sinclair presses a button on her phone. 'Could you come and show Ms Wiley out, please?'

Emma looks blankly from one to another as Mr Harper enters the room.

'What's going to happen? I mean . . .'

'Emma, you don't have to worry about it. I will inform your mother that it was a false alarm and that there's no need for her to come over.'

For a moment, Emma looks as though she's going to argue. But she knows as well as I do that there's nothing she can do.

I avoid her eyes as she follows Mr Harper out.

'Sit down, please, Henry.' Mrs Sinclair points at the chair in front of her desk. Then she looks at Mr Ward. 'You may leave too now.' He opens his mouth, but she cuts him off. 'Please.'

I withstand his dark glare as he walks past me. He wanted to cause trouble for Emma, for whatever reason. I'm sure of that as I sit down.

'Henry, I don't know what to say.' Mrs Sinclair walks up and down, on the other side of her desk. The way she often does when we have something to discuss. As head teacher and school captain. But now I've broken the rules and it's her job to punish me. 'How did those photos get onto your phone?'

'I took them.'

She eyes me, waits a second or two, as if she wants to give me one last chance to put everything right. I say nothing.

'Why, for God's sake?'

'I was scared. I've missed so many lessons. I didn't want to fail maths too. I know I'm borderline on the grades. And there's the uni application.'

'Yes, there is, Henry.' Mrs Sinclair sounds firm as she rests both hands on her desk and leans forward slightly. 'This is about your future, about university places. And I will have to make note of your deception. Worse than that, I've only just had to give you a warning. Do you understand what that means?'

I can only nod.

'And I would be prepared to overlook a minor incident, but cheating will not be tolerated at this school. This is breaking my heart, Henry, but I'm afraid you've left me no choice.'

I break out into a cold sweat.

I'm school captain. I'm her son's best friend. I've lost my sister.

Surely she can't . . .

But, Henry, what were you thinking? That you could get away with anything? That the rules don't apply to you?

Mrs Sinclair eyes me, shakes her head in disbelief and straightens up.

'Henry, I have to suspend you from classes at Dunbridge Academy until further notice.'

33

HENRY

There are heaps of things that scare me. Illness, death, losing someone close to me. Being alone. Downtime, having nothing major to do. And, apparently, being kicked out of school is another.

Mrs Sinclair's face is serious as I slowly stand up. Her voice echoes in my head.

I have to suspend you from classes at Dunbridge Academy until further notice.

Go upstairs, pack, clear my room. I want to wake up from this nightmare.

'I'm sorry,' I say, although that isn't actually what I mean. It absolutely isn't. It's capitulation of the worst kind, because I have no choice.

My voice has never sounded as flat. As if I don't care what

this means right now, when the opposite is true. I do care. I care more than anything.

What have you done, what have you done, what have you done?

The right thing. It was the right thing. Wasn't it? A moment ago, I'd been sure of that, but now I'm overcome by doubts.

I turn around. I grab the heavy black iron doorknob. I don't know how my legs carry me. I don't know how I push open the door and walk out of the head teacher's office without losing my composure. I don't know. I don't know anything any more.

I hear the voices in the corridor, the laughter that echoes off the high walls. The sounds of rapid footsteps on the old, uneven tiles in the arcaded walkways. Sunbeams fall through the panes of the lancet windows; dust glitters in the air.

Faces turn towards me, my fellow pupils smile at me, say, 'Hi,' the same as ever, and I don't reply because I can't. I run blindly past them. I have to get away but I don't know where to go. I no longer have a home.

The thought hits me like a punch in the belly, but it's true. For a moment I feel the need to stop and curl up. But I keep on running.

My feet fly over the tiles, taking routes that I could walk with my eyes shut. Across the courtyard to my dorm wing, brown brick façades, covered with twining ivy. High lattice windows, dark roofs, pointed towers. I see it all but feel nothing. Coming towards me down the worn stairs from the first floor are the fourth-formers; they slow as they recognize me, then run all the faster once they're past. The heavy dark wooden door to our wing is shut. I have to lean my whole weight against it as I reach for the key in my trouser pocket and open the bedroom door.

Silence.

And then I pull my suitcase from beside the wardrobe and start packing.

EMMA

I walk down the corridor and everything is a grotesque repeat of that moment weeks ago now. When Henry had learned that his sister was dead and he was in his room, packing. Just like he is now, according to his text. When the bell went for break, I immediately headed for the east wing.

'Henry?' I hammer on his door. I don't give a shit about anything else.

I take a step back as he opens it and I see the pain in his face. On the floor behind him is a half-filled suitcase; his stuff is everywhere. At least he hasn't finished packing, so that's one benefit of his stupid injured shoulder.

'Are you out of your mind?' I whisper.

'Emma,' he says quietly.

'Why did you do it? Why did you say it was you? Why did

424

you still have those fucking photos on your phone?' Henry doesn't flinch as I approach him. I want to pummel his chest with my fists. I want to hurt him. I want him to understand how badly he's screwed up.

'There was no alternative.'

'Of course there was an alternative! They had no proof. I didn't have the pictures any more. Mrs Sinclair was on my side. She would have believed me, she would have—'

'Emma,' he interrupts, and I want to burst into tears. 'It's no good, none of it. We'd have been found out sooner or later, and then things would have got even more complicated.'

'No, we wouldn't. Don't you get it?' I stare uncomprehendingly at him. 'Have you been suspended?'

'Rules are rules,' he says. It makes me furious that he's trying to stay so calm. When he turns away now, and runs his hand through his hair, it's the first time since he walked into the office earlier that I've seen any emotion in him. 'Hell, yes, I didn't think she'd really do it. I thought they'd take pity on me because of everything, but . . . It is what it is.'

'I can't believe it! It's all so utterly stupid, you could have—'

'I did it for you,' he says, and his words are like a punch in the guts. Because I remember them well. Except that last time it was me saying them.

Henry blurs before my eyes. 'And it's not like I asked you to, for God's sake,' I whisper.

'I know, Em.'

'So what happens now?' I wipe away my tears. 'Suspended . . . Does that mean thrown out?'

'It means I can't go to lessons until it's all gone to the Council.' I don't have to ask because Henry carries on unprompted. 'A committee of parent governors, former teachers and major funders.'

A spark of hope glimmers within me. 'So does that mean . . .?'

'In my time here, there've been a handful of cases that have gone to the Council. Two of them were over cheating. Both people involved left the school voluntarily.'

'You're school captain, they'll . . .'

'Emma,' is all he says.

'No.' I'm not prepared to accept that. This is Dunbridge Academy, Henry's home, his future, all rolled into one, and I've ballsed it up. I have to do something, I just have to.

'Theo's picking me up soon,' says Henry. 'I should finish my packing.'

HENRY

Maeve always found it kind of funny that Theo and his girl-friend rent a nice terraced house in St Andrews rather than a grungy student flat. It sounds more upmarket than it really is. The house is in serious need of renovation, but there's a small back garden. And it suits Theo and Harriett. They're happy here.

Theo's the oldest twenty-one-year-old in the world, Maeve said on his birthday at the start of last year. I was sixteen and didn't understand. In the meantime, I've turned eighteen, Theo's almost twenty-three, and Maeve is no longer with us. I hadn't been expecting Theo to have a photo of us up in his living room. It's one of the three of us, no Mum and Dad; I think it's from our Christmas holidays in Cape Town two years ago. Maeve had just finished her first term at uni where she'd discovered that nobody was fussed if you get your hair cut super-short and dye it grey. The dye washed out relatively quickly and then she experimented with being a redhead.

When she died, her hair was its natural colour. Dark brown, with a slight reddish tinge in certain lights. The same as Theo's and mine.

'Excuse the mess,' Theo says behind me. 'I never got round to tidying up properly after the last lot of exams.'

I eye the pile of papers on the dining table, which isn't quite as organized as the rest of his house. Everything else looks immaculate.

'You can sleep on the sofa.'

I owe him my life. Seriously. Theo picked me up without a word after I rang him.

'Thanks.' I stop in the middle of the room. I've never been

alone here with him and Harriett before. It's really amazing how different a house can feel depending on who's filling it. It was kind of nicer when my parents were here, or Maeve, who could always find the right words so that Theo and I didn't have to face up to the fact that we had nothing to say to each other.

On the drive away from school, he asked exactly what had happened. I told him the version of events that doesn't involve Emma in any way, and he didn't say a word. I'm sure that Theo is judging me. A school captain, who cheats in an exam. He'd never have done such a thing. But I'm not like him.

'I'll get your stuff from the car.'

'I can do it myself.' I turn around.

'Not with your shoulder,' he says curtly.

'I've got two arms.'

'Henry, just sit down. Do you need ice? You ought to be cooling that regularly if you're in pain.'

'I know that,' I snap. Why am I like this? Theo studies me briefly and reaches for my case.

I let myself drop into a kitchen chair as he vanishes out to the car. I rub my face with my right hand. I want to cry because everything's so shit. I've been suspended. I don't know what will happen now. Will it be just a few days before I have to face the Council? Will they let me back to school? Would that be all right, even if they did?

'Are you OK?'

I jump. How can Theo be back so soon? He peers at me as he comes closer.

'Yes.' My head aches. I want to sleep. At least that way I won't have to think about everything.

Theo sits on the chair next to mine, and then he gives me a hug. Just like that. I start to cry.

'I miss her too, Henry,' he says. 'And I'm no good at talking about emotions, but I'm afraid we'll lose each other now that she's not here.'

I'm scared too. And I should tell him that. But I can't. Why does talking get more and more complicated, the more you have to say? Maybe Theo could tell me that. He always was a man of few words.

'I always envied you two for being so close to each other,' he continues, to my surprise. At that moment, I realize that maybe Theo and I aren't quite so different after all. That I was jealous of him and he was jealous of me. Because it's true. There were three of us, but Maeve and I were a unit. Even though the age gap between us was bigger. Or maybe *because* it was. 'But I never meant to make you feel like I didn't care about you. The last few years have been so busy, I've always had stuff on, but now I regret not having spent more time with the two of you.' He laughs cheerlessly. 'I mean, when did we ever see each other once I left Dunbridge? In the holidays with Mum and Dad, but when else? Practically never, and we don't even live far apart.'

'I know,' I say. 'I'm sorry, I . . .'

'No, Henry, *I*'m sorry. I don't think things have always been easy for you, because of me. At school especially. But I'm proud that you're on the rugby team and that you're going your own way. I'm proud to be your brother. And I wish I'd told you sooner that you can always call me if you want to chat. But I'm doing it now and I hope it's not too late.'

My eyes sting. I shut them briefly. 'For ages, I thought I had to be like you to make Mum and Dad proud.'

Theo shakes his head. 'That's bullshit and you know it. Look at you, you're school captain.'

'I'm suspended,' I whisper. Theo falls quiet. For a moment, neither of us speaks, then I bury my face in my hands and can't help laughing. Because it's all so absurd.

'You didn't do it for no reason,' says Theo. I raise my head. 'Copying exam questions, it's not like you. You'd never do a thing like that for your own advantage.'

I bite my lip and shrug.

'Was it because of this girl?'

'Emma,' I say at once, although I hadn't wanted Theo to know how tangled up in this whole mess she is. But now I do want that. Because he clearly knows me a bit better than I thought.

'Emma,' Theo repeats. His voice is surprisingly gentle.

I sigh. 'It's complicated.'

'You don't have to explain, but I wanted to tell you that I've always admired you. Your selflessness when it comes to

430

helping others.' Theo gulps, hard. I can tell that it's not easy for him to say this stuff. When he looks at me, I get goose-bumps. 'You're like Maeve. And you always will be. There were days when I could hardly bear to look at you because I see so much of her in you.'

'I see her in you too,' I say, without a second's hesitation. 'Her sense of purpose and passion. What would Theo do? That's what she always asked if we were stumped.'

A smile flits over his face.

'It's not fair that she's not here. It never will be.' The words taste bitter, but I carry on. 'But Maeve would want us to go on. Together.'

'If you say so.'

'Maeve would have said so, too.' I wipe the tears off my cheeks with my sleeve.

Theo smiles. 'Yes, she would.'

34

EMMA

The gossip at school is off the scale since word got out that Henry's been suspended. I can hardly choke down a mouthful at breakfast the next morning, although that might have something to do with the fact that Mum's flying into Edinburgh this afternoon. Since Henry took the rap for me, it's his parents who've been invited to a meeting – a virtual one – with Mrs Sinclair, but Mum insisted on coming over anyway, once I told her what had really happened.

Tori and Sinclair are understandably speechless. And they still are, when I finally tell them, in the dining room, what really happened with those exam papers. We're late, and most of the seats around us are already empty.

'But that *is* his office,' says Sinclair. 'If that's where he told you to go, why wasn't he there, and why did he leave the exam papers lying around?'

I shrug. 'He says he told me a different room, 2150.'

Tori nods. 'That's the little meeting room. I've had to see him there before.'

'But I could have sworn he told me to go to his office.' I lower my voice slightly as a couple of fifth-formers walk past us.

'He did.'

I jump a mile. Tori, Sinclair and I all whirl around simultaneously. Grace is standing behind us. She's still holding her tray.

'I'm sorry, I didn't mean to listen in on you. But he really did say that. It was the other day when he filled in for Ms Ventura in chemistry, wasn't it? I heard him mention his office.'

I stare at Grace. 'What room number did he say? Do you remember that too?'

'2350,' she says, without a second's hesitation.

I turn to Sinclair and Tori. 'You see?'

'Maybe he made a mistake,' Tori suggests.

Sinclair looks at me. And then he says what I've been thinking. 'Or maybe he did it on purpose.'

'Why would he do that if the exam papers were in his office . . .' Tori stops. Her eyes dart from Sinclair to me and back again. 'Hold the bus, are you saying . . .?'

'So that Emma would see them,' Sinclair says.

'Wasn't the door locked?' Grace asks.

I shake my head. 'No. I knocked, and when I didn't get an answer, I walked in. And then those papers were lying there.'

'Whoa.' Grace pauses. 'So, he definitely did mention his office. And he even repeated the room number for you. I know that for a fact because I was making a video for my Insta, and you could hear him in the background.'

'Wait!' My cutlery clatters as I put it down. 'You've got him on video saying that?'

Grace looks at me. 'Yes, I – I wanted to make this reel and –'

'Have you still got it?'

'I don't know. I uploaded it without sound. But the original might still be on my phone.'

'Could you check?' My voice trembles. Grace is looking at me like I've gone mad. 'Please, it would make all the difference. For me, but especially for Henry.'

At that moment, she seems to put two and two together. 'Is this to do with why he was suspended?'

I hesitate, but then I decide that it would be best to tell her the truth. 'I saw the papers and knew they were for our maths exam. Which Henry would be doing too. And I was scared he'd just hand in another blank sheet of paper and fail it. I took photos of the questions.'

'Did Mr Ward catch you?'

'No. I'd been out of his office for ages, waiting in the corridor when he came round the corner.'

'Because he wanted to give you time to fall into his trap,' adds Sinclair.

'Anyway, I told Henry about it. We argued. I deleted the photos. But he had them on his phone too. Because I sent them to him . . . Yesterday I was called to Mrs Sinclair's office because Mr Ward told her I'd cheated. He couldn't prove it, but then Henry came along and showed them the photos on his phone. He said it had been him.'

'What?' Grace's voice is shrill now. 'But why would he do that?'

To protect me. I don't say a word, but she looks at me and I'm sure she understands. Because she's known Henry so long and that he'd do anything to keep others out of trouble.

'OK.' Grace puts her tray on our table and pulls out her phone. She scrolls for a few seconds, then holds it out to me. Tori and Sinclair jump up and lean in as I start the video. There's a selfie of Grace and Olive, then a shot of the hallway, and another view out of a window into the courtyard. In the background, you can hear the usual jumble of voices at break time. Laughter, snatches of conversation. I turn up the volume and hold my breath. Yes. It's not very clear, but it's Mr Ward's voice.

Kindly come to my office next Wednesday at five. Do you know where that is? Room 2350 in the old building.

I exchange glances with Grace, then hear my own voice repeating the room number, a 'Yes,' from Mr Ward, and then the video ends.

'He really did say it,' Tori murmurs, looking at me. 'That was no mistake, was it?'

'Absolutely not,' declares Sinclair.

'But why would he do that? Has he got it in for you?' Grace asks. I feel three pairs of eyes on me. Yes, but why? Because he wants me gone. Because since my very first lesson with him, there's been something about him that makes me nervous. Because I finally have to know the truth.

The others stare at me as I get up.

'I have to make a quick call.'

My fingers are sweaty as I dial the number I'd never wanted to call. But I do, and I'm almost surprised that he picks up right away. And that he agrees to meet me this same afternoon in a café in Edinburgh.

Mum's eyes bore through me as she gets out of the taxi that brought her from the airport to the school. To my surprise, she gives me a hug.

'What on earth were you thinking?' she asks.

I shut my eyes. 'I only wanted to help,' I whisper. My chest feels too tight to breathe. I've achieved the exact opposite. Henry's been suspended and is now with his brother in St Andrews.

'I honestly thought you had more sense,' Mum says, as the taxi turns. 'Photographing exam papers . . . God, Emma.'

'I know.' I clench my fists. 'It was wrong and I'm sorry. But it might never have happened if you'd told me the truth from the start.' When Mum hesitates, I know I'm on to something. 'Mr Ward didn't get me to go into that office by chance. One of my friends has a video of him telling me the room number, so I've got proof. But he says he didn't. He wanted me to find those exam papers.'

Mum keeps looking at me.

'Why would he do that, Mum?' I don't want to talk to her like this. But I have to know what this is all about. 'Why have I had the feeling – since my very first day here – that he wants to see the back of me as soon as possible?'

'Emma, this is all very—'

'Complicated, I know. But it's more than just something between you, Dad and him now. Henry's been suspended. For my sake. Because he's an idiot and took the blame and I couldn't prove it wasn't him. That's why I need the truth. So he can come back and finish his A levels.' Furious tears sting my eyes. 'We're meeting Dad at twelve in the Saint Giles in Edinburgh. You two can tell me everything there.'

He's already there when I open the door, and he stands up as we walk towards him. I can see the surprise on his face as he recognizes Mum.

'Hi,' I say, sitting down. 'Thanks for coming at such short notice.'

'Not a problem,' says my dad. His eyes are on Mum. I'm not sure when they last saw each other. I only know that Mum doesn't look half as shaken as I'd feared. I may be confronting her with her past but, at this moment, I understand she's built a new life and he can't hurt her any more.

'Hello, Jacob,' she says calmly, as she sits down.

'Laura.' He clears his throat and sits too. 'I didn't know you were—'

'I only just landed. Emma wanted the three of us to have this conversation and I can see the sense in that.'

I give her a sidelong glance.

'Fine.' My father nods. 'Then . . . How are you?'

'Very well, thanks.' She doesn't ask how he is, just tries to catch a waiter's eye. I can't help noticing that my dad is taking her in as she orders an espresso. He seems very different from how he was in Glasgow.

The waiter looks at me.

'I'll have tea, please. English breakfast,' I murmur, because that's what Henry would have ordered, and I miss him. It really hurts. I don't know what he's doing, only that he's with his brother. It's wrong for me to be sitting with my divorced parents in a café in Edinburgh, and not with him.

'How's school?' my dad asks, once the waiter's gone again.

I don't know if he's genuinely interested, even if he does seem like a different person now, sober and by daylight. I guess I should be glad that he even asked. But I've got no time for small-talk and pleasantries.

'I have a question for you both,' I say, instead of replying. I look at my dad. 'And I need the truth. It's important. For me . . . and for a friend who's in trouble for my sake.'

438

He studies me. 'And you're sure that I can help?'

'Yes,' I say. 'Alaric Ward, Mum and you. What happened between you three?'

My father looks from Mum to me. 'Biscuit, this is nothing for you to worry about.'

'She needs to know,' Mum says. 'All of it. Making a mystery of it has caused enough damage as it is.'

My dad looks at her.

'He's her teacher.'

'And he hates me,' I add. 'I need to know why.'

The silence as the waiter brings our drinks is unbearable.

'I'm the reason,' my dad says. Mum doesn't dispute that, just stirs sugar into her espresso. 'And I'm sorry, I really am. The accident, it was all my fault.'

'What accident?' I ask.

My father's face is blank. 'It was in the sixth form. Al had just got his driving licence and his dad let him drive his second car. There were five of us – your mother, two other friends, him and me. It was a Saturday night and we'd gone into town for a few beers. Al wasn't drinking, but on the way back to school, I persuaded him to let me drive. It was a country lane, never any traffic. He didn't want to, but everyone else thought it was a laugh. He gave in. I wanted to impress your mum, show off to him and the others. And then this deer ran across the road. He tried to grab the wheel, but I wouldn't let him. We hit a tree beside the road.'

He falls silent. I stare at him, I don't know what to say.
Even though I have a thousand questions.

'Your mother and the other two weren't badly hurt. Mild
concussion, maybe, but nothing serious. Me either, but Al . . .
The impact crushed the passenger side of the car like a fucking concertina. The footwell was just gone. Shit, I'll never
forget the way he screamed with pain. I was just glad when
he finally blacked out. Later, they said he'd been lucky they
didn't have to amputate his leg.'

The yearbook photos. Mr Ward suddenly missing, then
back again but walking with a stick. And my dad who disappeared altogether.

'Did you get expelled?' I have no idea where this calm
voice is coming from. Was the music stuff just an excuse,
not the real reason he never finished school?

'I ran away before they could throw me out. I was seventeen, I was scared. I'd almost killed my best friend, I couldn't
cope. The doctors said he'd be able to walk again but not like
he used to. He'd been one of the school's best runners. He
wanted to study sport science, it was his life, and I smashed
it up, just because I was trying to be cool.'

He wanted to study sport science . . .

Mr Ward's eyes when I run with Henry in the early morning. The tension between him and Mum.

I want to ask Mum why she never told me. I want to shout
at her, accuse her. But I don't. Not here, not in front of Dad.

They were friends. There was an accident. My dad was to

blame. That's why Mr Ward is so bitter. And the daughter of the man who wrecked his future comes along to his school, reminding him of what he'll never be able to do again.

'And did you never apologize?' I ask slowly.

My father shakes his head.

'Why the hell not?'

'Because I'm an arsehole, Emma,' he says, more loudly than I'd expected. 'I mean, look at me. I've got nothing. I walked out on your mother and I'm just a disappointment to you. Back then with Al, I was scared, I was out of my depth. I ran away like a wuss instead of facing up to my mistake and asking my friend to forgive me. I did everything wrong in life. I thought I could run away but the past always catches up with you. I realized that when I met a couple of people from our year. They said he wasn't doing well. He did get a degree, but not the one he'd wanted. He was bitter and was chugging pills like they were Smarties because of the pain, which never stopped.'

The tablets in his office. Mr Ward's nervous expression that time we saw him in the pharmacy at Irvine's. Hold on . . .

'You mean . . .?' I pause.

'I've seen a few people in the business get hooked on morphine. Especially in the States. You think you've got it under control, but it's the exact opposite. It destroys you.'

Morphine. Painkillers. Strong painkillers . . .

Mum nods when I look at her. 'I wasn't sure if you'd

noticed at the parents' evening. But I was afraid Al was on some kind of drug.'

I stand up. Dad lifts his head. 'Thank you. I . . . You've been really helpful,' I manage. 'Sorry, but I've got to go.'

'OK.' Maybe I'm only imagining it, but there's a flash of disappointment in his eyes for a second. It's too much for me. Because today he's so different from last time we met. Regretful, resigned. As if he wasn't as uninterested in me as I thought. Maybe because he's sober today. I have to think about what that means. Some other time, in peace, not now. Mum stands up too.

'How long are you staying?' he asks her.

'I don't know, Jacob,' she says, reaching into her handbag. The banknote she leaves on the table is as big as the unbridgeable chasm between them. 'I wish you all the best.'

He stands up, saying nothing. You shouldn't feel sorry for your own father. But I do when I grasp that he's the one who made choices he'll regret his whole life. It's not my story. I shouldn't judge. Accidents happen, people make mistakes. I should know. But my parents' past became my present when Henry and I were unwittingly caught up in something that could have been prevented.

And now I have just one job: to get justice done, to salvage our future.

35

EMMA

I'm feeling sick with nerves as we walk into Mrs Sinclair's office and Mum shakes hands with the head teacher. They make small-talk about her journey and so on as we sit down.

'Thank you for making time for us at such short notice,' says Mum.

'Not at all.' I feel Mrs Sinclair's eyes on me. 'I presume that this has to do with recent events in relation to Emma's maths mock?'

Mum looks at me.

'Yes,' I say. 'But mainly it's about Henry. Because it's not right that he got suspended. Please, you have to believe me, he had nothing . . .'

'Emma, we saw the photos of the exam papers on his

phone,' says Mrs Sinclair, and I can hear a regretful undertone in her voice.

'I know,' I say. 'But they were only there because I sent them to him. Honestly, Henry had nothing to do with it. He took the blame because he thought you'd be more lenient on him than on me.'

'I'd like to believe you, Emma, but unfortunately we found the photos on his phone and not on yours. And Henry admitted that it was him.'

I reach for my own mobile and wrap my fingers tightly around it. 'Yes, he did. But have you checked where Henry was at the time of my chat with Mr Ward?' Mrs Sinclair lifts her head. 'He was at rugby training. The rest of the team can confirm that.' Mrs Sinclair says nothing, but I can see a spark of hope in her eyes. She wants to believe Henry innocent. I just have to give her the proof. 'You can ask Mr Cormack. Please. My appointment was at five, which is the time training starts on Wednesdays.' I take a hasty breath and pull out my phone. 'I've got a video where you can hear Mr Ward telling me what time to come. And there's something else . . .'

Mrs Sinclair frowns but takes my phone as I push it over to her. Mum gives me a calming look. For a brief moment as Mrs Sinclair watches the video, I'm afraid that I'd only imagined Mr Ward's voice in the background. But, no, I hadn't.

'Hold on,' she says, as the film ends. 'Can I just . . .?' She plays it again. 'That's . . . He did give you the other room number, just as you said.'

'Yes.' Tears of despair sting my eyes.

'Where did you get this, Emma?'

'Grace Whitmore sent it to me. She was filming something else after class and happened to catch it.'

Mrs Sinclair nods slowly. 'But Mr Ward says he told you to go to the little meeting room, and not his office ... It goes without saying that I don't want to accuse anybody without good reason, but I almost get the impression that he wanted you to see the exam papers.'

'Me too.'

'But why would he do such a thing, Emma?'

'I think I might be able to help answer that question.' Now, Mum speaks up. 'And I'm afraid that this whole thing has less to do with my daughter than with my past history with Alaric Ward. He, Emma's father and I were all at Dunbridge together. Until an accident, years ago, in which Alaric was injured and after which my ex-husband left the school.'

'Oh, I didn't know that was you,' Mrs Sinclair says, to my surprise. 'I remember. It was so horrible. I heard about it at the time, even though I was at university by then.'

Mum nods. 'It was terrible. And it destroyed our friendship. After school, we went our separate ways. While I was at university, I got together with Emma's father and never expected to see Alaric Ward again. I didn't know he'd gone into teaching or that he was working here at Dunbridge. And even if I had known, I'd never have dreamed he'd make my daughter pay for the mistakes we made as teenagers.'

'I wish you'd told me all this straight away,' says Mrs Sinclair.

'I really should have done,' says Mum. 'Especially once I realized that Alaric was clearly still dealing with the fall-out from the accident. I wouldn't rule out the possibility that he's addicted to painkillers.'

Mrs Sinclair stares at her in amazement. 'You're aware that a suggestion of that kind could have serious consequences, Ms Beck?'

'Yes, and I wouldn't have mentioned it if I weren't concerned for the welfare of the pupils here at Dunbridge Academy,' says Mum. 'Let alone for Alaric himself.'

'I will look into all of this. If you are correct, of course we will take all necessary action.' Mrs Sinclair looks at me. 'So, Emma, I understand how complicated this entire business is but, with the best will in the world, it doesn't change the fact that you clearly did photograph the exam papers.'

'I know,' I stammer. 'And I'm really sorry. I never planned to do any such thing – you have to believe me. I would have left Mr Ward's office straight away, but I couldn't help it, because I was thinking about Henry. And I made a mistake, but I was so desperate. I didn't know how to help Henry, and I felt like he needed to pass these mocks. But it was wrong. We didn't look at the questions, not even once. I wasn't thinking, I was scared, but I'll take the consequences for my actions. But Henry – he honestly didn't have anything to do with it. You know he wants to be a teacher. He normally works so hard, and he deserves to do well in his exams. He was trying to protect me. But I can't let him take the blame for my mistake.'

Mrs Sinclair gives me a long look. 'As you know, honesty is one of this school's core values. But so are loyalty and willingness to help. And I understand that you weren't seeking your own advantage but were trying to help Henry. I have no way of proving whether or not you looked at the papers, but that doesn't change anything either way. I'm only wondering why you didn't come to me sooner with your worries about Henry, Emma.'

I shut my eyes but the tears still roll down my cheeks. 'I don't know.'

'He didn't even have to take these exams – we offered him the chance to skip them. He has plenty of time and support available, so there was no need at all for it to come to this.'

'I know that now. It was all a huge mistake. And I'm really, really sorry. I was honestly just trying to help, but I know I did it all the wrong way.' My voice is hoarse with tears. Mrs Sinclair doesn't reply, which makes everything feel even worse, if that's possible. She just looks at me.

'Emma, I'm proud of the way you have developed at our school,' she says in the end. 'And I'm a big advocate of second chances for anyone who means it seriously. Which you do, I can tell.' My heart skips a beat. 'I'm duty bound to suspend you for five days, but I don't consider it necessary to go to the Council about your return to school. And you will take on an extra duty until the end of next half-term. On top of which, because I have no way of knowing whether or not you and Henry did actually have an unfair advantage, you and your class will have to repeat the maths test to ensure that conditions are fair for everyone.'

I nod. Before I can open my mouth, Mrs Sinclair continues. 'And you may tell Henry to be back here for classes tomorrow.'

36

HENRY

It's my second day on suspension and I'm running out of things to do. Yesterday evening I ate with Theo and Harriett but I haven't seen either of them yet today, because I haven't got out of bed. Why would I? To do prep, or revise? What for? I haven't the faintest idea when or if I'll be allowed to set foot back at school again.

I groan quietly and roll onto my side. Emma isn't answering my texts and I'm starting to get worried. I'm about to start searching for my phone, which went down between the cushions during my *Outer Banks* Netflix binge, when I hear a muffled buzz.

Great. That could be her, and I can't find the bloody telephone. I dig through the bedding until I find it and pause as I see an unknown number. Then I take the call.

'Hello?' I say, stifling a cough.

'Henry, this is Mr Harper from the school office.' I'm unable to speak, but fortunately, he carries on. 'I'm calling on behalf of Mrs Sinclair to let you know that from tomorrow you are welcome to take part in classes again.'

'What?' I sit up. 'Tomorrow?'

'Exactly.'

'But what about—'

'Mrs Sinclair will speak to you as soon as you get back, but you're no longer suspended. Everything else can be explained once you get here.'

Emma . . .

What has she done?

I guess I should be relieved, but my only question is whether she's been thrown out of the school instead of me. I have to find out, but I'm pretty sure that Mr Harper wouldn't tell me.

'OK, I . . . Thank you. I'll be there.'

'Glad to hear it. See you tomorrow, Henry!' And he's gone. Surely Mr Harper wouldn't have sounded so cheerful if someone else had been suspended in my place. Or doesn't he care either way?

I immediately open WhatsApp and see Emma's messages.

E: *Sorry for not answering sooner. It's been total chaos. My mum's here and we went to see Mrs Sinclair. It's all sorted, Henry. You're not suspended any more!*

H: *Mr Harper just rang me! What did you tell them?*

E: *The truth, H.*

H: *Emma . . .*

E: *Everything's fine.*

H: *What about you? Did Mrs Sinclair believe you?*

E: *Yes, but I'm suspended for a week. I'm flying back to Frankfurt with Mum in a bit.*

I shiver as I realize what that means. Even if she's only going for a week, I don't know how I can go another day without seeing Emma. I'm about to text back when another message comes in from her.

E: *Can you meet me before I go?*

H: *Where are you?*

E: *In my room, packing. The flight's at five*

H: *Let's meet at the airport?*

E: *But only if I can run into you*

I smile. She's joking, so things really can't be as bad as all that.

H: *Maybe I can run into you – I'm quite fast now*

E: *Weirdo*

H: *I'll ask Theo if he can drive me*

E: *OK*

H: *Are you OK?*

E: No. Miss you. You OK?

H: You have to tell me everything. I love you

E: Say you miss me too

H: Thought that was obvious

E: ☺ Love you too

I drop back into the cushions and stare at the ceiling. I can go back; I don't have to leave the school. And neither does Emma. No idea how she managed it, but hopefully I can hear that today.

I jump up, run out of the room. I have to ask Theo for a lift to Edinburgh.

'Theo?'

There's no one in the kitchen either. Is he out? I cast my mind back over our last conversation and try to remember if he'd mentioned going to a lecture or similar. Then I catch sight of someone through the window. Theo's sitting out in the garden, in the cold. Smoking, maybe. His only vice, and one that Maeve never missed a chance to comment on.

He lifts his head as I open the back door and walk towards him.

'Another five minutes off your life,' I say, because that's what Maeve always said. The words taste stale on my tongue. Theo wipes his face with his sleeve. Just for a moment. But his eyes are red.

I stop. Has he been crying?

'I guess so,' he mumbles, stubbing out the cigarette, but his voice is rough.

'Are you OK?' I ask, cautiously.

'Fine.' He straightens up and tries to smile. 'Hay fever,' he says, gesturing vaguely at the garden.

I don't nod. It's December. And this is the moment when I understand that Theo's grieving. I knew it in my head. But it's only now that it seems real.

In the hospital in Nairobi, at Maeve's funeral, through all the weeks after her death – maybe I was just too busy with my own pain to get that it wasn't any easier for him, even if it looked that way from the outside. But now I do.

'Whoa, that excuse is so lame it could be one of Maeve's memes.'

Theo's lips twitch, but his eyes are glistening again. 'Yeah, I guess so.' He clears his throat. 'Let's go indoors.' Once we're back in the house, he asks, 'Did you want something?' and I suddenly remember why I'd been looking for him.

'I'm allowed back to school tomorrow,' I say.

Theo's face brightens. 'Seriously?'

I nod. 'Yeah. And I have to get to the airport. Emma's flying back to Germany later and I was hoping–'

'When's her flight?' Theo interrupts.

'Five,' I say.

'Good.' He nods towards my joggers. 'Get dressed properly and I'll drive you.'

37

EMMA

At the airport, I did run into Henry, straight into his arms, where he held me for a moment so that he could explain that he was still seriously angry about my idiotic actions, and then kiss me. I could feel his lips on mine for the whole flight, and although I was in Frankfurt, my thoughts were constantly with him. We Skyped every day.

I briefly considered messaging Isi and seeing if she wanted to meet up, but then I decided I'd be better off investing my time in the schoolwork I was missing.

By the time I fly back to Edinburgh on Sunday evening, I feel like I've been away for a month. Henry meets me at the airport, because he's crazy. After wing time, he creeps into my room. It's traditional.

'And he seriously never apologized to him?' he asks again,

as I tell him the story of Mr Ward and my dad once more, but face to face this time. I shake my head. 'That's wild.' He absentmindedly doodles a little pattern on my arm with his index finger. I lift my head a little way off his chest so that I can look at him. 'But it explains why Mr Ward was so weird to you,' he says.

'It really does,' I say. 'Has he said anything about it all?'

'Not to me, but he's more unbearable than ever. Apparently, he has to answer to the school authorities but even Sinclair hasn't been able to get anything else out of his mum. By the way, the others are super-pissed-off that we all have to do the maths exam again. Don't take any notice if there are snarky comments tomorrow.'

Really, I could hardly care less. I totally get it – I wouldn't be thrilled myself – but at the moment all that matters is that Henry and I are both still at this school. And that he seems kind of more together since his time with his brother.

'How was it at Theo's?' I ask.

'Fine,' Henry says. 'No, really. We talked about Maeve. Not much, but by our standards it was quite a lot. And he's been in touch since I've been back here.'

I wrap an arm around him. 'I'm glad, Henry.'

'Me too.' He puts a hand on the back of my neck. 'What about your chat with your dad? How did it go this time?'

I think about my answer before I speak. 'Different, not so bad. I think he is actually sorry for what he did. Not just to Mr Ward. But to Mum too. And me. It doesn't change what happened, but it felt a bit like closure when we were in that café.'

'That's good, Em. You don't need him.'

'True, I only need you,' I whisper, into Henry's jumper.

'That's not true,' he says. I lift my head in surprise. 'You only need *yourself*. Nobody else. But I'm a nice bonus.'

'Very nice,' I mumble. 'Will you go to the New Year Ball with me, then?' I ask. 'Tori told me about it,' I add, when Henry looks at me in surprise.

'Of course we're going to the ball together.' He says it like it's the most obvious thing in the world, and I love everything about that.

'Good. Cos Tori wants us to go dress-shopping in Edinburgh before the Christmas holidays. And you and Sinclair have to come too.'

'So she's going to the ball with him after all?'

'No, but she still wants him to be there.'

'Valentine won't like that,' Henry remarks. 'But he hates us now anyway because we got his uncle into trouble.'

'I really don't know what Tori sees in him.'

'I don't think she knows herself sometimes. But until Sinclair has the guts to ask her out, they'll never get it together.'

'We could help,' I suggest.

'I think that's something the two of them have to figure out for themselves.'

I groan. 'Why do you always have to be so sensible?'

'You mean, not looking at exam papers and nearly getting myself expelled?'

'Let's not talk about it,' I say hastily, even though we're clearly going to talk about this a lot.

Henry looks at me a moment. 'You'd do it again, wouldn't you?' he asks.

'I'd do anything to help you. But not like that. I'd go to Mrs Sinclair or Ms Vail and tell them I was worried about you.'

'I had a chat with her on Friday,' Henry says, out of the blue.

'Ms Vail?'

He nods. 'I kind of needed to talk and you weren't here.'

'And how was it?'

'Good, I think.'

'You could go to see her again. Even now I'm back,' I suggest.

'I've been thinking about it.'

For the first time in weeks, I can feel Henry's confidence returning. They're baby steps, but we'll take them together – in the right direction.

HENRY

Like every year, the run-up to the Christmas holidays seems to fly by. The days are stressful but it's OK. We resit the maths exam, and for the first time in ages, I feel like my mind can focus on something other than pain. My end-of-term report is better than I'd been expecting. Most teachers seem to have turned a blind eye to my catastrophic results in the weeks after Maeve's death – it's the only explanation, and it makes me feel like I still have a realistic chance of getting into St Andrews, which is a relief.

All the same, I'm dreading my session with Mr Ward. From the fourth form on, we have these guidance chats with our form tutors twice a year.

'Still keen on teaching, Mr Bennington?' Mr Ward asks, once I'm sitting opposite him.

I nod in silence.

'And still St Andrews?'

'Yes, sir.'

'Very good.' He leans back in his chair. 'Well, I think you'll make an outstanding teacher.'

I can see that he knows very well I was expecting almost anything from him but that. Last time we had this chat, he mainly concentrated on listing every possible downside of the profession and explaining all the reasons I'd be better off studying somewhere else.

'Have you started writing your personal statement?' asks Mr Ward.

'I haven't had time yet, but I will do soon.'

He takes a piece of paper from a folder. 'Well, perhaps this will help you a little.'

I frown as he pushes it across the tabletop towards me. *Personal Statement*, I read. *Maeve Louise Bennington*.

My heart is pounding. 'Is this . . .?'

'I shouldn't really show you another pupil's personal statement, but I think that in this instance it will be all right. After all, from what you tell me, you're not intending to apply for medicine.' His voice is as chilly as ever, but for the first time I can see something like sympathy on his face. 'And I think you should have the opportunity to read it.'

I grip the paper with both hands, almost as though he might snatch it back. But Mr Ward just folds his hands and rests them on the desk.

'I'll be leaving the school at the end of this term,' he says, 'which means we won't be colleagues here. All the better for you, I suppose, as you won't have to suffer me as a student teacher as well.'

I don't know what to say. 'Sorry to hear that' would be a lie. So I quip, 'Being your pupil was punishment enough.'

Mr Ward glares witheringly at me. 'From now on, Mr Ringling will be your form tutor. I'm sure he'll be delighted to write a reference for his star pupil.'

I smile innocently. 'That's nice to hear.'

'I thought as much.'

This is a game – he hates me, I hate him back. It has to be this way. He's leaving the school, maybe going to rehab, maybe not, it's none of my business. But it looks as though we'll still be lumbered with his charming nephew.

'So . . . anything else I can help you with?' Mr Ward is sounding snappy again, which is kind of a relief.

'No.' I stand up and put Maeve's personal statement into my pocket. 'Thank you.'

'Off you go then, Bennington.'

'Yes, sir.'

I'm grinning as I leave the room. It's only once I'm outside, walking down the corridors, that I'm gripped by the oppressive awareness of what I've got. Something of Maeve's. Words she wrote. It was years ago now, but I can still remember her spending weeks on this statement. Nobody was allowed to read it.

Maybe some day, Henny, she always said. *When I've stopped being embarrassed by it.*

Back then, I didn't understand what could be embarrassing for her. I guess I'm about to find out.

I check the clock and see that I've got half an hour before my next lesson. Is it wise to read this text right now? Who knows? It will probably make me cry. If it does, it does.

I hear voices on the stairs up to our wing. I could go to my room and read it in peace. I stop, level with the door to the tower. Or I could . . .

I glance around, then press the latch and climb the narrow spiral staircase. It's chilly up on the roof, but bearable with the last rays of the setting sun. I sit beneath the low parapet, which shields me from the wind. The view from up here is my favourite, but – more importantly – I only know this place because Maeve showed me. I remember sitting up here beside her when I was in the first form, and homesick every night.

'Do you know why you can't see all the way to Mum and Dad from up here?' Maeve had asked, staring hard into the distance. It was a clear day and you could see across the rooftops of Ebrington to the sea. 'Because the Earth is curved. But maybe, right now, we're standing in the exact same place as them, except that they're on the other side of the world.'

Back then, I didn't see any reason to doubt her words, so I believed them. I still believe it in some way, even though I know perfectly well that her geography was way out. Surely it's New Zealand on the other side of the world, not Africa. *You're such a spoilsport, Henny,* Maeve said when I told her that, a few years later. But she'd been smiling, so I smile too. I think about Mum and Dad, working a hemisphere away to save lives. I think about Maeve, who'd done the same. I think that although it's still not fair, at least she died while living her dream. She did the thing she'd been working towards all those years. It wasn't for nothing. Nothing was ever for nothing.

I lean my head against the wall and study the rooftops and turrets of the school, behind which the sun has set. It's only then that I look down at the paper.

I like to imagine myself as a bridge. I have always found it easy to be a go-between, a link. That is probably because I have two brothers, one younger and one older. Oh, the neglected middle child, you're probably thinking, but the fact is I have never felt neglected. On the contrary. Because I am always in the middle of the sandwich, I have someone to learn from and someone to pass things on to.

This is exactly why I want to be a doctor. I would like to be a bridge to get medicine to the people who need it. I would like to learn to help others. At this point, I could write about how fascinated I am by the human body and the miraculous way the heart beats and the mind thinks. That would all be true, but I think it is the most basic prerequisite for wanting to do this job. And I am aware that there are very many young people who want that. But those are not the only reasons why I am a good candidate. My reasons are the people I was lucky enough to meet as a child. Thanks to my parents, I grew up in eight different countries. I therefore speak six languages, three of them fluently. They also acted as bridges between me and my surroundings. They enabled me to satisfy my curiosity and expand my knowledge. Going to a boarding school has taught me to be independent, to take responsibility for myself and my brothers, and also for my fellow pupils through my work in the sick bay and on the peer mediation team.

I keep reading Maeve's words about her A levels and the volunteering she did during the holidays. It feels like a part of her that I can hold on to.

I like to imagine myself as a bridge.

That really was Maeve. A bridge-builder, a mediator, the person I always wanted to tell everything to. And she always will be.

I lower the paper and look up into the sunset-painted sky. Maeve never saw me play in my first rugby match, she won't be there for my prom or able to show me around St Andrews in my first year. And that hurts, but this pain has belonged to me for a while now, just as Maeve always will. I will no longer fight it. I will live with it. Today's a day when I'm confident that I can do this.

38

EMMA

'Purple, same as last time?' Sinclair asks, as Tori slips through the heavy curtains into my changing room with another floor-length evening dress.

'Shut up,' she yells, then lowers her voice to ask me: 'Does this colour clash with my hair?' She holds the fabric up to her long, coppery locks, and I immediately shake my head.

'I love it,' I declare. 'Definitely try that one.'

'OK. Could you . . .?'

I nod and unzip the dress she's wearing.

'Em?' I hear Henry's voice from outside. The short, green dress I'm in looks hideous, so I just stick my head through the curtains. 'Blue?' he asks, holding out a long dress in a dark Oxford blue. 'I think it would match my suit. Or would that look silly? I could . . .'

'No.' I grab the dress. 'I'll try it on. Thanks.'

'God, he's taking this so seriously,' murmurs Tori, as I pull the curtains properly closed again. 'Unlike a certain head teacher's son.'

'Do you two know we can hear you?'

'Shut it and get me a dress as stunning as this one,' says Tori, holding Henry's dress up to me experimentally. Her lips form a silent 'Wow!'

'I don't even know what you're looking for,' yells Sinclair.

'Just think, What would Harry Styles wear? and you'll be right every time.'

I hear Henry's quiet laugh and Sinclair muttering something as he heads back out among the rails. Tori and I slip into our dresses. She doesn't seem particularly satisfied with her choice, but when I glance into the mirror, she puts both thumbs up.

'Show them,' she whispers, giving me a shove out through the curtains. I almost stumble over the length of it, and stop outside the changing room where I can see myself in the mirror. And, oh, it really is pretty. It fits perfectly, and the colour makes my eyes bluer. I twist to one side slightly. Sometimes you don't know what you're looking for until you've found it. This dress is the one. I can't remember ever having worn anything so elegant.

Henry's sitting on one of the armchairs beside the mirror and looks up from his phone. He opens his mouth but says nothing. His dark green eyes wander from my face to my body and back again.

'He's speechless but would like to inform you that he finds you extremely hot.'

I laugh. 'Thanks, Sinclair.'

Henry has stood up. He wipes his hands on his trousers as he comes closer. 'Does it feel good?' he asks.

'Pretty good.' I turn towards the mirror. 'Very good, actually.' It's clingy fabric and you can see everything through it, but I don't feel uncomfortable.

'Looks pretty good too,' he mumbles, then walks round behind me. I see our reflections and, in this moment, it hits me. Henry in this dark polo neck jumper and tight-fitting beige chinos, his long legs. His hands on my waist. We're buying a dress for the New Year Ball in the middle of January, and we're going to it with our friends. This is actually real. Edinburgh, Dunbridge Academy. This is my life now, and I wouldn't swap it for my old one for anything in the world.

'How about brown, Tori?'

'That's not brown, that's sand.' I watch in the mirror as she takes another dress from Sinclair. 'But, yeah, not bad.'

A smile twitches at Henry's lips as he watches them. His brown curls are falling into his face – they've got rather long, and I hope he doesn't get a haircut over Christmas. The holidays begin next week, and we're going to be apart for a while. I'll be in Frankfurt and Henry will be with Theo, their parents and grandparents in Cheshire. I'm going to visit them there before term starts again. The thought of meeting his family makes me nervous, but I'm really looking forward to it, too.

'I have to get this one,' I decide, tugging at the dress slightly.

Henry seems a little absent minded as he studies me. 'You definitely have to get that one.' He runs his hands over my hips and his eyes meet mine in the mirror. I want to kiss him.

'Bloody zip.' Tori's voice comes through the curtain.

'Want any help undressing?' Sinclair asks.

'Ha-ha, very funny, now piss off.'

I laugh, look apologetically at Henry and flit back to join her in the changing room.

Epilogue

HENRY

'We've trained hard for today, lads. All the sweat, tears and discipline will pay off. When you go out there now, I want you to look around and remind yourselves that you're representing this school, the team spirit.' Mr Cormack's eyes sweep over us. 'Today we're not playing for our own sake. We're playing for the whole school. We're playing for your parents, brothers and sisters who've come to watch. You're going to make them proud. I've no doubt about that. So keep calm and focus. We'll build up the pressure right from the start, and then we'll get a result from this game.'

Mr Cormack steps back and Valentine launches into the team chant. The words echo off the changing-room walls, and they're transformed into pure adrenaline, coursing through my veins. There's a tingling in my fingertips as we finally run out onto the pitch.

It's February, the last match of the season, and the time since Christmas has flown by. I've been allowed to train again for a couple of weeks now, and my shoulder isn't bothering me any more. Luckily, I was free of the sling in time for the New Year Ball after the holidays. It feels like half a lifetime ago.

I breathe in the cold air and breathe out little clouds of white. The last few days have been frosty, but the temperature's risen a little in good time for the match. The pitch is no longer frozen and the game can go ahead. Despite the cold, every last seat in the stand is filled. The sky is blue, the sun is shining, and there's music blaring from the speakers as the spectators cheer and we run out.

I don't know if I'll play today. Mr Cormack's keeping me on the bench for the time being, but who knows what will happen? He got Dr Henderson to tape up my shoulder in advance so that I'll be ready to go on at any time.

The others slip off their tracksuit tops and I join the lads on the bench. I glance over to the crowd. It's not easy to find Emma among so many people. But then I spot her. She's towards the front with Tori and Sinclair.

Emma's wearing a navy-and-white school scarf and matching gloves. When we kissed earlier, a few strands of her blonde hair were peeking out under her cap with the school crest on it. When she sees me looking over, she forms her hands into a megaphone and joins in the chants of encouragement. It makes me smile.

Theo and Harriett are here too, standing on the sidelines with a few other old Dunbrigonians. They came especially to see the match, but Theo checked that I was OK with that. I'm more than OK with it. It means the world to me that he's here for me, and maybe that's why I'm hoping a tiny bit more that Mr Cormack will let me play.

Omar and Gideon are on the pitch with the rest of our boys. Hollington are not to be underestimated, but we've got the home advantage and we're off to a good start. It doesn't take us long to grab the lead, and for all of us to have jumped up off the bench.

I forget the icy temperatures. I forget everything as I yell the others on. The ref is fair, and by half-time Hollington are still miles behind.

'That was a strong first half, but we can't sit back now,' Mr Cormack urges the team, as we form a circle. I look into red, sweaty faces. 'We have to do the same thing again. Build pressure, stay patient and wait for our chance. Don't let them get into their stride, OK?'

Mr Cormack doesn't bring me on. I'm not sure whether he doesn't want to unsettle the others, or whether he doesn't have confidence in me to play yet, but it frustrates me more than I'd been expecting. The team is what counts, not me getting to stand on the pitch, I know that, but Theo's here and I want to make him proud. I want to prove to myself that I can do better than last time.

Gideon limps off with a nasty injury but Mr Cormack still doesn't bring me on. I'm itching to my fingertips to get a chance, especially when we miss touch from a penalty and Hollington catch up further. Twenty minutes from the end, they're in the lead.

Mr Cormack comes over to the bench. 'How's the shoulder, Bennington?'

'Fine, sir.'

He eyes me. 'Good. Warm up, then. You're going on for Ward.'

'For Val?'

'Aye, he's done for today.' Mr Cormack nods towards Valentine, who's breathing heavily, both hands on his knees. 'We want to focus our attacks down the left. Hollington are weakening and they haven't got anyone left to bring on. You can do this, Bennington.'

Val's not going to like this – since his uncle left the school, he's been worse than ever. Hardly surprising, I suppose, as he's lost his personal tutor to coach him through his exams in a few weeks.

Tori and Sinclair cheer as I run on. Emma copies them, but less enthusiastically. She's worried, I know, but everything's kind of different this time. My head is here, on this pitch, and I'm ready to give it my all.

I run till my body's glowing, and go through my stretches. Then Mr Cormack sends me on. Valentine glares at me as we high-five. Hollington have extended their lead with ten minutes to go but there's no way we're giving up. The others are tired, that's clear to see, but I make a clean break down the left touchline and score a try. The crowd cheers, but Hollington are still ahead and now I'm on their radar. This time, they're spreading their defence wider. They manage to get the ball off Omar and score a drop goal.

I'm buried under three Hollington players, the commentator's voice is ringing in my ears, and my shoulder is throbbing slightly. The ref says play on, which gets him booed, but, luckily, he awards us a penalty for an infringement at the breakdown. Omar misses. I suppress a groan and clap him on the shoulder as we line up once more.

Hollington don't score again but there are only two minutes left and they're still in the lead. I hold my breath as the forwards bind on. I have to stay alert as they tussle for the ball, which isn't easy, watching for it to emerge from the scrum. We keep possession and I start to run as it's passed to Omar. My heart is pounding, the crowd are screaming, and I've got space. Omar sees me, throws a fast, hard pass through the gap, I catch it, I've got the ball, and there's nobody in front of me.

There's nobody in front of me.

So I run.

SARAH SPRINZ

EMMA

I'll never understand how it's possible to pass that ball so
fast and so precisely from one player to the next. I feel dizzy
just watching. The rules of rugby are still a mystery to me,
but I'm getting the sense that whatever is happening right
now, it's a good thing. Dunbridge are still three points
behind and the clock is ticking down the last thirty seconds
of the match.

A cheer goes up as the ball whizzes through a gap from
Omar to Henry. The other team starts running, but Henry is
faster. Bloody hell, he's faster.

I don't notice myself jumping up. Screaming my lungs out
like everyone else. We clap and roar as Henry runs as if his
life depends on it.

Tori screams and grabs Sinclair's arm when they almost
tackle Henry to the ground. One of their players dives at his
feet, the tackle makes him stumble and slip on the muddy
grass, but he keeps his balance. They're gaining on him, but
he doesn't waste even a second looking back.

I feel like this stand is going to collapse any moment, with
all the jumping up and down. I yell. Tori and Sinclair yell as
someone catches hold of Henry's jersey just short of the line.
My heart is pounding as they fall, images of Henry in the
sick bay flash before my mind's eye, but this time everything's a bit different. It's Henry holding onto the ball and

474

breaking away before the two of them hit the ground, right on top of the line, and I can't tell if he made it. The referee blows his whistle. Everything happens at once, yet at the same time, it's like it's in slow motion as he awards the try.

Five points.

Five more points for Dunbridge Academy.

At the edge of the pitch, Theo throws his arms into the air, then picks Harriett up and spins her in a circle. The Hollington players sink to their knees, speechless, faces in hands, desperate glances at the scoreboard, which will prove, any second now, that we've won.

I've never experienced anything like it. The euphoria and community spirit. The whole school yelling, screaming, hugging, cheering. And my heart pounding as I see Henry pick himself up and look up at the scoreboard as it ticks over to show '32–30'. He's just getting back to his feet when Gideon, Omar and the rest of the team pile in and bury him again.

I squeeze past Tori and Sinclair and run through the crowd. I see Mrs Sinclair standing beside Dr Henderson and jumping for joy, then seeming to remember who she is. I see Ms Barnett and Mr Ringling clapping, Mr Cormack saying something to Henry and slapping him on the shoulder. I see Grace, celebrating with everybody else.

At that moment, Henry's gaze roams across the pitch to the sideline. To his brother, who's beaming with pride. Taking in the benches and the school buildings behind in the last rays of the sun. I see Henry panting for breath as he puts his head back and looks up. I only realize I'm crying when the tears blur my vision. But I keep running. I stop at the edge of the pitch, just for a moment, but then Theo gives me an encouraging nod.

I hear the shouting and cheering, and I get goosebumps as I step onto the grass. I run as fast as I can. The way I ran at Frankfurt airport. Crashing into Henry, falling in love with Henry, laughing with Henry, crying, falling, finding, growing, and feeling more than I've ever felt in my life. I run as fast as I did in Glasgow. Away from my dad and from the knowledge that we wouldn't have the kind of happy ending you get in films. Although maybe there'll be a different one, sometime, when I'm ready for it. I run, the way I ran with Henry in the pouring rain, before sinking to the muddy woodland path where I could feel the bitter sobs shaking his body. I run because it's the thing I can do best of all. But I'm not running after anyone who doesn't have room in their life for me.

Henry lowers his head and looks straight ahead, towards me, and although there are tears shining in his eyes, he's smiling as he spots me. He pulls away from his teammates, clears a path through the hands reaching out to clap him on the shoulder. He doesn't take his eyes off me; he raises his hands.

And I run, I run.

I run to him.

Thanks

Writing *Anywhere* felt like coming home. From the very first page, Emma and Henry taught me and gave me so much. It was a privilege to be allowed to tell their story and I'd never have managed it without a lot of people who helped, encouraged and sustained me. So I would like to thank:

Michaela und Klaus Gröner from erzähl:perspektive literary agency, for finding the best home for my stories that I could ever have wished for. Thank you for always having my back and being such a great help.

Thanks to the whole team at LYX, especially my wonderful editor Alexandra Panz, who worked on this project with me at all hours, sent me care packets before my exams, and always manages to keep me from a nervous breakdown every time I'm convinced I've submitted the worst novel in the world, yet again. I am very proud of us and of *Anywhere* and I'm looking forward so much to what is yet to come.

Thanks to Susanne George for her sharp linguistic eye. I'm grateful to Stephanie Bubley and Ruza Kelava for their trust in me and the chance to write this new series. I would like to thank Simone Belack and Sina Braunert for the world's best marketing, Andrea Berlauer for event management, Jeannine Schmelzer for the fantastic cover (and her expertise as a former boarder!), and Sarah Schneider and the whole LYX.audio team, who brought my stories out as audiobooks.

To my wonderful fellow authors. Gaby, for pretty much everything. Rebecca, because this time you were more than just a friend and colleague, but also sensitivity reader and expert adviser on all things relating to schools. Kathinka and Sophie for the virtual coworking sessions, without which I would never have either passed my exams or finished this book. Lena, for podcast-length voice notes and your kind words about Emma and Henry.

My parents and my brother, who brainstorm names with me and listen to my confused bursts of inspiration on plot (not that you really had any choice about that . . .). I owe especial thanks to my Mum/Mama for whole boxes of Hanni and Nanni books, which got me reading way back when.

To my beta readers Anni, Evi, Jule, Greta, Leo and Rebekka for giving me your time and your valuable insights.

To my friends for always having a listening ear, especially Leo (I'd have gone mad long ago otherwise) and Anni (Henry and you – what a team!), Simon for the visits to a certain boarding school, Daniela and Corrado for answering all my questions about rugby.

My thanks to booksellers, publishing interns, bloggers and reviewers for all your hard work.

I would like to thank my readers from the bottom of my heart. What you've done for me since *What if We Drown* was published is more than I could ever have imagined. I love your messages, reviews and replies so much. Believe me when I say that they carried me through the last few months. I very much hope that we will be able to see each other (again) at events some time. Until then, we will just have to keep dreaming of Dunbridge Academy – Tori and Sinclair are looking forward to it!

Trigger Warnings

(And spoiler warning!)

This book contains potentially triggering content.

This includes:
Death, loss, grief and bereavement,
substance abuse and addiction.

Please read this book only if you currently feel emotionally
able to. If you are struggling with these (or other) issues,
free and anonymous help is always available from MIND
(www.mind.org.uk) and Samaritans (www.samaritans.org).

Translator's Note

Translation research can be an interesting thing, and I am sure Google currently thinks I want to send my kids off to boarding school in Scotland, which I can assure them is very much not the case. It also frequently means knowing who to ask, and I am very grateful to the Goethe-Institut Glasgow's Stammtischlers for an entertaining few minutes brainstorming good Scottish words, even if a lot of them didn't make it into the text. Niall Sellar answered a lot of questions about posh Edinburgh schools and Professor Jo Drugan put me in touch with a group of fantastically helpful and enthusiastic translation students at Heriot Watt University. Particular thanks go to Ciara Bowen, Will Cassidy and Rebecca Smith for ensuring that the dialogue sounds natural for young Scottish people and not middle-aged English ones. My husband Dave acted as first reader, as ever, and answered a lot more questions about school rugby, while

Martin Wigg helped get the jargon right. Howard Smith was an invaluable source of information on boarding-school life, and Angela Hirons helped get Tori's astrology-speak sounding natural. Thank you all so very much!